Welcome to England

Father Ryan, bleeding from a cut on his forehead, was running toward them, but Tourret dropped the priest with a single blow across the throat.

Suddenly, he was engulfed in flames. Hovering over him, a dragon spewed out a fiery breath that fused wires with muscle and bone, sending hissing steam spiraling into the night. With a high-pitched, keening wail of pain, Bratton stumbled out of the churchyard to disappear into the village below.

The dragon hovered, recharging its flame. Atop its head, clinging to one large ear, Shamus Leafflyer searched for Tourret.

With a sudden roar, the dragon twisted violently, its right eye gone. Below, Tourret stood pointing at the flying reptile, pseudoskin removed from one finger to reveal the laser concealed within.

The dragon spat fire as it roared in pain, setting the roof of the church aflame. Its tail whipped about, connected with a corner of the centuries-old structure, sending large stones and sections of crossbeams flying. One small piece knocked Letty to the ground. A minute later, the burning roof collapsed. Screams of parishioners still trapped inside echoed in the night.

— from "Warriors of Destiny"

Torg
The Possibility Wars

The Near Now ... Later today, early tomorrow, sometime next week, the world began to end.

They came from other realities, raiders joined together to steal the awesome energy of Earth's possibilities. They have brought with them their own realities, creating areas where rules of nature are radically different — turning huge portions of the Earth into *someplace else.*

Now a primitive realm of dinosaurs and spiritual magic exists in North America, a fantasy realm of magical creatures and high sorcery invades the British Isles, and a theocratic Cyberpapacy™ springs up in Western Europe. A high-tech espionage realm takes control in Japan, a terror-filled reality of horrific monters dominates Southeast Asia, and a realm of Techno-Horror™ decends on Los Angeles. Egypt, along with much of Northern Africa, is a realm of 1930s pulp science fiction.

But Earth is not helpless. Standing between these Possibility Raiders™ and total victory are the *Storm Knights*™, men and women who have weathered the raging storms of change with their own realities intact.

TORG

The Possibility Wars™

created by Greg Gorden and Bill Slavicsek

Dragons Over England

WEST END BOOKS®

DRAGONS OVER ENGLAND
A West End Games Book/May 1992

First Printing: May, 1992.
Printed in the United States of America.

0 9 8 7 6 5 4 3 2 1

Library of Congress Catalog Card Number: 92-80513
ISBN: 0-87431-342-2

Cover Art by Daniel Horne

Graphic Design by Stephen Crane

Edited by Douglas Kaufman and Ed Stark

West End Games
RR 3 Box 2345
Honesdale, PA 18431

CONTENTS

Introduction

Ed Stark

The stories in this book focus on a few characters fighting, living, and dying in Aysle, one of the realms involved in the "Possibility Wars." As can be seen from these stories, set in the universe of the Torg roleplaying game, Aysle is the realm of fantasy and legendary adventure: monsters, myths, and magic all come alive in the realm of Aysle.

But why? Why is there a section of the Earth that has been turned into some fantastical place from European myth and legend? And, in a larger sense, what does this mean to the rest of the game world?

There are many different, and contradictory, answers to these questions, but, simply put, Aysle represents a land of magical conception. Not only can there be elves, dwarves, giants, or other magical creatures, but they can exist, in Aysle, without detaching themselves entirely from the world of twentieth-century Earth. The magic-using elf may use a calculator to figure out an arcane puzzle; dwarves invest on the

London stock exchange; and giants mix with half-folk and mythical creatures in modern-day crime syndicates. The point of reference is familiar.

It is this uniqueness, this mixing of the real with the unreal, that gives *Torg*, the game, its appeal. And, in these works of fiction, these "Chronicles of the Possibility Wars," authors are able to experiment with this "cross-genre" fiction. Elves and dwarves, pulp heroes and dinosaurs, cyberpunks and occultists — *Torg* has all of these and more. Aysle is not "pure fantasy" any more than the real Earth is pure anything at all.

But it is not just the presence of magic or technology that makes Aysle special. Blending the attitudes and interests of modern Earth with those of "medieval fantasy" can be fascinating for an author or a roleplayer.

And, of course, this can lead to some interesting difficulties, as is shown below when Baran DeFlorrs, a court official loyal to the crown of Pella Ardinay, discusses policy with Sir Harald Wallic, a representative of Queen Elizabeth II, crowned head of England. The conversation is an excerpt from a royal investigative treatise, published previously:

From: Treatise to the Court, 133
Author: Kelegor

(This conversation was observed and reported by an anonymous courtier. He insists that he had no choice but to overhear the conversation and he has omitted certain details on the grounds of security. These details have been filled in, in a fictitious manner, so as to confuse the agents of the accursed Angar Uthorion and his evil minions.)

Sir Harald Wallic: Your honor, sir, if I might have a

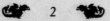

moment of your time?

(It is to be hoped that the reader will not find fault with the author for these repeated interruptions, but, in the interests of accuracy, I must humbly intervene. It is well known that Sir Harald, courtier to Her Royal Majesty Queen Elizabeth II, is of Scottish ancestry and, thus, has a strong native accent. In the interests of clarity, this accent will not be reflected in the author's reiteration of the following conversation. Likewise, only dialogue is presented here, though the author may include certain ... observations as the need arises.)

Baran DeFlorrs: Your servant, sir.

Wallic: Of that, my lord, I have no doubt. I thank you for your time.

DeFlorrs: Well, if your honor would be so kind ...

W: Ah, yes. Well, it has come to our — meaning certain friends of mine and I — attention that you are of a dissenting view regarding Her Majesty's — and by this, I mean Queen Elizabeth's — policy of half-folk citizenship.

DF: I suppose, my good sir, that by "dissenting," you mean "within the majority?"

W: Well, I do not think that has been established as —

DF: Established! It is obvious! Virtually all of the representatives favor the withholding of representation until this "Warrior of the Dark" business can be straightened out.

W: Virtually all of the *Ayslish* representatives, you mean ...

DF: Ayslish? Well of course I mean *Ayslish* — we are in Aysle, are we not?

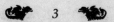

W: Technically, no, my dear Baran, we are *not* in Aysle — we are in England! Specifically, London!

DF: Ah, yes: "the last bastion of sovereign Great Britain!" I've heard the exclamation before. Your *Times*, I believe. What would the Queen — and *I* mean Queen Pella Ardinay *the First* — say to your words? Are we not united in our goals?

W: This "queen" of yours; this magical maiden; has caused more trouble than she —

DF: Now, now, Wallic; I do not believe you mean exactly what you are saying ...

W: *Of course I* — no, no; you are right, of course. Queen Ardinay, despite her origin, is an ... ally of the British Aysles. Damn! I mean "Isles."

DF: Ha, ha! Well said, well said!

(It should be noted that, at this point, the observer noted that Wallic looked decidedly uncomfortable and was visibly fidgeting, while DeFlorrs was of the calmest bearing.)

DF: So, we were discussing the halfies —

W: "Half-folk," if you please, my lord.

DF: Of course, of course ... pardon me. What were we saying about them?

W: Well, I was about to bring up that England has had a long history of equality within the masses, and Her Maj — *Queen Elizabeth* — feels that this should extend to our new ... emigrants. Regardless of race ... er, species.

DF: She does?

W: She does.

(At this point, Wallic has composed himself and DeFlorrs has taken a much more thoughtful expression upon his

features.)

DF: So the proposal is serious — even with the "Warrior of the Dark" leading the half-folk all across Scandinavia and Northern Scotland and whipping them into a frenzy?

W: Of course it is serious! There are a large number of half-folk still within the boundaries of ... the Light, as you call it. They are good, decent people — regardless of their looks — and should have representation under the Houses. Now more than ever.

DF: Oh?

W: Yes, yes, man — can't you see? A vote of confidence from the government is all they need ... a declaration of citizenry would establish us within their community. It would show that *we* are behind them.

DF: And the other minorities?

W: Hmm? Which? The dwarves? They have citizenship. And those elves who wish it — though there are precious few. And all have equal consideration under the law. If you mean the giants, they have —

DF: I do not. I mean the East Indians; the Irish; the European refugees; your own lower classes.

W: What do *they* have to do with anything? They have citizenship — those that qualify, anyway — and equal consideration.

DF: "Equal consideration" — bah! How many times is a man or a woman — a being of the same *species* as you or I — passed over for a job or an education simply because he or she is from what you call "the lower classes?"

W: That is pure rubbish; every man —

DF: Yes, yes, I've heard the rhetoric: "every man, woman, and child has equal rights and opportunity under the laws of England." Centaur sh —

W: Well, they *do* —

DF: "Pure rubbish!" Since when did a lad from Soho or Carnaby Street grow up to be King? Or even a member of the House of Lords?

W: That's —

DF: "That's irrelevant." Of course it is. Just as this "half-folk" issue is irrelevant. Half-folk are *half*-folk. Under the laws of Aysle, half-folk can join with Houses and come under their representation, but they *cannot* have their own. They are not *folk*. You discriminate meaninglessly: by race or gender. *We*, at least, have a *reason*. We allow those of our species — all folk — to be represented.

(For all intents and purposes, the dialogue ended here. Wallic rallied for a few more tries, but he was unable to get past DeFlorrs' logic. This is to be expected, as DeFlorrs has since been promoted to Her Majesty Queen Ardinay's Royal Barrister, and Wallic is still entrenched with the unpopular front of "England's men.")

"As can be inferred from the above excerpt, the 'Half-folk Citizenry Act of 1992 A.D./432 P.A.' was defeated resoundingly. It turned out for the good, as hundreds of these creatures immediately defected to areas of the Dark, strengthening Uthorion's forces with their own."

— Kelegor, Royal Historian

His Cool, Blue Skin

Caroline Spector

So much pain.

It pierces like a knife — and the blood. Nobody told me there would be so much blood.

Now the faeries come with their tiny hands, caressing my brow, saying words meant to soothe me, but I'm not comforted. The pain is relentless. I feel I'm washing away, caught in this circle of agony, the ebb and flow of my life stretched out in endless minutes of suffering.

They say it won't last much longer, but what do faeries know?

I want this to end. I cry out, and remember how it began.

* * *

It started with the storms. Terrific, pounding water crashing from the sky rocking the earth, making the world tremble. The lightning looked like huge grabbing hands and the thunder was deafening. I thought the storm lasted for days — maybe weeks. But I'm not certain anymore. Maybe it only lasted minutes.

Benedict said the storm was the beginning of the Millennium, the Apocalypse. He looked out the window as if he expected to see Famine, Plague, War, and Death riding down on the farm. There was a gleeful look on his face when he stared out the window, the expression of a wicked little boy with something to hide.

We'd come to England for our honeymoon.

I loved the accents, the bad food, the eccentricities. London charmed me.

But London made Benedict nervous. He said there were too many years there, that he could feel the pressure of history on him like heavy weights.

Eventually, we decided to rent a small farmhouse in the countryside. Quaint and rustic, we could pretend to be gentleman farmers, cozy in our cottage hideaway.

I like to remember that time — it didn't last long.

Everything changed. Except me.

I tried to talk to Benedict about it, but he just looked at me. Looking into those unblinking, ebony eyes was like staring into the abyss. He didn't know what I was talking about.

"Everything has changed," I said. "Can't you tell? You didn't use to be ... like this."

"Like what?"

"Like *this*. Blue."

Silence.

He toyed absently with his long braids. Crew-cut Benedict wearing a rasta hairdo.

"I think you should see a healer," he said.

"You mean a shrink."

"I don't want you to get smaller, I want you healed. You are obviously cursed by some strange magic."

"Bull."

That was one thing that hadn't changed. Benedict had always been good at putting off blame. It infuriated me when he did that.

"Look," I said. "I know this sounds crazy. You think I don't know how insane I sound? But I swear I'm not making this up. Things have changed. I remember microwave ovens, computers, television, CDs, for heavens sake. Now you look like a Smurf on steroids and we're living in fairy-tale land. Don't you find this disconcerting?"

He stared at me, silent and cold.

"I must go out now," he said.

* * *

My dreams.

They were vivid, full of omens and import. Bad dreams for a bad time. The first dream went like this:

She stands in a field of flowers. Her robes billow in slow-motion, hugging her, outlining her breasts, thighs, and stomach. In her hand is an obsidian crown. She raises it over her head then lowers it to her brow.

Hordes of foul creatures appear on the horizon behind her, led by four horsemen.

She could stop them, but she doesn't. The thrill of the power is in her now. A delicious wickedness — seductive and damning. She runs her hands over her body as this evil force flows through her.

In the end, the meadow is ruined, blackened and scorched beyond recognition.

She leans forward and I feel her warm, fetid breath.

Her face is a parody of beauty, twisted by her cruelty.

"Remember, I am Ardinay. I am Death."

Her voice is like fingernails on a chalkboard.

There's someone with me, a shadow, grey and vague in the background. He reaches for me, but his hands slide through me. I'm as insubstantial as a ghost. He tries to speak, but I can't hear him.

I woke in a sweat. Benedict was still asleep. I touched him, a reflex. His skin was cool, hard and unyielding, like a pebble under fast, running water.

The tears began then, hot tears in my frosty bed.

* * *

Benedict and I argued. He denied that the world had changed. These fights left me so frustrated that I often ran screaming from the room.

I began to mistrust him.

The local villagers knew something was wrong with me, too. They gave me strange looks when I went into town and stared at me out of their crude huts. They didn't think I noticed them looking, but I did. I could feel their eyes on me like ants crawling on my skin. It got so bad I didn't go into town after a while. Instead, I spent my time tinkering with the few items left from before the storms. My portable CD player still worked. When Benedict came home one evening I showed it to him. I even made him sit down and try to use the damn thing. It stopped playing the minute he touched it.

He told me I was a sorceress, that I was playing with evil magic and I must stop. He said I mustn't tell anyone what I could do.

I began to hate him.

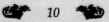 10

* * *

I had many dreams. I couldn't escape them. They were so real, and seemed to become more real as time went by. Sometimes I wasn't sure I was dreaming anymore. I don't remember all of them.

* * *

I stand on that familiar field. Ardinay is here. Clad in armor, she rides a huge horse. Her lance is drawn and aimed at someone. I think it's me, but as she charges forward, I see her rush toward a man. He looks like a Viking. Her lance strikes him. I run to him. His chest is soaked in blood.

I cradle his head in my arms. He looks at me. I'm drawn by his eyes. Seduced. I'll do anything for him.

"See what she's done," he says. "Save me from her."

"How?" I ask.

"Kill her."

"Who are you?" I ask.

"Uthorion. Angar Uthorion."

He coughs blood. It spatters my face like teardrops. The light goes out of his eyes, and I'm left holding his limp body. The pain of his death hits me in waves of agony. He is my life and Ardinay, that bitch, has killed him.

I lay him on the ground. A shadow falls across us. I look up. Standing before me is a knight clad in armor similar to Ardinay's.

"You are not supposed to be here," he says.

"Who are you?" I ask.

"Noble of the House Gerrik. Who are you?"

"Martha Ayers. From America."

"You are dead," he says.

* * *

One morning after one of those horrible dreams, I asked Benedict what he knew about Ardinay.

"Lady Pella Ardinay of the Houses?" he asked, surprised at my interest.

"I suppose. I've been having nightmares about her."

"Oh," he said. "Tell me."

Something in his voice made me cautious.

"I don't know. Just dreams. I've never heard of her, but I have this feeling that she's a real person. Pretty strange, don't you think?"

"I do not know what to think. I do not know you anymore, Marka."

"I told you, my name isn't Marka. It's Martha. Martha Ayers. Good god, Benedict, we've known each other for years. You know my name."

"I know that you are my lifemate and I do not understand this strange behavior."

"You and me both."

We stood and looked at each other. Even with all the changes, I still knew him. It was a queer sensation, as though reality were layered over by a fine film. In that moment I could almost see the truth, but not quite. Not then, not until later.

I'd never felt so alone. I came to England believing that Benedict and I were starting a life together that would last until we died. Now my life was slipping away from me faster and faster and I couldn't stop it.

* * *

I went riding my bike in the countryside one day. What I saw as I rode along scared me even more than when Benedict changed into an elf after the storms.

The countryside had turned into something awful. Green rolling hills and meadows had been transformed into scarred, blackened earth. The trees were twisted and gray beyond recognition and I could barely identify what type they were. When I stopped and touched one of them, it seemed to cry out. For an instant, I could have sworn I saw a woman's face in the bark.

All around me the trees sighed. Mournful sounds. I wanted to gather them together and ease their pain, but I couldn't. I couldn't help anyone. Not myself, not Benedict, not those wretched trees.

I began to pedal faster, as though I could outrun the terrible images I was seeing. That's when I came upon the group of dwarves. I'm not talking about little people, although they were. I mean real dwarves, with beards, crossbows, and armor. They stopped me, fascinated by my bike.

Their names were Diver, Wart, Ferris, and Brown Billy. I tried hard not to laugh as they introduced themselves. It felt good to laugh. It'd been a long time since I'd felt happy.

Diver was the leader of the group, outgoing and talkative. Unlike the others, he kept his beard short-cropped and neatly trimmed. Wart also liked to talk and had a sense of humor, but the other two, Ferris and Brown Billy, didn't seem to have anything to say. I wasn't sure if they were taciturn or just stupid.

All of them were dressed in shades of brown and gray. Their clothes seemed practical and sturdy.

They told me a lot about Aysle, which is where they said they came from. And they talked about Lady

Ardinay. They seemed to like her. I felt sorry for them, being duped by that woman. Obviously, she had deceived them into believing that she was good and kind. That she would take advantage of their trusting nature revealed a lot about her character to me.

They talked about the storms. Slowly, I began to understand what had happened to my world. Ardinay had invaded Earth and imposed this fantasy world on us. My dreams were signs that I had to stop her. I didn't want to be involved with this, but it was beginning to look like I didn't have a choice. If I wanted my world and my life back, I had to take some action to stop her.

I spent the afternoon together with the dwarves, and when I left, I felt better than I had since the storms.

Dwarves and talking trees were becoming commonplace to me.

* * *

"Join us," Mara says.

We stand in the field where the other dreams took place. This time it's covered in green grass dotted with delicate pink and white flowers.

Mara looks ultra-punk, her hair a white mane. She touches me with her cybernetic arm, pointing toward a castle in the distance I've never noticed before.

"I know you think Ardinay is the enemy, but she's not. Uthorion is deceiving you."

"Liar," I say. "He's my life. And you want to kill him."

"No," she says. "Uthorion is using you. Can't you see?"

"I don't believe you. He warned me about you."

I put my hand into my pocket, fingers closing around

the handle of a knife. I don't remember putting it there, but feel a surge of confidence at its presence.

"Please, listen to me," she says. "You're important to all sides right now. You're the balance. If you go to him, he'll use you up and throw you aside. But we need you. We will always need you. Every Storm Knight is important in this struggle."

When she calls me a Storm Knight something tightens in my chest. I feel my eyes sting with tears. Not of sorrow, but of joy. So much joy it hurts. I can't stand feeling the happiness.

"Shut up," I say and drive the knife into her heart.

Surprise is stamped on her face. She pulls me close.

"Beware of Uthorion," she whispers in my ear. "See what he is doing before it's too late."

Her lips brush my cheek and she sags in my arms. Once again there's blood on my hands.

"You have to leave."

I look up. Noble stands before me. The light dances off his armor. I put my hand up to block the glare.

"What are you talking about?" I ask, my voice raised and shrill.

"Your body is mine. You are dead. I need your body to finish my duties."

I feel queasy.

"I'm not dead. I don't know what sick part of my subconscious you are, but get the hell out of my dreams." I sound like a fishwife but I don't care. Some spook out of my id isn't going to scare the hell out of me.

He shakes his head.

"Something has gone wrong," he says.

* * *

I woke, but this time I didn't pull away from Benedict as I had before. I let my fingers trail over his cool, blue skin. I cupped his buttocks in my hands and slid closer to him. I reached over his hip and held him in my hand, stroking gently. Then harder. He rolled over and pulled me close.

"Marka," he whispered.

I put my lips on his to stop that name. Not that, not here and now. I wanted to put the events of the last few weeks out of my mind, to have my husband back, for everything to be like it use to be.

His mouth was warm. I bit his lip. He grabbed the back of my neck and ran his free hand roughly over my breast and then down. I wanted him. It made me furious.

He was searching my body with his mouth. Exploring me like a blind man.

But I was impatient.

Pushing him onto his back, I straddled him and gasped as he slipped inside me. I didn't want to think anymore. I let the feelings swallow me up.

Angry sex. We'd never made love like that before. When we finished I felt sad and drained as though I'd lost something precious.

When I woke the next morning, my body felt bruised and battered.

And Benedict was gone.

* * *

Days passed and Benedict didn't return. I would have been worried, but I had other problems. The villagers burned me in effigy. They did it right in front of the house. I don't know how they got so close without my hearing them, the fools. They thought they could frighten me.

Uthorion came to me nearly every night.

* * *

"They're peasants," Uthorion says.

We're lying together in the green pasture. His head is cradled in my lap and I'm stroking his hair.

"Ignorant sheep," he says. "Someone has to lead them."

He looks up at me, his blue eyes mesmerizing.

"We will lead them," he continues, "but first, you must stop Ardinay."

I laugh at the idea that I could stop anyone.

He slaps me. Hard. My head snaps back and I put my hands to my face, cowering from him.

"Never laugh at me, " he says. His voice is flat and cold.

"Please," I say. "I'll do whatever you want."

He tells me what I must do to stop Ardinay. I want to please him. I'm willing to do anything.

* * *

The dreams continued. I dragged around the house during the days, exhausted from lack of rest, jumping at shadows and the slightest noise. The nights were worse. When Uthorion wasn't in my dreams, Noble was. He showed me awful things and told me lies about Uthorion.

Noble wanted out of my dreams. He demanded that I relinquish my body, saying he needed it to complete his mission for Ardinay. It got more and more difficult to make sense of anything. I felt trapped in the farm house, stuck in a foreign country which had become far more strange than I ever imagined it could be.

* * *

Noble no longer stayed safely in my dreams. He was in my head all the time, talking, trying to control my actions, commenting on my thoughts. All I wanted to do was shut him up, but he wouldn't be silent. He kept nattering around in my mind.

"We should go to Oxford," he said.

"I'm not going anywhere until Benedict comes home," I said.

"Ardinay is in Oxford. She'll know what to do."

"I don't care who's there. I'm not leaving."

I stopped. There I was, standing alone in the middle of the afternoon, having a conversation with someone who wasn't there. I went to the bathroom and pulled out Benedict's shaving bag. There in the bottom was the bottle I was looking for: Valium.

I swallowed two of the pills. I would get some rest and relief from this endless nagging.

The dreams didn't come that night. I woke up groggy with a terrible taste in my mouth. But I felt clearer than I had for some time. What I needed was a few nights without the dreams and maybe things would begin to make sense.

* * *

I stayed on the pills for a week. Each night was a little ritual. Carefully, I placed the tablets on my tongue and let them dissolve slowly. The acrid taste was horrible, but I didn't want sleep to be easy. I was too afraid of getting addicted and not being able to sleep any other way.

During the day, I devised projects for myself. The main one was finding a power source to run the machines I could still work. I finally used the car battery for juice. The first thing I hooked up was the CD player and speakers.

It took me a couple of minutes to decide which album to listen to, then it came to me. I plucked the shiny mylar disc out of its jewel box and carefully dropped it into the waiting mouth of the player. I pressed the track number and then the play button. There was pause, then the familiar syncopated drums, yelping vocals, and piano broke through the night, shattering the pre-electric silence.

"Please allow me to introduce myself,
I'm a man of wealth and taste.
I've been around for a long, long, year,
stole many a man's soul and faith."

It seemed appropriate.

* * *

Eventually, I had to leave the farm house. Benedict didn't come back and the villagers were becoming dangerous. Even though they were superstitious, they were less and less impressed by my technological tricks. The few times I went into the village for supplies, I was armed. Bullets seemed to impress them, but they still harassed me when I was on the farm. They thought I was playing with evil magic and wanted me to leave.

But I was afraid to leave. Even with the danger from

the villagers, the farm was home now. Though I didn't want to admit it, I was still hoping Benedict would return. I felt so isolated. That's when the dreams returned.

* * *

We're sitting together in the field.

"You must find Ardinay, now," he says. He is emphatic. "You can't wait any longer."

"What difference does it make?" I ask.

"Are you questioning me?" he asks. His voice is deceptively soft. A chill sweeps through me.

"No. it's just that I'm afraid I might fail you."

He laughs.

"Rest assured, you won't."

Then he pushes me backwards onto the grass and we don't speak again.

* * *

I woke with the memory fresh in my mind.

I knew I had to leave. I wondered about Benedict. He'd been gone for almost three weeks by then.

I gathered up supplies to take with me. I didn't know what conditions would be out there, and there was no telling how long it would take me to find Ardinay and get close enough to her. I decided to take the horses. I didn't want to stand out too much.

I brought the pistol with me. It was an antique I'd found in an old wooden case at the bottom of one of the closets. It was a beautiful piece, inlaid with mother-of-pearl and gold. Much to my surprise, it was still in working order. There was even a small amount of shot tucked into a leather bag. The leather was so old it crumbled into dust in my hand. In one corner of the case was a small silver box holding gunpowder. I shoved the shot into my jeans pocket and tucked the pistol and powder into the inner pocket of my jacket.

I knew the villagers were out there in the dark watching me. Waiting. When I finished with Ardinay, I would come back and deal with them.

* * *

I camped out along the way to Oxford. Everywhere I went there were faeries, but not the sweet kind I read about when I was a child. Real ones, full of malice and rotten intentions. They spun webs around me. Their music drove me mad, but that's what it is supposed to do. Spriggins, brownies, Hedley Kow, cluricaun, fir darrig, goblins, kobolds, wichtlein, coblynau, pixies, bogie, phooka, will o' the wisp, puck, trows, Unseelie Court, Fachan, hags, black aunts, bogles, red caps, bean-nighe. I knew all these creatures. They were like intimate friends.

"Safe passage," they whispered. "Give us the little one and you may have safe passage."

I laughed.

"No little ones here."

"Safe passage, safe passage for the little one."

"Fine. Take it."

They wheeled away, screaming with delight. I didn't mind giving them what I didn't have.

I was two days out from the farm. My life there seemed like a faint memory. Each day out I got stronger. And I was changing.

I was going to Oxford. Ardinay was there, surrounded by her loyal idiots. She thought she was safe, coddled in that illusion. What a pleasure it would be to ruin her.

It wouldn't take me long.

* * *

I met the dwarves again. They seemed glad to see me, but you could never tell with dwarves.

They told me they were on their way to Oxford to lend support to Lady Ardinay. I mentioned that this was my destination, also. They just nodded their heads as though they knew already. When I pressed them to tell me how they knew, they shrugged and said they'd been keeping an eye on me. I was annoyed at this news, but kept it to myself. I didn't see any reason to provoke them. We agreed to travel together.

The conversation turned to arms. They showed me some of their weapons. Beautiful workmanship. A few months ago I wouldn't have understood a thing they were taking about, but now I seemed to have an innate knowledge

We discussed grips, proper position, heft, and the balance of a good sword. They asked if I would be willing to trade my pistol for one of their weapons. I agreed. What the hell, they probably wouldn't be able to use it anyway.

* * *

It was wonderful.

I never thought anything deadly could be beautiful. Diver said he would instruct me on the finer points of using the blade. We travelled slowly, taking time each day for lessons.

Diver was my primary instructor. He said he'd never seen anyone take to a blade the way I did. I must admit my spirits improved, even if every muscle in my body ached.

The countryside no longer seemed as menacing. Maybe I'd grown accustomed to the way everything had changed. There were small green buds on the trees, and even a few wildflowers peeking out here and there. I mentioned this to Diver, but he just grunted. Dwarves weren't interested in green things.

Maybe I was too tired, but that was the first time since the storms, except for that week at the farm, that I didn't dream. Part of me missed them, but what I felt most was relief.

Wart talked a lot about Ardinay and Aysle. His version of what happened was very different from what Uthorion told me. But what could you say about a man who only comes to you in your dreams?

I wondered where Benedict was. I asked the dwarves about elves' habits, but they just laughed. According to them, the only good elf was a dead elf. Though Wart wouldn't discuss it, I got the feeling that something awful happened back on Aysle between the elves and the dwarves.

* * *

While I was no longer bothered by Uthorion in my dreams, Noble was another matter. As I trained with the dwarves I could hear him in my mind. He tried to take control of my actions. His voice was in my head, telling me when to riposte, feint, and parry. There were times when it seemed as though he had taken hold of my body. When I fenced, Noble got stronger.

"Get out of my body," Noble said.

I was leaning against a tree trying to catch my breath after a bout with Diver. Noble's voice was clear and loud in my head.

"I'm not in your body," I said.

Diver looked at me with a perplexed expression on his face.

"Yes, you are," Noble said. "You don't realize it, but you're not supposed to be here. Why don't you go now, before things get even further out of hand?"

"Shut up," I said.

"I did not say anything," said Diver.

"Not you, him." I gestured at the air.

"Ah," said Diver. He gave me a long appraising look. "En garde."

* * *

After we had been traveling for a few days, I had some doubts about going to Oxford. I realized how stupid it was to kill Ardinay because of dreams I'd been having. I told the dwarves I had decided to go back to the farm.

They talked me into continuing on with them to Oxford. They convinced me that going back to the farm would just entail more run-ins with the villagers. Reluctantly, I agreed. Perhaps when I got to Oxford I could find a way back home to America.

The further we traveled, the better the country looked. In some ways, it seemed better than before the storms. The grass was more lush. The air was cleaner. All around me I saw new life. I didn't know a lot about wildlife, but even I could tell that things were different;

a vitality was in the air that hadn't been there before.

I mentioned the faeries to Wart. He shrugged like they were the most normal things in the world. The only time he seemed worried was when I told him about them wanting the 'little one.' Of course I pointed out that Benedict and I didn't have any children, so it didn't make any sense. He said faeries never made much sense, but it was worrisome just the same.

I was glad I'd met the dwarves. They gave me perspective on everything that happened, but even more so, they became my friends.

* * *

We traveled along the Thames. There were a surprising number of boats on the river. Most were fairly primitive — simple canoes, a few barges. I did see one motor boat. It looked strange and out of place to me.

We stopped at noon and ate. Diver insisted we spar. I didn't want to, since it had become too simple to defeat him. There was no point in fighting him anymore, except to work up a slight sweat.

The other dwarves teased him afterward. I felt bad that I was the cause of his embarrassment. I began to feel, again, that I should continue on my own.

And I thought more and more about returning to America. The impulse that had once driven me to Oxford had faded and in its place was a sense of responsibility to the dwarves. I looked at my situation and realized that there was nothing for me in England anymore. Benedict was gone, I had no family here … going home made sense. I missed America and was afraid. If England had changed to this, what had become of America?

* * *

Benedict came back the next day.

"Hello, Marka," he said.

"Where the hell have you been?" I asked. I tried to keep the anger out of my voice. I failed.

"Out. When I returned, you had left. I was concerned, so I came to find you."

"I'm touched. But it's too little, too late." It felt like a red haze had enveloped my mind, a curtain dropping down over everything and coloring it with my anger. I was surprised at my reaction. Even when we had fought before the storms, I'd always tried to placate him. Now I didn't want to; I was furious and I wanted him to know it.

"Since when does 'going out' mean disappearing for a *month*?"

Benedict shrugged. He squatted on the ground a little way from the fire. Something about him got my back up.

"What are you doing here? How did you find me?" I demanded.

He toyed with a piece of bark. I'd forgotten he did that, played with things as he thought: one of the little nervous habits that punctuated his life.

"I thought it best if I left. Things between us had gone ... bad. I went to the woods for solace. I found I could not forget you."

"Thanks for letting me in on the decision. You take off for a month, then pop up here and expect everything to be all right between us. Well, it won't work."

"You misunderstand me," he began.

"I don't misunderstand anything! I've put up with

a lot of crap from you, Benedict, but this tears it."

I struggled to get my anger under control. Maybe I was a little relieved to see him, but I wasn't about to let him know it. If he started talking, I'd probably go all soft, and that would be the end of it. Well, he wasn't going to get away with bailing out on me that easily.

"Please," he said.

This was a red-letter day. Benedict didn't use that word.

"Please, what," I said nastily.

"Please let me try to explain."

"Explain how you disappeared. Not a word where you were or when you'd be back, if ever. You left me in the middle of all those crazy villagers. You abandoned me, and now I'm just supposed to say 'It's okay, Benedict, you can come back.' Forget it."

I turned and started to walk away from him.

He jumped to his feet. The movement was incredibly swift. Benedict had never moved that fast, and I'd never seen him so angry.

"Do you think you are the only one who has suffered since the rains?" he asked. His voice took on a harsh, ugly edge. "You aren't as I remember you, either. The Marka I know is gentle, placid, and tranquil. She would never be in the forest alone, armed with dwarvish weapons. She would never have done what you did the night before I left. She would have waited for me to come to her."

So that was what was bothering him. Of all the Neanderthal ideas. Now I knew I was in the Dark Ages. But it might explain why he disappeared, somewhat.

"Well, I beg your pardon." My voice dripped with sarcasm. "I didn't realize your delicate sensibilities were offended because I initiated sex. Honestly, you're being positively Medieval."

He looked puzzled for a moment, then reached up and began toying with his hair. That was something Benedict did when he was thinking. Then he said haltingly, "It has been difficult for me. I am sorry I left. I should have stayed. What can I do now?"

I stared at him. He was right. It had been hard for both of us, not just me. Maybe when he left it wasn't malicious, just weak and stupid. A perfectly human reaction. Or should I say elfish.

"Please," he said. "We have both been confused. The best we can hope for is to start again. I am willing. Are you?"

Was I willing to try again? I wasn't sure — so much had changed and I didn't know what I felt or who I was anymore.

We stood there, opposite each other, motionless, for a long time.

Finally, I broke the silence.

"I'm willing. A new start, then."

He stepped forward, his arms outstretched. I rushed into his embrace. I wanted to try and put some of my old life back together. My feelings toward Benedict were so confused: anger, relief, love. I wasn't certain what I was feeling. As we embraced, the image of Uthorion flashed in my mind.

That's when the dwarves showed up.

* * *

Lady Ardinay and I are in a green meadow. I am dressed in my finest armor, my family crest tattooed into the smooth metal. She takes my hand and leads me toward her castle.

"We have missed you, Noble," she says.

My heart pounds. Her beauty is more exquisite than I remembered. Her touch is sweet fire on my skin. I pull her to me.

"My Lady," I say.

She puts her fingers to my lips.

"We have work to do," she says. "Come to Oxford and all will be put to right."

She kisses me softly. A silent promise. A holy vow.

"Unhand the lady, or I'll run you through."

* * *

The voice belonged to Diver.

"I said, let go of her." His face was flushed red and angry furrows creased his brow.

At the edge of our camp stood the four dwarves. They each had a weapon aimed at Benedict. Diver looked particularly nasty holding the pistol I'd traded him.

"Diver," I said, trying to keep the panic out of my voice. "This is Benedict. My husband."

His face looked as though he'd just bit into putrid meat. You would've thought I told him his own sister had married an elf.

"Martha," he said. "Why didn't you tell us your husband was … one of those?"

I could feel Benedict tensing up. Just what I needed — a sudden display of male macho. Or was it elf/dwarf macho? At any rate, I knew I had to cool things off, quick.

"Well, he hasn't always been like this," I said. "This just happened when the rains came. Before that he looked like me, but with a bad New Jersey accent. I mean, he wasn't always blue."

Diver looked unconvinced.

"Do you think I would bring an elf here if I didn't know him? I know how you feel about elves. I swear, he can be trusted. Now will you please put down those weapons? You're making me nervous."

Diver stood there with his feet planted and his face set in a hard frown.

"As much as I want to trust you, I have no use for elves. He can stay, but one false move and we kill him."

"Very well," I said. From the tone of his voice, I knew there would be no discussion. I hoped they would see that he was my husband and, as such, owed his loyalty to me.

I glanced at Benedict. He was looking at the dwarves as if they were something bad he had just stepped in. Then he looked at me and smiled, but it didn't quite reach his eyes.

* * *

"I think you might explain this."

Benedict and I were walking alone in the woods. Things hadn't calmed down at all back at the camp. I thought a walk would help ease the situation. Instead, Benedict was grilling me as if I were a common thief.

"There's nothing to explain," I said. "They're my friends. I met them after you left for parts unknown. I had to leave the farm. After you left, the situation with the villagers took a turn for the worse."

"But dwarves? Really, Marka, you know how they are."

"No, as a matter of fact I don't. All I know is they've

been good friends. Besides, I was having these dreams while I was at the farm and they've stopped now."

"Dreams?"

"Yes. Anyway, the dwarves were heading for Oxford to help Ardinay and I met up with them and decided to go along."

"Tell me about your dreams," Benedict said.

I hesitated. What I hadn't mentioned was that the dreams had started up again. They weren't as distinct as before, but I could still feel their influence. It frightened me, like I was losing myself.

"Just some stupid dreams," I said. "Really, they didn't mean anything."

"We set great store by dreamers."

"Is that the royal 'we'?" I tried to make the retort sound flip, but the whole conversation was getting to me. The more I thought about the dreams the more they held me.

"Look, could we just talk about something — anything — else?" I asked.

Benedict stopped and looked at me intently. He reached a hand out and held my arm.

"We could stop talking altogether," he said, pulling me closer. His skin smelled like a faint memory. His lips were a warm shock. I sank into the moment, releasing my mind from dark thoughts of Ardinay, Uthorion, and Noble.

* * *

I'm in the field again. It's raining. There's no sound except for the rain. A figure staggers toward me. I'm afraid. I want to run, but my feet won't obey.

Everything is moving in slow motion.

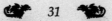 31

Then, Uthorion is in front of me. His hair is plastered to his head. The rain washes fresh spurts of blood from a cut on his face.

"Martha," he says. "Help me."

I start to pull away, but his grasp is strong. Panic is circling around in my stomach. I can't breathe.

"You're not real," I say. "Leave me alone."

"Martha, please, you're my only hope." The rain washes more blood off him. I can smell its hot, copper scent.

"Go away."

He pulls me closer. His hand slips up to my breast. Passion replaces fear. We sink toward the sodden ground, but he pulls away.

"Soon," he says. "You know what you have to do."

He leaves me there kneeling in the wet earth, hungry for him. Wanting.

* * *

Benedict woke me.

"You were having a dream," he said.

I pulled away from him.

"We should be heading back to camp," I said. "It's getting dark. I imagine they're wondering where we are."

"Why do you care?" he asked. "It isn't as though humans and dwarves have been all that friendly."

I shrugged my shoulders. I was feeling strange and off-center, as though I were still stuck in the dream.

Benedict slipped his arms around my waist.

"We can leave them. Why do we have to stay? We could go to Oxford on our own."

His voice was low and hypnotic. It would have been

so easy just to do as he said.

"No, we at least need to stay together until Oxford. I wouldn't feel right abandoning them like that."

I could tell he didn't like my answer by the way he stiffened against my back. I pulled away.

"I mean, they were really nice to me when you left," I said. I hated the pleading tone I heard in my voice. And the sudden weakness I felt, like I was losing control of myself.

"Yes, I understand," he said. "But after all, they are dwarves."

There was something about the way he said "dwarves." Bigots had a special way of talking about the people they hated, and that's the way Benedict sounded when he said "dwarves." It broke the tenuous peace between us.

"I didn't like the way you said that." My voice was tense.

"Said what?" His voice rose with innocence.

"Don't play naive verbal semantics with me, Benedict. The way you said 'dwarves.' It sounded really rotten. It just dripped hostility."

"That wasn't my intention," he said. "I will confess I have no love of dwarves, but … "

"Let's just drop it, okay? I'm not leaving them and that's that. If you want to leave when we get to Oxford, that's fine."

I looked at him and he pulled his mouth a funny way, like he wanted to say something else, but stopped himself.

"Let's go," I said turning to walk back toward camp.

* * *

The dwarves were sitting around the fire when we got back to camp. Wart was skinning a rabbit. Diver smoked his pipe, lost in thought. Ferris and Brown Billy were taking turns stirring a stew that bubbled away over the hot coals. There was a nip in the air that chilled me, reminding me that autumn was approaching. When Benedict and I came to England it had been the middle of summer; time had slipped away so quickly, I hadn't even noticed the change in the season until now. I walked over to the fire, welcoming the chance to warm myself. Benedict seemed indifferent to the cold.

The dwarves stood as we approached.

"Hello," I said.

They just nodded.

"I know this, uh, dwarf-elf thing is an awkward situation," I said. "So we've decided that once we get to Oxford, we'll split up."

"If that is what you desire," said Wart.

"I think it would be for the best." I couldn't look Wart in the eye when I said it because he would know I was lying.

Wart held his hands up as if to say, 'What can I do?' then turned his attention back to the rabbit. I looked up and saw Benedict poking through his pack. He was angry. I could tell from his gestures.

"Someone went through my pack," he said. "One of you filthy dwarves was trying to rob me."

Diver started to rise, but Wart restrained him. Brown Billy and Ferris glanced at each other, then at me.

"No one here is interested in your pitiful belongings," said Diver. "If you want to accuse people of deceit, best look to yourself."

Benedict's face was pulled into a mask of rage.

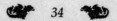 34

"Dwarves have always been an ugly scar on the face of Aysle. It's a pity Ardinay didn't get rid of you when she had the chance!"

"The Lady of the Houses would never harm the dwarves, and well you know why," said Diver.

"Old legends, little man. Only fools believe them."

Benedict smiled then, a thin curving of his lips which pulled his face into a feral pose. His eyes were black and hollow. I shuddered. He was a stranger to me, yet I felt compelled by him.

"Thieving scum," Benedict snarled. He pulled his sword.

"Do you think to provoke me?" asked Wart. "You know that is the coward's way, not the action of a True Son of Aysle."

Benedict held his sword at his side.

"Are you implying that I am not a True Son of Aysle — midget?"

I could tell from the expression on the dwarves' faces that this was a horrible insult.

"You know the legends as well as I. The creators made the dwarves, but there is no mention of elves. No, your kind are not of Aysle and never will be. It is no wonder you have aligned yourselves with that viper Uthorion."

"What lies you dwarves tell! It is no wonder the gods left after creating you!"

Everything was frozen for a moment after Benedict said that. Then the dwarves rushed him. Their short knives looked so small I thought for moment they wouldn't have any effect.

It was all over so quickly.

Benedict was bloody, his skin pale. I rushed to his side, kneeling as I touched his neck to find a pulse.

There was none.

"Oh my god," I wailed. "What have you done?"

Then a veil seemed to settle over my mind and the world was tinged in black and red.

I cradled Benedict's head in my arms, but it was heavy and kept slipping down out of my grasp.

"We had to," Wart said. "He was helping Uthorion."

"Liars!" I shouted. My voice sounded strange. Everything seemed to be taking place three feet away from me, like I was watching all this happen to someone else.

"Listen to us," Diver pleaded. He sounded like a small child.

"Why should I?" I was on my feet now. I didn't remember standing.

"Because we're your friends. We were sent to look after you. To help you. But you've been, well, a little strange. In fact we were going to tell you about your ... husband and his association with Uthorion when he showed up. Uthorion has been trying to use you to get to Ardinay. His spy was your husband."

"Bastards," I said. "Liars." My sword was in my hand. I didn't remember drawing it. I wanted to stop the pain in my heart, in my soul.

I was surprised at how quickly it was over. Again.

One swing and Wart's head hit the earth with a soft thunk. Brown Billy and Ferris tried to run, but I was on them in a flash. They were harder to kill. I stabbed at their backs, but made little headway. Eventually I ran them down. They cried out for mercy, but the rage was in me now, demanding and consuming. Mercy was an emotion I wasn't going to indulge.

Sweat trickled down my face, burning my eyes, as I ran back toward camp. I'd expected Diver to run, but he was still there.

"It was stupid of you to stay," I said.

"I'm your friend," Diver said. "I couldn't leave you now."

"You just saved me the trouble of hunting you down."

"Listen, you're being used," he said. His voice was rushed as though he knew he only had a moment to speak. "Your husband was an agent of Uthorion. I don't know why, but you're important. Uthorion has been trying to overthrow Ardinay for some time now."

"Wart already said this," I replied, "but I don't believe it. I'm not significant to anyone anymore. You've seen to that."

I took a deep breath. The adrenalin was fading. I began to feel weak and trembly.

"Martha," he said. "Haven't you noticed how you've changed?"

"Of course," I snapped. "That's obvious. Everything has changed. I'm tired of talking about this." I raised my sword.

"I am sorry we have to part this way," said Diver. His voice was sad.

Parries, ripostes, leaps, and bounds, thrusts, jabs, as though he knew this was for the last time. I had never seen him so graceful. But I knew I would win. After ten minutes, he was tired. I was barely breathing hard. Twenty minutes and it was easy to finish him.

I wiped my blade on the grass. My heart was beating a mile a minute. Unhooking my scabbard, I collapsed on the ground. I knew I had to bury Benedict, but I didn't have the strength to start.

I rested. I'm not sure for how long. The hammering in my chest subsided, but it was replaced by a dull ache, as though someone had hit me, hard, and left a bruise. I felt like crying, but I couldn't. There wasn't a tear left inside me. I was dried up and hollow as an old husk.

I stood up and walked over to where Wart lay. Retrieving his severed head, I placed it at the top of his neck. I folded his arms over his chest and put his legs together. Then I got the rest of the dwarves' bodies and laid them next to each other in a neat line.

"Four little dwarves in a row. Ho, ho, ho," I sang. I began to hum a little ditty to myself. Humming had always cheered them up.

"Now stay there. Don't run away," I said.

I turned back to Benedict's body. His arms were splayed at bizarre angles. His legs looked as though he were about to run. Gently, I straightened his limbs. His clothes were twisted about. I knew that would bother him. He had always been neat about his appearance, even after he turned into an elf. So I carefully tidied up his garments.

My hand brushed against something in his vest pocket. At first I thought it was an amulet, but the shape was wrong. I pulled it out. It was a carefully folded piece of parchment.

Curiosity killed the cat …

"Satisfaction brought him back," I said out loud.

I opened the parchment and read Uthorion's words to Benedict.

The paper fluttered from my hand. I couldn't catch my breath. Something was squeezing all the air out of my lungs. I put my head between my knees until the feeling passed. I wasn't going to let this overcome me. I wouldn't allow it.

I pulled myself together and went on. The sun had

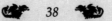

long since set when I finished their cairns. That night there were no more dreams.

* * *

It took another two days, but I reached Oxford.

It was astonishingly easy to get into Ardinay's castle. She was as beautiful as I remembered. Or at least as Noble remembered. I wasn't sure whose memories were mine anymore.

"My lady," I said as I knelt before her. She peered at me as I rose.

She search my eyes for a moment.

"So it is you," she said. She reached up and removed her crown from her brown. Relief swept her face, as if a heavy burden had been laid aside. "I've been waiting for you."

"And I have been searching for you."

"Have you come here to kill me?"

I was surprised by the question. So blunt and to the point.

"No. I discovered Uthorion's intentions and have come to tell you that the threat to your safety from me is over. But how did you know about his plans?"

"His Darkness Device helped reveal his plans to me," she said. "That is why Noble was sent on this mission — to prevent Uthorion from taking control of this Storm Knight."

"You knew?" I was stunned. "You knew that Noble would be placed in my body while I was still alive? You condemned him to this?"

Ardinay shrugged her shoulders. And I grew cold.

"Oh, my god. He didn't know that I would still be alive, did he? He thought he was coming into an empty body, but you knew. You knew I was alive and what would happen to Noble if we were to occupy this body at the same time."

The shock I was feeling — was it mine or Noble's?

"I had no other choice. Time was of the essence. He volunteered. 'Anything for you, my lady.' Those were his very words."

There was a mocking tone in her voice.

"What kind of person are you?" I whispered. I was filled with a horror I would not have believed possible. "He thought he knew you. He loved you. This is something Uthorion would have thought up."

Ardinay's eyes flashed.

"How dare you compare me with that swine," she growled. "I could exile you for such insolence."

"There was a time when you welcomed frank speech from your subjects. Or so I have heard. Perhaps your fascination with Uthorion's plaything has clouded your judgement." That was definitely Noble.

"Get out," she shouted. She regained her composure at once. Her voice softened. "I could banish you from Aysle forever for saying such vile things, but such is my mercy that I will allow you to stay and continue serving me."

"Serve you? You treacherous bitch, I would rather serve the foulest demon in Uthorion's court than consent to be under your thumb again," said Noble.

"Do not test me further, Noble. It is Noble now, isn't it? You always did have a way with words, much more eloquent than that peasant whose body you inhabit. 'Tis a shame you ended up in that body; I remember well how handsome you once were. And you were my favorite. Alas, all things end and so too has this audience."

She gave a curt gesture of dismissal. I was numb. Was she so secure in her power that she wasn't even afraid of me?

"You may leave," Ardinay repeated.

My hand dropped to the hilt of my blade and I knew in an instant that I could kill her if I wanted to; it would be easy. She was struggling with the dark powers of the obsidian crown: Uthorion's influence was in her much as it was in me, and her power was lessened by it. Images flashed through my mind. Images of Ardinay as Noble had known her with the love he still bore for her. And then there were my memories. What I had been and what I had become.

I had had enough of bloodshed. Nothing good had come of all these machinations except the loss of lives. Benedict for all his flaws had been as much a dupe of Uthorion as I had. And the dwarves. I would carry the guilt of their deaths for the rest of my life. Though Ardinay was supposedly on the side of good, she still thought more about the bigger issues than about the sacrifices of individuals. I was tired of being at the whim of her and her kind.

My hand slipped off the hilt of my sword.

"Lady," I said. "I hope you win your struggle."

Her face changed for a brief moment; I saw in her then what Noble had loved enough to die for. She nodded at me, in agreement, in recognition — I wasn't sure which. I turned and left her, and steeled myself not to look back. Not for me, but for him.

* * *

We stand together in a beautiful grassy field.

"I must leave," he says.

"You can't," I say. "That's death for certain."

"I can't stay here with you, like some parasite in your mind. I cannot be a voyeur in your life. Not alive, not dead."

"Where will you go?"

"The wind."

"You'll die."

"Perhaps."

"Don't you want to finish what you began?"

"Of course, but here I am powerless."

"Maybe there is a way," I say.

"How?"

I take his hands in mine.

"Come with me," I say. "I'll show you."

* * *

I travelled north for many months. It was almost time. The faeries will be coming. They were right, there was a little one. A babe. And he'll look just like his father with azure skin and dark eyes. Eyes black as the night. I'll name him Noble.

Our present to Uthorion.

Our revenge.

The Voyage of the Daria Marie

Greg Farshtey

Being a Chronicle of the Voyage of the Good Ship Daria
Marie, *late of Haven, through Treacherous Seas and Great
Perils, as Chronicled by Robin Treveylan, Second Mate*

I was a lad of but two and twenty years when first
I signed on board the *Daria Marie*, a frigate of no small
reputation among those who ply the Trade Seas of
Aysle. I had spent my youth as a farmer's son on the
isle of Liandar, the last refuge of that once-great House,
now reduced to so piteous a state as to be forced to
subsist on alms from the Bendes clan. My family's
fortunes mirrored those of the Liandars — each suc-
ceeding generation found life a harder burden to bear,
as the Dark encroached from every direction.

By the time I had reached young manhood, I could
see that little future awaited me in my homeland. I saw
my father toiling each day to coax a few sickly plants
from the blasted and barren soil, his calloused hands
working pick and shovel in an endless struggle with

the earth. He was bound to that ground by a thousand years of blood and sweat, but I felt no such ties — when the sun slipped from the sky, I would make my way to the water and dream of lands that lay beyond.

My opportunity to escape the island of my birth came one evening, late in the month of Endrak, when I made one of my infrequent journeys to the village. Living in so bitterly cold a region as we did, we could ill afford to run low on furs or flint, so I traveled to purchase supplies. But when I reached Ekim, I heard the sounds of great revelry coming from the tavern. My heart knew what that meant — a vessel must have docked, and its crew would be drinking ale and sharing stories of the sea's wonders.

My purpose in coming to town all but forgotten, I stole up to the door of the inn and peered inside. The spacious room was filled with the smoke of a hundred pipes, the air rich with the scent of exotic tobaccos from Elvenport and Vareth. In the far corner, a dwarf made sweet music on his pipe while an elven maid danced sinuously to the strains. My father would have deemed the goings-on no more than efforts to tempt the wrath of Dunad, but in my eyes, the tavern seemed the first sign of light and life I had seen in many a year.

A glance told me that the seamen who sang so boisterously and capered about the room were no pallid merchants or grim explorers. Their colorful garb marked them as Corsairs, the Coast Brethren who were the terror of the Trade Seas and the subject of a thousand legends. Most were the descendants of Crown War veterans, born and bred to the life of the sea; some, no doubt, were much like myself, men grown dissatisfied with their lot in life and willing to risk storm, sea monster and Viking attack to obtain a bit of freedom.

I longed to hear their tales but was at my wit's end how to approach them. No doubt they would laugh at my eagerness to leave Liandar and speak of terrible vortexes that waited to swallow land dwellers who dared venture out on to the waters. I was turning to depart when I felt a hand easily twice the size of my own clamp upon my shoulder. The next moment, I was dragged inside with seemingly no more effort than if I were made of straw.

"We have a spy in our midst, fellows!" my captor bellowed, as his companions laughed heartily. "What should we do with this stripling, eh? Who's for keel-hauling and feeding his guts to the gulls?"

A hearty chorus of "Ayes" went up at that, and in truth, I feared they might well be serious about their intentions. If so, I was prepared to make the cost of my life a dear one for them to pay. I turned to look at the pirate who held me fast and was surprised to see that he towered above me. His face bore the brutish features of a giant and he bared his teeth in a savage grin that sent a chill through my bones.

"Perhaps we should feed you to the Aquaticas, my fine lad," he snarled. "After all, you could as well be an agent of the Dalerons, come to lead us all to hanging."

I felt the blood rush to my face and anger crowd out all fear. There was no fouler curse that could be hurled at a follower of the Liandars than the name of Daleron, the family responsible for our exile to this miserable rock.

Heedless of my own peril, I lashed out with my foot and elicited a howl of pain from the brute. His comrades seemed to find this very amusing, one of them shouting, "Beware, Lon, this minnow has a bite!"

The giant's smile was gone now and he raised a fist

to cuff me, a blow I felt sure would take off my head. I braced myself for oblivion and am certain I would have found it had not a booming voice cried out, "Hold!"

Instantly, all noise stopped in the inn. Lon released me without even a snarl, dropping his hands to his sides in what I imagined was the closest a Corsair could come to an attentive pose. I turned my head to see what had so affected the sailors, and so had my first glimpse of Captain Basil.

As I remember it now, it was the eyes which first struck me. Slate gray, like chips of stone, with a piercing gaze that would give a dragon pause. His round face was ringed by a black beard, and though no giant, he left the impression that he could best any and all the men in the room.

He turned his glare upon me and rumbled, "What do you want here, boy? This is no place for the likes of you."

I do not know what made me say it — I had not come to the inn planning to sign aboard ship. But somehow I knew I was being extended an invitation I would surely regret refusing.

"I … I wish to join your crew, sir," I stammered, drawing myself to my full height. "I can work harder than any man and would ask nothing in the way of wages."

"That's all to the best, as I pay none. Every man-jack gets his share of the plunder we take," Basil said, grimly. "Is life on Liandar so bad, then? Would you leave your home and family, likely never to see them again? Think well on it, for we have no time for squalling babes on the *Daria Marie* — long for your former life but once in my presence, and you'll be naught but added weight for our anchor."

"I have no love for farming, sir," I said, with conviction born of observing the futility of my father's efforts. "I'll not shame your vessel, nor water the ocean with my tears, that I vow."

Basil approached me then and clasped my hand in his, with a grip sufficient to grind my bones to dust. "You have a strong hand, boy," he said, still unsmiling. "It so happens one of our lads was swept overboard in a storm near Scania last month and I had put in here in hopes of finding a likely sailor to take his place. Would that be you?"

"Aye, Captain, that it would," I said, thus writing the first page of my life's volume.

Basil allowed me to return to my home and bid farewell to my parents, though he forbade me to tell them upon what ship I would be sailing. Were it known the *Daria Marie* were in these waters, the Houses might well dispatch vessels to hunt it down. I moved like the wind down the pathways to the farm, all the while dreaming of discoving exotic lands and great treasures.

To my father's credit, he made no attempt to stay my departure. He walked with me to the edge of our land and said, "This farm has been a harsh mistress, Robin, my boy. It asks much of us, and gives back damned little. I have heard much the same said of the sea — but I am not fool enough to ask a man to turn a deaf ear to the song the waters sing. Go with Dunad, son, and may you find what you seek."

At dawn the next morning, I carried my few belongings on to the *Daria Marie*. It was a large ship, crewed by well over a hundred men and bristling with cannon. It flew the crossed swords of the Tancreds from its mast, but I well knew that banner would be replaced by the skull and bones of the Corsair as soon as the ship was safely out of port. As I smelled the salt sea air and felt the deck move beneath my feet, I found myself wishing we were already at sea.

I was stowing away my belongings in the cabin I would share with Lon (my company perhaps seen as a punishment for the giant) when I heard the voice of Captain Basil raised in anger. I hurried on to the deck, only to see the ship's master striking a crewman with brutal force. Already, one eye of the mariner's had swollen shut and blood was streaming from his nose and mouth. Scattered about the deck were feathers and stones the like of which I'd never seen before.

"I'll feed your miserable carcass to the kraken, I will!" Basil shouted, his face crimson with rage. "I'll have no sorcery on board this ship! By Rak and Ugorl, I'll beat the life out of you if need be!"

He might well have done so had not the first mate, an aged pirate named Arden, drawn him away and pacified with a few low-spoken words. The unfortunate sailor was led away by his fellows, and the objects which had apparently prompted the beating were cast overboard as if somehow unclean. That night, as the tropical breezes sped us toward distant Pelk Cove, I asked Lon about what I had witnessed.

"The Captain, he hates mages and their like," the giant said. "He won't bring the ship nowhere near the Mage Islands if he can help it. The *Daria Marie* is the only ship I know of that doesn't have a wizard to help fill the sails."

I was at a loss. "But surely to forbid the use of magic is akin to ordering his crew not to breathe," I said. "What could prompt a sane man to lay down such a law?"

Lon gestured for me to lower my voice. "There's a tale I heard told in Haven once, long ago. Captain Basil's wife, they say she was a witch-lady. She wanted the Captain to settle down on an island with her and spend his days digging in the dirt. She thought if he were rich, he would be content to stay — so she tried to conjure up a mountain of gold. When the Captain returned home, he found a Viking's treasure and her, raving and screaming. Her mind had broken, you see, from the strain of the spell.

"From that day to this, Captain Basil's carried a hatred of sorcery in his soul. It's worth your life even to sharpen your blade by magic on this ship."

"But what if we should be attacked by wizards?" I protested. "How would we defend ourselves?"

Lon smiled. "Don't you worry about that, boy. Captain Basil always says he's never met a mage who could cast a spell with cold steel sticking in his ribs."

Four years were to pass before the events which I will relate here. I worked my way up to the position of second mate under Captain Basil, learning much of the sea and sharing in a wealth of plunder during that time. I had begun to dream of one day having a ship of my own, and so set aside much of my gold toward the end of purchasing a sloop one day.

I also worked to become proficient at magic, despite Lon's misgivings and the feelings of the Captain. Though it was difficult to learn and impossible to practice in the open, we occasionally captured a merchant or a mage who would share some of his knowledge for an extra glass of ale or crust of bread. In that way, I eventually attained a small degree of mastery of the art, and felt more secure knowing I had a weapon so powerful and so easily concealed at my command.

There had been many changes in the Coast Brethren in recent years. The Council of Captains had been split as to whether to follow Lady Pella Ardinday's armies to the new world called Earth — Basil, of course, had voted nay, calling the strange bridge that linked our seas to theirs "more damnable wizardry." When Ardinay began calling for peace, civil war spilled from Earth back to Aysle, and Basil called for the crew to vote on which side to back, as is the Corsair way.

The men who sailed the *Daria Marie* were not cowards, but they were practical and they were pirates. They voted to support neither side, but take the money from either whenever it was offered. I was dismayed by this — having voted to work solely with the forces of the Light — but then I recalled that I worked alongside Corsairs, men who had no country or House to which they owed allegiance. Their only concern with the wars of others was how best to profit from them.

An opportunity to do just that arose some months later. We had looted a merchant vessel two days from Tradeport and the men were looking forward to spending their ill-gotten gains in the inns of Haven. It had been many weeks since we had put into shore, for there were few safe ports remaining. The return of Tolwyn of Tancred to Aysle, and her raising of an army to challenge the might of her brother, had led to every vessel that approached the continent being suspect. Tancred privateers were everywhere, and it seemed the *Daria Marie* would soon be forced to take her chances in Viking waters.

We were skirting the coast of Vareth lands when the seaman on watch reported a harpy approaching from the direction of the Folk star. It was odd indeed for a half-folk to fly so near a human vessel, for they were considered ill omens by sailors and were often shot for sport. At the look-out's first cry, three or four of the crew had moved to the starboard rail and were loading powder and ball into their rifles.

Viewed from the quarter-deck, it seemed certain that the creature was making for the *Daria Marie*, albeit unsteadily. I peered through my glass and saw that it carried a scroll in one claw. With both Captain Basil and Arden below decks mapping out our course, the matter was left to me.

"Lower your weapons!" I shouted to the crewmen, who turned to look at me in surprise.

"It's a halfling, sir!" one of them replied. "It's bad luck to let one too near the ship!"

"Nevertheless, you will not shoot," I said. "I believe that creature bears a message for the Captain — would you be responsible for its failure to deliver that message?"

The image of Basil enraged was sufficient to give them pause. Reluctantly, they allowed the harpy to approach unmolested. It swooped toward where I stood, weariness etched into its hideous features, dropped the scroll and soared back toward the shore.

I retrieved the paper and brought it to the Captain, who read it with great interest, then passed it to Arden. "We've been asked to transport some cargo, Treveylan," Basil said. "The money's sufficient for the task."

"Shall I see to the hold, sir?"

Basil laughed a short, harsh laugh. "Would that it were so, Robin. No, turn men out of three cabins and ready the quarters for visitors. And order the helm to bring us about toward the Metal star — we're making for Vareth."

It was later that day that I learned from Arden what

the strange message had contained. The people of Earth's kingdom called England were fearful, for the war went against them, and they desired to cement an alliance with the folk of Aysle. Accordingly, an ambassador and a small number of advisors had been smuggled up the bridge and were in hiding on the isle of Vareth, homeland of the Dark dwarves. The *Daria Marie* was to ferry the group to Elvenport to meet with the leaders of the elves and sign some sort of pact.

The amount of trades they offered was truly staggering, but did little to ease my mind. In my years at sea, I'd had little contact with the elves. It was said they were not a seafaring race, preferring to keep to themselves and be left alone by others. Elvenport was the only port of call for Freetraders in that part of the world — beyond that, the waters were filled with unknown perils, not the least of which were the elves themselves, who were said to sink every vessel that approached their lands.

Like most mariners, I had little trust in elves. They did what they wished, never sharing their reasons with others — it was said they would rescue you from the sea only to drown you the next eve. Many a man swore that their women were the most beautiful in all of Aysle, but Captain Basil dismissed that as the results of enchantment.

I had been among the Corsairs long enough to know that one did not refuse treasure when it was proffered — but I knew I would rest far easier when the familiar coastline of Haven was once more in sight.

We dropped anchor off the coast of Vareth when the night was some hours old. We dared not come too close, lest the dwarven frigates chance to be in the area. As it was, the dwarves among our crew were restless and agitated. Many of them had become Corsairs after having escaped the Vareth slave pens and disliked drawing so near the site of their former misery.

As prearranged, I lit a lantern and swung it three times over the railing, then doused its flame. The answering signal came immediately thereafter, followed by the soft sound of a rowboat moving through the water. Captain Basil ordered the ladder lowered to receive our guests.

They were indeed unique visitors in the annals of the *Daria Marie*. The first was an elf, tall and handsome with the trace of arrogance in his smile so common to that race. The second was Ayslish, clad in green and brown and sporting three stars on a patch above his heart. This marked him as a servant of House Gerrik, a noble clan of which my father had always spoken with the utmost respect.

But it was the third whose appearance struck the crew like a thunderclap. A woman, clad in raiment that I would wager was unlike any seen before in Aysle. Her dress and jacket were of dark material and finely cut and seemed to accentuate the lines of her body, yet did not seem intended to seduce. Her skirt revealed far more of her legs than was common among ladies, but her manner was cool and dignified just the same. Her hair was a fiery red, her features chiseled from ivory, and she wore spectacles with metallic frames.

If the men were speechless at this vision, Captain Basil was not. He turned angrily upon the Gerrik man, saying, "You did not tell me you would be bringing a woman aboard ship, Devin! I'll not have it!"

The elf interceded. "If I may, Captain, my name is Berut, a member of a faction in Elveim that wishes to see the Dark expunged. This woman is Catherine

Sinclair, a representative of Queen Elizabeth II of Britain. It is my understanding that passage on your vessel to Elvenport had been obtained, and I must confess I fail to see where the question of gender enters into the matter."

I could see Arden moving through the crew, calming those already thinking of feeding the presumptuous elf who dared to lecture their captain to the sharks. For his part, Captain Basil was having none of Berut's manner.

"You don't see because you've never set foot on a sailing ship, elf," Basil said. "Women on board ship are a curse, particularly when there's danger involved. If you think —"

"We do, Captain, but perhaps you do not," Catherine Sinclair said. If the crew was shaken before, they were doubly shocked to hear a woman — a woman — dare to speak thus to a Corsair. "You have been paid in full, in advance, for the use of your vessel. Whether I am man, woman or a Hebrides goat is irrelevant. And while I freely admit I have never sailed on so ... quaint a ship, I was born and raised in Dover. I daresay I know as much about the sea as any man aboard."

With that, I was quite prepared to throw the lass overboard and be done with it. But Captain Basil looked her up and down and actually smiled. "Aye, my Maggie would have said much the same. Very well, you may come aboard — but mind you, the first sign of trouble from any of the lot of you, and I drop you on the nearest sandbar and leave you behind!"

His warning given, Basil turned toward the crewmen on deck. "Why are you standing here? Hoist anchor and let's get underway — I want to be well away from here before sunrise."

I was given the "honor" of escorting our guests to their quarters. I found myself embarassed at the condition of the cabin Miss Sinclair was to occupy — a room that seemed perfectly fine for a seaman appeared at the same time to be no fit place for a lady, and I said so.

"Don't worry about me, Mr. Treveylan," she said, smiling. "I've stayed in worse places. Ever hear of Beirut?"

"You mean, your elven companion? No, I —"

My words were cut off by her laughter. "Forgive me," she said. "I'm not laughing at you. It's just the absurdity of this whole situation. If anyone had told me five years ago I'd be living an Errol Flynn movie, I'd have had them locked up."

It seemed clear that our conversation would of necessity be a limited one, since I did not know who Errol Flynn was or what, exactly, a "movie" might be, although I assumed it was some form of barque. In addition, I was beginning to find the scent of her — something much like the flowers that struggled to bloom in my mother's garden — distracting. Thus I wished her good evening and repaired to my cabin, there to spend a restless night dreaming of elves, ambassadors, and, to my surprise, the island of Liandar.

The swiftest way from Vareth to Elvenport was straight through the Living Sea, past the Mage Islands and then into the Trade Sea. But we were not to go that way — Devin Gerrik had cautioned us that enemies of the Light were aware of Miss Sinclair's presence in Aysle, and would surely be lying in wait for us along that route. This, coupled with Captain Basil's notorious dislike of the Mage Islands, led us to devise a course toward the Aquatic star and Tradeport. It would mean a far longer trip, but that could not be helped, it seemed.

The initial weeks were pleasant and uneventful. The warm weather typically found in the Trade Sea seemed to cheer our guests — all save Berut, who spent much time at the rail, perhaps thinking of home. Catherine — as I had been granted the privilege of calling her — often spoke of how pleasant the climate was here as compared to her native London. She seemed not at all nervous about her upcoming meeting with the elves, comparing their confusing behavior and complicated customs with certain Middle Eastern tribes she had encountered in the past.

We were flying the leonine banner of the Bendes, a family whose vessels could normally sail unmolested save by some rogue Vikings and the occasional Corsair. We saw few vessels beyond merchantmen — indeed, it seemed at times we had the entire sea to ourselves.

It was three weeks into the voyage when I came upon Catherine watching the sun slip into the Land Between. She never ceased to be amazed by Aysle, and was constantly questioning me about the stars and what lay on the other side of the world.

"You know, I think I will be sorry to leave here," she said, as the waves lapped against the hull. "This is really a very beautiful place."

"Aye, it is, and you've but seen a little," I replied. "But it would be far more beautiful if we had peace."

Her face clouded, and I regretted what I had said. "You sound like Devin. I think Oxford insisted he come to make sure I remembered my duty."

"I do not think you would forget." Indeed, I had rarely seen a woman so committed to a task. "And what of Berut? Does he not serve as a reminder?"

"There are times I think he would rather the whole

mission be abandoned," she answered, to my surprise. "I'm convinced he sincerely wishes an alliance, but he is doubtful one can be achieved between two so different cultures. And if I fail, well, I'm sure he will be considered shamed by it."

I considered this carefully. "Then do not fail," I stated at length. "Make your argument with the same force and clarity you used on the Captain to obtain passage on this ship. Elves are not skilled at debate — they have grown accustomed to others simply doing what they say because they wish it. You will be an … experience for them."

Catherine laughed. I had begun to like the sound very much. "I have been called many things in my time, Robin, but never before an 'experience.' I — Robin, look!"

Her expression had changed on the instant to one of fear. I looked toward our wake and saw that the sea had begun to churn, as if preparing to spew forth a great evil. I had seen that sight only once before, and knew all too well what it portended.

"Get below!" I shouted, pushing Catherine toward the hatch even as I rang the bell that would summon the crew.

"What is it? What's the matter?" she protested.

She had her answer in a moment. The waters seemed to explode and the hideous head and serpentine neck of a Draconis Aquatica reared up before us. Its scales glistened in the fading light, and Catherine's scream was lost in the horrifying screech of the creature.

Captain Basil and the rest of the crew had made it to the deck now, and I heard a volley of rifle shots from above. As the balls glanced off the monster, I thrust Catherine through the hatch and down the stairway leading to her quarters.

The ship shuddered as the dragon slammed its massive tail against the port side. It was a full-grown beast, perhaps 75 feet in length, resembling nothing so much as a huge snake. It was the terror of sailors everywhere, and this night the men of the *Daria Marie* had good reason to fear.

I raced below-decks to aid a gunnery crew in the loading of their cannon, then touched match to fuse to spark the explosion, even as my comrades did likewise. A score of cannonballs flew from the vessel, at least a few striking the beast and leaving it shaken. It dove beneath the waters and then rose up again, a sweep of its tail splintering the starboard railing.

Praise to Dunad, we had a strong wind and a fast ship. While the monster prepared for another attack, Basil ordered the ship turned about so that the port guns could be turned on the monster. A second cannonade drove the beast back beneath the waves and this time it did not rise again.

Damage to the ship had not been serious, but the price of our victory in lives had been dear. I found Captain Basil standing at the shattered railing, gazing into the depths.

"Twelve men, Robin. Twelve men stood at this rail and fought to defend their ship, and now all are gone," he said mournfully. "Swept into the sea in the blink of an eye."

"But they have been avenged," I said, attempting to comfort him. "The monster is dead."

Basil shook his head. "Would that it were so. But I saw little blood where it was wounded, and no serpent's corpse floats upon the waves. No, it's been hurt, but not slain. We can only pray that it has tasted enough of our steel."

Basil was not a man to place his trust in the gods, however — he ordered a doubling of the watch for the duration of the time we would spend in the warm waters of the Trade Sea, where the Aquatica thrived. Carpenters were set to work repairing the rail, while leaks in the port side were patched.

I was detailed to ensure that our guests were unharmed and found them to be so, if greatly shaken. Berut, in particular, seemed intensely disturbed by the incident.

"Perhaps Captain Basil was correct," he muttered. "Perhaps this was a poorly conceived plan."

"Aquaticas are native to this portion of Aysle, and they will attack virtually any vessel. We were extremely fortunate not to suffer more damage than we did," I said.

"Will we be so fortunate a second time?" Berut demanded, now pacing the cabin. "If Miss Sinclair should be killed while en route to Elvenport, think of the damage that would be done to human-elf relations? It would be catastrophic!"

"No one else will be killed," Devin Gerrik assured him. "Captain Basil knows what he is doing and will make certain we are all safe."

But Berut was not to be mollified. "This is your fault, Gerrik! You were the one who warned of hidden enemies, and said we could not take the most direct route!"

"Gentlemen! Stop it, now!" Catherine shouted. "We're all under strain, but bickering among ourselves serves no purpose. Mr. Treveylan says that such attacks, while ... unsettling ... are a common occurrence in these waters. But I have faith that the *Daria*

Marie and her crew can get us to Elvenport safely. If either of you wishes to debark, I'm sure Captain Basil could find a nice sandbar somewhere around here."

Catherine's words served to calm her attendants, but did little for her own nerves. She confessed later that the appearance of the dragon had frightened her out of her wits, but she knew from previous experience that it would not do to show that.

"I've survived as a diplomat because I know how to act as if nothing surprises me," she said. "I could have sat down with that dragon and negotiated a peace treaty, if need be. Then I would have gone somewhere and had a nice, quiet nervous breakdown."

"Your speech is strange, Catherine, but I believe I understand your meaning," I said. "When first I came aboard the *Daria Marie*, I had a great deal to learn — and the first lesson was not to let on just how ignorant I was of the sea and her ways."

"Did it work?"

"With all but Lon and the Captain," I replied. "Captain Basil knew a green youth when he saw one and took it upon himself to teach me all he knew of Aysle's waters. Lon saw to it that I did not get myself killed needlessly, say, by calling a fellow pirate a 'dirt farmer' in the heat of anger."

She smiled her first true smile since the dragon attack, and I wished I could make it last. Then I noticed she was turning over a large splinter of wood in her hands, probably left over from the carpenter's work. Once certain there was no one about, I took it from her and promised her a miracle.

This would be my first effort at sorcery before another, save for my "instructors." It would be but a minor trick, but more than enough to get me hung from the yardarm if Captain Basil caught me. I concentrated harder than I ever had before upon the stick of wood, and to my delight, tiny buds began to spring from the splinter. In another moment, flowers were blooming from what had been no more than a rotten remnant of the railing.

Catherine's eyes grew wide as first one, then another rose appeared, as beautiful as any ever grown in a garden. Hesitantly, she reached out and lifted the wood, then sniffed the scent of the flowers.

"They're wonderful!" she said, happily. "I've seen your people do magic before, but never anything like … they're so beautiful, Robin."

Suddenly, I wanted very much to have her in my arms, to rain kisses upon her face, and the Corbaal take all of Aysle. "They pale beside you," I whispered, reaching for her.

Her smile faded and her face seemed to grow very sad for a moment. Then her lips met mine in a kiss both sweet and tender.

Much later, I bid her good evening and joined Lon on the quarter-deck for our watch. The giant was muttering a prayer to Ugorl when I approached, so out of deference to him, I did not announce my presence until he had finished. Lon had never been a religous man, in my experience, but our encounter with the dragon had many of the crew turning to their gods.

"You're late," he said when finally he saw me. "I was about to find someone to replace you."

"I was … detained," I answered. No gentleman — not even a Corsair — would relate to another the words spoken between Catherine and I that eve. Lon seemed to be satisfied with my answer, at least he did not press the matter. He turned his attention to the stars that danced overhead.

"They care little about the stars in Lower Aysle, lad," he said. "They serve merely to light the way on a hunt or watch over the camp when the Dark things are about. Up here, folk read much into their positions in the sky or which was ascendant at birth. Tell me, Treveylan, under which star were you born?"

"My mother bore me in mid-Endrak, under the Fire star," I answered. "She said she knew the star whose gifts would be bestowed upon me, for it was fiercely hot that day."

Lon laughed. "Perhaps, little one, when we are back in Haven, you may wave your hands and light all the torches in the village, eh?"

I looked at him in surprise. It was unusual to find a giant — particularly on Captain Basil's ship — so well-versed in the magic skills one gained by birth. It was true that I had from childhood a talent for conjuring fire from nothing, one only harsh discipline at the hands of my father taught me to control.

I turned to answer Lon's jest and saw that he had the glass to his eye. He was looking off the starboard bow, but I knew not at what. Finally, he handed me the instrument and said, "There is something there, Treveylan, but I only get a fleeting glimpse."

I looked out into the darkness and immediately saw to what he referred. Out amid the waves a shape was moving, first rising, then falling, only to appear again. The motion was smooth and unhurried, and it reminded me uncomfortably of a revenant stalking its prey.

"Sound the bell, Lon. We'd best be prepared for whate'er may occur."

Captain Basil knew at once that a Draconis Aquatica

followed hard on our heels, and in the first light of dawn, the scorch marks on its scales became visible. It was the same creature that had attacked us before, come back to send us all into Dunad's embrace.

The cannon were readied and a hundred pairs of eyes watched anxiously as the serpent drew near and then retreated. It did not strike at us — strangely, it kept a distance between itself and our vessel, following in our wake for many hours. It would vanish for a time, only to reappear again, and we dared not let down our guard lest it seize the moment and destroy the *Daria Marie*.

For days on end, it remained thus — the dragon taunting us from just beyond the range of our cannon, the men slowly growing hollow-eyed from lack of sleep. Occasionally, the nerve of one would break and Basil would order him confined to quarters. Tension charged the air and small disagreements between shipmates became serious quarrels.

Mindful of the danger, Basil offered to put Catherine and her party off at Tradeport, but she would have none of it. Her spirit seemed to rally some of the men and we passed the home of the merchant fleet in better spirits than we had enjoyed in some weeks.

Alas, her bravery did not seem to extend to her companions. Berut continued to complain that the trip was folly, the dragon a sign from Elmiir that all would end in disaster. Devin Gerrik called upon the Captain to send a hunting party out to confront the dragon (a suicidal course, as any mariner knows), and resisted the idea of leaving the warm waters of the Trade Sea and risking coming under the eyes of the Vikings. Basil insisted that we would maintain that course, for Aquatica favored warm waters above all, being one of the few creatures capable of surviving in the Boiling Sea.

On the ninth day of Mesus, five months after we left Vareth, we came in sight of the isle of Skani, home of the Viking race. No sooner had our lookout made that known than a longship appeared on the horizon, bearing toward us with doubtlessly hostile intentions.

It is doubtful there is a sailor in all of Aysle who has not had dealings with the Vikings on some dark day. Fierce warriors who care little for their own survival in combat, they regard all vessels that pass into their waters to be forfeit. It is for that reason that merchants began to navigate to Elvenport via the Elemental star, a longer trip but one that kept one's goods out of Viking hands.

We still flew the Bendes flag, but little good would it do us now, it seemed. The Viking ship moved as if it had wings and was upon us long before we could make speed to flee. Indeed, the winds seemed to have died completely around our vessel, and Captain Basil paced the deck cursing the foul sorcery of the Vikings that had made it so.

Fear of the dragon was lost in the wash of hatred for Vikings that every Corsair feels. Cannons were loaded and sabres drawn from their scabbards as the longship's horrible dragon figurehead came into view. I stood at the rail, Berut and Devin by my side, their mistress already in her cabin with our best pistol shot as guard.

"They will demand a ransom, no doubt," Berut said. "I am sure we could meet their price."

"Vikings do not accept tribute from such as we," I responded. "They will capture the ship intact, if possible, slay the men, and take Catherine as a slave. Once they have stripped the *Daria Marie* of all its cannon and brass, they will send her to the bottom. That is the Viking way."

"This is why I called sailing these waters madness!" Gerrik snapped. "We could have slipped past Scania in the dead of night, with no Viking being the wiser!"

"We might also have sailed via the Mage Islands, had you not insisted we come this way, Gerrik!" Berut hissed. "Perhaps we could have avoided these past months of having a dragon as a companion."

At that, I ordered them both below. Neither looked to be worth very much in a fight, save when the opponent was the other. We could hear the war song of the Vikings clearly now, almost drowning out Captain Basil's exhortations to run the sea red with Viking blood. The winds had risen again, now pushing us toward the longship despite our best efforts to tack away.

It was then I saw a sight more bizarre than any in my years at sea. The dragon surged past us on the port side and rose before the Viking ship, its mighty tail smashing into the hull and sending a hundred warriors into the water. A blast of steam from its mouth seared those who stood against it, sending them too over the side to seek relief in the cool deep. Spears flung by the Vikings were useless against the beast, who seized the figurehead in its jaws and dragged the ship under water as a prize.

The instant the vessel disappeared beneath the waves, the winds returned to normal. Viking corpses, many in pieces, littered the waves, a grim reminder of a fate that might well still be ours.

Captain Basil had moved beside me at the rail and there was a gleam in his eyes I had not seen before. "It seems we have a protector, Treveylan," he said quietly.

"The dragon hunts us, harries us, yet will not let us come to harm at the hands of another. What does that suggest to you?"

"Perhaps the monster is mad," I offered. "It wants revenge upon us for its earlier defeat and will stalk us until the proper moment."

Basil nodded and drew upon his pipe. "Perhaps that is correct, and perhaps there is more here than we know. Bring us around to a new course — toward the Water star."

I confess to some surprise. Traveling that way meant turning back upon ourselves and moving between Holm and Bar'aan. There was no land there upon which we could safely deposit our passengers and we would be even deeper into Viking waters.

"You wonder if too many years at sea has driven me mad, eh, boy?" he said, a smile that made him look like Corbaal himself playing on his lips. "After you have seen to the wheel, bring Mistress Sinclair and her party to my cabin."

I did as I was bid, prepared for virtually anything to pass from Captain Basil's lips save for the words that were to do so. Catherine was puzzled by his decision, but I had explained that the dragon's leaping to our defense defied all legend and experience. The creature had returned to stalking us and seemed content to do so until Anglach Dornin, if need be.

Berut was convinced the Captain had come to his senses and would be turning back, a move he heartily endorsed. Gerrik was furious and demanded to know the meaning of the course change.

"First you defy all logic by leaving the Trade Sea, then you drag us even deeper into Viking waters. How much have the Dalerons paid you to betray us, man?"

I had heard all I cared to from Devin, who seemed to me more of a strutting fool than a true warrior of the Light. I brought my dagger to his throat and whispered harshly, "Remember where you are and with whom you sail, dirt lover. Better men than you have regretted speaking thus to the captain of the *Daria Marie*."

Captain Basil seemed unconcerned about Gerrik's words, however. He unrolled a chart for all to see and pointed to where we were at present. "For your benefit, Miss Sinclair, and the peace of mind of my Second Mate, I am going to explain our present route. As Mr. Treveylan could no doubt tell you, a Draconis Aquatica is many things, but it is not a hound — it need not track a vessel across hundreds of miles to find worthy prey, nor would it do so merely to gain vengeance for a few cannon shots."

"Then why has it been chasing us?" Catherine asked.

"Not us, madam; you. I am convinced that, through sorcery, this dragon has been induced to torment us and force us to turn back to Vareth," Basil said, his hatred of all things magical evident in the tone of his voice. "Were we to come within sight of Elvenport, I have little doubt it would attack and attempt to sink us. But for now, its master wishes only your defeat, not your death — that is why it slaughtered the Vikings before any here could come to harm."

Berut looked unconvinced. "And who is this mysterious 'master,' if I may be so bold as to ask?"

Basil fixed him with a glare. "When that is discovered, the sharks will feast well, elf. For now, we are going to dispose of our shadow in the only way I know, although it entails some risk to us."

Basil went on to explain his plan: Aquatica disliked the cold, so the *Daria Marie* would make for Ice Bay.

With a strong wind, we would make it by the end of Borl when the ice floes would be moving to cut off the waterway.

"If the Aquatica follows us in there, it will be slowed by the cold and eventually trapped when the floes lock together," Basil finished.

"As will we, Captain," Gerrik put in. "How will the ship escape the bay once the ice is in place? Or are we to make a life among the nomads of the Frozen Land? Perhaps a treaty of alliance could be signed with them?"

Catherine cut off his diatribe. "Devin, we knew there was a risk in undertaking this mission. If it means freeing ourselves from that creature, I deem the risk an acceptable one."

Perhaps only I could see the concern she concealed. I realized once again that such a woman, if born in Aysle, would surely have ruled a House by now.

The passage to Ice Bay did not go smoothly. The dragon made numerous attempts to turn us from our course and many a man perished in defense of the Daria Marie. But Basil would not be dissuaded from his plan of action and ordered a watch put on Gerrik, Berut and Catherine whenever they were not in their cabins to prevent sorcerous sabotage.

The air turned bitterly cold and, not for the first time, I wondered how those known as the Ice Nomads managed to survive in this region. No resident of my home isle could be unaware of the mysterious tribes that stalked the Frozen Land, as House Liandar was said to be the only one to have made any contact with the Nomads. No one knew where their loyalties lay, for few had the courage to venture into their domain.

Finally we saw the ice floes ahead, gleaming like

diamond chips in a setting of blue water. Captain Basil took the wheel and, with consummate skill, led us into the mouth of the bay and brought us about. We had arrived later than had been hoped due to the dragon's predations, so already the ice was beginning to drift together. Soon it would be impossible for the ship to sail out of the bay again for some months.

Now began the wait to see if the Aquatica would follow us. To do so might well mean its doom, thus I felt certain it would turn away and wait for us to emerge again. And to the dismay of Basil, that is exactly what it did, more evidence of a man's intelligence behind the beast's actions. We now had seemingly no choice but to return to the sea and battle the beast, or else risk being trapped in the bay until the thaw.

Captain Basil retreated to his cabin for some hours, then emerged and called for volunteers for a hunting party. I offered to accompany him, but was refused. "Someone must look after our passengers," he said, by way of explanation. Also refused were Devin Gerrik and Berut, for reasons Basil would not deign to state.

The party was gone for much of one day and they returned with the meat of winter wolves as well as hare and a species of bird with which I was not familiar, but which tasted quite good. Captain Basil also announced that he had made contact with the Ice Nomads and they had agreed to shelter us until the thaw or, if we wished, to guide us overland across the wastes to the vicinity of Elveim. This news was met with much rejoicing among the crew, but the diplomatic party seemed less than enthused. Catherine feared for her ability to survive so long a trek and felt certain her government would feel some ill had befallen her after so many months. Berut said much the same, and Gerrik simply muttered that savages like the Ice Nomads were not to be trusted.

For myself, I was fascinated by the prospect, if aware of the hardships an overland journey would entail. That night I visited the Captain and asked him how he had found the Ice Nomads to be and when we might expect to depart.

"We'll be leaving as soon as that dragon's dead, Treveylan, and not before," he answered, putting away the paper upon which he had been scratching with his quill. "I never saw an Ice Nomad the whole time we were hunting, nor was I looking for them."

"But you said —" I sputtered, now quite certain the old man had lost his mind.

"For the benefit of our guests, my boy," he answered. "If you wish to be a Corsair captain one day, you must learn the advantages of dishonesty in its proper place.

"If I am correct and one of the members of Miss Sinclair's party does not want her to reach Elvenport, he must act now before we can abandon ship and meet with the Nomads. That means the dragon must enter the bay and our original plan can proceed. The alternative is months spent in this barren hell, one to which I would not consign my worst foe."

After relating that to me, Basil swore me to secrecy. Only the other members of the hunting party were aware that no Nomads had been encountered and they had taken blood oaths not to breathe a word of it.

I left the cabin with a new respect for Basil and a new feeling of certainty that we would survive to make our way to Elvenport. The former would last for many years — the latter would be dashed in an instant, as I stared out to sea and saw the ice beginning to choke off the mouth of the bay.

* * *

Well into the hours of darkness that eve, the lookout reported that he had lost sight of the dragon. Immediately, men moved to the rails all over around the ship, lanterns in hand, looking for the slightest disturbance in the water that would indicate the monster's presence. We waited an hour, then two, with no sign.

Then the ship rocked, as if struck from the bottom. It was not unusual for such a thing to happen in these waters, where chunks of ice slammed into the hull all too frequently. But this felt most unlike that, more as if something were trying to raise us out of the water. Captain Basil ordered spiked nets to be lowered into the water and swept to and fro, in hopes of snagging the dragon.

"We've got something, Cap'n!" one of the men sang out, struggling to hold the net in place. A second later, the huge battering ram of a tail the Aquatica possessed broke the water and then slammed down again with tremendous force, sending a wall of spray crashing on to the deck.

"Release the nets!" Basil shouted, an order heeded by all but one, who had become entangled in the mesh and was fighting to keep from being dragged overboard by the angry beast. Without waiting for the command, I sprang down the ladder, cutlass in hand, and sliced through the netting that held my shipmate. He collapsed in my arms, bloodied by the spikes, as the net flew into the bay.

The dragon's head next appeared, to be met by a

volley from the starboard cannons. It responded by blasting blistering hot steam at the guns, turning them red hot and eliciting screams of pain from the men who manned them.

But it did not take a man of science to see that the Captain's plan was working. The beast was not sloughing off the shot as it had been before and its movements were stiff and labored as the cold began to take effect. A sweep of its tail cracked one of the masts and sent it crashing down, trapping unfortunate men beneath it.

At the rail, Lon readied harpoons. The giant had been practicing for much of the voyage, swearing he would ram the wicked spear down the monster's throat if he had the chance. He let fly with his and it buried itself in the soft flesh immediately beneath the creature's right eye, green blood spurting sickeningly from the wound.

I threw mine and saw to my delight that the dragon's efforts to dodge the missile were impeded by chunks of ice which had trapped the beast between them. My harpoon found the creature's eye as well, effectively blinding it on its right side.

"Fire!" Basil shouted, and the starboard guns that still functioned unleashed a deadly barrage at the creature. The dragon used its steam breath once more, but this time it was directed at the ice that had it pinned. The monster succeeded in melting much of the floe but fast upon it was more ice.

Lon and I launched harpoons anew, mine glancing off the scales of its neck and Lon's finding the inside of its jaw. The monster was now thrashing about wildly, blood and spray flying everywhere and the ice relentlessly crushing its body even as it threatened to do the same to our ship.

Again, the cannon roared and this time the monster seemed to have no will to resist the hot steel. With a screech, it twisted at the impact and then fell, the upper half of its body slowly sliding off the ice and into the water. All that remained behind was the bloody mark of its passing on the floe.

A yell went up from the Corsair crew as the dragon died, yet not all voices were raised in joy. I know not how, but my ears detected a scream that could only have come from Catherine. Snatching up a harpoon, I flew to the port side, all but abandoned as the crew had moved to see the beast expire.

A moment later would have made all the difference. Catherine — my Catherine, as I now thought of her — was locked in a struggle with a man and was slowly being forced over the rail. Though she fought bravely, strong hands were squeezing the life from her throat. There was no time to reach her — I hurled the spear with all I had in me and watched it tear through the side of her attacker, the force flinging him the length of the deck.

I was upon him in a second, wrenching the wheel lock he had drawn from his hand. In the light of the ship's lantern, I could see the bloody face of Devin Gerrik, his features twisted with hatred.

His scream of pain had brought Captain Basil and some of the others. Catherine choked out that he had assaulted Berut and left him for dead, then attempted to murder her when he saw the dragon had failed.

"Why, man?" Basil asked the dying betrayer. "You're a Gerrik — does the name mean nothing to you?"

"Why should it have any meaning?" he spat. "We have no riches, our lands are foul. We are forced to turn to the Bendes for aid. The Tancreds promised me I would rule House Gerrik if the Dark were victorious. They did not ask so much ... the defeat or death of a Core Earth witch and a shipload of murdering pirates. When the deed was done, a simple spell would have summoned a vessel to my aid and transported me home."

"Damnable sorcery!" Basil raged as life slipped from Devin Gerrik. He bent to his body and retrieved an amulet with the figure of a dragon upon it, then cast the charm into the sea. "See how it twists a man and blackens his heart!"

But I was no longer listening. I had taken Catherine in my arms and would hold her until the months of tension and grief had all spilled from her eyes.

Dawn found the situation even worse than I had feared. The bay was well and truly packed with ice and it seemed there would be no escaping for the Daria Marie. The days spent waiting for the dragon's attack had cost us dearly and it now seemed as if we would fail at our task to deliver Catherine and the recovering Berut to Elvenport.

"I put it to you men, as has always been the way of the Corsairs," Basil said to the crew that day. "We can attempt to force our way out and risk scuttling the ship; or we can cross the floes and take our chances in the Frozen Land until the ice breaks. Which shall it be?"

No one seemed enthused about either prospect and I was on the verge of volunteering a third course of action when Lon stepped forward. "There is another way," the giant said, glancing in my direction.

"Aye?" Basil answered.

"Treveylan was born in the month of Endrak. He has the fire knowledge, Captain."

I silently blessed the loyalty of the old giant. He

must have known I would offer to use sorcery to free the ship, and face certain hanging if Basil chose to enforce his strictest rule. Thus Lon had made the suggestion, offering to sacrifice himself on my behalf.

"Is this true, Mr. Treveylan?" Basil said, hell and damnation in his voice.

My mouth went dry. "Aye ... aye, Captain. I was born with the fire knowledge and I have ... some knowledge of its use."

"You know how I feel about sorcery on this ship," he said darkly.

"You may cast me to the kraken when we are free of this bay, Captain, but I will do what I must to save this ship and its crew."

"You threaten mutiny?" he demanded, slamming his hand upon the rail.

"No, Captain," I responded, feeling much like the young farmer who had confronted a sea captain in a tavern so long ago. "I plead for a hundred lives."

That afternoon I stood at the prow, Catherine and Lon by my side. Captain Basil himself manned the wheel and at a nod from him, I stretched my hands toward the expanse of ice between our vessel and the sea. Mustering all my will, I shot streams of flame from my fingers on to the ice, rapidly melting it.

The wind was strong at our backs and the ship moved swiftly through the channel I carved, inch by painstaking inch. The ice reformed behind us an instant after we passed and it took more strength than I thought I had to keep going. At last, with a crack like a rifle shot, the last floe split apart and allowed us to leave the bay and steer into the Frozen Sea.

My last memory of that day was Catherine's smile as the cheers rose from the crew. Her face dimmed before my eyes and I fell to the deck, exhausted.

It would be two days before I awoke again, to find us well on our way to Elvenport.

* * *

There is little left to tell of my story. The *Daria Marie* docked in Elvenport in the early days of Asten, much to the dismay of several Freetrader vessels already there. Berut immediately departed to notify his superiors of our safe arrival, while Catherine stood at the gangplank to bid me farewell.

"My work here is important, or else I would not leave you," she said. "Will we see each other again, Robin?"

I kissed her gently and ran my hand through her hair of flame. "Perhaps you might ask that the *Daria Marie* be hired to bring you back to the shores of Aysle, Catherine."

She smiled. "But next time, we go the short way."

She reached out and held me close to her. "I never thought I would fall in love with a pirate. It's so … Hollywood. And when my task is done here, I'l'l have to go back to London and somehow I know my old life will seem unreal after this. Do you … do you think you will ever come to my world?"

I looked at her and wondered if I could exchange the sparkle of the sea for that which I found within her eyes. "I fear it will be a long war, my love. And if the seas of Earth have need of one more Corsair, then I would be a fool to deny them."

We parted then with a pledge to meet again. The ship returned to Haven for repairs and much celebration of our victory over the dragon and the Dark. In the months that followed, Captain Basil and Arden would retire from the sea to live off their fortunes, leaving me master of the *Daria Marie*.

And on nights when the stars dance in the skies, I find myself wondering when the message will come that Catherine waits in Elvenport. And more, I wonder about the world that waits on the other side of that strange bridge of water.

Child of Thunders

Lester Smith

A rumble of thunder faded in the distance. In its wake lay a hush, punctuated by the fall of droplets from rain-washed leaves. The last beams of a summer sun slanted across the glade, filling the air with golden light. They lay in amber streaks across tree boles, and sparkled like candle flames on the wet grass. In their glow, the profusion of wild blossoms dotting the clearing seemed nearly to burn against the green of its lawn.

In the center of the glade, hovering lightly on dragonfly wings, a fairy maiden danced. She was hardly more than a handspan tall, clad in wisps of spider silk, through which her pale skin shone like luminous pearl. Her hair was dark as night clouds. Her arms gestured skillfully as she spun through a complicated series of *pas de chat* from classical ballet, but her legs hung limp and her face was lined with pain.

Abruptly, she halted her dance. Sighing, she gazed about the clearing, uncheered by its wealth of color and life. Eyes downcast, she fluttered to a mossy boulder set in the middle of a toadstool ring, and settled clumsily upon it, using her arms to arrange her crippled legs before her. Then, hands clasped in her lap and head bowed, she wept, quietly, while the sun set behind her in a blaze of copper clouds.

* * *

"The problem with most people," Duncan said, "is that they are like a watercourse, always taking the path of least resistance." A youngish man, no more than thirty, he rode his black mare with the easy grace of an expert horseman — reins held loosely, back straight, head high, rolling with the motion of the horse's gait. His gray cloak and hose were clean and well mended; the setting sun shone on his helm, chain mail shirt, and spurs, betraying their meticulous care. A dark, smoothly trimmed beard adorned his solid jaw, and brown eyes gazed coolly upon the surrounding woods from above a Roman nose. A bastard sword hung across his back, atop the cloak, its hilt within easy reach above his right shoulder. The handle of a long dagger hid among the folds of cloak at his left hip.

"But God," he continued, "wants us to stand firm, like lighthouses built on solid rock. That's all a hero is, Philip, just a person who stands firm in the face of trouble."

A few paces behind, a gangly youth rode astride a spotted mule. He too wore gray, but with no arms or armor except a dented buckler and ancient short sword hanging together from the pommel of his saddle. His cloak, tunic, and hose were at the same time both too big and too small. They hung loosely upon his bony frame, but his sleeve ends rode several centimeters above his wrists, and the cloak, while billowy, ended just below his knees. While he sat bolt upright in a flawed imitation of Duncan's nonchalance, his blue eyes darted frequently to the growing shadows beneath the trees, and strands of black hair clung to the sheen of nervous perspiration on his pale forehead.

"Yes, my lord," Philip stammered. "But — well, it's all very well to stand firm, but how does a person know for sure when he's standing for something right? Everyone always seems to think what they're doing is the right thing. How can you tell when you're right and not just being pigheaded or stupid?"

Duncan reined his horse around and glowered at his young squire. "You study. You listen to your elders, and you search your own soul. Eventually, you come to know for sure what's right and what's wrong. Trust me, people don't have as much trouble telling the one from the other as they'd like you to believe. Their real trouble is in not being brave enough to stand up for what they know is right, but spending all their effort instead on trying to justify the easy way out. But the easy way always leads to damnation."

The mule halted. Philip dropped his eyes and flushed beneath Duncan's fierce gaze. "Yes, sir," he said.

Duncan nodded, gave a grunt of approval, then turned his face toward the sunset. "Night's falling, but the moon's already high," he said, looking upward at the pale wedge hanging in the sky above the trail. "We have several more hours with enough light for our search. We'll keep going until we absolutely have to stop."

He fumbled in a pack for a moment, then drew out a bullhorn. He stared at it for a bit, turning it over in his hands as if reminding himself of how it functioned: a chemical reaction in the batteries would push an electrical current through a coil that caused the horn to resonate with an amplified version of whatever sound was fed into the microphone at the narrow end. He flipped the on/off switch and there was a satisfying, amplified click, followed by a slight ringing of feedback. Lifting the bullhorn to his mouth, he shouted, "Camigwen!"

The name boomed beneath the trees like a thunderclap. Philip flinched.

* * *

Eventually, she slept and dreamed. In the dream, she was eleven years old, living in Dublin. She was a pretty girl, though small for her age, with a dancer's posture and a poet's eyes. Her mother took her to see *The Nutcracker Suite*, and, noting her breathless fascination with the dancers, promised afterward to talk to Father about enrolling her in ballet classes.

Her father, a big, gruff fellow with a florid complexion and the manner of a ruffled crow, a man who eked out a meager living as "Reverend" O'Neil, pastor of a tiny Methodist church in the city, exploded.

"That's all the girl thinks about!" he shouted, tossing his arms in the air as he stalked back and forth across the scarred floorboards of their tiny kitchen. "Frivolity. It isn't enough that she spends her every waking moment with her nose buried in fairy tales. Now she wants to waste even more time, and our hard-earned money, on another frivolous pastime. When is she going to grow up and realize that you have to work hard to accomplish any good in this wicked world?"

Her mother hadn't answered, but simply sat grim-lipped, staring fixedly at her hands clasped on the kitchen table before her, quietly weathering the storm.

"And what good has dancing ever done anybody?" In her dream, he leaned forward and shouted directly into her face. "I'll tell you what it's done; it's led weak people to worship false gods, and to rut like animals before them!

"Life isn't about all play and fun, missy," he said. "It's a testing ground. Those who take it seriously and devote themselves to good works will end up with God in Heaven. But sluggards and dreamers will find themselves dancing right down the wide road to Hell!"

Eventually his tirade had finished, and her mother had gone the next day to work out a bargain with a dance studio, whereby they would give dance lessons in exchange for her mother's work as a janitor. Though the girl threw herself into the classes, she always felt secretly ashamed that her mother had to make such a deal.

* * *

Philip clutched the ample folds of his too-short cloak about himself and shivered. Roughly an hour had passed since sunset, and the damp night air was turning cooler. But it was the sight of the corpse that truly chilled him. He stood holding the reins of both mare and mule while Duncan crouched to examine the body. Both animals were skittish. They tossed their heads and pawed the earth, ears flicking at the slightest whisper of wind.

"A messy death," Duncan said. The words came out in something of a hush. He stood, cleared his throat noisily, and continued in a more normal voice. "He

was a traveling tinker, from the looks of things."
Duncan gestured toward a ragged pack lying a few
yards away from the body, with several dented copper
pots and a few tools spilled out. "I'd guess he died
sometime this afternoon. Must have met up with a
bear, the way he's been mauled. His rib cage has been
crushed like he was hugged to death."

Philip's eyes flashed white as the mule's. "Why's his
skin so pale?" he asked.

Duncan glanced at the boy, then back down. He let
out a deep breath. "Blood loss," he suggested finally,
"and shock."

Philip shook his head mechanically, his eyes fixed
upon the corpse. "It's all shriveled and puckered, too.
Like all the juices have been sucked out." He shivered
again.

"And look at the tracks." He let go his cloak to point
at the earth around the body. It was torn and broken,
as if a great spiked wheel had rolled across it.

Duncan bent and pulled a thorn out of the victim's
clothing, compared it with another he plucked from
the broken earth. "Not a bear, then," he said. "No
matter. We'll deal with it if we have to." He took the
mare's reins and remounted. The animal sidestepped
nervously, but quieted a bit when he patted its neck.
"Right now, we have a mission to finish. We'll stop and
bury the body on the way back."

Philip tore his eyes away from the dead man, looked
up at Duncan, then at his mule. Stiffly, he walked to its
side and hoisted himself into the saddle.

Duncan gave him a reassuring smile, then turned
the mare and headed onward down the trail. The mule
lurched forward, trotting to catch up.

* * *

In her dream, years passed. She lay in a hospital bed, awash in a haze of pain. Her father was speaking again … something about mercy. Slowly, the words solidified.

"All discipline seems harsh at the moment," he said. "But in the end, we see it as God's mercy." His voice trembled somewhat, and he cleared his throat loudly.

She struggled to remember what had happened. She heard the sound of pages turning, then her father's voice again, this time more formal, more mechanical. "'Now no chastening for the present seemeth to be joyous, but grievous,'" he read, "'… nevertheless afterward it yieldeth the peaceable fruit of righteousness unto them which are exercised thereby.'"

She had been somewhere. She remembered staring out the window of a train. Going where? The rest of the dance troupe had been with her. They were going to perform somewhere … in Belfast! She remembered the station, the crowds of people, the anticipation of seeing the city.

She remembered the bomb blast. The people screaming. "That's how you have to think of this," her father said. "I know it's difficult right now, but you'll come to see God's wisdom in it. It's just a way of getting your attention, of removing the temptation to waste your life."

She tried to lift her head. A blaze of agony flashed up her neck and detonated inside her skull, then ran back down into her shoulders. Her spine felt on fire. Her arms pulsed with pain. She couldn't feel her legs.

Her heart seemed to stop when she realized the fact. "But it's not the end of the world," her father was saying. "You'll see that. There are a lot of good works for you to do even from a wheelchair."

She screamed …

* * *

Philip looked again at the sky. The moon had crawled its way down the heavens. It hung on its side like the hull of a gleaming silver ship sailing the rustling treetops of the wood. The course they followed had grown wilder. The trees crowded closer to it on either side. It was dark beneath them, and patches of shadow spilled out across their path, masking stones and roots that made their mounts stumble.

"Are you sure we're headed the right way?" he called toward Duncan's back. "If we are, your sister sure picked an awfully out-of-the-way spot to live. There haven't been any lights of houses or smoke of fireplaces, no signs I could see that anybody at all lives anywhere around here." He raised his voice again, called "What should I be watching for?"

"She has to come to us," Duncan answered. "There won't be any house or fire to see." He halted the mare, took the bullhorn from his pack again, and examined it before turning it on and shouting into it, "Camigwen!"

The night's raucous chorus of crickets and tree frogs immediately fell silent as if the bullhorn had stricken them dead. Only the whispering of leaves in the evening breeze remained. Duncan sat with his head turned to one side, straining to hear any reply to his call. Philip licked dry lips and peered intently at the trees all around, watching for signs of anything approaching. His hands clenched the mule's reins.

One by one, the frogs and crickets regained their

voices. Philip let out the breath he had been holding. Duncan glanced at him, cleared his throat, and clucked to the mare, turning her head once more down the path.

"We'd best make what distance we can before the moon sets completely," he said over his shoulder as the mare resumed her gait and Philip kicked his mule into motion.

They rode on in silence for several minutes, during which time Duncan glanced back repeatedly at his squire. Philip followed gamely, but the boy's tension and fear were evident in the manner in which he sat atop the mule, the way he clutched the reins, the jerking of his head when a startled rabbit skittered through the underbrush. It was obvious that the battered corpse they had found earlier in the evening had spooked Philip considerably.

Duncan drummed his fingers on his saddle, rubbed a hand along his bearded jaw. "I suppose I ought to explain about Camigwen ..." He spoke loudly, to carry back over his shoulder above the clopping of hooves and the rasping of crickets. "... why she's out here, why there'll be no house or fire to spot. It's something of a story."

Hearing no reply, he continued. "Camigwen is my junior by nearly ten years. I was out of the house, off to seminary, before she had grown very old, so there wasn't much chance of us being close. She was something of a dreamer, never seemed to have her feet quite on the ground. It rankled our father something fierce. He was a preacher, a stern man, full of fire and brimstone, but his heart was in the right place — though Camigwen could never see that. As she came into her teen years, they clashed quite a lot, neither one really hearing the other, just generating a lot of heat.

"She was always our mother's darling, though. Mother said Cami had a spark of something few people possess, that she saw deeper than most. The way Mother put it, 'Many people don't even look for Heaven. Of those who do, most settle for just a hope of it. But Camigwen actually catches glimpses of Heaven now and again, whether or not she recognizes it as such.'

"So from the time Cami was seven or so, Mother did what she could to provide the means for her to explore whatever current interest she had, whether it was music lessons, or art supplies, or dance classes. And as Cami got older, and Father grew more impatient with her flightiness, Mother did what she could to defuse their fights.

"It was dance that most captured Cami's heart, though. By the time she was seventeen, she had become quite accomplished — good enough, in fact, to join Dublin's most prestigious dance troupe. Mother died shortly thereafter — a heart attack — and Father and Camigwen seemed to take their pain out on each other. Father disapproved of Cami's dancing, said it was irreligious, and they fought about it frequently and bitterly. Finally, Cami moved out of the house and in with another member of her dance troupe — a male member. I think she did it just to revenge herself on Father.

"Then the dance troupe went to Belfast to perform, and an IRA bomb exploded in the train station when they arrived. One of the other dancers died; my sister suffered burns over thirty percent of her body and a spinal injury that left her legs paralyzed.

"She took it hard. Father went to see her a couple of times at the hospital in Belfast, but she threw such a fit that they had to insist he stay away. I had been to Indonesia, working with a missionary group, and came back to see her, but she made them turn me away too. When her burns had healed, they moved her to a private facility to treat her for clinical depression. I stayed on with Father in Dublin, hoping we could all patch things up eventually.

"Then the invasion came, and as you know, the world changed ..."

* * *

The battered gray cab had dropped them off across from the Bond Street Private Hospital. While Duncan paused to pay the cabby, his father found a seat on a public bench and sat frowning across at the facility, his big, age-freckled hands resting heavily on the head of a scarred oak cane. When Duncan finished, he helped the old man to his feet and escorted him across the street, through the wrought-iron fence, and up the path to the hospital's lobby entrance.

"I'm going to see her this time," his father said, half to himself. "I don't care what the doctor says. It's about time she faced up to reality. No more of this molly-coddling."

Duncan just nodded. Once inside, he seated his father and went to the desk to announce himself. The receptionist rang up a nurse, who went to tell Camigwen O'Neil she had visitors.

All too soon, the nurse returned. "I'm sorry," she said, "but Camigwen still refuses to see you. We had hoped that maybe this time.... But we can't force her. You understand, I'm sure."

The elder O'Neil's face began to turn livid. "Father

…" Duncan began.

"No!" cried the older man. "I'll not be turned away again like some beggar on the doorstep! Tell me which room she's in, missy, or I'll search every one of them till I find her." The nurse shrank back as he brandished his cane at her.

Duncan laid a hand on his shoulder, but the old man shook it off. "I mean what I say! Someone had best take me to her right now!"

"Please, Mr. O'Neil, calm yourself" the nurse said. Duncan saw the receptionist watching the altercation — and then she picked up her phone. He tried to usher his father to a seat, but the old man would have none of it.

"'Honor thy father and mother,' the Book says!" The elder O'Neil was shouting to the lobby in general now; he trembled with rage.

Duncan saw a pair of orderlies enter from a hallway. Their eyes were on his father. Vainly, he tried again to calm the old man but was shaken off. The orderlies were getting closer.

And then a ripple seemed to pass through the air. Duncan felt a wave of dizziness wash over him. All movement froze for just an instant, then resumed, but with differences. One of the orderlies stumbled, caught himself, began shrinking in stature even as his limbs and torso thickened, splitting the seams of his uniform. The other orderly shouted in horror at the sight, then fled. Duncan heard people screaming at a distance, but his eyes were on his father.

When the wave passed over him, the Reverend O'Neil stiffened with a jerk. His eyes rolled back in their sockets, all the color drained from his face, and then he simply folded up like a marionette whose strings had been cut. His cane clattered noisily to the floor. Duncan caught the old man as he fell, knelt holding him to his chest. Stunned, he felt for a pulse — there was none. In stupefied shock, he scanned the lobby for someone to help — it was empty. He couldn't seem to catch his breath; he didn't know what to do. A sense of isolation crushed him down like a huge weight. Then he remembered: Camigwen was somewhere nearby. I have to find her, help her, he thought. Laying his father on the floor, he went to the abandoned receptionist's desk and flipped through the registry till he found the entry "O'Neil, Camigwen, 103."

Something heavy struck the front of the building, and bits of plaster fell from the ceiling. There was a squeal of pain from just outside the main door, followed by a rumble of wicked laughter. Duncan ran back toward the stairs, fought his way up them through a scattering of panicked people coming down. By the time he had climbed the flight to the first story, the whole building was shaking with repeated blows from various sides. He caught a glimpse of a huge head and shoulders through a window at the end of the hall and wondered, dizzily, if he were going insane. But he pressed on toward room 103. The only thought in his mind, through all the madness, was the absurd notion that he must reach Cami before she left her room.

Of course she hadn't. When he entered, she was sitting in a wheelchair, staring out her window. But the light seemed to play tricks with his eyes. There was a prismatic glow radiating all around her, and she was constantly changing sizes. Before he could say anything, before he could move, she settled on one. He blinked, and she became a tiny thing hovering in the window, with the light glinting on a pair of dragonfly wings sprouting from her back. Then she flew out and away, while Duncan hung in the doorway, stunned.

Suddenly, an eye the size of a dinner plate peered in the window at him. He grabbed up a straight chair, threw it, and fled. Back down the stairs he ran, then out a back door. A trio of "men" two stories tall were demolishing the hospital with clubs the size of oak trees, grabbing up people as they fled the building and tearing them limb from limb, or stamping them to jelly on the lawn. Duncan prayed fervently not to be seen, desperately thought of himself as invisible. Somehow, he made it past the giants without being spotted.

Over the course of the next several hours, he fled through a city of nightmare. Fantastic armies of giants, dwarves, and even Vikings marched through the streets, demolishing whole city blocks, herding the native populace before them, or simply slaughtering the people where they stood. At the outskirts, Duncan joined up with a handful of survivors, most on foot, a few with bicycles — engine-powered vehicles had all ceased functioning. Together, the refugees fled into the surrounding countryside, hoping to find aid and maybe even some sort of answers to the impossibilities they had witnessed.

* * *

"... I headed back to Dublin, my home city." The moonlight glinted on his helm as Duncan turned to glance back at Philip. His saddle creaked with the movement. "A few days later, one of Lady Ardinay's aides came through. After talking with me, he told me I was a Storm Knight. Then he spent a few hours teaching me something of what that means, outfitted me with this sword and armor, and assigned you to be my squire. I've tried to be faithful to that calling.

"But I didn't give up on looking for my sister. I've been tracking down stories of fairies being spotted in Dublin, and yesterday I even managed to talk to one of the Celosia, the plant fairies. He said that there had been a strange fairy in town a few weeks ago, a sad one with dead legs. She stayed with the Celosia for a fortnight or so, then left town headed west down the trail we're following now.

"I didn't get the impression that she was going anywhere in particular, so she's not likely to be traveling fast. As long as we keep pushing, we ought to catch up to her. But I don't really know what signs to look for. I just have to hope that she'll answer the bullhorn when she hears it."

Duncan halted the mare and turned in his saddle to see what effect his story had had on his squire. Philip was staring at him; the moonlit half of his face looked thoughtful. Then suddenly his visible eye focused on something beyond Duncan and he stiffened.

Duncan spun, reaching across his shoulder for his sword.

* * *

… Camigwen jolted awake. Hazy nightmare after-images clouded her mind, making it difficult to focus. Her heart was hammering, and she was chilled. Her right arm had fallen asleep where it was curled beneath her head. Her wings felt stiff.

Clumsily, she pushed her torso upright by reaching across with her left hand, then began kneading and flexing her right arm to restore circulation. Her wings snapped open and closed a trio of times in quick succession. As the dream images faded, her pulse slowed to normal. She rubbed sleep from her eyes.

Night had fallen. A low crescent moon silvered the glade, its light reflected from thousands of separate water droplets on flower petals and grass blades. They sparkled like stars among the sharp-edged shadows.

It was a lovely sight, but a lonely one. Camigwen sighed. Her heart hurt, and there was no one to talk to about it. She was cut off from friends and family by a gulf far greater than mere distance. Her mother might have listened to the little fairy-woman, might even have understood a little, but she was gone. That left her father and brother, one too fossilized in his private version of Truth to hear her when she was still human, the other too ... what? Too busy with his own life? She couldn't really say.

Duncan was so much older than she that they'd never been more than strangers spawned in the same house. But one thing was certain: Duncan had never seen things the same way she had. He had been dutiful where she had been independent. Duncan's had been the way of peace, but it seemed so dull to her. Better to burn out quickly, painfully bright, she thought, than to plod along dumbly like a shackled sheep.

She smiled wryly at the thought, jeered herself for growing melodramatic and alliterative. It always happened when she thought about her family. The problems involved there changed with a glacial slowness, if at all, and thinking about the situation was just so much useless spinning of wheels on ice. If only she had someone to talk to, someone to serve as a sounding board for her unspoken thoughts. But that was exactly the problem. She couldn't imagine anyone who could hope to empathize with her situation.

The crippling had been difficult enough, but she'd always known deep down below the anger and hurt (and the simple, but profound, disappointment of a lost career), that there had been other people who had suffered similarly. Even though she couldn't talk to family at the time (for fear of their self-righteous pity), and couldn't bring herself to talk to friends (for sheer jealousy that they could dance while she no longer could), the simple fact that there were other cripples living reasonably normal lives at least lent her hope of eventually overcoming her helpless rage.

But this! How did one come to terms with such a thing? In the space of a few scant heartbeats she had been transformed from a flesh-and-blood human woman into a being of sheerest fantasy. What human was there in history that she could point to and say, "That person understood what I am going through, and survived it; therefore there is hope for me"? There was no one.

Worse yet, there were none among the fairie. She had gone looking. When the change had occurred, and once she recovered from the shock of shedding her wheelchair like a chrysalis and being reborn as a creature of flight, she had joyfully searched for others of her kind. Finding them had been easy enough — for one who knew the signs from a childhood full of fairy tales. Joining them had been something altogether different.

Over the course of her search, she had met fairies of earth, of sky, of water, fire, and metal. She had even talked with a brownie who had strayed from the invading cosm itself. While none had done her lasting harm, none had welcomed her either. All struck her as somehow less than real, as if they were nothing more than personifications of whatever element they were attuned to.

The closest she had come to fitting in was when her journey led her back to Dublin (drawn, undoubtedly, by a subconscious desire to return "home"). She had met a band of Celosia there, and captivated by the beauty of their work with flowers, she had joined them for a while. She had even learned something of their magic, as attested to by the richness of the glade she currently occupied, by the ring of toadstools that warded her from nocturnal hunting creatures.

But tending garden did not long fulfill her need for purpose, nor did the company of the Celosia satisfy her desire for companionship. When, out of a desire to share another type of beauty, she tried to teach them something of classical dance, they had watched her movements in total incomprehension. They might as well have been nothing more than bees. And if she could not share the beauty of dance with them, how could she hope to share the pain of her past?

She sighed, and looked again around the glade. Tomorrow would be another day just like today. The sun would rise, the plants would drink it in, the sun would set — and she would dance and then stop, and be sitting here once again, thinking the same thoughts. She wondered, idly, how long a fairy lived.

The still air was suddenly shattered by a shout. "Camigwen!" Her thoughts scattered like a handful of dropped pebbles. For long moments the fact that it was her name that had been called did not even register. Then it struck her whose voice it was … and how dangerous it was for him to be stomping about this far from civilization in the middle of the night, advertising his presence to everything with ears and some few horrible things without.

Spitting a curse, she leapt into the air and flew toward the sound of her brother's voice.

* * *

Duncan pulled his sword clear of its scabbard and brought it up to a ready position as he twisted in the saddle. The mare turned in response to a nearly unconscious pressure from his knee. He cast about for any sign of threat, wondering what it was that had caused Philip to react, and remembering all too easily the mangled body they had discovered earlier.

Then he spotted it — something tiny and luminous coming through the trees ahead and to the right of the path. From the way it bobbed about, it could easily have been a lantern. A very dim one, perhaps. Before long, it reached the path, and then it came more rapidly toward him. If it was a lantern, he couldn't make out the shape or size of whomever was carrying it. Then he recognized the source of the light and lowered his blade.

Camigwen halted a meter beyond his mount's head, hovering on a level with his own eyes. Though he could not make out the finer details of her face, he clearly recognized the angry hiss of her voice, even above the furious buzzing of her wings. Her fists were clenched tightly on her hips as she spoke.

"What the hell is the matter with you?" Duncan, heart pounding at the look of her, considered how best to answer the question. Before he could settle on a reply, she continued.

"Is it that you're trying to get yourself killed, and

that poor boy behind you? There are wild things out here, Duncan, and you're plodding along in your usual 'damn-the-torpedoes' manner, shouting through a bullhorn, for Christ's sake! Why not just tie the boy to a tree and cut his throat, then strip yourself naked and lie down to sleep beneath the body? Something entertaining's bound to find you then!"

Despite himself, Duncan flushed at her ridicule. He could hear Philip shifting uncomfortably in his saddle, then the sound of the mule being guided to a more respectful distance. His ears began to burn, and he was thankful that the darkness hid the fact.

"I came looking for you, Camigwen. And now I've found you," he said simply.

"What made you think I wanted to be found?"

Duncan didn't answer the question. "Father's dead, Cami," he said.

She dropped several centimeters in response to that blunt statement, then returned to her original elevation. But he noticed that her glow had dimmed somewhat and her arms hung more loosely. Her eyes were downcast.

He continued, "There're just the two of us now. I ... I don't want either one of us to forget that we're family. So I've come to take you back to Dublin with me. There's work to be done there; we're fighting the invasion, and we could use your help."

Her glow regained some of its intensity, and she squared her shoulders defiantly. "I've already had one father, Duncan, and believe me, that was more than enough. Nothing I ever did — no, nothing I ever was met with his approval. I'm not about to subject myself to another twenty-some years of seeking yours."

He frowned and raised his left hand from his sword

hilt in a gesture of negation. "I don't know what you're talking about."

"No? You've always been so sure of yourself, Duncan — and that's damned irritating to those of us who see life as a mystery. Your kind wants to put fences up around everything. 'This is okay to think about, but that isn't.' Or maybe it's just that you want to put everything in a box, to say that you have all of existence nicely labeled and separated into two camps — Good things on one side, and Evil on the other. And the funny thing is, your worst enemies are all just like you. You preach conformity to a religious truth, they preach it to a scientific one, or to a social one, or whatever.

"Well, I don't find life so conveniently divisible. And I don't want to. I don't trust your labels. I don't trust any of your answers. I want to be free to find my own. And I'm sick to death of that desire for freedom being characterized as 'rebelliousness,' or 'intellectual laziness.' I'm sick of people preaching at me. All I want from all of you is to be left alone."

Duncan simply stared at her. He sighed. "Are you quite finished? I have no idea where that all came from, but if it's a theological argument you want, I'm ready to give it to you!" His face heated in the darkness. He hadn't expected this kind of reception, but he certainly knew how to handle it.

"Have you really searched your heart, Cami? Have you seriously thought about your motives? Is it that you aren't sure of what's right? Or could it be that you're afraid to come back with me?" He paused, thoughts coming together into an inevitable truth. "Afraid because you think that if we defeat the invasion things will return to the way they were, and you'll be back in a wheelchair?"

Camigwen glared at him. When she spoke, her voice was low and fierce. "I am not so stupid, nor so self-centered as you seem to think, Duncan. I didn't say I don't care about right and wrong, but that I don't trust your definitions of them. That you could even think I might be so shallow just proves how far apart we are." She gritted her teeth. "So why don't you just turn your horse around and get the hell back where you belong?"

Duncan clenched his jaw, then shook his head. "All right," he said, "I will. If you're so blind with resentment that you can't recognize the significance of the trouble I've gone through to find you, then there's nothing I can do. I've got work to do in Dublin, and it's time to be getting back to it."

He wheeled his mare about and started back down the path the way he had come. "Let's go, Philip," he said as he passed the boy.

"What about that thing that killed that man back there? It could be prowling around someplace nearby." Philip said.

Duncan halted his mount and spoke back over his shoulder. "If you're worried about Cami, she said she doesn't need us, that she's perfectly able to take care of herself. And I'm not afraid of it, so don't worry about traveling by night."

"Well … that's not what I meant," Philip said. "I meant … shouldn't we do something about it?"

Duncan remained facing toward the east and Dublin. Cami flew past him and turned to look in his eye. "What 'thing' is he talking about, Duncan?"

"It's just a bear," he replied quickly. "It mauled a traveler a few kilometers back. We found the body. But I'm sure you can handle it without our help."

Camigwen's voice was icy. "If it mauled a traveler,

you can't just let it to run free. It's sure to kill someone else. Yes, I can take care of myself, but destroying a rogue bear is a bit beyond my abilities."

Duncan crossed his arms across his chest. "Are you suddenly dictating to me what I should do, after arguing so eloquently against people shoving 'right and wrong' down each other's throats? I have other, more important duties."

Philip again withdrew to a discrete distance as Camigwen glared at Duncan. The buzzing of her wings grew more furious. Tension hung thickly in the night air. Duncan glared back at her, then cleared his throat as if to speak.

Philip screamed. Cami made a startled leap back and upward. "A Green Man!" she shouted as Duncan wheeled his mount around. The mare caught a glimpse of Philip's assailant and reared in panic, tumbling Duncan out of the saddle to land heavily on his back.

The impact knocked the wind out of him. His diaphragm locked up, and an ache began building toward a crescendo in the region of his kidneys. Dimly, he could hear the retreating hoof beats of the mare in one direction and of the mule in the other, could hear Philip's desperate pleas for help and the sound of something crashing through the underbrush. He rolled to hands and knees and forced himself to stand, fighting for breath, and feeling like a total fool.

"Stay back, Cami," he managed to gasp, but she was already following the retreating sound of Philip's cries. Duncan launched himself after her.

Branches tore at his cloak as he ran, choking him. He reached up with one hand and ripped the ties loose, let the cloak fall, ran on. Now the branches slipped across his chainmail without finding purchase, but left scratches on his face and the backs of his hands. He didn't slow his pace. Philip's cries were growing nearer — and more desperate.

Soon, Duncan could see a figure bulking blackly ahead of him. It broke into a clearing, and the last of the moonlight fell upon its mossy back. Its armed were wrapped around a human-sized bundle, carried like one might carry a baby … or a haunch of beef.

Duncan put on a last burst of speed, raised his sword above his head with both hands, and swung it down with all his might.

It was like chopping into a tree trunk. The blade wedged deep into what felt like wood. Then the creature dropped Philip and spun about to face him, and the sword was wrenched from his hands.

The Green Man looked like a walking stump, its surface scabbed with cracked, barklike skin and patches of unhealthy looking moss. Its face was hideous — entirely too large for its body, with ragged-edged knotholes the size of Duncan's fists for eyes, and a snarling mouth whose corners reached down well into what should have been its chest. Its short legs and feet were gnarled and spiked like clustered roots, and its arms were twisted limbs with multiple long, twiggy fingers that sprouted wicked-looking thorns, many of which glistened darkly with Philip's blood. Duncan could see the point of his sword projecting upward and forward on one side of the creature's head like some sort of bizarre pencil tucked behind its ear.

Snarling, the Green Man took a rapid step toward him and swung with its right arm. Duncan ducked, but one of the twig fingers lashed across his face, leaving a bloody gash that narrowly missed his left eye. Meanwhile the creature had stepped forward once again, closing with him — it was quicker than he would have suspected. As it lifted its right arm to hammer down upon his head, Duncan reached out with his mind to feel the possibilities surrounding him. He seized one.

When the blow landed, he had leaped safely to one side. The Green Man recovered and turned toward him. Again Duncan seized a possibility, and again the creature's blow missed. But Duncan knew he couldn't keep this up forever. Eventually he would use up all his "luck," and the Green Man would crush him.

Twice more it swung, and each time he manipulated reality in order to evade it. Each time grew more difficult; Duncan could feel his grasp of possibilities dulling. He tried once to tear his sword free and received a ragged gash across his palm for his trouble. But he knew the sword would be of little use against the thing's tough hide anyway.

Now the creature began to stalk him, convinced of his helplessness against it. Duncan retreated slowly. Resolving to drag things out as long as possible, he worked to stay just out of its reach, and hoped desperately for a miracle. His ability to shape possibilities was nearly exhausted, but he racked his brain for some last trick that he could pull to seriously hurt the thing. Unexpectedly, he felt another force drawing possibility energy into itself. For a moment, he feared that it was the Green Man.

Then he spotted Camigwen hovering in the center of the clearing. Her normal pale luminescence had intensified to a brilliance that rivaled the moon's. Even from a distance, Duncan could clearly see her features locked in concentration, and he could feel the possibilities being siphoned into her being. The distraction cost him, however. The Green Man lashed out again and struck him on the helmet, sending him sprawling. The blow made his head ring, and he felt blood running from his nostrils. Duncan blinked his eyes to clear his vision, tried futilely to lever himself up from the ground. His head threatened to come apart as he did so. Helplessly, he heard the creature's heavy tread approaching, saw its rooty foot rise, watched in horror as prepared to stomp down on his ringing head.

Duncan braced himself to die. Suddenly, a green nimbus sprang into being around the creature's rear leg. Camigwen flew closer, gesturing downward with splayed fingers, and the rootlets of that foot began burrowing into the soil beneath. Duncan forced himself to roll onto his belly, just out of reach of the other foot as it struck the ground. He took a ragged, hopeful breath — Camigwen was using the plant magic of the Celosia to root the creature to the ground! Painfully, he began struggling to his hands and knees.

The Green Man gave out a booming howl. It turned to face the fairy, took a step toward her with its free foot, then that one too rooted itself to the earth. Cami grimaced in fierce concentration as she drove the roots deep into the soil. Then, with a cracking sound, the creature's legs began growing together, forming into a trunk.

But the Green Man had not given up. Fighting the growing rigidity of its body, it reached painfully backward and grasped the hilt of Duncan's sword, working the blade free from its lodgment. Determinedly, it twisted its torso to face Duncan again, then strained both arms upward to lift his weapon high in the air, intent upon bringing the sword forcefully down upon him. Duncan knew that when the blow landed it would cut him in two, but his aching head could not force his limbs to move him any further out of range.

But Camigwen was fairly crackling with energy now. Though she was eclipsed by the Green Man's bulk, her fairy glow blazed like a corona with the possibilities she was manipulating. Even through his haze of pain, Duncan could feel the electricity in the air. Dimly, he recalled her reading him tales of Cinlums, the fairies of elemental air, summoning storms to destroy crops. He wondered if a gust of wind could blow him beyond the sword's reach.

The sword began its downward rush, but the Green Man was too late. With a deafening crack of thunder, a bolt of lightning arced from Camigwen's body to Duncan's sword. Duncan was blinded by the flash.

A few minutes later, when his vision returned, Duncan saw the Green Man's smoking remains, a wide crack splitting the thing in two from top to base. Its arms had been burned to mere stubs, and the only sign that remained of his sword was a scorched hilt smoking in the grass before the blasted stump.

Duncan scanned the area for Camigwen and soon spotted her glow, quite diminished now. She was lying, dazed, off to his left, just a few meters away. He crawled to her on hands and knees, saw that she was breathing normally. A few minutes later, when he had recovered enough to stumble back to where Philip had been dropped, he discovered to his relief that the boy was still alive though bleeding from dozens of cuts and punctures. Retrieving his discarded cloak, Duncan began tearing it into strips and binding the worst of the wounds.

By the time he had finished, Camigwen had recovered. He found her staring at the Green Man's remains.

"That was a wicked thing," she said, her voice

reminding him of the little sister he had barely known so long ago. Duncan nodded, then regretted it. He wondered if his head would ever stop pounding. When the throbbing had subsided to a dull ache, he turned toward his sister. "You're a stormer, Camigwen," he said softly. "You shouldn't let it go to waste."

She looked him in the eyes, something odd and tender in her expression. "What about you?" she said. "You're a stormer. Will you let that go to waste?"

He started an angry retort, then bit it back. He suddenly knew exactly what she meant, and it galled him. Finally he gave a bitter laugh. "The brave hero," he said. "I told myself my duties as a Storm Knight were too important to waste time on a rogue bear. I knew it couldn't be a bear. I … I was just afraid, I guess." He looked up at her, eyes glistening in the light she cast. "That's not like me, Cami."

"I think it is," she said softly. "I think you've been afraid all your life—afraid of father, afraid of standing up for yourself. That's why you've followed so closely in his footsteps. You've used 'duty' as an excuse to avoid doing a lot of things."

He remembered his boastful words to Philip earlier that evening. "I guess I'm hopeless," he said sadly.

"No!" she cried fiercely. "No! I saw you be brave when it mattered. The world has changed completely, and we all have another chance. I said you'd once chosen to be like father, but it's not too late to take a new direction … to try something daring."

He smiled with genuine pleasure. "I think you're right." He stood, feeling strength come back quickly to his aching limbs. "I'll find the horse, and take Philip back to Dublin. He'll help me remember how to be brave."

Cami lowered her eyes. Eventually she sighed. "I'll need both of you to help me to remember myself."

"What?"

She looked up again. "You were right, a little, about me — about the ... the wheelchair. My wanting to stay here is the same as your not wanting to deal with the creature of the woods.

"Look, enough idle chitchat." Her wings buzzed with renewed vigor. "We need to get Philip back to Dublin, and you look the worse for wear yourself. There's blood all over your face, and your eyes are turning black. Don't worry, I know the way."

"But —" Duncan said.

"You stay here," she added. "I'll go fetch the mounts. Fairy charms are useful for such things."

Duncan smiled.

Warriors of Destiny

G. D. Swick

"*. . . now that a people have come amongst us who know how to make them, we shall have martyrs aplenty.*" — The Archbishop of Cashel

"Ye've lost yur mind, Letitia Blossomwalker!" the leprechaun known as Leafflyer shouted. "First, ye make a friend o' one o' the Big Feet, then ye bring her to our clan counsel, an' now ye want to make a deal with a dragon an' use leprechaun gold to seal the bargain! Ye've lost yur mind, Letty."

"Hush yurself, Leafflyer," Letty shot back. She gestured at Elizabeth O'Cleary, the human sitting beside her on the fallen trunk of an ancient oak. "This lass could no more harm us than she could turn into a bird. She has some magic in her, aye, like her people once had before they turned away from the land, but she does'na understand it. She couldna use the magic to harm someone even to defend her life. I'm tryin' to tell ye that the land is in danger an' —"

"If so, the danger comes from where it's always

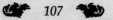

come from—the Tall Ones, like her!" Leafflyer shouted, pointing an accusing finger.

Elizabeth cringed. Why was Letty's friend yelling at her? Everyone seemed to yell now, ever since that mean priest Mr. Tourret came to town. Was it a sin to think a priest was mean? Well, he *was* mean, even if he was a priest like Father Ryan. Father Ryan yelled now, too, even during Mass. I liked it better when he talked about loving each other and everybody left the church smiling. *I don't like going to Mass anymore. Forgive me, Jesus.* She crossed herself reflexively.

She was still wearing the dress and jacket she had worn to Mass that morning. Her feet dangled a few inches above the ground as she sat on the oak trunk. At nineteen, her body was slight, but she still towered over the leprechauns gathered about the clearing. Her flat face, slanted eyes, and wide lips showed the features common to those, like herself, born with Down's syndrome. Nervously, she began twisting a strand of her short, brown hair. Tears sparkled in her slanted eyes.

"Ye'll be leavin' Elizabeth alone, Shamus Leafflyer," Letty said, noticing the tears. "If I hadna met her, I mightna have heard o' this Tourret until it was too late. When he speaks, I hear a winter without end rise up howlin' an' shriekin' in my breast, an' a demon voice speaks along with him. The land sent Elizabeth to us for a reason. Now hush an' listen!"

"Dinna be hushin' me, Letitia. I knew ye for a thousand seasons before we all laid down to take our great nap an' — "

"Please listen to her," Elizabeth said, the tears no longer held in check. "Please listen about Mr. Tourret. Well, he's really Father Tourret; I mean he wears a collar and says Mass, but he doesn't act like Father Ryan. But

Father Ryan doesn't act like he used to and now something's happening to Mr. M'Kenna, too, and he was already so sad, and that Jeremy Bratton scares me and ..."

Confused by her racing thoughts, her tongue unable to keep pace, she lapsed into silence and sat staring down at the oak trunk, tears sliding along her cheeks.

There was a shamed silence from the other leprechauns. "Elizabeth," Letty said, laying a reassuring hand on her friend's arm, "why dinna ye make some flowers, the way I taught ye to? I'll make these contrary old fools listen."

Elizabeth nodded and stared at her cupped hands, trying to concentrate on roses so she could make one appear between her fingers, but instead, she kept seeing what had happened at the churchyard in Neary's Parish that morning. Around her, the arguing began again. This wasn't like the other times she had sat here with Letty, just the two of them. It used to be so nice here, she thought, her mind drifting away from the shouting leprechauns ...

* * *

Elizabeth walked through the fields west of Neary's Parish under a robin's-egg sky and clouds like great balls of cotton. As she left the last of the houses behind, she remembered what Letty had taught her about walking and, closing her eyes, imagined her feet getting lighter and lighter. Soon she was barely skimming the grass, pretending to be a butterfly borne lightly along on the breeze.

When she reached a stand of trees near a bend in a small stream, she slipped beneath their branches and sat on a carpet of leaves.

"Letty, I've got breakfuss," she called, her wide, thick tongue slurring the words.

There was the smallest stirring of leaves in a patch of flowers and the tiny woman, wearing a dress and jacket of emerald green, emerged to climb onto a root beside her.

"Good mornin' to ye, Elizabeth."

"Good mornun, Letitia. See what I've got?" Elizabeth asked, handing a pastry to her friend.

"Aye, wait a moment," Letty said, breaking a leaf from a mint plant and dipping it into the pouch slung on her belt. "Chew on this, lass, just like before so we can speak in the proper old language instead o' that abomination yur people came up with while mine were nappin'."

Elizabeth took the leaf into her mouth. She knew her friend wasn't making fun of her talking, the way some children had done as she was growing up. Letty had explained to her that leprechaun ears were sensitive enough to hear the voice of the land, and the "abomination" of English was not pleasing to those ears.

Together they munched their breakfast, Elizabeth finishing what Letty couldn't hold. Afterwards, they sat in the shade while Elizabeth dripped multicolored stars from her fingertips, watching them sparkle and disappear in the sunbeams that danced through openings in the branches.

"Teach me how to make flowers again, Letty. I forgot."

"Now, lass, it's just like makin' those stars or walkin' proper. All ye have to do is picture what ye want — a rose or whatever — an' then imagine it bloomin' between yur hands."

Elizabeth thought. She imagined the roses that grew in the churchyard, small red blooms with golden crowns in their centers. In her mind one such rose opened from dew-speckled bud to full blossom. An identical flower began to appear, dimly at first, then ever more brightly, between her cupped palms. The rose's petals turned blue, then deep purple. Its golden center took on a velvet red appearance.

"I've never seen a flower like that one, lass, but it's a beautiful thing."

"I wanted it to be special," Elizabeth said, "'Cause I wanted to give it to you."

The leprechaun looked away and ran a hand across her cheek. The rose disappeared as Elizabeth became engaged in trying to make flowers with stars on the end of their stems.

A shadow crossed over them, chilling the glade where they sat. Tree limbs shook wildly, leaves dipping and swaying like mad ballerinas. Through breaks in the leafy canopy, they could make out a long red body and the movement of great canvas wings.

"So the dragons have returned, too. Ah, that I could have lived without," Letty said.

"What's wrong with dragons? I thought it looked pretty, what I could see of it."

"Oh, I suppose dragons are all right in their own way," Letty replied. "Some are good, some are bad. But no leprechaun likes to see those great worms pokin' about. They're fond o' gold — an' so are we."

"I think I remember Father Ryan preaching about gold once. He thought it was a bad thing."

"Among yur kind an' the dwarves, I suppose it might be, for ye've forgotten why ye want it so much. Even before our people started our nap, yurs had turned gold into somethin' to trade amongst yurselves, to buy trinkets with, forgettin' why it was so valuable to begin with. An' the dwarves were even worse."

"Why *do* you want gold?"

"Because it's magic, lass! It is the most beautiful of all metals an' as such it has magic powers. It's gold dust I dip the mint leaves into so ye can speak in the proper old language. Leprechauns remember the value of gold — an' so do dragons."

"Father Ryan sometimes tells me stories about magic silver."

"Oh, aye, trust the Tall Ones to corrupt the real magic an' then try to make somethin' out o' second best. That's what happens when yur built so far from the ground. Ye lose sight o' the true nature o' things."

"Do fairies like gold? I've seen fairies dancing in the meadows at night."

"Fairies, ha? Those bubbleheads don't keer for nought but their dancin'. Gold means no more to them than it would to a butterfly. Come to think of it, a butterfly probably has more sense. It certainly can pay attention longer. An' lass, ye be keerful about bein' outdoors at night. There's more than leprechauns an' fairies waitin' in the mists. M' cousin Grassweaver saw a banshee a fortnight ago an' I'll bet m' pouch o' gold that come winter, the pooka will be roamin' the hills causin' mischief again. We little folks have nought to fear from them, but 'taint safe for Big Feet like yurself."

"Letty, how come I never saw fairies or leprechauns before? Mama and Papa told me stories about them, but I never saw one until I met you."

Letty sighed. "The magic went away for a time, lass. No leprechaun wants to live in a world without magic. But we trusted the land to return things to their proper order an' we just lay down to sleep until it did. Now an' again, some o' us would wake up and wander about for a bit to see if the magic was back, then return to the dreamtime. But recently, we all began to wake up, like flowers peekin' out through snow in the spring. We could feel the change. The magic isna as strong as it was before, lass, but I feel it growin'."

Elizabeth thought about that, her face tight with concentration.

"Could you teach me how to use magic to make Father Ryan laugh again? He used to smile and joke with me when I cleaned the rectory for him. Now he almost never smiles and on Sundays he shouts a lot during his sermon. People used to leave Mass happy, but now they look like they do when they leave a funeral. It's been like that since Mr. Tourret came to town. He scares me."

Letty hugged herself, as if warding off a sudden chill.

"What's this Tourret like?"

"He looks mad all the time, like Mrs. O' Dell's mean bulldog. He talks to Father Ryan a lot and afterwards, Father starts to look mean, too."

The leprechaun pulled her arms tighter together. "The land is tryin' to tell me somethin', Elizabeth. I'd like to get a look at this Tourret. Where d'ye think I might find him?"

"He'll probably be at Mass on Sunday. Can leprechauns go to Mass?"

Letty laughed heartily. "Lass, the religion hasna been thought up yet that can hurt a leprechaun. Ye wear somethin' ye can hide me in an' meet me by the bush that hangs over the wall in the corner o' yur churchyard. Now ye'd best be gettin' home, but take the leaf out o' yur mouth first. Yur people dinna appreciate proper talkin' these days."

* * *

"By this time, it was gettin' stuffy under Elizabeth's jacket inside her church," Letty told the other leprechauns. "I had to get a breath o' air, so I peeked out.

"The Tall One that Elizabeth sets such store by — Father Ryan, she calls him — was speakin'. At first, he sounded pairfectly normal. At first ..."

* * *

"Much has happened in recent months," Father Ryan was saying, "to challenge what we accept as true. We have learned that life does exist on worlds beyond the Earth, worlds that now claim part of our planet as their own. Even here in Ireland, mythical creatures walk the land. Acts of magic have stepped out of children's fairy tales to become a part of daily existence. All of this has forced us to accept possibilities that once we would have scoffed at.

"I have come to believe we live in a new Age of Miracles, a time when God will speak directly to His servants as he did to Moses and Abraham, a time when faith can move mountains literally as well as metaphorically. This time of tumult challenges us all to re-examine ourselves and the world around us with an open mind. Remember that as you listen to our guest from France, Maurice Tourret."

Tourret, dressed in black robes, stood in a smooth, flowing motion. His tall, slim body gave him the look of a ferret standing on its hind legs, sniffing the wind.

Long, black hair did nothing to dispel the image. His feral eyes glinted in the light, black and deep as the bottom of a well. When he spoke, his English seemed tinged with a hint of Irish brogue, despite his French origins.

"Brothers and sisters, you will find little comfort in the sermon today. Comfort and complacency lead to the fires of Hell itself! It is indeed an Age of Miracles you now live in, miracles long denied you by villains I will soon name. I have been sent to lead you into the fold of the GodNet, where you will hear the voice of God, not just in your hearts, but with the same clarity you hear my voice now."

Trust him. He speaks the truth.

Letty bit her lip to keep from screaming in pain. A second voice was tearing at her eardrums, cold and lifeless, coming from everywhere at once in a crackling, grinding echo. If the Tall Ones' machines could speak, she told herself, surely this would be their voice. But no one else seemed to hear a thing.

Trust him. Follow him.

Tourret raged on, spewing anger and damnation, and always the metallic, grinding voice demanded *Trust him. Follow him.*

"Oh, God," he beseeched, "these humble people have sinned, led astray by false prophets. Give them a sign, Lord, to show them the truth of the message that I bring to them. Steer their great faith onto the right road. Give them a sign!"

From somewhere within the church came a loud gasp, followed by a shriek. Other voices quickly joined in.

"The cross!"

"Blood! Blood on the cross!"

A great rustling from the sudden stirring of hundreds of bodies echoed through the room. On the wall behind Tourret's head hung a crucifix. A dark red liquid was sliding in rivulets across it, creating large drops that vanished as they fell. Throughout the church, worshippers were on their knees, crossing themselves and appealing to a variety of saints.

Trust him. Follow him.

"Yes, blood," Tourret shouted, pointing at the crucifix. "First the blood, then the faith. It has been ever thus! In blood you shall be redeemed! I come to bring you the message that has been hidden from you. You shall break the limitations of the body of Adam through cybertechnology and find the powers the Lord intends for those who follow the True Way of the Cyberpope. You will speak directly with God. Father Ryan, are my words true?"

The Father leapt from his seat as if catapulted. "Yes, oh, yes, it is the truth! The Voice of the Burning Bush, The Voice that gave the plans for the Ark, has spoken to me. It foretold the arrival of Brother Tourret and spoke of how Neary's Parish shall be the birthplace of a new and greater hope for all Ireland. God can and will speak to the ears and not just the hearts of those who trust in Him and his true servants. This is the new Age of Miracles of which I spoke, and we shall spread its message across the land!"

Sobs, joyous shouts, and frantic questions mingled noisily.

Trust him. Follow him.

"Follow us now to the churchyard," Tourret shouted, "and you will see even greater miracles!"

With Father Ryan beside him, Tourret led the congregation into the churchyard. A young man stood among the tombstones, a dark figure under a grey sky,

his jacket gleaming wet in the drizzling rain. As he turned
to face the crowd, there were gasps of recognition.

"Jeremy Bratton," someone muttered.

"Yes," Tourret said, "Jeremy Bratton of your own
village. One of your own lambs, gone from your flock
nearly ten years, now returns as a ram to lead you to
better pastures.

"Brother Bratton has already converted to the True
Way. He stands before you as living proof of the
strength and power that await all who will open their
eyes. God gave us a brain to develop the technology
that now leads our bodies and minds to a higher
evolution. It is only due to a plot of deception, an abuse
of your faith, that this information, this higher calling,
has been denied you. Jeremy, show your friends what
gifts await them."

Slowly, with a sly grin, Bratton removed his jacket,
then his shirt, his undershirt, to stand bare chested
before the crowd. No hair grew upon his torso, no scar
or wrinkle marred its perfect surface. His face was
unnaturally smooth with no lines of worry or laughter
to hint at what lay behind it.

Finally, he removed his gloves. The sharp intake of
breath into a hundred lungs created a hissing sound in
the stillness. Bratton's left hand was a metal claw,
glistening blue-black in the pearly light.

From beneath his robes, Tourret produced a throwing knife and hurled it at Bratton's chest. It struck
between his breasts, bouncing off harmlessly. Without
a word, Tourret pulled a wheellock pistol and fired.
The bullet flashed as it ricocheted from Bratton's torso.
The crowd muttered like rising waves hissing onto
shore.

"Interdermal plating," Tourret shouted, sweeping

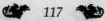

his arm toward Bratton. "A Heaven-sent gift to make human flesh as strong as the Will of God!

"Behold now the wonders of the left hand of God!" he shouted, tossing a stone to Bratton. In seconds the stone was powder, crushed in the unrelenting vice that was Jeremy Bratton's left hand.

"Behold God's Right Hand as it will mete out justice to the unrighteous!"

Bratton pointed his right index finger at the base of a bush overhanging the wall around the churchyard. A quick series of flashes from his fingertip were accompanied by a flat CRACK-CRACK-CRACK. The bush toppled, hung for a moment on the ancient stone wall like a drowning victim going down for the last time, then tumbled out of sight behind the moss-covered stones. Silence and a burning smell hung in the air.

Bratton turned to face the crowd again.

"You all remember me," he said. "I grew up here among you, before I went north to work in the factories and see a bit of the world. Well, I worked and I saw."

He slammed a fist into the claws of his other hand with a sound that reverberated against the church walls.

"I saw that no Irishman is ever truly free as long as our country is divided, with someone not of Irish blood sitting on the other side of the Irish Sea and deciding Ireland should be split in two. And I saw that others felt as I did. I joined them and we made things unpleasant for Englishmen and Orange alike, unpleasant enough that I had to flee to France or rot in an English prison. For years I stayed there, staring across the grey water and dreaming of my green home and cursing the English who kept me from returning to it.

"Well, now the English know what it's like to have

someone sitting above them and determining their fate. Pella Ardinay dropped her Maelstrom Bridge on them and brought her dwarves and elves and all the rest from Aysle to make England her colony. If England was all she wanted, I'd say let her take it and best wishes. But she dropped a bridge into Belfast too, and *that* belongs to Ireland! With the help of God, we'll throw out these new invaders *and* the damned English, and Ireland will stand free and united!"

"What are you offering, lad, the IRA?" someone asked. "It's been dead around here since before you were a gleam in your father's eye."

"Not the IRA! No, Neary's Parish will be the birthplace of a new hope with an old name — a new *Fianna Fail* — the Warriors of Destiny!

"This time, we will win the war, for God will truly be on our side. Brother Tourret," he growled, "continue your sermon."

"Your old friend and my new one speaks the truth," Tourret said, pacing among the headstones. "Although I am not of your soil, I share your country's long hatred of those who seek to impose their will on others by force. Did Lady Ardinay ask the permission of a single Irish soul before dropping her bridge on your green island? Do you think she'll ask permission whenever she wants to rearrange your land and your water, your people so that Ireland will be 'a little more like home' to her and her kind? Do you think the masses who fled their homes in Belfast to live in tent cities left behind all they owned without good reason? They were fleeing Lady Ardinay's terrors — terrors that will soon come to your village, to your wives and children, unless you stop them where they are and then drive them into the sea!"

There was muttering among his audience. Some shook their heads in agreement.

"Pella Ardinay does not fight alone. She is aided in her dream of conquest by your unseen enemy, a glib, scheming mocker — the false pope of Rome, who gives his evil blessing to those who oppress you!"

"You can say what you like about the English or that woman Ardinay, Frenchman," growled a middle-aged shopkeeper, "but we're pious people here, loyal to God and loyal to the Church, for they're one and the same! And don't you be forgetting that again, blood on the cross or no."

"Hear him out, Laurence Pearse," Bratton said quietly.

"Thank you, friend Jeremy," Tourret continued. "I do not question God nor your faith in Him, but your trust has been shamefully abused. Did the Church you placed your faith in ever aid you in overthrowing your yoke of English slavery? When your brave ancestors were defeated at the Boyne, did not the Vatican rejoice for your oppressors with a High Pontifical Mass and *Te Deum* for bloody William of Orange? Do you think Rome will help you now? Has a single Pope ever called upon the good Catholics of England or any other country to rise up for you?

"No? You were told the meek shall inherit while others stole what was yours. Now, at last, the Cyberpope, Jean Malraux I, has come with a flaming sword to drive your enemies from your land like sinners from the Garden of Eden!"

"I've heard enough," said Laurence Pearse. "The rest of you can listen to this heretical blather if you want, but I'm leaving. I've trusted in the Catholic Church all my life and I'm not about to change just because some Frenchman wants me to." He started away from the crowd, toward the road.

No one was certain how Jeremy Bratton got to Pearse as quickly as he did. One second he was standing near Tourret, the next he had a hand around Laurence Pearse's throat, holding the stout shopkeeper six inches off the ground. Pearse's feet churned and he dug at the vise-like fingers while his face flushed dark red.

"Release him, Jeremy," Tourret said. "Let the Hand of Righteousness fall upon him that he may see his error and repent."

Bratton opened his fingers and Pearse dropped to his knees, gasping for air. Tourret approached, grasped the man's head and, looking skyward, prayed.

"Oh, God, this man knows not his folly for he has long been misled by the heretics of Rome. Show him the suffering that awaits him if he refuses the truth of Your Word as revealed through the Cyberpope Jean Malraux I, Vicar of Christ."

Suddenly Pearse stiffened. His eyes widened as spasms rippled across his face. A few of his neighbors started forward to help him but were restrained by others when Jeremy Bratton stepped forward.

"No, no," Pearse muttered, "please, no, no, nuhaahh!"

His scream continued to rise until the cyberpriest released him and he fell face down into the wet grass.

"Better a man should see Hell while he lives and turn from it than to live in ignorance and learn too late his soul is eternally damned. Brother Pearse will recover to tell you what awaits those who refuse the True Word."

As he spoke, Tourret moved among the crowd,

which quickly shifted to give him room. He stopped in front of William M'Kenna, a large man in his early forties who ran a bakery. M'Kenna's ruddy face was lined with deep wrinkles, like barren ground cut by dry creek beds. His clothing bore stains and signs of recent neglect. It was obvious his shoes hadn't seen polish in months.

"Brother M'Kenna, you were good enough to come this morning after all."

"You and Tim Ryan pestered me enough this past week. I told you I'd come to your Mass and I came. But I also told you I'd been Protestant all my life and when I needed God, He was busy elsewhere. I won't be troubling Him again, so keep your rosary beads to yourself. And don't waste your time showing me Hell. I've already seen it."

"We of the GodNet can show Heaven as well, brother M'Kenna," Tourret said softly. He placed his hand on the baker's head. Moments later, M'Kenna began smiling. Joyous tears sparkled in his eyes, and a half-laugh, half-sob, escaped his lips. Then he wrenched his head free.

"Don't ever do that again, Tourret," he gasped, trembling. "I don't need you to remind me of what I've lost, to make me see what I can't touch. Keep your Heaven because I don't give a damn what you papists do. Or the Protestants or the bald-headed Hare Krishnas, for that matter." His eyes darkened. "But if it's war you're going to, give me a gun and I'll join your bloody army. If I'm to worship a god, then I'll serve Mars. At least in war death makes some kind of sense, doesn't it? *Doesn't it?*"

"First the blood," Tourret whispered, "then the faith."

* * *

Letty paused for breath before continuing.

"An' through all this was the demon voice tellin' one an' all 'Trust him, follow him,' but ye'd have sworn I was the only one hearin' it for all the attention the Tall Ones seemed to give it."

"I never heard it," Elizabeth said.

Letty twisted to face her.

"Are ye certain, lass?"

Elizabeth thought. Sometimes remembering was so hard. It was like there was a big black stone in her mind and when she tried to remember things, they hid behind that stone.

"I'm not sure, but I don't think I heard it. Are you mad at me for not hearing it, Letty?"

"No, lass, o' course not. Perhaps only leprechaun ears could hear it, although it was worse than a banshee to me."

"Demon voices," Leafflyer said. "Flesh that canna be cut or hurt. Blood flowin' without flesh around it. Ye may be right, Letty. This is unnatural even for the Tall Ones. But to ask the aid o' a dragon an' to pay the beast with gold ..."

"Not all dragons are evil, Shamus, but I'll not be beholden to any o' them, good or bad. A debt owed to a dragon is a terrible thing, for they always collect their due one way or t'other. We'll pay this dragon up front an' honest, because we canna fight this fight by oursel's. We've all amused oursel's playin' tricks on the Tall Ones at times, but like Elizabeth's, our magic willna let us do real harm.

"This is no game. I feel it as surely as I can feel a change o' weather comin'. There'll be no place for leprechauns in the land this man desires. An' I'd rather deal with an honest, gold-lovin' dragon than see the land die under creatures that speak like machines."

In the end, she had her way. Negotiators were dispatched to find the dragon's lair and arrange the least odious deal for the great reptile's aid.

* * *

Jeremy Bratton, Maurice Tourret, and a second Frenchman sat inside an abandoned farmhouse. A variety of electronic equipment surrounded them.

"I still say this is the wrong place to begin our revolution," Bratton said. "These people are too set in their ways. We may win over a few, but in the cities we'd find hundreds to rally to the cause."

"No, Jeremy," Tourret responded, "your tiny hometown is a perfect base. Here, we will be near the southeast coast in an unassuming area between the ports of Arklow and Wexford, which will make smuggling our equipment much easier. 'Tourists' travelling to the resort at Courtown northeast of here won't be questioned for carrying large amounts of luggage, and the Wicklow Mountains to the west are a traditional haven for those who seek shelter from the queen's minions. This is a perfect place for us to begin. Besides, Jeremy, you forget your Irish legends. Was not Saint Patrick rumored to have landed near Arklow? I'm certain we can turn that tradition to our favor at the appropriate time."

"Alec," he continued, turning to their companion, "your hologram of blood dripping from the cross was most effective."

Alec nodded in response. "The locals have been suitably impressed today."

Bratton gave a dry chuckle. "Especially when Maurice's 'miracle' fingers made that fat fool Pearse think he was staring into Hell."

"What is Hell if not our worst fears come to life?" Tourret responded airily. "Using electronic impulses to stimulate the subconscious, producing hallucinations based on personal phobias, offers a unique new tool for converting heathens. I'm proud to say I am one of the pioneers in this area of holy research. Of course, pleasure centers can also be stimulated, as I tried to demonstrate with brother M'kenna."

"Why did you single out William M'kenna? When I lived here, he was the most peace-loving man in the county and Protestant to boot."

"Have you ever looked into the eyes of an animal lying dead beside the highway, Jeremy? Vacant eyes, without a trace of light or life — M'Kenna's eyes. He is not the man you knew. He is an empty vessel and we shall fill him. Is that not the mission of The Church? In fact, it would be a Christian act for you to visit him this afternoon. Take him his weapon."

When Bratton had gone, Tourret reached beneath the long hair covering his neck. From an input jack concealed there, he removed a chip that allowed him to speak in acceptable Irish brogue and to summon millions of bits of information on Irish history, customs, and culture in nanoseconds.

"Ah, it is good to speak in a civilized tongue again," he said in French. "So, Alec, what is the status of your surgical equipment?"

In answer, Alec lead him into another chamber where aged brick walls now enclosed an impressive operating room.

"I'll have finished the last tests in a day or two. The

generators and backup generators all survived the trip in fine shape."

"So you are nearly ready to begin the conversions?"

"Soon, although I still have my doubts about operating in this hovel under such primitive conditions. This is more like a back alley hack shop than the cyberconversion chambers of The Church's hospital in Avignon. We may lose our first few converts until I can work out the bugs."

"Then we must not perform the first operations on those we deem most important. In fact, I think I have the perfect subject for your first surgery — that idiot girl who cleans the rectory. Implant whatever cyberware you choose in her, so long as it doesn't make her dangerous, of course. Perhaps in some small way she can serve The Church. If there is a flaw in your system, best we find out with one whose loss will be of no consequence."

"Exercise caution, Maurice. These people have not had the benefit of our enlightenment and do not see her imperfections as an affront to God. Her death could work against you."

"Then I must not be the one who is blamed. How long has it been since God spoke to Father Ryan?"

Alec grinned. "Several days. I'm sure the good Father is fervently praying for the next visitation."

"Then, by all means, let us answer his prayers. Reveal God's plan for Elizabeth O'Cleary to him tonight."

* * *

Elizabeth struggled to count the coins in her hand, wrestling with change a third grader could have handled with ease.

"Huere," she said triumphantly, handing over the coins, her thick tongue giving the word two syllables.

M'Kenna took her offering, giving in return a bag of pastries and the only genuine smile he was likely to have that day.

"Tell your parents I said Hello," he told her.

"I will. Hullo, Doctor O'Donoghue," she said cheerfully to the short, grey-haired man entering the bakery.

Doctor Gavin O'Donoghue lifted his hat and smiled in response as she left with her bag of cheese pastries tapping against the leg of her corduroy jeans.

"You know, William, a small preservation spell, like many housewives use these days, would keep your pastries fresher than those bags."

"It'll be a cold day indeed when you find me using magic, Gavin, I've seen what happens to those who use it — they change." M'Kenna said. "Speaking of change, how's Pearse?"

"He'll live, although I doubt he'll ever talk above a whisper again. It's the damage to his mind that worries me. He's nearly comatose from shock. If I had better control of magic, I suppose I might know how to cure him, but by the time I learn what spell's applicable, it may be too late to repair the damage."

"You put a lot of bloody faith in something you never had till recent times, Gavin. If your magic is so all-powerful, why don't you use it to give that sweet child that just left here a more normal life?"

"I wish it were that simple, William. But her problem is a form of Down's syndrome called translocation. One of her chromosomes is joined to another, giving her an excess of genetic material, causing mild retardation. How could I begin to sort out her genetic makeup? It's not like a broken arm where I can cast a *mend* spell and join the bones back together. Or like a tumor, where I can reverse a *growth* spell to make the tumor shrink away to noth —"

He paused, saw the pain in his friend's eyes, and looked away. "I'm sorry, William. I didn't mean ..."

"I know what you meant. You meant that now you can wave your hands a few times and just magic the cancer right out of a body. Well, isn't that wonderful? Too bad your magic didn't come to you a month sooner, now isn't it?"

"Will, you know magic's only been possible since Lady Ardinay's realm came to Earth. I just didn't have this magic skill —"

"You trusted other magic before, Gavin. You called your spells surgery and chemotherapy then and they didn't work near so well. One damned month, Gavin — you'd have had your new spells and Janie would still be with me. One damned *month*!"

"There's no guarantee of that, William. She was so far gone. Sometimes we just have to accept God's Will —"

"'God's Will?' I've heard that from everyone in this town! If God has a Will, none of us are the beneficiaries. Suffering, Pain, Despair, and Death —those are the four gospels, and I'll tell you, Gavin O'Donoghue, a time is soon coming when a new Acts of the Apostles will be written. It'll be written in blood and leave no doubt in anyone's mind as to what God's Will is!"

Abruptly, he left the shop and strode purposefully away, leaving the doctor standing sadly in the empty store.

* * *

"They're goin' to do what?" Letty asked.

"Convert me," Elizabeth answered. "Father Ryan and Mister Tourret say it's a wonderful thing that God chose me to be the first. Letty, what's 'convert' mean?"

"It means no good if Tourret wants it. God chose ye, indeed. How do they get that, I wonder?"

"Oh, God told Father Ryan so. Last night, at the rectory."

"Humph. When is this 'conversion' supposed to take place?"

"Sunday night. Father Ryan is calling another special Mass that evening to tell everyone. I'm not supposed to let anybody know before then, but I wanted you to be there. Do you think God will be mad at me for telling you?"

"I'll tell ye what, Elizabeth," Letty said, patting her friend's hand. "Take me inside yur jacket when ye go to clean the rectory this week. I'll jump out an' wait for God to speak to yur Father Ryan again. When He does, I'll ask Him m'self if I can come along. How's that?"

Elizabeth nodded happily. "You're my best friend, Letty."

"Aye, lass. Well, there's no better friend than a leprechaun. An' no more stubborn enemy, exceptin' maybe a greedy dwarf."

* * *

"It jammed on me again," M'kenna said.

He held out a Belgian machine pistol for Jeremy Bratton's examination. Bratton made a show of examining the pistol and then handed it back to M'kenna.

"I told you; you're firing too long at a time. Use short bursts. Soon I'll have better weapons for all of you, direct from the Cyberpapacy's own suppliers, but these will have to do for now."

Bratton looked around, reassured himself that his other trainees had left the practice field.

"Tourret wants you to attend Mass again Sunday evening and bring your weapon. Conceal it under your coat, he said."

He held up a hand to stop the questions forming on M'kenna's lips.

"If you want to go to war, William, you've got to learn to follow orders without question."

* * *

"Without question," Letty said, "this Tourret won't idly stand by while someone mucks about with his plans. If I succeed in stoppin' him from takin' Elizabeth, it will mean war between us."

"Protectin' the land is one thing," Leafflyer said, "protectin' yur friend is another."

"She's one o' the Always Children, Shamus. Abandonin' her would be like abandonin' the land itself, to m' way o' thinkin'. I must be with Elizabeth that night, doin' what I can. Is there ought the rest o' ye will do to help?"

"Ye know we won't abandon a member o' our own clan. We'll dance the Sacred Rings for ye that night to ask the land to aide ye, but ye've said yurself we're not warriors."

Just then a mournful, shrieking cry came through the mists, bone-chilling in its sheer loneliness. When it died away, Leafflyer looked at Letitia.

"I hope it's not yur death the banshee is foretellin', Letty Blossomwalker."

* * *

Father Timothy Ryan sat on the edge of his bed in the rectory, looking about at the mementos of sixty-two years of devotion: a small bookcase filled with scholarly theological works; an iron crucifix given to him by members of his first of many small parishes; a bottle of holy water from Lourdes; a trunk filled with odds and ends. With the brevity of phrases chiseled on a tombstone, his possessions told the story of a quiet, dutiful life. Dreams of glory won in service of the Lord that had filled his head as a young man had been stored away long ago in a musty, dust-covered corner of his mind.

Until The Voice came.

Like summer thunder, The Voice had come to him one night, foretelling the arrival of Maurice Tourret and holding forth a shining promise. The holy army of his youthful dreams would become real. Led by Saint Timothy Ryan, it would sweep the devil's legions before it like leaves before a whirlwind.

His reverie was broken by a knock at the rectory door. He opened it to admit Elizabeth O'Cleary and her parents. After Father Ryan reassured them of God's beneficence in choosing Elizabeth for this holy calling, her parents left to take their seats in church. When she was left alone with the Father, Elizabeth kept glancing around the room nervously, as though she were looking for something. Clearly, she was agitated, perhaps even frightened.

Suddenly, a whispering rush like December winds in the dried bones of sinners swept through the rectory. Then, The Voice came.

"Elizabeth, why do you cringe from Me? Have I not

chosen you from all others to carry out My works? Speak, girl."

Father Ryan gasped, grabbed Elizabeth's hand, and took them both to their knees.

"What is it, Father?" she asked, trembling.

"The Voice of God, child. Indeed, you are chosen."

"It scares me. It sounds awful. I don't want to be chosen."

"Do not question My choices, girl!" The Voice thundered. "You were centuries unborn when I came to Moses in a flaming bush! I did not consult you when I appeared to Saul of Tarsus in a light so bright he was blinded! As they served, so you shall serve.

"Reassure My chosen one, Timothy Ryan, then lead her into My holy service."

That takes care of that, Alec thought, switching his monitor from the rectory to cameras hidden within the church. Let Ryan worry about calming her.

Elizabeth was sobbing.

"Don't cry, Elizabeth. You have heard the Voice of God. It's wonderful!"

"No, it isn't. It's scary and mean. I don't want God to sound like that!"

"Child, child, don't say such things. The Voice of God is great and it promises greatness to those who heed it."

"It promises to make ye the greatest bloody fool in all o' Ireland, Tim Ryan!"

The Father leapt to his feet, his eyes sweeping the room. Who …

"Over here." The small voice was coming from the sofa cushions. "Here, tryin' to keep that great grindin' voice yur so in love with from smashin' m' hearin' for all time."

A tiny woman dressed all in green was glaring up at him. *Saints preserve us*, he thought — *a leprechaun*?

"Watch your heathen tongue, woman," he said, his faith giving him courage in the face of the unknown. "Whatever pagan deity you may worship, you'll show respect for the Christian God here."

"I've no quibble with yur God, Ryan. It's the fools He suffers to exist that vex me. He must have thrown ye together on an off day wi' whatever leftover parts were close t' hand. Does yur pride deafen as well as blind ye or do ye just not care when God's voice speaks with the grindin' o' a machine instead o' the sweet whisper o' the land?"

"Machine? What are you muttering about?"

"Machine, aye. Ye might ken that yurself if ye weren't puffin' yurself up like a bullfrog and croakin' about how God drops by to talk to ye personal-like."

Righteous anger flashed in the priest's eyes. He took a step forward, one hand poised above his head to squash the blasphemous pagan, but Elizabeth darted in front of him, dropping to her knees by the sofa. She put a protective arm around the leprechaun.

"Help him to hear, Letty," she said urgently. "Use your magic to let him listen to the land like you do!"

"You know this creature, Elizabeth?" the Father asked, perplexed, his hand still upraised.

"She's not a creature, she's my best friend. Please let her put some gold in your ear. Gold isn't bad, you know — it's magic!"

"Lass," Letty said, touching Elizabeth's cheek, "it's not that simple. I can magic ye to talk the old language, but so far as I know there is no spell to hear the land with — it's just a thing I can do. What would I mix with the gold to work m' magic on?"

Elizabeth bit her lip, then jumped up and ran into the bedroom. In seconds, she was back, carrying the priest's bottle of holy water and the crucifix she had lovingly dusted so many times while cleaning the rectory.

"Let me have some gold, Letty. Please."

"What are ye thinkin', lass?" Letty asked as she sprinkled gold dust onto Elizabeth's fingertip.

Father Ryan, unwilling to further delay the evening service by upsetting Elizabeth again, watched bewildered as she mixed gold dust with holy water in her palm. She daubed the mixture on his ears, then put the cross into his hands and closed his fingers around it.

"God made the land, didn't He, Father? So doesn't the land talk with His voice? Maybe with the gold and the holy water and the cross, you can listen to the land like Letty does."

He sighed and closed his eyes. If pretending to listen would calm Elizabeth so he could take her to the service, what harm could it do?

He began to smile. He pulled the crucifix closer, as if he were embracing a loved one. His smile widened; then, suddenly, he fell to the floor, covering his ears.

"Stop! Stop!" he screamed, twisting in pain.

Elizabeth knelt beside him. Seconds later, he stopped shaking and looked at them through tear-filled eyes.

"A miracle! I swear I heard snow melting and the sound of seed pods bursting. It was like a symphony until another voice nearly burst my eardrums."

He screamed again, covered his ears, and curled into a ball.

"Again. A voice repeating Maurice Tourret's name, telling me to trust and follow him."

Suddenly, his head jerked up.

"It's gone, all of it. I can't hear the symphony any

more."

"The lass has magic in her," Letty said approvingly, "but she canna make it last long. Still, she let ye hear the sound o' the land — an' that *other* raspin' voice. Now tell me, Tim Ryan, which one do ye choose to worship?"

The priest stared at some distant point for several minutes, as if watching a phantom army on a battlefield only he could see.

"Come, Elizabeth," he said at last. "The congregation is waiting."

Distractedly, he dropped into a pocket the crucifix his first parishioners had given him. Then, taking Elizabeth's hand, he led her from the rectory with the leprechaun following.

"Letty," a voice whispered as they crossed the churchyard.

"Shamus Leafflyer? What are ye doin' here?"

"Ye may be a fool, but I couldna let ye face the Tall Ones alone. I've seen yur Tourret an' Bratton now an' I've heard yur demon voice. It pains me to say it, but ye were right about them."

"Are the others here?"

"Nay, they're dancin' the Sacred Rings for ye. Calm yurself a bit an' ye'll feel the land's heart beatin' louder as they dance. Oh, there'll be fine magic tonight."

"I hope so, for it's tonight we must end this. Shamus ..."

"Aye, I know what must be done. Watch yurself, Letty Blossomwalker."

He sprinkled gold dust on a large leaf lying nearby and, true to his name, rode off on it as it leapt into the wind.

* * *

Maurice Tourret, watching from an alcove behind the altar, was both pleased and annoyed. The church was filled to overflowing. Jeremy Bratton and William M'Kenna would provide crowd control, if it became necessary. But where was Ryan?

Suddenly, hushed whispering among the worshippers dropped into silence. Father Ryan had entered through the main doors and was slowly walking down the nave, Elizabeth by his side. They ascended to the altar together. Father Ryan gazed out across his congregation.

"In the twenty-fourth chapter of the book of Matthew," he began, "we are warned that 'false messiahs and false prophets will appear, performing signs and wonders so great as to mislead even the chosen, if that were possible.'"

Tourret stiffened. What was that fool up to?

"Like most of us," Father Ryan continued, "I dreamed of being more than the reality of my existence, harboring hopes that God's plans for me would more closely match my dreams for myself.

"So when I heard a thunderous voice calling me to the greatness I dreamed of, I was far too ready to let myself believe that the God of the Old Testament Who spoke directly to servants here on Earth had returned, and had chosen me as He chose the prophets of old. I didn't dare look too closely for fear the miracle I had hoped for would vanish. I convinced myself my willingness to believe was an act of faith, instead of pride."

Tourret clenched his hands and cursed. What to do now?

"Tonight, one whose childlike faith remained true opened my eyes — and ears — to the truth. 'Where the carcass lies,' Matthew's gospel also tells us, 'there the vultures gather' — vultures like Maurice Tourret and his Cyberpope! Their 'religion' is the way of deception and death! Forgive me, dear friends, for what I tried to lead you into. Dear God, forgive me."

"Heresy!" Tourret screamed, rushing onto the altar. "What have the devil and his servants in Rome done to you, Father?"

"It's you who have done it, Tourret. You and my own sinful pride."

Tourret turned to the congregation. "Satan has stolen the Father's soul! The Trickster knows what miracles will occur tonight and fights to prevent it!

"Come with me, girl," he said, roughly seizing Elizabeth's arm.

"Let go of her." Father Ryan placed himself between Tourret and Elizabeth.

"You forget yourself, old man."

"That's true, Tourret. I forgot I swore to serve a loving God. But you helped me to forget, didn't you, with your tricky little messages? 'Trust Tourret. Follow him.' How many times a day do you play that tape? Have you had the entire town listening to subliminal suggestions that we follow you like lemmings? I have heard your message, Tourret. I. Have. Heard."

The Frenchman's lips pulled back in a canine snarl. He swung at the older priest, but Father Ryan grappled with him and they fell together, struggling on the altar.

Churchgoers rose from their pews, muttering and shouting. Before they could act, William M'Kenna froze them by firing a machine pistol burst into the rafters. Bratton rose from his seat and stripped off his gloves menacingly.

"Stop!" Elizabeth cried, tears running down her cheeks. "Please stop. Why can't it be like it used to be when everyone was happy?

"Remember how we used to smile and shake hands and hug each other after Mass? How we'd help each other when we needed it? Remember when Mr. M'kenna used to smile and nobody carried guns? We loved each other!"

Her thoughts whirled as she sought a way to show them what she felt. *Like makin' those stars or walkin' proper. All ye have to do is picture what ye want.* But when she tried to latch onto the happy images that had filled her mind moments before, they fled to hide behind the black stone.

No, she thought, go away, stone, go away. In her mind she flailed at the solid black barrier ... and found herself moving forward through a thick, dark fog. She could see nothing, but from somewhere voices were singing in the old language, their rhythm seeming to guide her as she moved through the blackness. Then she was entering a place of intense light and waiting in it like mislaid toys were the images she sought: Neary's Parish before Maurice Tourret came.

Inside the church, the air began to swim like heat waves before the altar. Elizabeth, now smiling brightly, eyes closed, moved her hands continuously as hologram-like scenes began to dance, fade, and reappear in the air in front of her.

The congregation watched a movie in which they themselves starred, with scenes of smiling worshippers shaking hands at Mass; neighbors working with one another to repair a car or plant shrubs; William M'Kenna and his wife, Janie, laughing with friends in their bakery.

With a snarl, Tourret tried to lunge for Elizabeth, but Father Ryan held him tightly.

"Bratton, M'Kenna! Kill the little witch!"

"Run, Elizabeth! Run for the side door!" Letty shouted from hiding. Elizabeth, snapping out of her dream state, began to run.

Jeremy Bratton was charging forward, tossing aside those who got in his path.

Elizabeth ran out into the night air, ran blindly along the side of the church, raced smack into a hedge bordering the road in front of the building, and fell to her knees. She looked up and saw William M'Kenna standing over her.

"Good job, M'Kenna," Bratton said, racing up, Tourret close behind him. "Now finish her."

M'kenna looked down the barrel of his weapon at Elizabeth. Elizabeth, the child he and Janie never had. The little girl they had saved the largest pieces of gingerbread for. The young woman who still brought her childlike awe and unquestioning love to him whenever she visited his shop. He turned to face the other two.

"You'll not harm this child, Jeremy Bratton. Go on and fight your war, but she's not to be a part of it."

"Then stand aside and I'll do the job, M'Kenna. Don't make me kill you, too."

M'Kenna laughed ruefully. "So much of me's been dead so long, any wee bit you might finish off wouldn't even be noticed. But you'll not harm Elizabeth." As he finished speaking, he triggered a burst from the machine pistol.

Bullets ricocheted from Bratton's interdermal plating. A few sent sparks flying from his head, punching holes through the thinner armor of his cheeks and throat and shattering the ball of sensors that served as his right eye. The impact knocked him to his knees, silicone lubricant streaming down his face like tears.

Then M'Kenna's pistol jammed.

"For that, you won't die clean, M'Kenna," Bratton said, his voice rasping like a file on metal. He fired the flechette pistol built into his index finger. Clouds of razor-edged triangles whined through the air, ripping into M'Kenna's legs. As the baker dropped, screaming, Bratton turned to Elizabeth.

Father Ryan, bleeding from a cut on his forehead, was running toward them, but Tourret dropped the priest with a single blow across the throat.

"Nothing personal, girl," Bratton said.

Suddenly, he was engulfed in flames. Hovering over him, a dragon spewed out a fiery breath that fused wires with muscle and bone, sending hissing steam spiraling into the night. With a high-pitched, keening wail of pain, Bratton stumbled out of the churchyard to disappear into the village below.

The dragon hovered, recharging its flame. Atop its head, clinging to one large ear, Shamus Leafflyer searched for Tourret.

With a sudden roar, the dragon twisted violently, its right eye gone. Below, Tourret stood pointing at the flying reptile, pseudoskin removed from one finger to reveal the laser concealed within.

The dragon spat fire as it roared in pain, setting the roof of the church aflame. Its tail whipped about, connected with a corner of the centuries-old structure, sending large stones and sections of crossbeams flying. One small piece knocked Letty to the ground. A minute later, the burning roof collapsed. Screams of parishioners still trapped inside echoed in the night.

Wildly the dragon spun about, disappeared in the darkness to the west. Minutes later, the ground shook violently as it lost its battle to stay in the air.

Tourret stood silhouetted against the flames of the church. In the village below, other fires were springing up, spread by the wild beating of the dragon's wings. Behind him, Father Ryan struggled to rise from where he had fallen, but Tourret's attention was fixed on Elizabeth crouched at the base of the hedge. A flying stone had scraped away part of the Frenchman's face, revealing the cybercircuitry beneath. There was a loud click as he closed one hand and three spring-loaded blades extended from the back of his wrist.

Elizabeth searched for magic, tried to make Tourret disappear, tried to find anything to make him stop, but her mind was again filled with the black fog.

"You little idiot," he growled, "you can't begin to know what you've done with your half-witted magic. I'll slit your belly like you were a rabbit."

"You'll have to kill me first."

The Frenchman spun around. Father Ryan stood breathing heavily, clutching the iron crucifix he had pocketed earlier, the way a child clutches a teddy bear after a nightmare. His eyes had a glazed, half-mad look.

"I'll stop your devil's work even if I die in the process. My faith is solid now as the iron in this cross."

"The iron of your papacy against the steel of mine, eh, Father? I'm sure there's an allegory in there somewhere," Tourret laughed. In a blur of motion, he swept his arm up, burying his wristblades deep in the priest's side.

Father Ryan gasped. Blood began trickling from his lips.

"O Lord," he cried out, "do not desert me as I deserted You."

He grabbed for the cyberpriest, shoving the crucifix

into the exposed wiring in Tourret's face.

Sparks flew. Electricity coursed through the iron molecules of the cross, travelled through the Father's body, returned to Tourret. The cyberpriest stiffened as wires short-circuited. Paralysis seized his cybermuscles and froze his diaphragm, shutting down his lungs. Mouth open, the crucifix burned into his face, he expired locked in deadly embrace with the Irish priest, both bodies sparking with what some would later call electricity and others would swear was holy fire.

Elizabeth stumbled to her feet. Dazed, bewildered, she wandered away from where Doctor O'Donoghue was desperately using magic to try to stop the bleeding in William M'Kenna's legs. Picking her way around stones knocked from the church, she found Letty groggily trying to stand.

"Ooooh," the leprechaun moaned. "What happened?"

Letty's face twisted in horror as full consciousness came rushing back.

"Leafflyer!" she shouted. "He was ridin' the great beastie. I've got to get to m' people!"

Unsteadily, she began staggering toward the west. Elizabeth scooped her up and began to run, letting herself become the wind, her feet flying over the grass below.

In minutes, they reached what was left of the leprechauns' forest glade. Trees were broken and uprooted. A long, deep trench showed where the dragon had plowed the ground in its crash landing. The trough ran directly through the place where the meeting hall had been. Some ways off, the dragon's body lay, parts of trees sticking out from its scales, its blood soaking into the soil.

"Leafflyer!" Letty cried. "Grassweaver! Is anyone alive?"

"Not many."

A leprechaun hobbled from under a bush.

"Grassweaver!"

"We were dancin' the Sacred Rings when the beast fell among us. A few escaped, but most were right in its path."

"An' Leafflyer?"

"I had a glimpse o' him ridin' the creature down, tuggin' on one ear as if he could turn it away from us. It was a valiant death he had."

"Letty," Elizabeth said, "Can I —"

"Go back to yur people now, Elizabeth." The leprechaun wiped away tears. "Go back to yur people an' leave me to bury mine."

* * *

Elizabeth trudged out of town under a listless grey sky, a pack slung over her back. The acrid smell from burned buildings still lingered in the air, over a week after the conflagration. She passed the church where repairs were well underway, supervised by priests sent from Arklow. Many new graves lay like raw wounds in the cemetery. Two of them contained her parents.

She had gone to visit William M'Kenna where he was recuperating, a sheet laid over the stumps of his legs.

"Gavin says he'll soon have the abracadabras cast on a platform he's building for me," he told her. "Swears I'll zip around better than I did on what he called my 'fat, middle-aged legs.' Guess I'll be using magic after all, if I want to get about. Some of the townsfolk are getting up a local guard to watch the coast road and the farms hereabouts, and they've asked me to coordinate it. They haven't found Jeremy Bratton's body yet and some of our village lads haven't been seen since that night at the church, either. We're thinking they may be off playing Warriors of Destiny and we don't want them stirring up more trouble around here. Ah, to think I threw in with that lot. What would Janie have said?"

He paused and looked into Elizabeth's eyes. "I saw her, you know, child. Not just a memory like Tourret showed me or what you conjured up in the church; I really saw her.

"When Gavin was working on my legs there by the hedge, I sort of floated above and watched him for a bit. Then I saw Janie, nothing separating us but a wee stream, her standing under the trees on the far side. But when I went to cross over to her, she just kept waving me back, saying 'Not yet, not yet.' Then I woke up here without my legs. But I almost made it to her, Elizabeth. I almost made it to her."

She left then and slipped out of town unnoticed. She stopped at the ruined glade.

"Letty, I've come to say goodbye."

With a rustling of leaves, the leprechaun emerged to sit on a jagged stump a little way off.

"So yur goin' travellin'?"

Elizabeth nodded. "I guess so. Maybe the people who made us unhappy will do the same thing in other towns and maybe I can show people how things used to be, like I did here."

"Aye, yur a dreamweaver, that's for sure. An' a powerful one, too. I haven't seen such a dreamweaver amongst yur people since long before ye brought in the machines an' we lay down to take our great nap."

"Doctor O'Donoghue says I have some extra something in my body. Is that where my magic comes from? 'Cause, you know, Letty, I feel different ever since that night —" Elizabeth hesitated, looking around at the wrecked glade.

"Anyway, I feel kind of like something inside me came unstuck, like water running through a drain after you unstop it. I still have trouble saying words sometimes, but when I try to remember how to do things, it's easier now. Most of the time, anyway."

"I suppose the magic might have been sleepin' in ye an' when ye needed it badly enough, it woke up. Makes no difference, long as ye got it."

They sat in silence while a butterfly flitted among the broken flowers. Elizabeth saw small mounds like the new graves in the churchyard.

"I'm sorry about your people," she said softly.

Letty nodded. "The fairies came to dance over them an' helped me plant seeds amongst them. Fairies aren't such a bad lot, for bubbleheads. Even the banshee came to sing a dirge."

"I heard it." Elizabeth said, shivering. She lifted her pack. "Well, I'd better go."

"Where are ye headin'?"

"I don't know. That way, I guess," she said, pointing west.

The leprechaun sighed and climbed down from her stump. Silently, she began plucking leaves from mint plants and slipping them into the pouch on her belt.

"What are you doing, Letty?"

"Well, I don't intend to put up with that abomination yur people speak all o' the time. It's bad enough I'll be hearin' it from the other Big Feet without listenin' to that squawkin' at night when we're alone."

"You mean you'll go with me?" Elizabeth was incredulous.

"Dreamweaver ye may be, but few Tall Ones are likely to pay much attention to what a young one is sayin', especially if they think she's a bit fairy-brained. Ye'll need someone with experience to teach ye the ways o' the world. Besides, without remindin', ye'll forget how to walk proper an' go squashin' every grass blade an' cowslip beneath yur great feet! Now hoist me up onto yur shoulder so I can slip into yur pack if we run into anyone."

From her friend's shoulder, Letty surveyed the broken glade one last time.

"I would like to return in the Spring, though, to see the flowers bloom over their sleepin' places."

"We'll come back," Elizabeth said. "I promise."

"Like the *Fianna*, we'll come home when Eire's shores are safe, eh, lass?"

"Who were the *Fianna*, Letty?"

They started off across the fields.

"Ah, dinna yur people teach ye nothin'? Let me tell ye about when I was a wee bit younger than I am now ... "

Gypsor's Luck

Bill Smith

"Aye, you're right, Fred. Gypsor's in fine form tonight."

Bakkeris had to scream to be heard above the sound of the crowd. He looked up and over the bar, squinting to try and see who Gypsor had targeted tonight. The smoke from the dwarven pipes interfered with his vision of the scene, but from the way Gypsor swayed and smiled, bouncing from hoof to hoof, Bakkeris could tell that Gypsor was trying his best to make a favorable impression.

Grabbing a pair of freshly washed mugs and trotting over to the keg, Bakkeris pulled the handle, allowing the ornately carved ceramic mugs to fill with thick, brown ale. He had to smile to himself. A filled tavern, a happy clientelle, Gypsor in rut again and a full cash box. What more could one ask for? "A few more weeks like this one, and we'll be back in the black. Soon the *Satyr's Pub* will be ours."

He looked back over at Fred, one of the regulars at

the Pub. In the past few weeks, he had become a good friend of the barkeep, always drinking enough to justify his permanent spot at the bar, and never causing any problems. He also had a good nature about him, even if he was a little dull-witted and coarse. "I tell you, Bakkeris, you let that half-folk pester your paying womenfolk like that, and business'll go bad."

"You're just jealous that the pretty ones pay more attention to someone who's half goat than someone like you, who's half in the bag."

"You know, I should rip out your ..." Fred's brow creased as he thought about what word would be most appropriate. He thought hard. Real hard. "Give me another ale, now," he mumbled as he took a deep drought of the beverage, his previous threat now a million miles from his inebriated brain cells.

Bakkeris turned to pull the filled mugs out from under the keg, and carefully navigating around the slick spots of spilled ale on the floor, he placed the mugs on the bar in front of a pair of centaurs. Bakkeris smiled at the one on the left, who was older than his companion. His hair, both on head and his horse-half, had tinges of grey amongst the fine brown. Bare chested, and rippling with muscle, he still could stand up to any "pups" who tried to give him trouble.

"So, Adriag, who's your young friend?"

Adriag layed a handfull of small silver coins on the bar, and took a deep drink from his mug. Sighing with satisfaction, he slapped his companion on the shoulder. "Bakkeris, always a fine ale here! This young steed is Jonn, my brother's eldest. I'm out here showing him the exciting spots of this fair city of Oxford. At least, after we've had a few here, first. Isn't that right, Jonny-boy?"

The younger centaur seemed uncertain of how to respond. He smiled sheepishly, and slowly reached out to his mug.

Bakkeris made a slight hand gesture, murmering, "here," and the pile of coins slid toward the bartender, off the bar and into a chute running the length of the bar, about one foot below the bar's top.

"Handy parlor trick you've got there, Bakkeris."

Bakkeris looked up with a quick smile. "I'm not much one for magic, but that little trick just comes naturally to me. Birth magic and all."

Taking out his bar rag to wipe off some spilled liquid, he leaned over to the younger centaur, and whispered, "You'd do well to just relax a little. Have fun. Have a few too many. And, if its the ladies you're interested in, go watch Gypsor over there. He'll teach you something if anyone can."

Gypsor was closing in for the kill. His twinkling eyes were always the bait, but that smile just sealed the deal. He could tell tonight he would be ... doing well. The three human young ladies at the table seemed thoroughly entranced; their dates were not nearly so entertained.

The humans were all obviously Core Earthers, probably college students taking a break from their studies. The one woman who Gypsor was most interested in, primarily because her date was obviously the most distressed of the bunch, was named Karen. Her striking blue eyes and light brown hair made her quite pleasant in appearance. Too bad she wasn't more ... *compatible*.

"...and then, just as it seemed that the guardsman was going to fall for it, my friend Bakkeris over there —"

pointing a finger at the thin, balding human at the bar, who looked up and waved, as if on cue, "— comes around the corner screaming, 'Gypsor, where the hell did you go?' It was all down hill from there, and I ran for my life."

The women all laughed, and Karen, in a move deliberately calculated to get her date's attention, leaned over and rubbed the satyr's hand. The glare Gypsor got from the woman's date, Doug his name was, made him all warm inside. "Crash and burn" was the oft repeated phrase the half-folk had heard, and that's exactly where Doug was headed.

Gypsor decided to have a lot more fun with the situation. Leaning in to the young woman, *my, her perfume is effective*, he offered, "My lass, let me be back in a moment. If you'll excuse. Can I get your friends a drink?"

He quickly nodded to all of the other people at the table, while not taking his eyes from hers. Doug grumbled something about a strong ale, and the others also ordered some of the Pub's trademark brew. Karen simply smiled and laughed some more.

As he worked his way back to the bar (ignoring all of the calls of other patrons; being a barmaster was so difficult), he could hear Karen comment to Doug, "He's so funny and charming …" *Bingo!*

Leaning up on the bar, he screamed down to Bakkeris, "Hey, Bak, get me five ales and a *sleeping dragon*, Pronto!"

A human, probably a factory worker by trade, with a flannel shirt and worn blue jeans, asked, "So, is she yours?"

Gypsor cocked his head, and asked, "So you noticed, huh?"

The worker laughed and took a deep drink. "Noticed! I've got twenty trades riding on you! Go get her, man!" Gypsor heartily slapped the man on the back, with a deep laugh, grabbed the tray, and headed back across the bar.

"Here we go, an ale for all of you, and a sleeping dragon for the lovely lady." Gypsor put on his most charming smile, as he placed the glass in front of the woman. Karen was ready to play along.

"I didn't order a drink."

"No, my lady, it is on the house. I, Gypsor, your most humble and unworthy barmaster for the evening, offer it to you. Drink it in good health."

The satyr heard Doug mutter, "I don't believe this."

Gypsor quickly excused himself from the table, and looked over his shoulder. Doug had grabbed Karen by the hand, and, quickly scooping up their jackets, was leading his friends out of the bar.

As soon as the group left, the bar seemed to become as silent as a crypt. Gypsor seemed to be the center of attention, as he just stood in the center, taking orders for drinks. Seconds later, when it was clear that Karen wouldn't be coming back, English pound notes, and Ayslish trades and lemays started passing from one client to the next on virtually every table, amongst cries of, "Damn satyr!" and "I knew he would push his luck too far! Now, give me the money!"

As mid-morning rolled into early afternoon, Bakkeris examined the pile of bills in front of him. "Look at this — ale permits, tax forms, bank agreements, fire insurance, magic insurance, liability insurance, bills for new mugs and napkins and who knows what! Why didn't I think of this before I got into business?" Gypsor casually strolled by, puffing on one of the cigars he had bought earlier in the morning.

"C'mon, boss, you knew we were getting into this. Besides, how are we doing money-wise?" He turned and pulled out a seat, his hooves clacking on the hardwood floor.

Bakkeris wiped his brow. "*We* nothing! You know as well as I do that your signature isn't worth a pile of dragon spit. We're getting by — a few more weeks like this, and we'll be in the clear."

Gypsor smiled. "Good! How much did we clear on the bets last night?"

Bakkeris pulled out a bulging pouch, holding it up to show its heft. "Nearly 300 lemays for each of us. Everyone was sure you were going to show that lass an *unusual* time."

"And I will yet, I promise!"

"What do you mean? Do you think her boyfriend will ever bring her back here again?"

"He wasn't her boyfriend, or at least if he was, he isn't anymore. I took her heart, or at least that's the way she feels. I'm irresistible. Proven fact. Law of nature, like magic. That kind of thing."

"You know you should have been a minotaur. You've got more bull in you than most cattle."

A few seconds later, the door to the *Satyr's Pub* opened, to let in some of the cool breezes from outside. A human, wrapped in a concealing cloak, entered cautiously. Gypsor turned to follow Bakkeris' gaze, as the mysterious figure headed straight for the two. Quickly pulling off the hood, Karen smiled and nodded at Gypsor. "I wanted to come see you. I wanted to apologize for Doug. He normally doesn't act like that. You were so nice, buying that drink for me and all."

Gypsor flashed Bakkeris a quick smile, and silently mouthed, "I'll be back later."

Bakkeris admonished the satyr, "Oh, no you don't. You've got work to do." Then, to Karen, "I'm sorry, but Gypsor has work to do ..."

Gypsor literally leaped from his chair, placing himself between the door and the young woman. Putting on his most charming smile, he explained, "Karen, my dear, I will be free after three this afternoon. May I call upon you then, and where?"

Bakkeris was content to let the satyr finish his plans without an observer. Returning to his stack of papers, he once again set about tallying the figures from the night before. A few minutes later, Gypsor returned, bearing a smile a mile wide. "And this afternoon, I, Gypsor, will once again have the delights of female companionship. Mithorl once again smiles on me."

As Bakkeris set back to work on the finances of the *Pub* and Gypsor returned to cleaning up from the night before, a trio of dwarves entered the small tavern. There were three of them, each with long beards and of indeterminable age. Utilizing his most sophisticated mannerisms, Gypsor seated them near the fireplace and took their orders for lunch, while Bakkeris took up his turn, in the back of the tavern at the fire pit.

Behind the kitchen doors, and far from prying ears, Gypsor commented to Bakkeris that these dwarves seemed unusual. "I tell you, Bakkeris, they're not our usual customers. They're wealthier than you or I can imagine. Listen to how they talk, and look at what they're wearing. Gold watches on chains! Finely tailored suits; probably from London! And, I heard them talking about their business — I can't figure out exactly what they do, but whatever it is, it's a valuable piece of work. They're talking about guards and looking out for thieves and trouble-makers. And, if they're so wealthy, what are they doing here? We aren't exactly an aristocratic neighborhood around here."

Bakkeris sighed with irritation. "Gypsor, my friend, you worry too much. They're just here for a lunch. Be yourself, and keep them entertained. If they're as wealthy as you say, you'll receive a good tip for your trouble!"

Within minutes, the dwarves had a fine meal before them, and, from what Gypsor could piece together, they were merchants on their way back from London. Gypsor was trying his best to be charming without being overbearing. This was a finely practiced art for him, but he hadn't dealt much with dwarves, so he didn't know their peculiarities, or what kind of humor they appreciated.

While Gypsor prattled on to the travelers, Bakkeris went back to his bookkeeping duties. He tried not to eavesdrop on the conversation, but here and there he picked up a snippet of conversation. The lead dwarf was named Dwurgven, while his companions went by the names of Hisgarg and Voladikyn. They seemed to be enjoying the satyr's company (it was hard not to appreciate his easy-going nature), so he decided to let well enough alone.

With the meal nearly concluded, the dwarves ordered a last round of ales before heading out on the road again. Gypsor, in all of his efforts to be impressive, found himself concentrating far too much on charm and not enough on dexterity. He nearly tumbled a full mug of ale on Hisgarg, but his reflexes helped him catch the mug, spilling only a few drops and none of it on the customers.

Gypsor, as was his custom, commented, "Mithorl once again smiles on me."

This comment piqued the interest of Dwurgven. Absent-mindedly adjusting his long, stringy black hair, he asked, "Who is this Mithorl you speak of, friend satyr?"

Gypsor was taken aback that any folk, such as humans or dwarves, would take any interest in a minor, and almost forgotten, god of the half-folk. "Mithorl is my true god, the god of revelry, luck and happiness. The true god of the satyrs. These days, our kind haven't had much to celebrate, but I feel that we must carry on his story."

Gypsor's storytelling skills were at their peak, and after Gypsor had related his tale, Dwurgven sat back seemingly appreciative of the satyr's unusual beliefs. Gypsor was shocked when Dwurgven casually commented, "You half-folk and your silly gods! Do you really believe in him? I'd never heard of him before I'd met you."

"Well, of course you haven't. All your lives you've been led to believe that my kind are little more than savages. Ignorance is bliss and all. Not meaning any rudeness, but folk like you are the only ones who can do something. Look at the condition of my people. The folk can't even see fit to declare us 'full-folk.' We are 'half-folk,' with not even 'half-rights.' Think of it — we have no rights that you have. It's an ancient tactic — if you want to exploit someone, just make everyone else believes they are no more than savages. Ignore their art, their culture, their beliefs. Portray them as beasts, and, sure enough, they will be treated as such!"

Dwurgven showed no anger, nor any other emotion. He just looked at his other friends, and commented as if Gypsor weren't even present. "Well, no wonder they are treated so. No ability to talk rationally; always getting emotional when cooler heads are necessary. And his belief — a god of revelry, indeed! Sounds like some myth that would come out of a wild feast or orgy."

As he headed back toward the kitchen, Gypsor muttered, "Mithorl wouldn't have it any other way, either." He noticed that Bakkeris had retreated to the kitchen. As soon as he walked into the back room, his human friend grabbed him.

"Hey, Gypsor, calm down. Relax a little."

"Well, I know I shouldn't blame you, but I've got every right to be angry about this. I only hope someday all of the other folk realize how ignorant their attitudes are."

"Someday they will my friend. But, for now, keep your mouth shut. Let me take care of these people! Stay in the back."

Gypsor's eyes widened with half-curiousity, half-fear. "What is wrong?"

Bakkeris stepped back, and looked down at the floor, unable to look his friend squarely in the eye. "Did you not recognize their accents? It took me a while. At first, I thought they were from Haven. Then it dawned on me. They're from Vareth. Then I started to listen to their discussions about their business. It wasn't too hard to figure out that they're ..."

"Slavers."

As early evening approached, Bakkeris found himself continually looking at his timepiece. "Where the hell is that satyr?" Gypsor had been known to be a little late, especially when he was out with a woman, but he was almost always on time for work. *Almost* always. That was why he still wasn't worried.

That is, until Karen came through the door to the *Satyr's Pub*. She came up to the human and asked, "Where's Gypsor? I'm supposed to meet him here in a few minutes."

From Karen's reaction, Bakkeris could tell that he wasn't hiding his concern well. "Gypsor hasn't been back yet. He was supposed to be here over an hour ago. I thought he'd still be with you."

Karen blushed quickly, but then concern quickly returned to her face. "He left my place about two hours ago."

Gypsor's first sensation was that of a rocking motion. Not the smooth rocking of a ship at sea, but a sudden bumping and jolting. His head seemed to pound with the uneven rhythm of the bouncing ride. He'd had hangovers like this before — not often, but once or twice. Now, as before, he vowed never to drink again. *Wait a minute! I wasn't drinking! I was just going down an alley, when I got hit over the head. What have I gotten myself into?*

The satyr opened his eyes. It took him a minute to focus, but as things came into view, he wished he had never opened his eyes. He was in a slave cage wagon, nearly twenty feet long, with iron bars every few inches. It was barely tall enough for him to sit upright, no where tall enough for him to stand. Around one wrist and one ankle was a chain, anchored to the floor the cage.

Gypsor quickly looked around, and even though it hurt immensely to do so, pulled his head up straight to get a look at his captors. Two horses pulled the heavy cage, with four dwarves in the front seats, two acting as drivers, and the other two paying careful attention to the "passengers" in the cage. There were maybe 20 of them in all, mostly dwarves, but a few gnomes and goblins were also penned up. All were chained to the floor like Gypsor. Most were asleep, or more likely unconscious, and probably thankful for it, too. Gypsor was the only half-folk of the bunch.

The wagon was being pulled along a decaying paved road, the pot holes accounting for the rough rocking motion. A road sign up ahead read "Moorestock —15." It seemed to be morning, but with the thick haze, he couldn't tell for sure.

Gypsor felt a trickle of water run down the side of his head, and reached up with his unchained hand to wipe the mist away; his hand came away covered with blood. For once, Gypsor was glad that he didn't have a mirror with him.

Then he took a closer look at the dwarves. He didn't recognize the two guards, although he did recognize the weapons they were toting — they were called "AK-47's" and from what he had heard, they were able to spit thousands of hunks of metal in a few seconds. The dwarves seemed eager to use them. Gypsor decided that he didn't want to learn anything more about them.

The one driver he didn't recognize either, but the assistant was none other than Voladikyn. As he stirred, one of the guards called out, "The halfie's awake, sir. Shall we club him back down?"

The dwarf turned to face the satyr, a satisfied grin on his face. Grooming his thick red beard with his chubby fingers, the dwarf laughed. "No, no. He seems docile enough now, aren't you? Aye, Gypsor, Mithorl has indeed smiled upon you. You are now honored enough to become one of our slaves! If you had kept your mouth shut at your friend's tavern, none of this would have happened. In the future, you should be more careful when you share your political thoughts. But, you know, a half-folk with a big mouth will never be missed, and no one will take the time to investigate your disappearance. You brought this upon yourself. Welcome to your fate!"

Gypsor passed out again, this time with the evil laugh of the dwarf echoing in his ears.

* * *

The previous night at the *Satyr's Pub* had been horrible for Bakkeris. All night he had been tortured by the thought of Gypsor in trouble, but he couldn't just close the tavern. He was so anxiety-stricken that he couldn't sleep.

By now, midmorning, he still didn't know what to do.

As soon as dawn broke, he began his hunt for his friend. First, he called on some of the satyr's favorite haunts. Meeting with no success, he checked in with Ardinay's Home Guard. They had no reports of any kind, but thanked him for his effort, and promised to look into it "once they had a chance." From their manner, he could tell they wouldn't have a chance for days, or possibly weeks. Bakkeris was infuriated — had it been a human, an immediate search would have been called. Unfortunately, Gypsor was not a human, and as far as the Home Guard in Oxford was concerned, he wasn't even a person. His case would have to wait, behind the petty robberies and thefts that troubled "important folk."

With that, Bakkeris had decided to talk to his banking representative, in the hopes of getting a small extension on his loan payment. An exhaustive search of the city would certainly shut the *Satyr's Pub* down for at least a couple of days, and that income would make the difference between covering the monthly payment and foreclosure. The loan officer was courteous, and sympathetic, but nonetheless unable to grant an extension.

And now, his troubles overwhelming him, and his best friend in the world missing, Bakkeris was unable to decide what to do.

"All I ever wanted was a chance to settle down, and enjoy my life, instead of scrounging. If I leave to go look for him, I'll lose everything." And in that moment of self-pity, Bakkeris realized that he really had no choice. He locked the door as he left the *Pub*, headed for the "Mixed Quarter," where the dwarves, and some half and lesser folk lived. It was as good a place as any, for Gypsor had many friends in those neighborhoods. In the window of the *Satyr's Pub* was a small, hand-lettered sign that read, "Closed Until Further Notice."

* * *

Bakkeris wished he'd listened more to Gypsor when he'd talked about his adventures in the city. Now he found himself in the Mixed Quarter, and he was worried that his ignorance of the neighborhood would get him into trouble — quickly.

Bakkeris knew that Gypsor was quite an explorer, and seemed to know every nook and cranny of the city. By contrast, Bakkeris had gotten over his wanderlust when he was younger. These days he tended to stay close to the tavern and his apartment over the bar. It was a quiet lifestyle, and one he much preferred, for three years serving under Uthorion in his various campaigns had quite beaten the adventurer out of him.

And now, fate was about to force him into that lifestyle again.

When asking directly about Gypsor proved useless, Bakkeris decided to start investigating the slaver angle. The encounter with the dwarves were the only unusual thing to have happened late, and Gypsor knew the streets well enough to avoid random crime. This tack was either going to work, or get his throat slit.

As he turned down another darkened alley, on his way to yet another meeting with a shifty merchant he knew of, he heard a rattle of garbage cans. He took a quick step backward, sinking his foot into a deep puddle of cold muck, and he remembered the last time he had felt so alone and in danger. A quick moving shadow off to his left allowed him to see a flicker of light off a knife blade. He started looking for defensive positions, or an exit.

Three figures, tall enough to be humans, emerged from behind crates. Two were about twenty feet down the alley from him. One was barely five feet from Bakkeris, and he cursed himself for not being more observant. One of the far figures lowered his hood, showing himself to be a young human teen, with stringy brown hair and a ruddy complexion. "You're out of your neighborhood aren't you, old man? Don't know where not to go? That's okay, 'cause we'll give you a lesson you won't forget." The man-child then pulled a small pistol out from under his cloak, while the other two thieves produced knives from under their cloaks.

Bakkeris didn't want to fight, but he knew that going down peacefully would still result in his death. On the other hand, his combat training would come in useful. He tried to back himself around so that he could watch all three of the punks at once, but his reflexes were no longer what they once were. The youth nearest him grabbed him by the neck, and made a quick flick with the knife blade, leaving a trail of blood down Bakkeris' left forearm. The gun-wielded thief laughed menacingly, as Bakkeris tried to think of some way to get himself out of this situation. He twisted quickly, shifting the lower half of his body to the right, throwing the punk over his hip and into a pile of garbage. The punk got one last slash in, and it dug deeply into him, but there was one less thief to worry about, at least for the immediate future.

The gun-wielding youth laughed again, with a taunt. "So, the old man wants to fight. Cut him, Robert!" As the other knife-wielding thief closed in on Bakkeris, a blast of light exploded in the alleyway — someone's portable light spell had chosen this moment to malfunction and cease working. Taking advantage of his tremendous luck, Bakkeris rushed the thief, who was momentarily blinded by the flash. Tumbling back into the other thief, the knife dropped at Bakkeris' feet while the gun went spinning into the air, landing in a pile of garbage.

Bakkeris leaped for the gun, but was tackled by the first thief that had injured him. He felt a sharp sensation in his back as the boy thrust the blade into him. Blindly swiping back with the captured blade, Bakkeris knew he made contact as a shrill scream broke the air of the alley. Bakkeris tried to see what had happened, and saw the boy holding his abdomen. Then, he looked to where the gun and landed, and found himself staring down the barrel of the pistol, levelled at his forehead by one of the youthful punks. Bakkeris prepared for the death blow and closed his eyes, but the scream was not his. Looking up, he saw that the boy had dropped the gun as an arrow had pierced his hand.

The boys seemed ready to surrender now that an unknown foe had joined the battle. They pulled back down the alley, as a deep voice announced, "Run back to your mothers to nurse your wounds, little human pups."

With the boys long gone, a solitary figure emerged from the shadows, bearing a short bow and a quiver of arrows.

He was a satyr. He had dark brown hair, a little darker than Gypsor's. He was also younger, probably not even out of his teens yet. Aside from his bow, he had a sword and knife scabbarded about his waist.

"You almost died, you know. Not even carrying a knife. Not a wise thing to do around here."

Bakkeris was trying to think of an appropriate response, but all he could get out was, "I know. Thank you."

The satyr seemed to have a sly grin on his face. Extending a chubby hand, he helped the human back up to his feet. "I'm Bendas. I noticed you wandering around a few blocks back, and figured you might get into a … situation like this. You know, you really stand out around here."

Bakkeris looked incredulously at the satyr. "And you don't? And besides, I didn't want to come down here, but I'm looking for someone."

Bendas went to search for the pistol and the dropped knives. He found them, and wiping the blood off the blades, he handed them to Bakkeris. He pocketed the pistol for himself. The satyr's eyes were lit up with curiousity. "That is interesting. You think that if the dwarves know anything they'll tell you?"

"For a price."

"You got that right. Give me a few coins, and I can clue you in."

"Look, Bendas, I appreciate your help. I'm indebted to you. But, I've got things I've got to do, and I don't have time to play games. So, if you don't mind, I want to get out of this alley before the Home Guard shows up."

Bakkeris managed to get halfway down the alley when he heard the satyr call out, "It's about the satyr that got clubbed yesterday, isn't it?"

Bakkeris turned to face this ever mystifying individual. "You know about Gypsor?"

"So that's his name? Yeah, I know something about him. You really set the underworld around here spinning. Asking around about 'buying a couple of slaves, and where you could get one.' No one's going to believe that someone dressed like you is going to be buying slaves. And coming straight to this neighborhood. That's like screaming, 'Hey, all you dwarves, I know you're all slavers, so come help me or else.' Not a polite thing to do. You were lucky these common thieves got to you before some of the hired help found you.

"Anyway, I found out about what happened. Your friend was kidnapped by a dwarven slaving company. He's being sent to the mines of Moorestock, in Wales. This wasn't easy to find out, you understand?"

"Okay, Bendas, I'm doubly indebted to you. What do you want?"

"Let me help. This may seem strange, but your friend is well known among our kind. Think of it as kind of my job to make sure he's okay, at least for now. There's a lot in it for me, so don't think I'm doing it for charity."

Bakkeris considered the stranger's words. "Motivation is not what matters, it's action. I could use your help. I guess it's off to Moorestock."

The grinding screech of metal on metal no longer registered in Gypsor's fatigued mind. Between the injuries sustained in his abduction, and the fatigue of the ten hour work day, he was incapable of anything beyond reactive thought. He no longer thought — he just understood and acted.

He pushed another cart up the steep rails. This was his tenth trip of the day, his first day in the mines. Each journey, over a half mile up an unyielding incline, had taken a tremendous toll on the spirit of the satyr. His first day. He wondered how many more days there would be.

Each trip brought a fortune of nearly incalculable worth to the surface, feeding the coffers of the Vareth slavers. The ore carts were filled with precious gems, including diamonds, rubies and emeralds, but the satyr seemed immune to the charm of the wealth he moved.

He considered himself lucky. It was grueling work, but he could handle it. He was surprised to see how quickly his military conditioning returned to him. He was thankful as well. He could have been sentenced to permanent mine duty, which was even more grueling and certainly more dangerous, with hardly any food or water, and certainly no chance of escape. Now, with his assignment, he might be able to escape.

He had quickly learned the rules of the slave camp. He learned to ignore the pleadings and complaints of those around him. The dwarven guards had already shown an incredible callousness toward life, from those of the dwarves to that of the lesser and half folk. The guards had made it clear that nothing was to stand in the way of production. This was graphically made clear to him, and all of the other new slaves, during one of his early trips.

When he arrived at the bottom of the mine shaft and began shoveling the gems into the cart, Gypsor saw that one of the goblins had fallen. Gypsor could easily see the severity of the injury, and the guards had brought the poor creature to the rails, near Gypsor's mine cart, where a healer had been summoned. After a cursory examination, the healer had declared that the slave would die within the day, and it wasn't worth bringing him into town for healing. The guards dragged the slowly dying goblin over to Gypsor's fully loaded ore cart, and just threw the body on top of the gems, with a gruff, "Get that body out of here before it starts stinking up the place."

Gypsor heard the dying creature's dying words.

"Kalim, help me ..."

Kalim. A lesser folk god of corruption. But, a god who had promised to protect the faithful nonetheless. Kalim, Dunad, Shali and all of the other gods of Aysle ... even Mithorl. They had promised to protect. How much the people of Aysle had given in the name of religion, and how little they had received.

Where indeed had the gods and their promises of protection gone?

* * *

Moorestock was a small village, with little more than a few dozen houses, a small market, and a pair of pubs. This particular evening was foggy and damp, and Bakkeris felt chilled to the bone, despite the thick cloak he wore. Bendas showed no signs of discomfort, but instead pranced about with excitement.

The two of them were an odd combination — one, a retired foot soldier turned tavern keeper, and the other, a young urban adventurer. Bakkeris was here out of duty, friendship and more than a little guilt; Bendas' motivations remained a mystery. They had come to take on almost impossible odds, to tempt fate and all that might be. To possibly die to save a friend. It seemed so noble in the myths, and so frightening now that he was living the life. One thing that his years of combat experience taught him was that skill had very little to do with survival on the field of battle. More often than not it was pure, blind, stupid luck.

The worst part of the situation was that they had convinced themselves that they were ready to take on a group of dwarven slavers, probably sanctioned by House Vareth itself.

Bakkeris could see that the cold had finally gotten to the young satyr. "Well, my friend, it seems we have arrived. Our best bet is to lie low and stay out of sight. Once we spot one of the dwarven slavers, then we can simply follow them back to the mines, and proceed from there. A good plan?"

"The best we can hope for."

Picking a grove of trees not far from the village, the two travelers set up a quick camp. It was far enough from the village that a camp fire wouldn't attract any attention, and while they had to walk nearly a mile to get close enough to observe the village, the security was a fair trade.

Bakkeris took first watch shift and carefully made his way toward the village. After several hours of watching through his spyglass, with no sign of the dwarves, the town quieted down. He knew that things were shutting down for the night and there was no point in a continued vigil. Besides, one would have to watch the other while they slept so they wouldn't be attacked by any animals or creatures.

When Bakkeris returned to camp, Bendas' hunt had turned out to be successful and he had already cooked a rabbit stew. With the stew and hardtack consumed, Bakkeris finally spent some time learning about his companion. Bendas seemed to be the most *driven* individual he had ever met. Most people seemed to wander through life, falling into whatever they managed to stumble upon. Bendas, from his tales of wandering Upper Aysle as a young teenager, to his stories of his life in England since the invasion, seemed to have a certain sense of destiny about him. It was not that the satyr was even aware of this, it was just that his events all seemed interrelated somehow, by a sense of constant knowledge and luck. And, for a satyr, he was remarkably sedate.

Finally the conversation turned to religion. Bendas looked at the campfire rather than Bakkeris. "Tell me, Bakkeris, whom do you worship?"

"No one."

"You don't worship a god? That's unusual for a human."

"Bendas, from what I've seen, I have no reason to believe that the gods care about us. I was raised to believe in Dunad, and it was explained that it was my duty to Dunad to join the armies and fight for the honor and glory of Aysle. Little did I know that the honor included slaughtering children in their beds, and killing enemy troops who surrendered. After that I came to the conclusion that the gods, if they existed at all, were too busy to care about us. There is too much suffering in this, and all of the other worlds."

"Bakkeris, you are a bitter man. Do you not believe in a higher purpose?"

"Oh, I believe in a purpose. But it is a purpose that we must take upon ourselves. It is entirely in our hands. If we become evil, it is not because of the gods; it is because of a choice we have made. If we save this world, it is because of a choice we have made. I, for one, am done making those choices, for they always seem to be the wrong ones. And what of you, who do you worship?"

"In many ways, I feel aligned to Mithorl, the satyr god. There is more to it though. I feel we make our own gods, and, when we do, they are real; they are in us. I agree that our fate is truly in our hands and not someone else's. I must rest now, Bakkeris, my most intriguing friend."

The night passed uneventfully. As morning approached, they took up their positions just outside the village. The unlikely partners watched the town for several hours, by which time the morning mist had burned off. It had turned into a fine, but chilly, fall day.

Finally Bendas exclaimed, "I think our quarry has revealed itself!"

Bakkeris followed Bendas' directives, adjusting his spyglass to look far down the road. Over his right shoulder he could hear Bendas commenting on the scene. "It's those three dwarves coming into town. One of them has been injured and must be a slave. Look at the rags he wears. I bet they're bringing him to a healer. But look at the other two dwarves — see the objects bulging in their packs. You can see the rifle barrels. They've had to hide them going into town. Fortunately for us, it will take them a few moments to get those rifles out of the packs."

"Bendas, what are you talking about? You sound like you want to attack them. That wasn't the plan!"

"Come, Bakkeris, look at the situation. The slave will be able to guide us there, and tell us what they're defenses are like. Besides, if we can stop them now, we won't have to fight them at the mine. Follow me!"

Without another word, the satyr was running toward the road and the hiding spot they had found the previous day. Bakkeris didn't like the idea of changing plans like this, but Bendas' logic sounded reasonable.

The two companions carefully crept up to an ideal hiding spot along the road. A series of high reeds gave them excellent cover. Bendas gave Bakkeris the pistol, while he notched an arrow into his short bow. Being careful to stay out of sight of passing farmers and townsfolk, they still had to wait at least an hour for the dwarves to return the way they had come.

The dwarven guards marched right up to the reeds, with no awareness of the ambush that was waiting for them. The taller dwarf, on the left, was discussing the merits of the new slaves that had been brought in. He was in mid-sentence when Bendas counted a silent "three" and the ambush was sprung. The dwarf on the right went down as a bullet struck him just below the chin, while the other dwarf was taken out by an arrow in the chest. It took less than ten seconds for Bendas and Bakkeris to drag the bodies into the reeds, where they could be hidden. The startled slave didn't know what to say, but simply nodded when the two attackers told him that he had been freed from his slavery. The dwarf was still too terror-struck to respond when asked about the location of the mine, but after a few minutes, he reluctantly agreed to lead the human and satyr to the mine entrance.

* * *

With some prompting from the dwarf, Bakkeris and Bendas decided to scout the mine area from a small hill nearby. It was close enough to allow observation of the mining in process, but far enough away that guards seldom patrolled the area.

As the trio watched the slaves pushing carts filled with gems, Bendas realized that he had stumbled upon a fortune. He started pumping the dwarf, Indric, for information. The poor dwarf barely had time to answer one question before another was thrown in his direction. Bakkeris quickly learned that the gemstones weren't natural to the area, but there did seem to be a wealth of them. He surmised that they were created during the axiom wash. Once the gems were discovered by the dwarves, the Vareths, led by Dwurgven, quickly set up a slave mining operation. Dwurgven wasn't actually present most of the time, leaving the management of the mine to Voladikyn. There were at least a dozen armed guards on duty at all times, with about half at ground level and half beneath the surface.

Bendas noted that the layout of the mine was simple, and not truly geared toward defense. The mine itself was a simple hole in the ground, with rails running from a loading ramp on the surface into the mine. There were two modern trucks parked at the loading dock, one appearing to be partially full. There were two buildings, both approximately the same size. The nearer one seemed to be the quarters for the guards, as many off-duty guards milled about the area freely. The further building, Bendas surmised, was home to the slaves. Ringing the entire area were poles nearly thirty feet tall and topped by powerful Earther spotlights. Bakkeris spotted the small power generator, situated behind the loading ramp.

About every half hour, a pair of carts would emerge from the mine, loaded with gems. It was then that the two schemers both spotted Gypsor. "There he is! He looks like he's surviving, at least," Bakkeris explained.

Bakkeris quickly formed a plan. "First, we should use these new rifles to eliminate the guards on the surface. If we are lucky, we can also get Voladikyin. We should wait until they are changing shifts, since that's when it will be most difficult for the guards to control the slaves. In the confusion, we may be able to sneak into the compound. We may have to sweep the mines, but if we can set the slaves free in an open revolt, we may be able to force the guards to surrender."

It was late in the evening before the next change of shifts. The dwarves had activated the spotlights that ringed the mining camp, lighting the entire area. While the dark would provide superior cover for the initial assault on the guards, it was quite likely to be a hindrance if they had to fight their way into the mines.

Bendas checked over both guns, making sure that the ammo clips were full and the guns hadn't been damaged in the combat earlier that day. He gave

Bakkeris a quick tutorial in the use of the automatic rifle, and hoped the human would catch on quickly. He would have to.

The half-dozen guards suddenly changed their patrol route, diverting two to the slaves' quarters, and the other four going to the mine entrance. It was then that Bakkeris knew it was time to act. Bendas was ready to open fire every second, but Bakkeris wanted to wait until Gypsor was outside, and out of harm's way.

First the slaves coming into work were lead to the entrance of the mine. Numbering about fifty, most of them were dwarves, although there were a few goblins, as well. All of the poor slaves looked to be in wretched health, and a few had obvious injuries, as they walked with pronounced limps or leaned to one side. They had only rags for clothing and were chained together.

As they reached the entrance to the mine, they were released from their chains and forced at gunpoint into the mine. Then the workers whose shift was complete were brought out, escorted by yet another guard. Battered and bloody from their work, many showed injuries they had received, apparently on that shift. One of the dwarves fell to his knees, and pointed to his calf, begging for mercy. His leg had a huge wound, and it looked like it was becoming infected. One of the dwarven guards called the healer over to take a look — and circled around behind the dwarf, clubbing the helpless slave over the head with the butt of his rifle. That act of cruelty was too much for Bakkeris to stand. "This is too much. Let us act now."

Bakkeris and Bendas sighted their guns, Bakkeris taking aim on the guard who had just clubbed his fellow dwarf, while Bendas was concentrating on a group of five guards standing just outside the entrance.

They opened fire.

Gypsor was near the mine entrance, and was looking forward to a reprieve from the hard labor. That was when he heard the thundershots, which took him a second to recognize as shoots from the dwarves' guns. He could see out into the lit compound, and saw three guards fall. His fatigued mind raced as he finally figured out that the camp was under attack. The slaves outside fell to the ground, trying to take cover from whatever they could, while the four surviving guards pulled back into the cave entrance.

One guard, seeing the perplexed look on the satyr's face, screamed, "This is none of your concern, dirt slave. Back into the mines." With that, Gypsor felt a rifle butt smack him under the chin, and he fell flat on his back in the dirt.

Up on the hillside, Bakkeris saw that the attack had started well, but things looked like they might deteriorate quickly. "The slaves are trapped in the open, and Gypsor hasn't come out yet. I thought we'd get most of the guards at first. Now what do we do?"

Bendas, wild-eyed from the excitement of battle, ordered Bakkeris down the hill. "We must go around to the sides. They can't shoot us from here, but we can't get them either. We need to draw them out or else it will just be a standoff. We need to knock out their lights."

Bakkeris led the way, counting on his years of wilderness training to get him through the darkness. The guards, still unsure of where the attack had come from, hadn't fired blindly into the darkness. He had to be silent, for if he tripped or made any other noise, the guards would be able to gun him down. Easing down the hill, he checked for roots, loose rocks, or anything else that might cause him to trip and reveal his position. Bendas seemed to lack his companion's caution, but still managed to navigate the hill with no trouble, as he hopped on his goat-feet from rock to rock without a misstep.

As he approached the perimeter of the camp, Bakkeris aimed at the power generator and fired. Suddenly, a huge explosion lit the night sky, and a ball of flame reached skyward. Electrical energy was unleashed in the open air, and fragments from the generator cut into Bakkeris' skin. For a second, his position, and that of Bendas, was revealed to the guards in the mine, and they opened fire on the two attackers. Bakkeris dropped to the ground just as the first rounds richoted off the rocks behind him. He heard Bendas scream in pain behind him.

As the fire died down near the power generator, he screamed back to Bendas. "How badly are you hurt?" It took a second, but Bendas replied,

"It just knocked me silly for a second. Got me in the arm. Hurts ... but I'll live."

Bakkeris decided that the best cover was available in the backs of the trucks. Running at full tilt, he jumped onto the side of the truck, trying to scramble over the side before the guards in the mine saw where he had gone. Just as he threw his left leg over the lip of the dump truck, he felt a sharp pain in his right calf. Looking down, he saw the dwarven healer had somehow snuck up on him, and stabbed him with his dagger. The surprise of the attack made him lose his grip on the truck, and as his rifle clattered into the gems inside the back of the track, he fell flat on top of the dwarf.

Scrambling for the knife, which had fallen out of the dwarf's now-crushed hand, Bakkeris settled for several blows to the jaw and temple.

The battle done, Bakkeris set to crawling back within the truck. However, the previous incident revealed his position, and as he crawled over the top of the truck, he was greeted with several bursts of automatic rifle fire, all of which bounced off the side of the truck. Unscathed, but shaken, he landed on a pile of jewels the likes of which he had never seen before in his life.

Gypsor saw the huge explosion, and the highlighted form of Bakkeris and his satyr companion. "By Mithorl, he has come to save me!" As Bakkeris climbed into the back of the truck, Gypsor saw that his human friend had left himself terribly exposed. The four guards had taken cover behind a mining cart just at the entrance to the mine, and their aim was almost true. A split second later, and Bakkeris would have died. It was then that the satyr noticed the empty mine cart not fifty feet down the mineshaft.

Carefully pulling himself to his knees, he crawled back to the empty cart. Bracing himself properly, he started to push. With each step, he placed more power and more speed in each of his strides, gaining momentum.

The guards were caught completely unaware when the mine cart smashed into them. However, the effect was exactly as Gypsor intended. Two lay unconcious, and probably dead from the way their bodies arched. The other two were crippled with pain, but Gypsor quickly ended their lives with a burst of fire from their dropped and forgotten rifles.

Just as Gypsor was ready to go outside, gunfire once again rang in his ears, this time coming from deep in the mine shaft. Gypsor knew at once that the guards were killing the other slaves. Grabbing a rifle, he started pushing the mining cart back down the shaft. Just then he was joined by another satyr, much younger than he. "Hello, Gypsor! It is a grand adventure we are in, is it not?"

Gypsor studied the face for a second, for it was eerily familiar. Then as he and his mysterious new companion simultaneously jumped into the mine cart, Gypsor muttered, "My god ..."

"Nope, just an avatar. Oh, duck, by the way!" Pulling Gypsor down, the mine cart steadily picked up momentum. Bendas readied his weapon. The two listened for the sound of gunshots, and they steadily got louder and louder as the cart raced down the shaft. Finally, the shots were very clear, and they leaped up, opening fire on the completely surprised dwarven guards.

Leaping from the cart into the shaft, they saw little else beyond the blackness of unconsciousness.

* * *

Gypsor awoke with a start. He was in a bed, back at his apartment above the *Satyr's Pub*. His head was bandaged, and hurt like, well, a hangover. Sitting at his side was Karen (*Oh, how am I going to get rid of her?*), while Bakkeris and Bendas sat on chairs at the foot of the bed.

"I'm alive, you're alive; I'm home, and ...," looking

at Bendas, "… you're…" Bendas put his fingers to his mouth in a *Shhh!* motion, and Gypsor ended with, "…someone I haven't met yet."

Bakkeris explained, "My friend, this is Bendas. He is responsible for saving your life. He has got to be the *luckiest* person I've ever met. When we attacked the camp, he was out in the open. Should've bought a plot in the cemetery for that boy, but he saved your life down there. When you jumped out of that mine car, your broke one of your ribs and punctured your lung. He managed to use the healer's medicines and bring you back to life. Damndest thing I ever saw."

Gypsor had a million and one questions he wanted to ask. Bakkeris was already several steps ahead of him. "We've still got the *Pub* because of those jewels that they were mining. The rest we gave to the families of the slaves — most of them survived, thanks to you. Then, we called in the town militia and threatened to bring Lady Ardinay's army into town to do a sweep of the slavers in the area if they didn't do it themselves. It is truly amazing what happened over there."

Gypsor was overwhelmed by it all, but first he had to talk to Bendas alone. "Bakkeris, Karen, honey,"— *CRINGE!* — "could you excuse me and Bendas for a minute."

When the two satyrs were alone, Bendas started explaining. "I know what you're thinking, and no, I'm not Mithorl, *exactly*. I'm a part of him, and I was sent here to look out for you."

"Why me?"

"Because you really believe. You're one of the last and I, *he* needs you. He wanted you to know that he cares for his people. And, besides, without worshippers to host great feasts and orgies, things just aren't what they should be."

"Bendas, thank you."

"It was all part of my job. I'll see you … sometime."

With that, the smiling satyr seemed to change form, become a ball of pulsing blue energies. The form seemed to expand slightly, and give a hum, and then it slid into and through the ceiling. For the first time in a very long time, Gypsor felt fulfilled.

Three Soldiers

Douglas Kaufman

She had a quick hand, and that saved her.

One moment, Lieutenant Muriel Guinne had been deep in conversation with the Captain, hunched over the soggy back of her mount, paying negligent attention to the heath on which they rode. The next she was tilting backwards as the mare reared frantically away from a wild boar erupting almost underneath her hooves.

Cause and effect fragmented. *Not wild*, flashed her brain, *they wear the red pennants of battle-trained beasts.* The thoughts came even as frenzied whinnies sounded on all sides. Her fingers caught, clung to a fistful of mane; gleaming tusks slashed at her ankle, and she could smell the sharp musk of angry animal, close — and feel simultaneously the bunching of muscles under her. A scream rose, agonizingly close, and the whfff and thud of a crossbow quarrel hitting home, and she was flying, her own hair and the mare's mane whipping her eyes to tears as she struggled to see.

Ambush!

Her knees tightening painfully on the horse's heaving flanks, the Lieutenant felt blindly for the loose rein. She caught the slim leather strap in her free hand, but kept her hold on the thick hair of the mane. Was that pursuit, or another bolting soldier thundering behind her? The Lieutenant twisted in her saddle, pulling the mare's head around with her. Her heart thundered on, even as her mount slowed. Close on her flank, the Captain fought his own mount's head.

"'*A' tuirc dubh!*" she cried, forgetting that he spoke no Gaelic.

"Regroup!" he ordered, and swung around to face the ambush site.

The once-desolate heath writhed with activity. The Lieutenant guessed, with sick certainty, that their enemy outnumbered the living members of the Company more than two to one. Knots of men struggled in the grayish light, their gestures desperate. Laying her heels hard into the mare's sides, the Lieutenant charged back into the fray.

The Captain tucked his crossbow against his saddle-brace as he rode, and cranked back the string in rapid, economical motions. The Ayslish in the Company were crossbowmen, every one. That thought gave the Lieutenant hope — they could shoot quarrels more rapidly than she had seen farmers shoot rabbits, back in the old times before the invasion.

Her talents lay elsewhere. As she rode, Muriel Guinne shivered as always she did when she began to channel the fey blood that was her curse, and her only weapon. Training should have made it easier, but it did not.

In her mind's eye, she read the spell from stained

vellum. Gripping with her knees only, she loosed her hold on reins and horse hair. Up! her arms lifted, the one for balance, the other sketching jerky, whirling motions in the air.

A tingle like static electricity along her nape told her that the spell was charged. Even as she aimed the metal coin in her fist, deep in the Lieutenant's mind the awful knowledge that *she was using magic* smoldered and burned at her soul.

There! A huge boar paused in its charge to snort indignation at its victim. The Lieutenant flung her left hand, first two fingers and thumb outstretched.

At the snap of her wrist, the coin leapt forward. *Ah well, another five pence lost.*

Simultaneously, Muriel felt a moment's tearing pressure, as if the tips of her fingers were caught in suction tubes — as if the nails and the skin were being ripped away. She had steeled herself against the pain, and still she gasped. But even as the breath hissed through her lips, the sensation was gone, replaced by the throb of blood rushing back into her digits.

The gobbet of force, small, silver, fast in a way her mind still skirted uncomfortably — it was not a coin any longer, it was a weapon, and magically powered — the gobbet of force slammed on target, into the broad flank of the boar. The boar bowled sideways.

Scrambling to his feet, the Ayslish soldier that was its target did not look to see if the enemy was merely wounded or actually dead. He lunged for his horse's bridle. The Lieutenant, too, charged on, looking for another target.

There! A pair of hideous swine gored a fallen mount, while the trapped bowman valiantly cranked his weapon for a final shot. Right, and left again, Muriel recited, and swung, and flung her bullets. The two spells, worked nearly on top of one another, all but seared her fingertips with the heat of fast metal. Muriel clenched her jaw to contain a groan, and squinted to see how true was her aim.

The shrill squeal of a wounded boar sounded counterpoint to the bullets' airless whistle, but the second beast held its ground. The Lieutenant circled her arm to fire again.

Too fast to see, dark streaked with gold plunged from the sky. The soldier screamed. Heavy wings beat against his back and head; sharp talons rent his chest.

The Lieutenant turned away from his death cry.

And looked up at her own attacker! She had an impression of huge weight, a crimson flash — then she loosed the bullet.

The bird screamed just above her, deafening. Blood-wet feathers rained down upon her. Pinions rasped against her temple.

The bird did not strike. It angled away, flying low and heavy.

"Air attack!" she screamed. The mare needed no urging to gallop, and the Lieutenant let her mount have her head.

No men opposed them. Tardily, her brain made the observation. There were the black boars below, huge eagles above ... but no men. Somehow, that made the ambush all the more devastating. They were merely beasts, which struck and struck again, showing no mercy.

Half a hundred of the Company, Muriel estimated, had been lost in the first seconds, their horses broken and gored, their riders pulled down into a maelstrom of fiery-eyed death. Others of the Company fled accidentally into the deceptively flat landscape of the moor.

In the best of times, the bleak landscape bore the pocks of sudden pools, of solid-looking peat that sank under a man's weight, of shifty, glacier-tumbled boulders crusted in dank moss. Since Uthorion's sundering, there were patches even more sinister, where Aysle-outer, as Muriel's teacher had termed it, still held sway.

Muriel saw the Captain ahead of her, attempting to rally the Company. But their attackers were too thorough. Whichever way he turned, the boars hammered the soldiers out of formation. Whatever organization he accomplished, the eagles splintered into bursts of fleeing men. There was no place to hide or defend in the broad, blasted valley of the moor. Troops charged away, and dropped out of sight impossibly fast.

Faster than she could repeat her only spell, a brace of eagles harried her east, and east again. A boar charged, and her bullet spanged off a stone, wide of its mark. The mare stumbled. The Lieutenant was thrown.

She landed with a fusillade of scratches in a tuft of heather, the mad, red eyes of her enemy bearing down on her, no coins left to hand and no time or strength anyway to call another spell. Muriel waited for death.

The boar charged, its rank smell overpowering, its fetid breath fogging the wet air as it came — whfff! and the tearing thud of bronze-tipped wood driven powerfully into flesh.

Blood foamed in the gaping jaws.

The boar took four more strides, stumbled, then cartwheeled over its own shoulder as its heart pumped and the blood ran out of its veins. Its rough hind leg kicked limply into her ankle. Then it was still.

The echo of its hoofs resolved into the drumming of a horse's gait. Looking up, still numb, the Lieutenant glimpsed a familiar Ayslish uniform.

"Muriel! Lieutenant …. Are you hurt?"

Mentally, Muriel felt the sag of relief. Not only was she, herself, saved, but the question she had not dared to form, that of her lover's health, was blessedly answered as well. Pether was alive!

He had survived, and won through to her side across the hideous beasts and the chaos of the battlefield. Joy dizzied her. She drew in great gulps of air, finally remembered to answer his question. "I'm still breathing."

"Hop up, then, there's more chasing this way." He offered his arm, and she gripped it, set her foot atop his, and swung up onto the horse behind him.

"My mare."

"We'll see if we can catch her."

The Lieutenant look back over her shoulder. The heather was trampled and broken so that she could see the boars that came after them now. They could outrun the beasts, but they were alone. The Company was scattered. She held on tightly to her rescuer's waist.

"Have you seen the Captain?" she yelled at the back of his head, over the pounding of her heart and the horse's hooves.

"Aye, not long past. I think we're on his trail."

Muriel felt the tension of battle drain from her, to be replaced by the huge weight of loss. Pether guided the horse by whatever instincts and knowledge he had, and she did not notice their passage.

Instead, her mind replayed the events, like movies, on the black screen of her closed lids. Why had she not recognized the moorscape of her earlier nightmares?

What use was a seer who could not read her own prophecies? Bitterly, Muriel wished that Tolwyn of Tancred had not assigned her to the Company at all, but had left her in Glasgow to rot.

The trapped soldier's death scream echoed in her head. Her fault, his death was. Her fault all their deaths.

They had been more than 100 strong, and now they were two.

"Don't moan, sweetling. You should know we Ayslish aren't so easily vanquished," Pether tried to cheer her. "Your first ambush, is it?"

"I killed them all."

"Nay, they've just scattered into the hills. Look there, a broken stem, and there. That cobble's recently turned. The Captain passed this way. We'll find him."

"And then?" she asked, her tone dull with hopelessness.

"Well, were it me, I'd head back to that last decent town, and wait for the stragglers to come out of this blasted heath. There are a lot of clever men in the Company — they'll figure it out. And we won't be so feckled uncomfortable, skulking in this raw brush."

"I wish I had never come."

He squeezed her hand against his waist for a moment. "Sweet, 'tis not your fault. Turn your mind from blaming, and put your thoughts to work on what we might have for supplies tonight, once we've got your mare and the Captain on hand."

Muriel tried to do as he suggested. But her thoughts, turned resolutely from the battle, wandered to the question of their future progress. Should they retreat and regroup, as Pether suggested? They were ordered to clear the remnants of Aysle-outer from this sector of Scotland. Surely that was a needed task.

But if she were to choose for herself, Muriel would rather head south and east. There were tales of a Soviet psychic working in the lowlands. Such a one might ken a way to help her cope with or damp her visions. She would give anything to stop the dreams.

This last thought occupied her mind until at last the two soldiers caught up with their commander. The Captain had glad words for them, along with — joy! — Muriel's mare and all her gear that had been tied to the animal. Muriel's spirits would have lifted further had he not insisted that they three return to the ambush field, and try to puzzle out the location of the rest of the Company.

* * *

Tracking was hopeless. Indeed, just being in the same location as the attack gave Muriel the creeps. She felt eyes watching her. She felt spells crawling on her skin. The Captain looked at her expectantly.

"All right, I'll try your *seeing* for you. But it does not always come …" *And I cannot always interpret when it does*, she finished silently.

Standing on the edge of the slough, Muriel emptied her mind of all the images she'd caught during the day. She'd learned this at least, when she was apprenticed: every image a photograph, carefully tucked behind the glassy sheets of acetate, and clipped into the three-ring binder of her mind's eye. When all the fragments of her memory had been neatly catalogued and filed, she had a clean, blank room. No distractions.

She let her breathing settle, too, pulling air from deep in her belly, pushing it back out in slow, measured counts. She detached herself from the act, bottling up her fear, tamping her anxieties as smooth as the hard earth floor of a shepherd's winter hut. It was all defense.

She was deeply, bone-achingly afraid of the nightmares she'd always had. But her Captain had ordered her to *See* what she would see. She could not refuse an order.

So she layered over her fear with the calm techniques of her apprenticeship, and waited, trembling, for the *Sight* to come.

The wind whipped rawly at her hair. She smelled the rank rot of peat bog and spilled blood, and the wet weight of clouds before a storm. A wee bit of rain, they'd be getting — Muriel cursed her wandering attention. She stood so long, waiting, that her feet grew numb, and her balance shifted.

But no vision came.

Taking a step forward at last on pins and needles, the Lieutenant's just-opening eyes met Pether's concerned gaze, then the Captain's.

"Nothing. I —"

"You tried, Lieutenant." His words were kindly, his manner thoughtful. His gaze swept the blasted moor, and the lowering clouds, and came back to the three of them. "We head north, as we were, and hope that the lads have the good sense to remember their march and their orders. Mount up."

He turned to his own saddle, laying hands on the pommel with surprising determination. Muriel watched him fling himself onto his gelding's back before she remembered that she was heading out, too. She had failed to gain a vision, as she had failed often in this patchwork land. It just proved to her again how useless was this "gift," this curse, really, called the

Second Sight.

As they rode, heads into the wind, The Lieutenant recalled the first time she had *seen* the future. Gran had been telling tales of the old feuds Clan Gunn (the English spelling of Guinne) had fought with Clan Keith in the fifteenth century — tales of pride and treachery culminating that night in the murder of the Gunn and many of his men while they were at prayer. Big-eyed, Muriel and her sisters Sorcha and Morag had begged for more. But Gran had been firm — they were not to hear the resolution till the morrow. Now they were away to bed.

How many times had she wished that her night-mares were simply the result of bloody Highland histories and an overactive little girl's imagination! But Muriel knew better now.

Then, she had only had terror. In the close darkness of the thatched cottage attic where she and her sisters slept, Muriel dreamed of battles. Dark armies thundered down from the hills. Dragons flew over Dornoch Firth, belching not fire but frost, and stinging icy winds. Calum — her brother Calum with the jumping biceps — took eight-times-great granfa's claymore from the ceiling beam it had been nailed to all these years ... and tried to defend the cottage.

Even now, Muriel's eyes filled, remembering the image of her strong brother run through and bleeding. She had awoken shrieking her wee head off. And gran had come to soothe her, and hold her to her breast, and ask what had frightened her so.

"'Tis the Sight you have, bonnie lass. Ye ken more than your sisters," she'd explained when Muriel had at last poured out the details of the dreadful dream.

"Make it go away," she'd demanded.

"I can't, bairn. 'Tis a gift ye're given."

Of course, her mother had scoffed at gran's nonsense. Dragons were a fantasy. No one in the 20th century would come down from the hills raiding, certainly not sword in hand.

But the nightmares hadn't stopped. Her mother had forbidden tales of the Highlands, and gran had died several years later without Muriel's getting any closer to stopping the ugly scenes. After that, Muriel had suffered the occasional sleepless night in dread and silence, hoping that if she ignored the visions, they'd go away.

Instead, they came horribly true.

Calum was killed with a broadsword when the Ayslish invaders came. Muriel saw her two little sisters spitted like so many lambs. How she escaped … well, it was the Sight that saved her then. A sorcerer among the invaders saw the curse in her somehow, and claimed her for his own.

Against all odds, Muriel later remembered, he was a just man. He taught her the language of the invaders. He taught her their customs. At times Muriel thought she'd come near to time traveling, so backwards were their notions of things.

Most importantly, he'd taught her magic. She had a skill, he said, for divination, but Muriel refused to use that skill. Hadn't it killed her brother? Hadn't it brought her pain without ending? For in the newly conquered lands, Muriel discovered that the dreams were more frequent, more vivid. They almost always involved someone around her, someone close. Seven times out of ten, they foretold such bad things — injury, despair, ill luck — that she was loath to put them into speech.

Her dreams foretold, but there was nothing she

could do to prevent their occurrence. The transformed Scotswoman was sure she could do without.

Instead of pressing the matter, as was his right, her sorcerer taught her an alternate skill that he called apportation, and she, telekinesis. He taught her to move objects with her mind. He'd showed her a spell he called "bullet," that let him throw small metal pellets at the rabbits in the heath where they were camping. He told her she could do the same.

For several hours, Muriel had been stumped, cold, and resigned to failure. She had come back into the sorcerer's cave, ready to admit defeat. Then one of her visions came.

Desperate to dispel the horrible scene, Muriel lashed out. Almost unconsciously, she had wound her arm in the great circles she'd used in childhood to propel her brother's slingshot. There was a tingle like fire along her nape, and the seven-sided 20p piece in her left hand heated like a train-track just run. Startled by the sudden change in the metal, Muriel let go. The coin whined through the cave air, ricocheted off the far wall, and buried itself in a bundle of furs.

There was silence in the cave for over a minute. Muriel refused to look up, sure her teacher had decided on her death.

"Guess you've learned that," was all he said. Footsteps receded; Muriel looked up to see him, almost too casually, lean over the furs. "And tonight we'll see how you do at mending beds. But for now, I think a light spell."

He wasn't going to acknowledge the error. Muriel remembered to breathe again.

It was not long after that the Lady Ardinay made court at Oxford, and declared the usurper's minions outlawed. Muriel's apprenticeship to the sorcerer was traded for her Lieutenancy — for the greater good of Aysle. There were times she wished she still toiled in that cave.

* * *

The night came black as pitch, black as death ... black as a witch's heart. Even the wet fog, hanging like a vast swath of cashmere in their way — with none of the roil and swirl of most fogs — seemed black in the star-hidden night. It was a wonder they could see at all. The Lieutenant spoke a soft word, and the three reined to a stop.

"I don't like the looks of this," Muriel said. Her voice — normally fluid and lovely, soft yet resonant — dulled to sad echoes in the fog-entombed night. "This is an unnatural fog. It doesn't *move*."

"I can't see a bleeding thing," growled the Captain. "I'll trust your Second Sight, Lieutenant. If you want to go around, lead the way."

"That's just it," she piped. "I have no visions that might guide us. The fog extends as far as I can see in both directions. It might take hours to go around."

"Damn!" The Captain stirred within his cloak, and his horse stepped skittishly sideways, then forward. "We've been separated from the Company for hours. Why didn't the bleeders regroup and wait for us, as per orders?"

"Perhaps they think we're dead, Captain," said Pether.

"Fools!" spat the Captain. "But you may be right." He turned. "Lieutenant, it's time to gamble. Give a hail, and we'll see if we're lucky."

The Lieutenant nodded, and then said "Aye," when she realized the Captain could not see her in the velvety night. She moved with easy grace, drawing a silvery horn from a scabbard at her side as she dismounted. The horn's sides were inlaid with sworls of silver and bright gold that the eye could barely follow. It's a dwarven *thing*, she would say to those who asked. *I got it when I apprenticed to a sorcerer for a time. Would you like to touch it?*

Slowly, she raised the horn to her lips and blew a long, sweet note that echoed resoundingly, even in the dead night air. Its tone was high and pure and joyous, and they felt their hearts uplifted by its song.

"Well sounded, sweetling," said Pether, "but will it be of use?"

The question hung in the air along with the vast echoes of the horn, and the Captain began a sigh of despair like the hundred others he had uttered that night. But this one he did not finish — for sweet and loud and piercing, the sound of another horn came boiling through the fog, and the sighs of despair turned into shouts of joy from three throats.

"Hai!" cried the Lieutenant, and "Bloody good!" shouted the Captain. "Tallyho!" called Pether, his voice filled with a heartbreaking hope.

Perhaps the others were waiting just over the next hill.

And again the horn-sound came from out the fog, high and clear and alive, summoning them to battle, to life, to aid. The Lieutenant winded her own horn, then sprang to the back of her horse, and cried, "Follow me! This way!" before galloping, almost madly, directly into the heavy, ominous mists.

* * *

The fogs had closed around them like the fist of a giant, and the Lieutenant reflected that perhaps such an infernal denseness could play tricks with ears as easily as it had with eyes. They had been riding for nigh unto half an hour since hearing the horn-blast, and she would have guessed the sound to have come from half a mile away at the very farthest. But still there was no sign of the Company, and further horn-calls yielded no answer.

Her misgivings grew stronger as she studied the path they were taking, winding cold through the mysteries of the moor. At first it had been an easy route, chosen mostly by the horse, in the general direction she wanted to go. Then it narrowed, seemed almost to be a dry stream bed frozen into the harsh earth. Then it began to branch and twist as gorse and heather pressed close around them. Soon it was a single track winding through a damp and musty bramble. The horses' hoofbeats grew ragged, beating out an irregular tattoo as they fell into line more by instinct than guidance.

"Let's try a light, Captain," said the Lieutenant. "The ground has flattened, and I feel there are no more boars about." Her misgivings about their trail had turned into confusion and dread as she felt the path twist and turn under her, until she could not tell what was around her. Also, the ground was getting stonier, and her horse's footing was not as sure. She drew rein and, as Pether struck sparks with flint and steel, Muriel dug out her chip of mirror to catch and expand the light. This spell, too, pained her, with a dull aching behind her eyes. Magic always hurt, when Muriel used it. The sorcerer had had no cure for her pains. But the results, now, justified the discomfort.

Light! It had probably not come to this isolated glen, here in the midst of Scotland, since the invasion. Light! It glowed gently from the mirror's surface, grainy and thick, and Muriel had to remind herself that the fog was almost gone here, that the pearly volume of light that surrounded the three soldiers and their mounts was all her own doing. Light! It filled the air around them, illuminating bush and horse and house and …

"By all the Gods," breathed the Captain. "Where in the name of Love-Lara are we?"

It was indeed a house, small and black as the night had been, nestled crookedly into the cleft of the hill. Ragged, inward-leaning stone walls rose no more than two meters, and were capped in a steep, soot-blackened thatch. The front door sunk almost into a small patch of bog, and from the middle of the thatch, a thin spiral of smoke (black, of course) puffed away into the night. There were no windows, nor any sign of life within, save for the smoke.

Beyond the crofter's cottage, at the grainy edges of the magelight glow, huddled a similarly mean building — from the position and the mucky yard, it must have served as a stable.

The Lieutenant noted obstacles, angles — and dropped the mirror from her palm back into her pouch. The light winked out.

Pether's voice broached the darkness. "A hermit!"

Muriel opened her mouth to supply the term "crofter" but found her throat would not work. Fear closed it tight as a fist within her, a stronger fear than when the boars had set upon them with their slavering tusks. At least then she had taken comfort in her eyes, her sword. Now, though it was only her own feelings and not a true Seeing, she felt that nothing she did could save them from an awful fate. Her hand tightened on Pether's, crushingly.

He spared her a swift grin, his eyes bright glints in the blackness. "He'll offer us shelter or feel the edge of our blades!"

The Captain snorted at such bravado. "Not under my command, he'll not. Lieutenant, what say you of this dwelling?"

"Sir." At last, she could force her tongue to move. "It is a crofter's cottage, sir, and the Highlands are dotted with them like sheep. What fealty its owner pledges ... I cannot guess."

"Then caution is our watchword. Think you that any within have marked our approach?"

That was a hard question to answer. Likely, Muriel thought, the Captain'd know that better than herself, coming from a world where magic was commonplace. They could have been seen, heard, smelled, felt, or detected by magical means. Her vision gave no details. She told him as much.

He grunted. "So. As any good soldier must, I suggest reconnaissance. Pether, you take the horses back down the path. Lieutenant, you and I will scout the barn. We need a better picture of who lives here, and what the resources are, before we commit ourselves to action."

It felt good to be out of the saddle. Pether took the reins from his love's hand efficiently enough, but she could not gauge his mood in the darkness. And then it was just herself and the Captain, moving carefully around the brambly yard of the croft.

Muriel's heart beat louder than the occasionally rumbling thunder. She concentrated on the mental image she'd gleaned from the brief span of magelight. Swing wide now, to avoid the scraggly garden patch off the south corner.

Astringent mint scented the air, marking the space to avoid. The down, slowly, slowly, till the sucking mud of the stableyard announced her safe arrival.

Ahead of her, the Captain stopped. Muriel stopped too, stock-still, listening for any change in the atmosphere.

The Captain waved her into the little stable. Like the house, the walls of this building rose barely two meters before they gave way to steeply angled thatch. Inside it was close with the scent of hay and grain and cow ... and blacker, if such was possible, than the black night they had left.

"Lieutenant, can you conjure just a small light?" The Captain's order sighed against her ear after a long pause. Muriel knew her eyes would never adjust. Silently, she rummaged in her small kit for flint and steel, and the little scrap of mirror. It was always trickier for her to juggle all three components of the spell in the dark, but she managed on the fourth try. The headache flared again, and a small glow leaked from her cupped hands.

There were stalls for four horses, but they stood empty, abandoned. The hay in the tiny loft was unbaled, but clean. A small, ragged Highland "Coo" chewed its cud in the box stall in the far corner. The Captain poked his sword up into the hay rick once or twice, but his action was perfunctory. Muriel could see in the grainy glow that he was satisfied that the appearance of poverty was in truth the actuality.

As they came back into the yard again, big, heavy drops spat down from the black heavens.

"Likely it'll be sheets before long, eh, Lieutenant? Your famous English weather."

"Scots," she wanted to correct, but didn't bother. The Captain had served Lady Ardinay in Oxford. He still thought of the whole island as England, and who was she to be correcting Ayslish when not even the English tourists could keep their geography straight? Tourists. That was a lifetime ago and more.

As if in answer to the Captain's prediction, a near clap of thunder smote the hillside, and the rain, as if unleashed by the sound, flooded down.

"That's tipped our hand. Let us find the lad and the animals. We'll stop here, unless your Sight forbids it?"

Did she dare tell him of her feelings, pretend it was a Seeing so that he'd pay heed? No — foolish. She was being foolish and unprofessional. "I see nothing sir, bad or good," Muriel reiterated wearily. Cold rain slapped her face, and crawled along her collarbone under the Ayslish cloak. Never had she felt so useless. Dread receded to a tide of self-pity.

The Captain repeated his instructions to Pether. They were not to make anything of their military address or station. It was even possible that this isolated cottager was unaware of Lady Ardinay's uniform, although the Captain did not hold out hope of that.

The younger man appeared on the brink of argument, then shrugged. "Aye, sir. Who is to knock, then?"

They had progressed almost up to the dwelling. In the drumming rain, Muriel thought one could hide the approach of an army a thousand-fold stronger than three soldiers.

But the door was opening.

"Hail!" Pether cried, jolly as he let go his lover's hand and strode forward in the downpour. "Hail and well met! We are three travelers in the —"

"And greetings," said a silky voice. The door was fully opened, and in its frame stood a tall, narrow woman. She was not young, but not old. She wore black and her hair was black shot through with gray. She clutched a twisted walking stick in one hand, and leaned upon it heavily as if her skinny legs would not support her weight. Her eyes burned with green fire.

"What would you with me?" she asked, looking up at them ingenuously. "I have little wealth and my food is yours for the taking. And why are warriors out in the moor on a night such as this?"

Pether seemed taken aback, as though he had expected someone fairer to answer the door. The Lieutenant too felt nonplussed, since she had expected something far more foul. Only the Captain recovered his wits sufficiently to speak.

"Greetings, lady. We are three travelers who have been separated from our companions. It seems certain that we will not find them this night, and the weather turns unkind. Will you lodge us? We have our own provisions."

"Certainly," the woman said, her eyes flickering neatly across their equipment and mounts. "I've a small barn. You'll forgive me not hauling these frail bones out there myself, but arthritis has me twisted up in this rain. You should find all you need for your horses there. There's a torch just inside the door if you've no other lights with you. Come in when you've settled the beasts." She withdrew into the shadows, and the small door thumped shut.

Muriel fired up her light spell for the third time. The

rain pounded in rhythm to her heart and head, but at least this time there was no need for secrecy. Once inside the stable, the glow spread to fill the tiny structure. The sketchy details of her quick recon were thrown into sharp relief as light caressed the spareness of the structure. Muriel concentrated on holding her hand steady, and let Pether wipe down her mount with a twist of hay.

While the men worked, she looked. The cow mooed low, and Muriel wondered if she was fresh, and if they'd have milk tonight, perhaps even cream.

Now that she looked closely, the animal wasn't an evil-tempered Highland Coo at all, but a winter-shaggy, golden Guernsey. One horn twisted crazily wide from her head, that was all.

Muriel sighed. Guernseys were good milkers. She could almost taste the milk, rich and sweet, on her tongue.

"Lieutenant," the Captain said softly. Pether called her name. She shook her head, still feeling a low dread that made her dizzy.

"Captain, I —" she began, but didn't know what it was she was going to say. She reached for Pether's hand again, as they made ready to dash for the black cottage, but he did not notice and isolation surrounded her like a dark cloak.

The house's interior was small — smaller than it would seem from the outside, if such was possible. They came through the door into a small small hallway, where a lone black cape hung from a peg in the wall. The soldiers' cloaks soon followed suit. Leading from the hall, an opening in each wall: one way lead to a tiny kitchen, with a table just big enough for four; another way to a tiny bedroom steeped in darkness.

The final way was too black to tell.

The kitchen had a stove, with a small kettle hanging over it and a smoky fire lit beneath. There were no windows in any of the walls, and the smoke smelled acrid and sour and strangely pungent in the still air. The light from the hearth and a single candle on the table provided the only illumination, dancing fitfully on the worn sides of three teacups crowding on the tabletop.

"Seat yourselves as best you can," said the woman, her face eerily lit from flickering fire-shadows. "I'm just pouring tea." She vanished, without a sound, into the darkness.

"*Witchee*," muttered the Lieutenant, saying an Ayslish word for black magic. She had come to recognize such things during her brief stint as the sorcerer's apprentice. Pether smiled at her and shook his head. "She's not ugly enough," he whispered. The Captain frowned and stared into the fire, saying nothing. Several moments later, the woman returned, bearing a chipped china teapot, that had surely once been a bride-gift, sloshing over with water.

"You're far afield, warriors," she said, eyeing the Lieutenant speculatively as she placed the teapot on the table. "Aye, the garb maybe different, but I ken a doughboy when I see one still. Is it the weather that brought you lost, or trouble on the moor?" Her voice arched upward, as if leaving a third possibility politely unsaid.

Muriel was too startled to hear the sly innuendo. The three cups on the table, the full pot of tea ... this crofter had known they were coming! The memory of her gran's wizened face swam before her eyelids. Second Sight? It was common in the Highlands once.

The Lieutenant could almost forget her uneasiness. This crofter might have the Second Sight! All of the questions she'd wanted to ask her gran flooded back into Muriel's mind. Perhaps this woman could do for her what her gran had not had the time to, could teach her how to block out the disturbing thoughts and nightmarish visions that Muriel felt to be her curse.

The Captain nudged her shoulder, and handed her a slab of hardtack and a thick chunk of cheese.

"Drink up, lass, you're trembling with the damp."

The Captain's voice was concerned, yet casual, Muriel noted. He waited until he'd taken a couple of chews off the trail rations, and a swallow of hot tea before he turned his attention to the woman's opening sally.

"Doughboys, are we? Aye, but a long time ago. What would a knot of soldierboys be pursuing, up here in the backyard of beyond?"

"I was thinking you'd lost yourselves," she parried with that sly grin. "I shouldnae have to warn you, sir, that Second Sight is strong in Highland veins. Why play guessing games? Ye're nae local, and ye've not asked after those that are. Even without the gift, I'd be a fool not to recognize a uniform when I see one.

"But come, I've offered my hospitality and my hearth, such as it is, and I've a curiosity about what drives you here on this dismal night. I'd hardly guess it was to seek my services." She smiled the table round, and Pether, who had stopped chewing about midway through her speech, took up his rhythm again with an answering grin.

The woman smiled at him, a fondness in her eyes that the Lieutenant did not like. The smoke made her throat burn, but she felt it might be dangerous to drink the tea until the woman did. If only she had warned the men! The air of the cottage was close and sleep-inducing, and it must be slowing her wits, too. Muriel pinched herself surreptitiously.

Her hostess admitted to the Second Sight, though! Muriel felt each breath she drew flutter with hope — and wariness. Who was she, this crofter? How would the Captain answer her? Doggedly, the Lieutenant lowered her concentration to the food in her hand. He was the experienced campaigner. Let him play the scene as he would.

"Your services?" he asked, ignoring the questions of soldiery and uniform completely. The woman paused, as if to acknowledge the shift. Then she agreed. "Aye. Some call it fortune-telling, and some witchcraft, but even the scoffers have had occasion to change their tunes. I do a brisk business at lambing time. But that's not what you'll be wanting to know about. No, not the lambing for you."

The woman sat back against the wall in triumph. Her smug face said that she expected capitulation.

But the Captain was not giving it. He lapsed into silence, paying strict attention to his meal. The three soldiers ate, and warmed. Steam rose from the edge of Pether's woolen cloak, nearest the fire of the three of them. Apart from their chewing, all was silence.

At last the Captain set his teacup, with a gentle click, into its saucer.

"Thank ye kindly for the tea and shelter. 'Tis late, and we must make an early start come morning, so we'll away to bed if it pleases." He rose, and Muriel thought with a start that he meant for the three of them to sleep in the stables. Hastily, she too rose. Pether drained the last drops from his teacup, and gave the woman a polite nod as well.

"Here now, no need to send yourselves out of doors on a night like this. 'Tis a wee bit tight, but at least the house is warm. You're angry that I called you soldiers, but we're on the same side."

The Captain did not answer her, but Pether smiled and said "Oh?."

Pressing her advantage, the woman directed her wheedling at him. "There's dark things on the moor at night. You're safer in the cottage."

But Muriel's lover had fastened on the woman's previous statement.

"What side are we both on? What do you mean?"

"My clan has stood with Scotland since before the Bonny Prince, and we'll stand with her against the darkness through eternity." Her tone had the ringing quality of oath. But then it turned crafty once more. "But better still, I've a gift you might like the use of. You said you lost your companions. Well, finding them is a task I'd undertake for you. To convince you of my worth, like.

"Ah, skeptics. Do you not believe I have the power? Let me find your party. 'Tis a simple enough task to look for them. A boon."

"Can you see the future, woman?" Pether's tone was sharp. Impatient Ayslishman!

"Aye," she replied, knowing she had hooked his interest.

"Truth, Captain, such a glimpse could do us good." Pether seemed oblivious to his confirmation of the woman's suspicions. "We could observe the enemy's positions, even spot another ambush ... in this blasted moor we need every advantage."

It seemed to Muriel that the woman encouraged

Pether too much. But that was no reason to abort the Seeing, that was simple jealousy. Her own Sight was too erratic — and loath though she was to admit it, a part of her wanted very much to experience the controlled vision of an experienced Seer. She would at least see how it was done. Perhaps she could pick up a technique, a strategy for taming her own cursed gift.

When the Captain met her gaze, his eyes asking if she advised going with the other woman's plan, Muriel reluctantly nodded yes.

Somewhere outside a night bird called a shrill call, and the woman cocked up her head like a cat's ears. "The storm is passing — that's is a good omen for our beginning." She gathered up the cups and teapot, and swept into the darkness behind them.

Muriel listened for some sound of the kitchen or the cupboard, but there was only the spitting sussuration of the fire in the hearth. Startlingly fast, their hostess was back, bringing a tiny brazier, some pouches of herbs, and a silver bowl. She set her materials on the tabletop, and reached down to the table's foot. Muriel caught a flash of scarlet, and stifled a cry in her throat. Red! The same color as the decorative jesses of the attacking eagles. The same color as the pennants on the black boars.

The woman smiled possessively, and spread the fine crimson cloth across the rough table. "Is is not beautiful? India silk, my gran says. See the embroidery? It was her best shawl."

And as Muriel looked closer, she saw that the fabric was patterned with leaves and flowers in an Indian manner. Her heartbeat settled a little in its racing.

Coincidence, surely? The color stained her mind, but it was merely chance that the pennants of their attackers had been the same hue, merely a Scotsman's quick prejudice, where color and pattern had been badges of allegiance through the centuries.

Muriel had memorized the setts of all the Sutherland tartans as a wee bairn, and had been made much of at ceilidhs for her precocious talents. She had been able to tell what clan any tartan belonged to, even the obscurer hunting colors. Surely this sensitivity was mere over-reaction.

"I need a thread from your coats. Just a thread, no more," the woman reassured when Pether looked alarmed. "'Tis a contagion, to allow me to find similar clothing more easily. Just from one of you, laddie, there's a good man."

The request fit what Muriel knew of magic, and apparently what Pether knew, too, for he surrendered a scrap after that initial hesitation. Muriel's senses were bowstring taut, watching the little ritual gestures the woman made with the thread, and her herbs, and the silver bowl.

She had never been taught to use her gift — gran hadn't had the time, or the inclination, maybe. She had refused the sorcerer's help out of perversity and terror. Now, she needed desperately to learn.

The woman rolled the woollen thread back and forth between her fingers, then added a few snippets of leaves. Chamomile? Was that the crushed blossom? And now she added three hairs to the bundle, twisting them into a knot.

Odd. Muriel's preparations for a Seeing had always been mental. Maybe the crofter, too, suffered pain, and she used the drug …

Drug.

The woman's voice whispered low words that shimmered on the edge of Muriel's understanding, but the Lieutenant was no longer focussed on that part of the ritual. Her mind buzzed. Her eyelids were heavy.

Drug. Contagion.

This was not the Second Sight at all! The familiarity Muriel had been feeling was not for her long-ago memories of gran, but the more recent recollections of the sorcerer's teachings.

The woman was *witchee*, black magic! She had lulled the three soldiers into her spell and even now worked the ritual to keep them ensnared. Before, the Lieutenant had felt uneasy. Now, it seemed like dire peril. She said to the Captain, "There is danger here, we must go," but when she opened her mouth to speak, the smoke from the stove-pot came in and wrapped her tongue in fog. Her muscles were soft and tired, and she could not move. Somewhere, the *witchee* began a soft, low chant that numbed the Lieutenant's brain, and the room and all within began to drift sideways as a dream.

The chant grew louder, and dark smoke began to curl away from the chimney and toward them, blocking out the firelight, which glowed black and red in intermittent pops of ash and spark. It curled around their faces and enveloped them in a whispering miasma of no-sight and heavy smell. It darkened and lightened, and the Lieutenant knew it was in time to her own heartbeat. She struggled to raise an arm — could not — attempted speech — could not. Then a rest, to gather her strength for one final attempt to break the spell.

She tried opening one eye, cried out loudly at what she saw — Second Sight indeed! — for the house was gone, Pether and the Captain were gone — around her was a green meadow on a bright day, with a cool breeze blowing through her outswept hair. Red and blue motes sparkled and dove at the edges of her vision, but when she turned her head to look *at* them, they disappeared.

Two beautiful children approached across the grass, bearing fistfuls of buttercups and daisy blossoms that spilled through their tiny fingers.

"Mummy, look," cried one little girl, "look at the pretty flowers!" And they were, more beautiful than the Lieutenant ... no! my name is Muriel ... more beautiful than Muriel had ever seen.

"Mummy, oh, Mummy," said the other adorable cherub. "Thank you for bringing us here. I love you, mummy." Muriel's eyes filled with tears.

The scene stayed blurred even after she wiped her flowing eyes with the back of her hand, and now that hand was clothed in a familiar crossbow gauntlet, and the two children before her were not children at all, but Pether and the Captain, standing in the field, holding behind them the horses which she had not noticed before. Her body tensed even before her mind realized the pleasantries were over.

"We ride south," the Captain pronounced.

"South!" Pether exclaimed. "Don't be a fool, sir! That's where the enemy is. We three stand no chance against their whole force. Better to go back."

"Back!?" roared the Captain. "You coward! The rest of the Company is somewhere nearby, and we've got to find them. That's all that matters — that the Company stay together."

"The rest of the Company is dead," Pether said softly. His features wavered. The red and blue motes of possibility streamed like manic fireflies at the edges of her vision.

Muriel's breath caught in her throat. As he argued, her love's face contorted with exasperation. But there was another element, a more frightening vision by far. For Pether's features shrunk and stretched like odd funhouse parodies. His skin erupted with pocks and wrinkles. His eyes became rimmed with red. Muriel remembered the horrifying transformations that accompanied a person's devolvement to Aysle-outer all too well. As Pether's handsome face became a loathsome caricature, she realized she was seeing something the sorcerer had once tried to explain. Pether was facing a crisis of being — and coming out on the side of Aysle-outer.

On the wrong side. Shuddering, Muriel closed her eyes. More of the *witchee's* trickery? When she looked again, Pether's expression was normal — grave, not gruesome. Muriel stifled a sob, unsure what to make of the restored features.

"Why can't you see that? We may as well return home and make something of our lives." Pether looked meaningfully at the Lieutenant as he said this. Once, his smile would have filled her with hope. Now she cringed, waiting for the axe to fall.

"Our lives are nothing without the Company!" the Captain cried, dragging his sword from the scabbard with a shivery rasp. "Will you do as I say, or shall I kill you?"

Pether's own, slimmer sword seemed to leap from its scabbard and suddenly it was flashing forward and down in a screech and a bind and a thrust, leaving the Captain face down, dead in the mud of Rannoch Moor.

"No!" screamed the Lieutenant, but the scene did not end in answer to her command. It did begin to move faster and faster, like an avalanche jumping dizzyingly along; she and Pether mounted their horses in frantic haste, rode away at frenzied speed, and found a home together through the blur of the dream. The scene jumped! again, and Muriel was back on the meadow with the lovely children, and now Pether was approaching, all broad smiles and outstretched arms and a fine leather tunic embroidered with the sigil of a swordsmith. Their children ran to him, and Muriel saw how it would be, if only they would turn back now and leave the moor, leave the service of the lady Ardinay.

"But the Captain need not die," she whispered to herself, and a voice somewhere laughed and a cloud rolled over the sun and in the new darkness the Captain came striding over the hill, and they were back on Rannoch Moor, standing as they had the first time, with the Captain's sword roaring from its sheath as he cried, "Will you do as I say, or shall I kill you!"

Only this time, Pether fumbled for a split second at his sword-hilt, and the Captain's blade did not hesitate in its downward arc. Pether's head separated from one shoulder and he tumbled heavily to the ground.

"No!" screamed the Lieutenant, louder than before.

And now the scene moved again, faster and faster, but this time the Captain and his Lieutenant rode to find their Company — and did — but the battle with the enemy was a disaster ... more boars set upon them ... flying beasts that cast poisoned darts ... an ambush ... retreat cut off ... death to all.

The message of the dreaming was obvious: trust the Captain, face disaster. Trust Pether, and return to a life of beauty, peace ... children. It's what you want, eh?

And then they were back, all three of them, but not in the kitchen of the small black croft. Instead they all three stood, with the witch-woman off to one side, on the top of a dry hill, with the grass around them browning, crisping to hay in a bright bright sun. The Lieutenant knew that what had come before was a dream that each of them had experienced in a different way. This reality twanged with the electric tension of magic — a different kind of Dreaming, that all would share. What happened here would be real.

"You saw it," Pether said softly. "We all saw the two visions." His eyes met Muriel's for a brief second. "Captain, it need not be that way. Let's all of us go back."

"You believed it," the Captain said sadly. "I'm sorry for that — for both of you, perhaps. But you're right — it need not be that way. You're free to go back by yourself, or with the Lieutenant if that pleases her." He adjusted his sword-hilt, leaning his weight on it as though a great burden crushed him down. "I'll find the Company alone, or die trying."

But Pether reached quickly for his own sword as he saw the Captain touch at his, and it hissed from the scabbard through the Captain's desperate parry and the blood leaped forth to stain the Captain's tunic as he staggered back. A voice that was not wholly Pether's laughed as he advanced catlike, sword held high, his own hate and aggression coming forth more power-fully under the *witchee's* spell.

Were his features changing? The awful transforma-tion she had seen in the dream was fresh in her mind, but Muriel could not be sure. Harsh shadows hid his eyes.

The Lieutenant knew she had split seconds to make a decision: she could try to intervene in the fight, to keep Pether and the Captain from killing each other, to get to her companions in the haze of magic and unite them against the *witchee* … or she could attack the woman direct. She feared the wild magic of the other, in this reality of dreams.

The Lieutenant's own sword came free; as she stepped forward and saw the *witchee's* look of alarm she knew she had chosen rightly. Her sword whistled close to the woman's ear, and the dark sorceress had only time to writhe away, her form beginning to fade like smoke.

And then insects were all around, the writhing smoke a cloud of gnats, and their bites were fire. Pether and the Captain made inarticulate sounds of rage, their swords clashing again and again as the Lieutenant flailed helplessly, being bitten, being weakened. *Do I have a chance?* she thought desperately. *How can I fight a magician in a reality of magic?* And the question was its own answer: with magic of her own.

And what was her magic? Her coin-throwing spell was useless against the cloud of attackers, and she had no divination that would isolate the woman from her living "smoke screen." Gnats flew into Muriel's eyes, blinding her as she moved, sinking to her knees now, hearing the Captain and Pether killing each other and she could not believe that there was nothing she could do to save them —

Could not believe.

How could a woman — even as skinny a one as the *witchee* — shrink small as a gnat? There had to be some trick, some illusion. Hadn't the sorcerer said that transformation was only like to like in size? Could the witch be all the gnats at once?

But that was still not enough to equal one person. Then perhaps she was invisible — the Lieutenant swung great slices through the air but her blade met no resistance.

Which just couldn't be.

There had to be a body here! Muriel pictured the last position of the *witchee*, and holding the image in her mind like a paper target, swung again. She pictured the blade thrusting forward at the woman's skinny frame. She saw the pressure of metal on flesh. Her belief gave power to the magic of her disbelief. Flesh surrendering—

The *witchee* screamed and flew back, back into the writhing combatants, and as she did the other insects vanished like so many sparks; Pether and the Captain ceased their struggle, and the Lieutenant rose to her feet, all pain forgotten. Running now, she moved forward, her sword again upraised.

An explosion sent her staggering back, and there were two Pethers there, staring and goggling at each other; then, one leaped upon the other and they rolled, mixing until the Lieutenant did not know which was real, which was false. She stepped forward, uncertain.

The two identical men broke from each other's grasp, stood, eyeing each other with mistrust and fear. The Lieutenant tried to see a difference, but there was none. The perfect disguise.

And the witch had already proven that she could do two spells at once. A fear began rising up in Muriel, a terrible fear of the future, of death, of hate. She could run and run and leave Pether and the Captain to their fate, and save herself. Why throw her lot in with the Ayslishmen? What good had their Lady done her?

Bitter self-hatred welled up also — for Muriel knew that she had been running from herself for a very long time. Should she blame the Ayslish for her Sight? Wasn't it her desperation to learn more of the Sight that had brought them to this pass? That had made her eager to experience what she thought would be a Seeing?

With a gasp of effort, turning to a sob in mid-stroke, knowing that in seconds she would run and run and run and never come back and the *witchee* would win and the Captain would die and ... Muriel drove her sword hilt-deep into the belly of the right-most Pether, the stunned look on his/her face melting into woman/man and then witch. The dark woman made a hideous coughing noise and pitched face forward in her chair, the sword hilt now protruding from her breast, spilling a dark dark blood onto the table, which sucked it up thirstily like a desert sand.

Pether stared at her through the smoke of the tiny cottage, fright in his gaze, stared at the wounded Captain, who smiled and grunted, "We're safe now, thanks to the Lieutenant."

* * *

"She was one of the enemy, then," the Captain mused. "Did she know we were coming? Did she have Second Sight?"

"No," Muriel sighed. "Not at all, I think. She had illusions, and mind-trapping, but no Sight. She knew we would come because her mind-trap was part of the ambush, cast across the moor. Other members of our Company may have come here earlier in the night, and been killed by her visions, group by group, as we almost were. Others might be on their way even now."

"Then she's done us that small favor," the Captain muttered. "Let's ride a ways away from here and wait a few hours for stragglers." With that, the three soldiers mounted their horses and followed back along the way they had come, toward higher ground. They rode in silence for a time.

"Won't you tell me, Muriel, how you knew which was the real and which was the false?" Pether leaned close and whispered the words, as they rode away from the cabin in the moor, their three horses' hoofbeats sounding as one in the cool morning mist.

The Lieutenant did not answer, nor would she. How could she tell her former lover that her stroke was unguided, that it mattered not which one she killed — *witchee* to end strife, or Pether to save the Captain — and that the witch's fatal mistake had been to show Muriel that in the land of dreams, true souls were bared ... or that she herself was not, truly, Muriel, but the Lieutenant?

Companions

Ed Stark

"Ged ouda heah, ya bloody freak*!!"*

Hasifar looked up from the street vendor's wares, a look of surprise on both their faces. He was holding a head of lettuce in one hand and had been caught in the midst of passing a beat-up trade over to the woman.

A rock struck his flank; it hurt, but he was more surprised than anything else.

"Dis is a 'uman village, freak — gedoudda here!"

It wasn't hard to spot the missile thrower. He was standing in the middle of the cobbled street, his face bloated and red with anger.

Anger? Hasifar thought. *What have I done* now?

The source of his bewilderment started swearing and jumping up and down. Hasifar thought he looked insane. Apparently, the other villagers thought that the sight of a screaming man waving a shillelagh and entangled in a long, gray woolen scarf was rather odd also. Windows and doors were opening, despite the coolness of the spring day. People were staring and pointing.

The man stooped and picked up another stone.

"That is quite *enough!"*

A voice boomed out from the northern side of the street. The red-faced man, the crowd, and Hasifar all looked.

It was the chief of the Home Guardsman, Korin MacKay. He was decked out in his uniform and, not for the first time, Hasifar noticed how impressive he looked. His uniform was always immaculate, whether he was rousting a drunk at three a.m. or hunting through the moors for a goblin raiding party. MacKay's mutton-chops and whiskers made him look older than Hasifar thought he could be, but that lent him authority. Even his very slight paunch, well-hidden in his muscled frame, made him look like someone to be listened to.

"What," Chief MacKay enunciated, "the 'ell is going on here?"

Everyone stared, accusatory, at the red-faced man with the shillelagh. He held another rock in his right hand.

MacKay didn't waste any time. He strode right up to the stranger, no weapon in hand, but everyone suddenly became very aware of the Chief's wheelock dag — which was in its regulation holster — and the billy club that swung at his hip.

The stranger noticed, too.

Everyone relaxed; there would be no further trouble.

Hasifar, however, wanted to know what it all was about. He trotted up to the stranger, stopping about two and a half meters away. The chief had already arrived, but that didn't stop the scarf-bedecked man from shooting one more glare of pure hatred at Hasifar.

"In the man's face," MacKay then absorbed a lion's

share of his attention.

"What's all this, then," he barked. "Where do you get off, throwin' rocks at our citizens?"

"*Citizens*?!" the man squealed in an acidic voice meant to be heard. "You call that ... *thing* ... a citizen?!"

The hackles on Hasifar's neck were rising. Normally mild-mannered and quiet, he felt he'd had about all of this he could stand. He started forward.

MacKay shifted between the stranger and Hasifar almost imperceptibly and, with a quick hand gesture, waved him off. That cooled Hasifar's ire somewhat. He knew MacKay would take care of things.

Still, he didn't back off.

"He is a citizen of this village," MacKay stated coolly. "Just as he is a citizen of Queens Pella and Elizabeth, and he is protected under the same laws that protect you."

Hasifar got some brief satisfaction from hearing the ice and the implied threat that both surrounded MacKay's words. *Shut up and move on*, he was saying. Hasifar liked that.

Apparently the man didn't. He squirmed under the Chief's gaze. He fidgeted. He began muttering to himself.

Hasifar's neck hair went straight up ... and he had no clue why.

Suddenly, the stranger jumped back from MacKay — a foolishly sudden move; MacKay's billy club was out in a flash.

The stranger, his scarf whirling around him, his face florid, waved his shillelagh high in the air and screamed, "Not *me*! *Him*! He's the Outsider! The Filth! The Putrescence!" Then his voice lowered dramatically, "Drive him from *our village*!"

Hasifar began to chuckle — but uneasiness overcame him. Out of the corners of his eyes, he could see the people of the village, who had been returning to their work and their homes after the disturbance, coming back out. They were moving towards him slowly.

No one else was laughing.

"MacKay ...?"

Chief Guardsman MacKay turned towards him. There was a look of pure hatred on his face. It was growing more florid by the second, and Hasifar had a brief insane flash of thought:

I wonder if they're related.

Then MacKay swung his club.

It was a strong swing, but slow and wild; Hasifar had no difficulty in dodging. "MacKay!" He shouted, "What are you *doing*, by Dunad?"

There was a roar from all around him. Villagers started moving quickly. They were picking up rocks and vegetables and sticks, and a few even drew their belt knives. Hasifar looked around wildly.

They've all gone mad! He thought, as he dodged another attack by the Chief Guardsman.

Hasifar knew he'd have to do something quick. He could probably take out MacKay, the way the man was moving, but the crowd would be on him. He decided to run for it. But where?

The crowd was in a semicircle now, yelling and cursing him. Friends he'd known for months were starting to toss rocks and other objects at him. Even the vegetable dealer he'd just been talking to was breaking off a fence post to use as a club!

"Monster!" someone screamed.

"Half-breed!"

"Foul Creature!"

"Kill!"

"KILL!"

"KILL!!!!"

That last scream came from the entire crowd. Ducking under yet another blow from the chief, Hasifar brought up his right fist, from the shoulder, into the man's jaw. He straightened like he'd been poleaxed and started to go over. Just before he collapsed, Hasifar thought he heard him gasp something, just barely heard over the roar of the crowd:

"Get out of here, Has ..."

Whether real or imagined, Hasifar took the advice. He charged at the stranger, who stood in the weak point of the semicircle. He only half-intended to run him down — he wasn't thinking very clearly — but the man jumped out of the way with astounding agility. As he did so, he swung his shillelagh.

Hasifar felt a screaming pain along his left flank, and was only barely able to keep from passing out! *Gods! I've been witched!* His mind screamed, but his legs kept on moving.

Vaguely, Hasifar was aware of the crowd pursuing him, hurling missiles and insults at him. He was sure that a few hit him in the back or the rump, but he didn't feel them at the time. All he felt was the flaming pain of the stranger's weapon.

Despite the pain, he quickly outdistanced his pursuers and continued away from the village and into the moors. His instinct helped him regain his senses there — if he ran too fast he could hit a sinkhole and break a leg, and then it would all be over.

He figured later that he had gone almost ten miles before stopping to think. That was about when the fire in his side went away — completely. So completely it was almost a shock. He didn't even have a "phantom ache" there.

But he did feel the missiles that had struck him. Those thrown by his friends.

Half-breed. Foul Creature.

Monster.

The stranger's words blended with the townsfolk's, and that blended with the Chief's attack and the pain of betrayal and fear. He had been happy in the village. So happy.

Hasifar wept. Big, salty tears.

Tears the size only a centaur with a broken heart could manage.

* * *

Hasifar spent the night out on the moors thinking about what had happened. It had rained the day before, so even he was unable to start a fire (and keep it going) with the damp fuel at hand. Somewhere along the way he got some sleep.

While he slept, he dreamed.

The dream was of the Old Days, back in Aysle; the Aysle he had been born to. He remembered the hardship under Ardinay/Uthorion, and he remembered how his tribe had hidden in one forest only to be driven to another. Their tribe kept getting smaller and smaller, until only a scant three dozen remained.

His father Faratril was one. He was sad. Hasifar dreamed of the night after his mother, Marhas, and their chieftain fell fleeing the troll guard sent to hunt them out. His father had had to contain his grief and lead the tribe, or they all would have been lost. Young

Hasifar had tried to be strong, so his father could be, but he had cried all night.

"Hasifar," his father had said, waking him out of yet another vision of his mother's bloody death, "always remember — but do not hate. While the trolls, and Ardinay, and all those who fight our tribe may deserve our hate, it does not help us. Hatred makes us blind and weak, and our enemies strong."

Hasifar nodded and let his tears flow, but he could not help but hate. Looking into his father's eyes, he knew that he could not help it either.

The dream passed on.

His mind moved to the day before the Invasion. Ardinay had said that all the half-folk, even their tribe of centaurs, would be free citizens if they agreed to join. His father, still secretly hating, suppressed his hate and made a choice for the tribe: they would join.

Hasifar had come close to hating his father then.

But he obeyed. And it was good that he did.

After the initial rush of the Invasion, Hasifar found that his father had conceived a plan. He had united with some others of the half-folk, forced into service with Ardinay, and, at a certain time, they led their peoples over to the side of Light.

They found they were not alone. Many dwarves had joined the light, and even the mysterious elves seemed more interested in fighting against the Dark than for it. Plus, many of the Houses of the Humans were not so loyal to Ardinay as was once thought.

Still, they were outnumbered.

The day the legends came true, Hasifar's father died.

He died quickly and unremarkably; more like a soldier in the field than a chieftain or importance. An arrow took him in the throat, shot by some unknown archer. Hasifar was grieving when the messenger came:

"Tolwyn has returned! Uthorion, who had possessed Ardinay, is defeated! Good Queen Ardinay has returned!"

The armies of Light cheered for news of their victory.

Hasifar wept for his father.

The tribe, what was left of it, joined with the armies of Light to destroy Darkness forever.

Hasifar left.

He had not wandered far, and his dream reflected that. Soon, he found himself in the small village in Scotland that had been his home for so many months. Initially received as strange, and an outsider, he still made himself quickly accepted. His friendly, giving manner; his willingness to work hard and for little more than food and shelter; and his inoffensive healing and useful magicks all made him welcome in the transformed town.

Until the Stranger arrived.

In Hasifar's dream, the Stranger was larger and more lively; the townsfolk small. The centaur's confused and grieving mind saw the betrayal as coming from within, and the Stranger as a mere agent of its surfacing. His mind raced past half-imagined slights and veiled insults, and he saw The Truth.

The villagers had *always* hated him.

But there was a nagging in his mind. A whiskered face with an honest, sad expression. It seemed to be telling him something, but he couldn't hear. He strained, but his dream-ears heard only the curses and insults of the mob. The throwing of stones. The running. The fear.

The Staff of Pain.

Hasifar jolted awake. His upper torso was sweating profusely. He left his light jacket on, however, because he knew the moors were cold.

Looking down his flank, he saw he had accidentally shifted his weight, straining his left rear leg-muscle.

He struggled to stand, and the pain receded to a dull ache.

"Centaurs weren't made to sleep on the ground," he jibed himself. He was shocked to hear his normally smooth voice crack and break. He coughed. *No, no phlegm; no cold.*

He shivered again and pushed It back in his mind. It could wait.

Over the next few days, Hasifar found himself wandering northward. He didn't know why, only that south represented the village and other humans and betrayal. He'd never been north; maybe things were better.

Every night he dreamed about the mob.

* * *

Everywhere Hasifar went, he saw signs of the Ayslish civil war. Homes were burned, farms pillaged, and whole villages put to the torch.

But Hasifar's heart had grown hard. These were *human* villages, he told himself. *Folk*, not *half-folk*.

But still, even his heart was moved to pity and, in those brief moments, the mob was forgotten.

But there were reminders.

About two weeks after being driven from the human village, Hasifar was in Northern Scotland, near the eastern sea. He couldn't remember the name of the water — the humans of this world had such unusual names for their places and things — but as he gazed into the gray morning mist, he felt almost at peace.

But then a cry rang out. Hasifar pivoted his torso around so that he faced almost one-hundred and eighty degrees around.

He was tense and ready for attack. Many times since he began his journey had he encountered humans — and they had greeted him with such animosity and fear that he now avoided them completely.

But the scream had caught him unawares, during a moment of peace. He peered into the mist and listened, hoping that his superior hearing could catch more cries, so he could help.

And more came. It was a shrill voice, higher than even a marechild's. To Hasifar's quick ears, it sounded like the voice was screaming in pain as well as fear. It was a long way off.

Without thinking, the centaur grabbed his make-shift bow and his newly fletched arrows and started to gallop towards the sound. If he was correct, the sea air had carried the noise nearly a mile.

Hasifar could get there in two minutes.

But, as he grew nearer to the sounds of the cries, he started to pick out other noises. Deeper, but guttural, voices — laughing and taunting in man's language. He heard the shrill voice cursing — Ayslish curses, of a nature even Hasifar did not recognize. He also heard the impact of rock on wood and, yes, there it was, on flesh.

Anger flared in the centaur's heart. *A stoning!* No matter what sort of creature this was, man, half-man, or enchanted, he would not put up with a stoning — not when he could do something about it.

225

At a full gallop, Hasifar was able to string his bow and knock an arrow — his torso was steadied by his great back muscles. He leapt over a narrow creek and ran over a thistle bush, but he did not slow. Less than two minutes after he'd heard the first scream, Hasifar was on the scene.

He saw a circle of men surrounding a weathered, gnarled tree.

Despite the season, the tree had few leaves and its branches were withered. In one perched a large bird.

The men were laughing, so caught up in their sport, they did not hear the centaur come out of the mist. Perhaps they felt that the nearness of their village — only about a hundred yards through the mist, Hasifar could barely see — protected them so well they needn't heed noises of the early morn.

More fool, they.

One man, a fat, ungainly one dressed in strange clothes, stooped for a rock.

"Li'l birdie," he mocked, "'ere's some suet for ye!" He swung back to heave the stone.

An arrow sprouted from his neck. Great gouts of bluish-red blood began to spew from his throat as he dropped his stone and fell to his knees. The man's mind did not even seem to register the pain; his face was surprised until it hit the turf.

The other men froze, staring at him. Hasifar clicked his rear hooves loudly on a nearby stone to get their attention. They turned slowly towards him, and Hasifar sneered at their surprised expressions.

"Now, don't you know it isn't nice to throw stones at little birds, boys?" He taunted, pointing his already-knocked arrow at the nearest one's chest, "away home with you or you'll have to be punished."

Two of the men, nearest the centaur, started to back away, but one in the rear screamed, "It's another half-breed; a *murderer* — *kill it!*"

That was all Hasifar needed to hear. His hard heart sang in his breast as he loosed arrow after arrow into the men — now they'd see what an enemy they'd made! Stone *him*, would they?! They would suffer! The men tried to fight back, but their hastily-cast stones were no match for the centaur's bow. Arrows came with unfailing precision, piercing hearts, lungs, throats and eyes. A few decided to charge Hasifar, but they fared no better. Armed only with knives and clubs, he was able to dance around them and rear up, crashing down on their heads and shoulders with his unshod hooves. All the while, he kept loading his bow and firing, screaming curses that even he did not hear.

"Stop it, ya damned mule; stop it!" A voice came to him from above, out of the red mist. He knocked another arrow and pointed it towards the sound.

No. A voice in his head said faintly, that isn't right …

"Hey, whoa! *Whoa* horsey!" The shrill voice called, "Watch it with that thing!" The mist cleared and Hasifar looked around. No humans stood near the tree or the trampled bush, but at least seven lay stretched out on the earth. He turned his right-front hoof; it was standing on another's head, covered in blood and brains.

"What's come over me?!" he moaned. He felt himself swaying, as if he was going to faint or be sick at the very least.

There was a loud fluttering and a soft crash, and a voice spoke to him from below.

"I dunno, mate, but you'd better help me up or the villagers'll be here soon!"

"The villagers?" Hasifar asked hollowly.

"Cor! Whatcha think, mate? All that roarin' an' screamin' won't bring 'em out in droves? 'Ere, help me up." Hasifar looked down. On the ground, near the base of the knotted tree, he saw the "bird" the men had been taunting. It had a bird's wings, and a bird's feathers, and even a bird's legs and claws, but its torso was human.

"A harpy!" Hasifar said, awakening from his shock.

And it was a harpy — a true, Ayslish harpy, not one of the sorcerous constructs of the Invasion. She had no arms or long legs; just wings and legs and claws. She looked as if someone had stuck a small woman's upper torso and head onto a vulture.

"Well, I ain't no swallow — African *or* European!" The harpy fluttered its — no, definitely her; male harpies do not have breasts — wings anxiously. "Get me onto your back, or we'll never get outta here!" The idea of a harpy perched on his fine roan back made Hasifar step back in disgust — and it shook the last of his battle-fever out. "You, ride me?!" He exclaimed in disbelief.

"What, are ya blind, you refugee from a glue factory?! Canna see me wing's busted?" It was true. The harpy's left wing had been damaged somehow. That was why it — she — had taken refuge in the tree, presumably. "Or had you intended t'leave me 'ere after goin' t'all the trouble to save me?"

That was true, Hasifar, admitted to himself. Rather than go the step further and admit to her that he didn't know what had prompted him to gallop to the rescue, he merely trotted over to her and lifted her onto his back. She was remarkably light for such a comparatively large creature — indeed, she was probably larger than most vultures, though her wings were obviously built for flapping rather than soaring.

Still, there was much fluttering and squawking as she got settled onto his back. And she smelled. Hasifar wrinkled his nose and held her gingerly, trying not to imagine what her greasy feathers were doing to his fine coat.

"'Ere, now! I ain't some saddlebag, you damn horse!" She screeched, "I need something to hold onto or you'll buck me off!"

"If you don't keep quiet," Hasifar said sternly, "I shall buck you off for certain!" Then, remembering that he was supposed to be saving her, he mellowed his voice a little.

"Don't worry; you won't fall off my back unless I want you to."

"Well, see that I don't, stallion." Hasifar's fine ears noticed that the harpy's voice was losing some of its shrillness also — good, he thought, perhaps she was just scared, too.

The centaur was as good as his word. Even though he was inclined to gallop as far and as fast as he could to get away from the scene of the ... battle — both for his own peace of mind and their safety — he walked, then trotted, then cantered, then galloped, letting her get used to the smooth, rolling gait. Centaurs, his father had always told him, do not take passengers lightly, but when they take them, they keep them.

Thinking of his father softened Hasifar further. He found himself feeling glad to have this new companion, and he began to chat with her amiably.

He found he was right about her mood. When he started talking, she seemed to relax, and her voice settled into a bird-like soprano. It was sharp, and quick, but there was melody to it.

As it turned out, they had remarkably similar experiences.

Falen, as the harpy was called, had been part of a large flock in Aysle that had, for the most part, tried to keep out of the civil war. They did not care if the humans slaughtered each other, but they got drawn in all the same.

At first, Falen's flock had thought its aerie home protection against Ardinay/Uthorion's conscription attempts. But then, as he prepared to invade this new place, "Earth," they found his need for a reliable air force outweighed the difficulty of getting to it. He called in his mages and his other loyal flyers and sent them to the aeries of the harpies to talk.

Unlike his approach to the land peoples of Aysle, Uthorion treated the harpies reasonably well. He needed their loyalty, for, though they were not good fighters in the sky or out of it, they were excellent scouts and spies. He treated them to the bright baubles they favored and gave them choice meats — not the scavenge-pickings they were used to.

Still, Falen's aerie had had it better than most, and they still chose to sit out the war. They told Uthorion/Ardinay, as politely as a harpy could, that they were quite happy sitting in their nests and he/she should mind his own damn business.

So Uthorion invaded without the harpies of Falen's aerie …

But he did not forgive them.

The day of the big Invasion, Uthorion sent dragons against the harpies. The burned the slopes and they burned the woods and, when they could, they burned the harpies.

"Now," Falen sighed, "my people live by stealing

and by migrating … their ancestral home forever ruined.

"But I was young and angry," she continued, irony in her shrill voice, "I wanted vengeance against the Queen of Flame.

"I told my grandmother good-bye and left my chick to her, and sought out the enemies of my enemy.

"When I came down the Bridge, though, I was disappointed.

"Uthorion, I was told, had been 'n possession a' the Queen's body. *Cor!* I thought I had troubles," Falen let out a loud cackle that jarred Hasifar's sensitive ears. "Anyway, I decide th' best way t'get back at this Uthorion was to help 'er Rightful Majesty in the war." The grimy harpy's expression darkened, "But I found I wasn't needed as much as I needed, ifin you get my meaning." Hasifar nodded; he understood all too well.

"But I figured; hey, at least I won't get killed — an' this Uthorion'd be punished anyway, right? The Army of Light was all ready to take him on." She cackled again, but this time without humor. "Damn! What a sorry lot that is!" Hasifar had heard virtually nothing of the Army of Light. He hadn't tried to join up, but it was more because he hadn't thought of it than anything else.

"So I joined the Post. S'funny, y'know? The Post is run by those strange Earthers — the one's who was invaded upon. But they seem more ready to accept us than our own people."

"I don't know about that," Hasifar said bitterly. He was tired of walking, now, and he was starting to remember his troubles.

"Hey, I know, laddie," Falen said, her voice sympathetic.

"What I meant was, they accepted us right off when our own look at us down their noses — even to a tall one like you." There was something about Falen that made Hasifar smile, even though she was reminding him of his treacherous friends.

"I suppose. But they turn in the end." Falen looked at him sharply, "Yeah, that's right. On you too?"

He nodded sharply and stopped, "This looks like a good place to camp."

"I dinna mean to get yuir back outta shape," Falen said, her brogue strong with concern, "Y'asked me to tell you what happened to me, din ya?"

Hasifar nodded again, "I guess so. It just ... hurts."

"I know, laddy, I know." Falen jumped down and started to pick at the rough Highland grass with her long claws. She was able to pull out the dry, brown grass that lay under the wet green, so it looked like they'd be able to have a fire. Hasifar went off in search of game.

It was good for Hasifar to get away on his own, he felt. He'd rescued Falen only this morning, and now he was feeling close to her and becoming immersed in her troubles. He had wanted to harden his heart, not open it to anyone that came along, half-folk or no.

Still, it was good to have a companion. She was already proving helpful, and the day went quicker. Of course, it would go quicker still if she didn't smell so bad ...

It only took the centaur about forty minutes to bag two hares and a small, un-Ayslish rodent. He wasn't sure what it was, but it looked edible. He trotted back to their camp.

Falen was gone.

Panic rose in Hasifar's throat, but he fought it down.

"Falen!" He called. *Damn the bird! Where was she?!* "Falen, where are you!" He jogged around in a circle, hoping he could hear her, but he could not. He'd just found her, she couldn't be …

"Squawk!" Hasifar stopped—the sound came from just above him, in a nearby tree. But that was impossible … Falen's wing was broken; she couldn't …

"Hey, horsefur! What's th' big idea, wakin' me up! I almost fell off my perch!" Hasifar looked up. There, about twenty feet up, perched Falen. Her wings were folded around her naked torso, but her brown-haired head peaked out from the top. Her face was not very happy; it was the face of someone woken out of a sound sleep by a child yelling "Fire!" as a prank.

"Uh, sorry, Falen," he apologized, "I thought you'd, uh …"

"What, flown off? Wi' this?" She flapped her damaged wing, wincing in pain. "Now that wasn't very bright!" Hasifar could not tell which of them she was referring to.

"Then how did you get up there?"

She waved her good wing at the trunk of the tree. "I climbed, mule-brain!" Hasifar looked. There were deep gouges in the trunk, undoubtedly made from her razor-sharp claws. Still, it must have taken her a half-hour to get where she was.

"Any more foolish questions?"

"No. I'll go get supper started."

"If you got rabbit, don't cook mine!"

Ugh. "All right." He walked towards the camp.

Despite all Falen's blustering, Hasifar realized then how scared she was. It was one thing for him — big, strong, and fast — to be on his own, but she was small, relatively weak, and unable to fly. It would be like him with a broken leg — helpless. She had climbed the tree, probably in terror. Her kind were never comfortable on the ground, he figured, and she must have been about panic-stricken.

She hid it better than Hasifar thought he'd be able to.

He found that Falen had managed to put together a substantial amount of tinder before she went up the tree, and there was plenty of deadwood around. Taking a stick in hand, the centaur passed it over the tinder, muttering an incantation he did not understand.

He felt the wood grow warm, then hot. When it got to the point he thought was right, he dropped it into the tinder.

Instantly, the tinder and the wood caught. He tossed a few more sticks on the fire, and it started to burn merrily.

"That's quite a handy trick, my lad." Falen had come down behind him. She looked worn out, but hungrier than she was tired. "Where'd you learn to do it?"

Hasifar shrugged, idly skinning one of the conies. "My father bought it from a mage in Aysle. He taught it to all the tribe who could learn."

Falen nodded. "My gramma was the same way. Anythin' she saw could be used, she took fer th' aerie. 'Course, she never found anythin' like that." Finishing the first rabbit, Hasifar was about to skin the second when he saw the light of the fire reflected in Falen's hungry eyes. She looked gaunt, predatory, but also very tense and wary.

He held the skinned coney out to her. "Here. I've got to cook mine and ... whatever that is. I've got a couple of roots, too." Falen practically snatched the rabbit out of his hand. She looked like she was going to tear into it right there with teeth and talons when she looked up at Hasifar's face. A wave of something like concern passed across her eyes and she said, "Thanks. I'd better go off; you don't want to watch." He nodded and she turned and hopped off, one claw clutching the rabbit and the other bouncing her along the ground. He heard a wet smacking in the darkening night.

When Falen returned, Hasifar was just about done cooking the other two pieces of meat. He'd also gathered some water from a nearby creek and he was trying to heat a few potatoes and some greens without much success.

He was amazed at Falen's appearance.

The centaur had steeled himself for her return — undoubtedly covered in grime and now blood from the corpse — but he was not prepared for the shock.

She was clean.

Her hair, her skin, her face, her feathers and pinions — even her claws — looked as if they'd been neatly groomed.

There was a dampness about her that suggested a recent dip in a cool stream.

Falen saw his surprise and cackled — it was the same laugh, but from this creature, it was different.

"Surprised? Or didna you think harpies washed?" Hasifar looked at his meal, embarrassed. He heard her laugh again, knowing her bolt had hit the mark.

"Well, honestly, I didn't."

"A'course we do, laddie; otherwise th' filth'd get in our wings and we'd lose our flyin'! Hae y'ever truly seen a 'dirty bird' … for long?" Hasifar had to admit that he had not. Falen explained that harpies had always been scavengers … not necessarily by choice, but by design. They weren't powerful enough to hunt big game, and very seldom fast enough to catch small prey.

But they were smart enough to live off what others killed.

"A'course, we're also smart enough t'have huntin' parties … I'm sure ye've heard about them … and trappings, but we really aren't all that suited or inclined. We've never mind bein' nature's clean-up crew." And, since harpies were scavengers, they tended to have a great tolerance for spoiled or near-spoiled meat — but seldom did anyone have tolerance for them.

"So we've got a tradition that's almost harpy law. We don't eat our fill 'til we're safe — so we won't be too heavy to fly — an' we never clean until after we eat. It takes time to do proper, and y'never know when a fresh corpse'll turn up." Falen laughed again — and it was definitely a laugh, not a cackle — at Hasifar's discomfort.

Centaurs, Hasifar decided, were naturally fastidious.

"But when we clean, we clean — make no mistake. Back 'ome at the aerie, there are some harpy faces you'd call beautiful! But not out in the open," she smirked, "jes' like a centaur with two weeks a'trail-mud don't look all that handsome to a clean harpy." Both Hasifar and Falen shared a laugh at that, and the centaur agreed to wash up after dinner — though Falen could not quite understand why he washed his hands beforehand.

After he'd finished the two creatures — the non-rabbit, he decided, wasn't all that bad, though neither he nor Falen could put a name on it — he reached for one of the heated potatoes.

Falen looked at him curiously, "Whatcher gonna do with that, laddie?" she asked.

He grinned, "Why, Falen-lass, I'm gonna eat it," he said in his best imitation-brogue, taking a large bite out of the hot tuber.

It was hot, and it was filling, but that was all that could be said for the potato. But, it did provoke another reaction he hadn't expected.

"Yeeucccchh!" Falen retched, turning and flapping off into the dark. He heard faint coughing in her direction.

"What's wrong?" he called after her, scorching his tongue on the potato.

"You — eatin' that ... root! I thought ye' were kiddin'! I thought only 'umans ate dirty, nasty roots!" There was a stunned pause, and then both the harpy and the centaur began to laugh.

* * *

The next day it rained, so the harpy and the centaur sought cover under the eaves of a wood growing nearby. The stand was small, and unusual — most of the Highlands was plains and moors; this tree-growth was odd.

Still, it kept them drier than they would have been.

All morning, Hasifar spent his time examining Falen's wing. As near as he could tell, a stone had shattered one bone and seriously bruised another. The hollow bones were fragile; if it could be healed at all, it would take time.

Or magic.

After he'd done all he could to ease Falen's discomfort, he helped her into a tree and went hunting. Falen had offered to go with him, as her eyes were even sharper than his ears, but he told her to rest.

Truthfully, he wanted the time to think. The harpy's wing looked pretty bad. Falen said that harpies with busted wings seldom recovered — the bones might mend, but the torn muscles seldom regained their strength and coordination. Her mother, Hasifar was told, had been "sent down" after both her wings were crippled by orc slingshot.

The more Hasifar talked to Falen, the more he admired her, and the more he hated the men who'd done this to her. He wished he hadn't killed them — that he'd crippled them and then tortured them. They deserved to have their eyes put out, and their tongues slit, and …

There was a noise off to his left. Hasifar froze, his four knees slightly bent, ready to rear or run.

He listened. It was a soft rustling, maybe a hundred yards off. It wasn't the noise of an animal moving through the brush — it was too quiet even for that. No, whatever it was, it wasn't traveling; it was preparing —

A bolt of lightning cut a large branch of a tree not two hands from Hasifar's head. Fighting his natural instinct to rear, the centaur stood his ground and let fly with an arrow. He knew it would go wide, but maybe …

"Yow!" A piping voice came from the brush. Either Hasifar's shot was luckier than he deserved, or he'd startled the lightning-thrower.

Not knowing what to expect, the centaur charged. He hoped that whatever the trick was, his enemy wouldn't have time to do it again. He leapt over brush and ducked branches, and came to the spot he guessed the noise and the lightning had come from.

There, lying on the ground, was a little … person. It

was naked, which showed that it was obviously neuter. It's skin was a metallic blue and it had whitish hair. It looked like a thin man-child that had nearly died of exposure.

Except for the wings.

Attached to its back were small, thin, crumpled wings. They looked like transparent butterfly wings, only they were narrower — and crushed. Some giant hand had pinned them back and almost tore them from the creature's back.

From its shoulderblade protruded a brown arrow. A pool of blood welled around the wound.

It's face was contorted in pain. Eyes shut, it gasped, "Finish it, ye damned *affal*. Ye might as well end it 'ere."

Hasifar was suspicious of a trick, so he knocked another arrow. "Why'd you shoot at me, cyprium?" He'd heard about the lightning masters, the cyprium faeries, but he'd never seen one before. Back in Aysle, faeries were shy of humans and half-folk — when they weren't stealing from them or plaguing them with pranks.

The faery's eyes popped open in anger and pain, "Why'd *you* clip me bloody —" It stopped short and looked amazed at Hasifar.

It started to cry.

"Damnmedamnmedamnme —" it started to moan. Silver tears streamed from its eyes and the blood around the arrow — red, but shining with a near-phosphorescence — started to pump blood.

Well, Hasifar thought, *if it was going to pull a stunt, it would've done so by now.* Putting his bow and arrow away, he came forward and leaned down to the faery. It was apparently either delirious or uncaring of its fate, for it didn't resist as he picked it carefully up.

The arrow had found its way into a major artery — Hasifar thought. Having never seen a cyprium before — much less treated one — he didn't know what to think. But he knew the blood had to stop flowing. He started to gallop back to the camp.

"Damn me fer a fool," the faery moaned. It was near-unconscious. "Killed by a horse-rear for a bolt misdirected. *Quillus signar menta.*"

When Hasifar reached camp, he was greeted by a frightened squawk and many questions by Falen, all of which he ignored. He got out his newly-gathered bag of herbs and makeshift bandages and got to work.

"I don't know if this will work," the centaur said to himself. "It's lost a lot of blood and this isn't an *enchanted* spell."

"What," Falen squawked worriedly, "what d'you mean? Who's that?"

Hasifar kept right on working. He had to *try*.

Pressing a wet bandage around the arrow wound, he broke it off cleanly about four inches from the faery's chest. It moaned and turned in its pain.

"Hold it down," Hasifar barked. The harpy moved to comply.

Using his belt-knife, he started to work slowly at the wound, all the while muttering strange words his father had taught him. *The spell is on the arrow, not the creature*, he thought, *so this part will work.*

He was right, though it cost him. The strain from working the spell almost caused Hasifar to pass out — but the arrowhead cleared the wound without damaging the patient further. Blood started to well up.

He packed it with more bandages and started muttering another spell. *This* has *to work*, he thought, *it has to.*

Something went wrong. Either the spell was not

constructed to clot faery blood, or Hasifar wasn't doing it right. The faery lurched and bucked in pain, almost throwing Falen over. The blood continued to well past the soaked bandages.

"No!" Hasifar insisted, "this isn't *right*. It needn't die!" He muttered the spell again, quickly and with more force of will. He was near exhaustion. Whether the spell worked or not, this would be his last attempt.

Just when Hasifar thought he was going to pass out, he felt a snap — a loosening of bonds he hadn't known were there. He felt stronger, yet more tired, and he willed this strength into his spell.

The blood clotted. The faery stopped bucking and lapsed into sleep.

Hasifar collapsed.

* * *

Another day of rain passed, but Hasifar was eager to get going. He felt very active the next day, and it seemed to him that waiting around, doing nothing, was dangerous.

After the cyprium faery woke, though, it became apparent that they could not move yet. The faery — a male of its species named Spheros — had lost a lot of blood and Hasifar had no spell that could replenish that quickly.

Spheros' spell was hauntingly familiar. He and a *corum* — the cyprium word for a small family-like group of workers — had taken up residence near Edinburgh, Scotland. They had worked with the Earthers, cooperating instead of stealing as was their normal practise. They found that, by "charging" electrically things humans called "bat-arees," they could bargain for food and other human-made luxuries. And so, they passed the first few months of the war happily.

But then things started to go wrong. A messenger came to town. He said that Uthorion and the forces of the Dark were strong in Europe and in parts of Ireland and northern Britain. Edinburgh might have to send men to the war, like it or not. He also said that half-folk and enchanted were joining with a new force in Europe, a woman known only as the "Warrior of the Dark."

Things went from bad to worse. One day, the Edinburgh people were trading peacefully with the cypriums, the next they came at them with clubs and spear and nets. The *corum* were caught by surprise, and had to kill dozens of their attackers to allow their young to escape.

But the *corum* did not. Somehow, the humans had gotten ahold of enchanted weapons and nets, and they managed to trap almost all of the fairies. Once in the nets, the cypriums found their magic useless; the nets absorbed the lightning.

Then the humans who had been their friends taunted and tortured them cruelly. The first thing they did was crush the fairies' wings, making it impossible for them to fly away. Then, they manacled them to great "bat-arees" and deprived them of food until they produced charges.

"Many of me people died," Spheros said, "rather than submit t'those who'd betrayed our trust. They starved t'death rather than help." Spheros let out a long, ragged sigh. "But all the while, they implored those of us who were weak to keep chargin' the 'umans' bat-arees and to survive. And escape."

Both the centaur and the harpy nodded. They felt

they had heard the story before. "Finally," Spheros continued, "it was decided that at least one a' us should escape and get help. The 'umans couldna stop rumors gettin' to us. Rumors o' the Warrior. She was fightin' alongside half-folk an' enchanted, against the so-called 'Light' armies. She had naught o' Uthorion, but Ardinay, curse 'er name, called 'er a rebel an' an outlaw 'cause she banded wi' half-folk agin her own kind."

Hasifar looked sharply at Falen. They had discussed the Warrior of the Dark — or just "the Warrior," perhaps — before. Neither were sure what to make of her.

"Anyway," Spheros continued, oblivious to the by-play, "I was chosen by lot t'go. My mission is t'get to the Warrior an' tell her that almost half a' *corum* o' faery-folk — an' more, when the word gets out — will join her in her fight. If she'll rescue 'em."

The cyprium's small face took on a haunted look, "If any're left," he muttered.

* * *

That night, the three decided that they would try to cross the water to the east and make it into Europe. There, they could look around and possibly contact the Warrior (Hasifar still added "of the Dark," mentally) and see what rumors, if any, were true about her.

Hasifar also made a startling discovery. Caught up in his own thoughts, he barely listened to Spheros' long account of his capture, imprisonment, and escape. Falen, however, was very interested — her limited movement ability was making her eager to do something, even if it was listen to another being's troubles.

"... an' then, all a' the sudden, the 'umans broke into our cave, torches an' hearts aflame. We were so startled, they were on us before anyone reacted.

"Dessus — that's our *corum* spokesfaery — took a spear in the gut. It was a wood spear with an enchantment, I guess, 'cause he wasn't able to fry 'is killer. A shame, that; a faery should always have company on 'er way to *Shevar*.

"But Mrishin did. 'E went berserk, shootin' bolts o' lightning through the cave. It dinna hurt us, o'course, but I think 'e killed half-a-dozen in as many seconds. But the big 'un, the one wi' the scarf an' staff, started —"

"What?" Falen squawked, "What did you say?" The alarm in her voice brought Hasifar to full attention.

"What is it?" the centaur asked.

Spheros looked back and forth between them. "I was jus' tellin' how the leader o' the group signalled 'em t'use the nets —"

"No, no," Falen snapped impatiently, "describe th' leader for Hass."

"Okee. 'E was a biggun, mebbe 5'10", an' about two hundred pounds. Havin' a long cloak-an-coat, I couldna tell for sure."

"Tell him what the human was wearing," Falen prodded.

"'E had this long gray scarf. It were almost alive, twistin' in th' wind. An' he waved this short staff around like a maniac. I don' think the 'umans knew it, but it was a magic staff — all gnarled an' twisted wi' spells."

Hasifar went rigid. "That man matches the description o' the spaleen what ran Hasifar outta 'is village," Falen explained to the confused faery.

"Ah! But 'ow is that possible? Ye were only run out

a fortnight or so ago weren't ye?" Spheros queried. "Me people were enslaved months agone."

"But what about th' scarfed man? Has he been there all the time?"

The cyprium thought. He looked at Hasifar. *The centaur looked like he'd been caught by a will-o'-the-wisp*, the faery thought; *all starin' an gone ...*

"Yeah ... yeah," Falen looked intensely at Spheros, and he relented, "well, no, I guess not. It seemed like it, though. 'E were the one that enchanted the cages weekly, though; he couldna hae been gone for more than a week at a time."

"An' a human couldna hae gotten from Edinburgh to Hasifar's village an' back wi'in a week." Falen looked puzzled.

"Unless he were one'a them Earthers — an' went outside Aysle." Spheros provided. But he still looked troubled, "But e'en then, 'e'd have difficulty."

"Not if he was a wizard."

Both Spheros and Falen looked up. Hasifar had spoken, but he was still rigid, and his voice reflected the hollowness within him.

"A wizard could do it. A wizard could do it all."

* * *

A little more discussion, and the centaur, the harpy, and the faery came to a decision. "We'll have to join the Warrior," Falen said, "if there's a wizard behind both yuir outcastings, there must be somethin' evil afoot."

"But what?" Spheros, originally strongly for the sea-crossing, now was in doubt. "*Why* would a wizard do all this? I mean, I kin almost see the mess in Edinburgh — we were 'elpin' the people there resist the Invasion — but what about Hasifar? Sounds t'me 'e was all for sittin' out th' war."

Hasifar, having decided to cross the water, took no part in the discussion. He was readying the trio's meager supplies.

Falen, however, was still debating. "Kin y'not figure it?" Spheros shook his head, and Falen continued in a very low voice, "'e's a *stormer*."

"A *what*?"

"I fergot; y'weren't involved much in the Invasion," Falen explained. "When we were gearin' t'come over — e'en though I wasn't *with* 'em, I heard — the parties were t'keep their eyes peeled for those that did the ... near impossible." Falen glanced over her wing at Hasifar. "I think Hass moved hisself inta that category when he saved you."

Spheros looked first surprised, then shocked, and then a little ill — at least Falen interpreted the paleness of his silvery-blue skin as discomfort. "I were that close?"

Falen nodded, "Not only that," she continued, almost whispering now, "but 'e used a spell 'e was *certain* couldna work. It was a general 'ealing spell — *not* a surgery spell. But it did. Yuir breathin' 'ere 'cause *that centaur is a stormer!*"

Just then, Hasifar came up, and both dissembled into a discussion of the best way to cross the water to Europe.

"If either o' us could fly," Falen put forward, "we could go across an' get help."

"As it is now, I don't think either of you will be flying for quite a while." *If at all*. His mental voice added cynically.

Both the former fliers looked uncomfortable, and,

for a moment, Hasifar wondered whether they sensed his unspoken thought.

No. They don't know.

They put together the rest of their things in silence and Hasifar helped the two onto his back.

"We'll have to make for the shoreline, and hope to find a boat we can ... acquire." Hasifar's voice sounded strange, even to himself. Stronger than ever before, but also ... somehow sinister.

No, I'm just worried.

Hasifar walked carefully through the woods, listening for any noise. He heard nothing except the gentle *clop* of his hooves and the occasional crunch of a branch or dried leaves. He was filled with an eerie sensation. He became very aware of the weight — however little it was — of his two companions.

Leave them.

He stopped. "Did you hear something?" Hasifar asked.

Spheros said, "Nothing. What as it?" His voice was scratchy in the centaur's sensitive ears.

"It sounded like ..." *what business is it of yours?* "No ... it was nothing."

The woods seemed endless, and there were so many irritations. Hasifar's back was growing stiff, keeping it level for his passengers. Occasionally, he would misstep, and he could feel the harpy's claws and the cyprium's fingers grope for balance.

"'Ow much farther, Hass? It didna seem this far goin' in."

The harpy's voice broke the silence and irritated Hasifar. "Shut up. I'm listening." He said sharply.

"Well, excuse me, laddie."

A long pause followed.

"I think we're almost there, Falen."

"Thanks, Hass."

"Sorry." Then, "I'm feeling a little worried."

"Why?" Broke in Spheros. *His voice is like squeaky chalk,* Hasifar thought. *Why'd I have to save* him?

"Hass," Falen said, her voice concerned, "you've stopped. What's wrong?"

The centaur's torso pivoted to face his two passengers. "Get off my back." He said coldly.

Falen looked up into her friend's face, and what she saw was not pleasant. It was still his face, but not friendly or even worried. It looked like the face he wore back when he saved her from the stoning—but the one he turned towards his victims. Quickly, she slid off his back.

But Spheros was not moved. "'Ere, now, Hasifar; what's goin' on? We been walkin' for less than an hour — it canna be time for a break yet."

"'We been walkin''?" Hasifar mocked, "Well, since 'we've' been walking, I guess 'we' won't mind sitting." And with that, Hasifar bucked strongly, trying to shake the little pest off his back.

But Spheros held on tenaciously. "What're you doin', y'mulehead? Y'wanna *kill* me?!"

Falen screamed, "Jump *off*, Spheros! He *means* it!"

But the cyprium was adamant, "No, Falen; we've got t'get goin' before any more mischief is made on our behalf, an' I'll be *damned* if I'm gonna let some *horse-flies'* dinner slow us down 'cause his back's tired!"

That did it. Hasifar saw again the red mist come across his eyes, "All right," he yelled, "I've had *enough*! Be damned, will you?! All *right!*"

Hasifar lowered his human torso and performed a maneuver known to his tribe as the "centaur's roll." It was a deadly buck that no horse could even duplicate. He bent almost to the ground and then flipped his horse's body over, sending it crashing to the ground. Using his muscular human arms, he was barely able to continue the motion that would leave him upright.

The maneuver worked. The troublesome faery had to jump or be squashed. And it turned out to be a combination of both. The faery jumped as the centaur's lower half flipped around, but he was unable to get away from the crashing bulk entirely.

"Yaaah!" Spheros screamed as his leg was crushed under the centaur. Falen screamed also, half-running, half-flying to the faery's side.

"What th' *'ell* didya do *that* for, Hass?" she yelled as the centaur righted himself.

Hasifar looked down at the little beings below, and an urge to strike out with his hooves became almost overwhelming.

No, that isn't right.

The thought was like a cold bucket of water in his face. The red mist cleared, and he saw his two friends, one in great pain, on the turf below.

"Spheros! Falen … are you all right?"

Spheros continued to writhe, muttering curses in his native tongue, but Falen looked up accusingly.

"Ye coulda *killed* him, y'horse's ass!"

Her anger was a flame, but Hasifar fought the inferno that threatened to consume him again.

"I … I didn't mean to, Falen," his voice trembled, "I don't know what came over me."

She studied his face, and then, as if reserving judgement, said, "Well, help me with 'im now — if ye can."

"I can."

Hasifar went and found two dried sticks, each about

the size of Spheros' broken leg. Then, despite the faery's curses — at least he didn't shoot lightning bolts — the centaur studied the wound.

"It's as I thought; a clean break."

"'Ow bleeding considerate of you, *zurchus dra*!" The cyprium cursed.

I deserve that, Hasifar thought, but he continued, "I think I can fix this. I know a spell we use to bind legbones together — but it takes two to cast it."

"What do I do?" Falen asked. Her voice was carefully neutral, but it still stung.

"I'll actually cast the spell, but I need you to hold one stick against his lower leg — the unbroken one."

She gripped the stick in her left claw and hopped over. "Like this?"

"Yes. Now — whatever happens, *don't move that stick*! I'll do the rest."

Hasifar tried to put all the strange anger and pain out of his mind as he worked himself up to the spell. He'd never done it before — it was a difficulty procedure, and if he didn't do it right, he would be worse off than before.

After a few mumbled phrases, Hasifar touched the end of his stick to Falen's, then to Spheros' whole leg, then the broken one. Then he placed it beside the leg like a splint. Over the next hour, he repeated the procedure many times. By the end of the process, he was exhausted.

Spheros' eyes opened. "Th' pain's gone!" He looked down at his leg. Aside from a few purplish-silver bruises, it looked whole.

"You can stop holding the other stick now, Falen," the exhausted centaur breathed. He felt like he'd run for days and been put away wet. His irrational anger at his companions had totally blown away like it had never existed, leaving only a hollow ache.

"Spheros," he said haltingly, "I'm *so* —"

The cyprium jumped up, his eyes bright and his grin wide, "Ne'er you mind, horse- ... *Has*. Ne'er you mind. Y'made it better; that's all I need t'know!" The cyprium hopped off, presumably to stretch his leg out.

Hasifar turned to Falen, "I really *don't* know what happened, Falen. Honest."

She looked him over again and stretched her wings. "I dunno, Hass. Seein' y'put him back together ... that was the most sincere hard work I ever saw anyone do. But before ... y'looked so —"

"I know," he broke in bitterly. "From my side, it looked to me like you were *parasites* — little loafers taking advantage of me. I ... I felt like I had to be rid of you."

Falen considered, and then nodded. "I think I understand — better than you do."

Hasifar was confused, "What? What's going on, Falen?"

"Hae ye ever been prone to wild fits, Hass?" She asked bluntly.

"Huh? No ... at least, not 'til now."

"An' yuir friends in th' village? Were any o' them irrational?"

It hurt to remember, but, "No. Not to speak of."

Falen stared at him, "Yet, one day, this stranger shows up, an' all the town goes wild an' tries t'kill ye. Isna that suspicious?"

Hasifar felt a sinking feeling in his stomachs. "I ... I've tried to block it out, Falen." Then he crumbled under her stare, "Yes. I guess so," he concluded in a small voice.

"The way I figure it, Hass, this wizard cast a spell on the town — bringin' up in 'em the prejudice an' hatred they already had … but only in a little quantity. Then, he used his powers to focus it all onto you — the most 'different' one in th' village."

"So they don't really hate me?" Hope flared in the centaur's breast.

But Falen looked troubled. "I canna say. Spheros tells us that the Edinburghs' — if I hae th' name right — kept right on hatin' an' usin' the fairies right after the Scarfed Man disappeared — sometimes for days. If that's true — an' I don't think it's not — the mage must have some sort o' long-term spell that makes 'em …"

"That makes them blame *us* for what happened!" Hasifar said when Falen ran down, "That would be the easiest! Alter their memories a little, focus on the hate they're feeling — it could be done."

Falen nodded.

"Oh, those poor people!" Hasifar put his head in his hands.

"Now, remember laddie; they are na completely innocent — they had th' grain in 'em afore he arrived."

"But we all have some anger in us! Some prejudice!" A light dawned in Hasifar's mind, "Even me! When I hurt Spheros! *That* was the wizard."

Falen gulped. "We've *got* to get out of here — if he's nearby —" Her voice trailed off.

* * *

The trio got their things together again, and, this time, Hasifar took off as fast as he could. Apparently, the Scarfed Man, as Falen called him, had cast a spell on them to go 'round in circles, so as not to leave the forest.

But it had, apparently, worn off. Hasifar ran for clear daylight and then on to the sea.

When they broke through the trees, they were of one mind: they would get across the water, somehow, and meet with the Warrior. *She* would know what to do about this wizard who plagued half-folk and fairies. She could help them save their friends from his spell.

Back under the eaves, a figure stepped out from the trunk of a tree. It was wrapped in a whirlwind of living cloth, and, in its left hand, it held a short, gnarled stick.

It spoke: "Well, that wen' well, I ken." The voice was gravelly.

Another voice answered from a nearby tree, "Yes." This was a clear woman's voice — strong and powerful. "But he did not kill the faery. That would have made him completely ours."

The shape with the gravelly voice waved its stick, and another figure stepped out of a tree. This one was tall and thin, and had either a dragon's head or a helm made to look like a dragon's. It wore a long, black cloak.

"He will be ours," the gravelly voice said. "He shall join the Dark, whether he will or nil. The harpy can be lost in the passage, and the cyprium ... I have plans for it." The voice chuckled evilly.

The wind hissed through the trees, and the clear voice spoke, "You'd better get them a boat — we wouldn't want them to give up looking. And get me back across — I want to be there to meet ... them."

"Of course, Warrior."

"Of the Dark," the clear voice reminded.

"Of the Dark."

Evil laughter rang out and was suddenly hushed.

Myth Reality

Lisa Stevens

Culann shifted his body to give him a better view of the sidhe. His muscles, stiffened with disuse, strained as he moved. Around him, his people lay quiet, their pale-skinned bodies disturbed only by the breathing of deep sleep. Dust lay thick over the sleeping forms. Culann searched through his mind, sorting through the jumble of thoughts there as he slowly came to full consciousness — he had been forced to use magic to preserve his people. It had been — how long?

His eyes swept across the sleeping form of his soul-mate, Fionna. Time had not aged her handsome features. Culann remembered the moment he had first laid eyes on her at the Grove of Durne. They had both been sent there to meditate with Danu. He had tried to talk with Fionna, but she had fled at his approach. For weeks, he haunted the Grove, waiting for her. Then one day, she returned. Eventually, they had become friends, and then something more — more like one than two. When they had been declared soul-mates, it was the happiest day of his life. Gazing back toward her, he let his eyes roam over her sleeping form, taking in every detail. Culann's eyes misted over. He ached to touch her. It had been too long.

With awkward movements, Culann swung into a sitting position, dust falling from his clothing. He filled his lungs with air. What had awakened him? Letting his powers fill him, Culann allowed his awareness to wander for a moment. Ah, he could sense the magic! Since the days of Cath Maige Tuired, he had not felt so invigorated. It seemed that all was not lost: the humans had obviously lost ground in the battle to take Hibernia. The other Tuatha tribes must have resisted their advances. The humans would pay. But how long had it been?

With multitudes as numerous as blades of grass, the humans had come. And with them, they brought their religion — a religion that left little room for the beliefs and magic of the people of Hibernia. The Tuatha-de-Dannan had fought, but for every human they had slain, three more sprang up. They had swept the Tuatha before them, until finally the Children of Danu had been forced to take refuge in their sidhes, magical shelters built by their mother and goddess, Danu.

Living under the ground, the Tuatha had learned to exist without the fresh air and warm sounds of the surface world. A truce had been made and so the Tuatha-de-Dannan learned to coexist with the humans — one below the earth and the other above. Occasionally, the Tuatha aided those humans they deemed worthy, but mostly they harbored ill will toward those who had shut them off from the surface world.

Then the magic had faded. Slowly at first, but with increasing speed, the force that kept the Tuatha alive was drained from the world. As a final measure, the goddess Danu had given her children a powerful spell which would keep them alive until the day the magic returned to the world. But how long?

As his senses became more acute, Culann felt something. Anger. It roiled up inside of him. Instinctively, he knew it wasn't his own anger, yet it threatened to overwhelm him, forcing reason to retreat beneath its barrage. Somebody must pay! Then he felt something else — much more subtle, almost unnoticeable: fear. It wasn't the simple fear of losing a friend or of being caught doing something wrong, but rather the fear of dying, of being extinguished. Suddenly, Culann bent over, clutching at his stomach. Pain!

Something was dying and Culann felt the anguish of its death-throes. But what could possibly be so powerful? In a burst of insight, Culann recognized the voice that cried out to him in anger, fear and pain. How could he not? Next to his Fionna, it was the voice he, and all Tuatha, most cherished. It was the Earth. She was calling out to her people.

The humans must be responsible for this. Culann felt the Earth's anger, fear, and pain, and they became his. For this, the humans would pay dearly. The Earth had awakened her people to free her from this misery!

With a sigh, Culann surveyed his people. Soon they too would awaken and then, for the first time in … well, in a long, long time, the Tuatha-de-Dannan would ride the surface of Hibernia. And this time, the humans would perish!

* * *

Aubrey McDaniell clutched Sean's hand tightly.

She was nervous. Really nervous. On the other side of this curtain lay the gathered members of Parliament. They say that war makes strange bedfellows — well, nothing could be stranger than the spokesperson for the IRA addressing Parliament. The butterflies in her stomach threatened to erupt from her abdomen. Nervously, she brought her hand up to her lips and nibbled her index finger.

"You're on, Brea," Sean whispered to her with a smile, lightly pushing her through the curtains and toward the podium.

As she emerged into the room, Aubrey, or Brea as her friends and family called her, felt the weight of hundreds of eyes upon her, sizing her up as two duellists would when they come face to face for the first time. Summoning up all her inner reserves of strength, she marched toward the podium, her eyes trying to take in each person in the room in turn.

As she reached the podium, a chorus of coughs arose from various parts of the room accompanied by derisive snickers and stifled laughs. To her left, someone blew his nose. Fighting down her rising anger, Brea organized her notes and gathered her thoughts. Her speech could have a decisive impact on the war and she would be damned if she would let a bunch of stodgy old coots ruin it for her, and themselves for that matter.

Eying the crowd with her steel blue eyes, Aubrey began.

"Ladies and gentlemen of Parliament. Good afternoon. It may seem strange that I am addressing you like this, but war makes strange bedfellows and I believe you will all agree that an alliance of the IRA and the United Kingdom will be just that — strange. As all of you are aware, Britain and Ireland were invaded by an army that can best be described as not being from this world. They come from another cosm, as they put it, and their sole purpose is total domination of our fair countries. They take no prisoners. They don't fight with conventional weapons. Indeed, they seem to wield the magic of our myths and legends, making them formidable opponents indeed. Our weapons and other technological contraptions fail to work in areas where their forces hold sway. Only through sheer persistence and courage have we been able to hold them back until now. But even courage and persistence will fail in the end unless we can join ourselves into a common force and repel them with hands and minds united."

"Why are we listening to this bloody Irish terrorist?" a voice said from the back of the room. "I for one won't cast my lot with an Irish terrorist and a woman to boot." An older man rose from his seat and started to walk out.

Brea thought quickly. "Lord Dunsbury, isn't it?" The man stopped, his back to Brea. "Don't you know that for these invaders, there is no Irish, no Scot, no Brit, no Catholic, no Protestant, no man, no woman, no lord, no working man? There is only death and death does not play favorites. Death has no prejudice. These invaders are from another world. They have different morals, different values. They worship different gods. To them, a dead Irish terrorist is the same as a dead British lord. The same.

"I know that in the past, I would have gladly put a bullet into you, just as you would have gladly watched me hang. But in the light of these invaders, I would gladly call you brother, Lord Dunsbury. I would gladly embrace any one of you. For we are all human beings.

We are all Brits, Scots and Irish today. We are all Christians. We are all men and women. They," and here Brea paused for effect, "they are *none* of those things. Last week, I led a patrol of our forces, *our* forces, against the enemy. Against us they had a creature from nightmares — a monster. It tore through my patrol, cutting off limbs and heads, spilling entrails. Bullets and knives couldn't stop this monster. Few of us escaped. Those that did will always bear the memory of their comrades dying under the claws of that beast.

"These invaders must be made to pay for what they've done — the slaughter of helpless people, the destruction of villages and homes, and the perversion of the world as we know it with monstrosities of all sorts. These invaders come from another place, another time, and *their* world leaves no room for *ours* to exist. It is either them or us, ladies and gentlemen. I've seen their handiwork first hand. I've seen the blood and destruction, the tortured bodies, the women and children strung up like animals. All this I have seen and now I plead, no I beg of you: unite your forces, *our* forces, and fight this evil in our midst, which threatens to destroy *all* that we hold sacred. Long live the Queen! Long live Britain and Ireland!"

Brea let the final words linger for a moment. The silence was broken by Lord Dunsbury's clapping. For a moment, the rhythmic beat of his hands matched the hearts of all in the room. Then the assembled members of Parliament exploded into thunderous applause. Brea had to smile to herself. They were actually *applauding* her! Times had sure changed. As the applause died away, Brea realized with a start that she had done it. Britain was on its way to becoming united!

* * *

Culann pulled up sharply on the reins. His white horse snorted with eager anticipation, throwing its head from side to side. It was all Culann could do to keep it reined in — or to keep himself from kicking his heels into the horse's flank and galloping off across the countryside. A warbler took off from a bush as the mounted party drew near, its flight a wonder to behold.

It had been such a long time. How long, Culann still wasn't sure, but in some vague, imperceptible way, the world around him felt different. The birds sang different songs, the smells on the breeze were touched with odors that Culann couldn't identify, and the animals they'd encountered seemed much more pensive and afraid. Yes, things had changed.

Culann felt a touch on his arm. Turning, his eyes met those of Fionna.

"What are you musing about, soul of my soul? I would wager a guess that you are troubled by the Earth's changes and what has brought them about. Better it would be if you would muse about something useful, like finding us a decent camping spot before darkness falls." She flashed him a smile, which Culann returned in kind.

"You always were able to read my thoughts, flower of my life. Yes, it's the changes in the world that trouble me. But more so, I am concerned about why we have awakened and what that means for us — for you," Culann returned, squeezing his soul-mate's hand in the process.

"Don't worry about me, my love. As long as I have you, my life has everything I could possibly want."

Fionna smiled at Culann as she leaned towards him and they kissed. When they broke apart, they rode for a space with eyes only for each other.

Suddenly, Fionna's eyes lit up. Pointing to a nearby knoll, she spoke excitedly to Culann, "My dearest, isn't that our bonding tree?"

Culann turned toward the knoll and sucked in his breath. For there were two ancient oaks, their trunks and branches intertwined and reaching far into the sky.

"May Danu guide my thoughts, they are beautiful," Culann whispered. "Almost as beautiful as you, my love. But they are so large, so old. Have we been gone that long?"

The approaching gallop of a horse broke Culann's reverie. Shifting his gaze forward, Culann awaited his scout's report.

The young Tuatha rider saluted briefly.

"Father, I've spotted a village ahead, but it seems to have been destroyed. I detected no sign of the enemy, though I didn't ride in. I felt it more important to inform you of the location than to scout it out myself."

"How far, Tadg?" Culann replied, thoughtfully rubbing his chin.

"Just over that rise, sir." His son pointed.

With a wave of his hand, Culann set the party into motion. His Tuatha numbered thirty warriors. They all carried finely crafted bows and swords, with light lances available when mounted on horseback. Their armor was highly decorated. Each helm was wrought with the finest silver inlay and designed around various animal motifs — lions leaping to the attack, eagles swooping for the strike, wolves on the prowl, and boars charging.

As they progressed, Culann could feel the Earth's pain again, only this time it was more intense. The village: something had happened there that caused the Earth to recoil in anguish.

The Tuatha war band crested the rise. Below them was a seaside village, its small fishing boats bobbing at their moorings. The cry of a sea gull could be heard as the smell of salt air, mixed with something else, assaulted Culann's nose. Now he could see that the small houses which made up this village had been burned, the charred shells all that remained.

With their senses heightened to battle wariness, Culann led the Tuatha band into the town. The alien architecture and strange materials that made up the dwellings were readily apparent, but what held Culann's full attention was the horrible carnage in the center of the village.

Spitted on tall poles, over two dozen humans — men, women, and children — had been horribly mutilated and their bodies left for the gulls to feast on. Culann nearly doubled over with the Earth's pain.

"Cut them down and see to their burial," he ordered his people through clenched teeth.

Who had done this? Looking at the nearest body, Culann could tell that it was human. Could the Firbolgs have returned to Ireland? Or perhaps the Formorians? This wasn't their style, but someone — or some *thing* — had slaughtered these humans.

There were other questions as well. The humans wore strange clothing and much of the village felt strange to Culann. The men weren't wearing armor. Surely the men of this village would have fought to protect their homes. Also, the houses in the village obviously weren't made of the thatch and mud that

Culann was familiar with. Everything had a foreign feel to it, like the tales of someone who had visited lands far across the seas. More questions — but where to find the answers?

As his people cleaned up the massacre, the Earth's pain lessened as if the Tuathas' ministrations had soothed its injuries.

A commotion brought Culann back to full alertness. Tadg was holding a little human boy by the arms, lifting the lad clear off the ground as he kicked and struggled to get free. The boy's eyes were laced with anger, wonder, and a touch of fear. Culann smiled at the mop of red hair which constantly fell in front of the boy's eyes — a human of Hibernian stock for certain. As Tadg approached his father with the boy, the youngster stopped his quest for freedom and sized up the elder Tuatha with interest. Smiling to himself, Culann was pleased that the lad didn't display the fear that he had expected. Perhaps this one could be a source of information.

"What's your name, lad?" the head Tuatha queried.

"Bono," the young boy answered distractedly, obviously more intrigued by the wolf on Culann's helmet than the questions the elder Tuatha was posing.

"Bow-No. What kind of a name is that, boy?" Culann smiled. "Does it mean you're too young and small to shoot the short bow?"

"My daddy named me after the rock band; you know, U2," the boy replied, for the first time looking Culann in the eyes.

Shaking his head in bewilderment, Culann said, " 'Me too'? My Father didn't name me after any band of rocks. My name comes from my grandfather's surname."

Repressing the urge to ask why one would name a son after a band of rocks, Culann said, "So, Bono, you look like an intelligent and courageous young lad. Can you tell me what happened here?"

"Are you an elf?" Bono asked, ignoring the elder lord's question.

A smile crossed Culann's face. The humans of Hibernia had called his people that long ago, along with many not-so-pleasant nicknames.

Before the Tuatha could respond, Bono went on. "My brother played an elf a game. He was a fighter and a magician and a thief. He killed a dragon once. Boy, did he get a lot of treasure! He was really powerful. Are you a fighter and a magician and a thief?"

"Hold on boy. Did you say that he was a thief? And the dragon, where was the beast lairing?"

"Yeah, he was a thief, but also a fighter and a magician. I think the dragon laired near a big forest next to a big town, but I forget its name." Bono fired off replies to Culann's questions about as fast as the Tuatha could propose them. "They didn't let me play, just watch, 'cuz I was too little."

Puzzled even further by Bono's strange replies to his questions, Culann's anger built up. "Young man, you *do* realize that many people were killed here? It is very important that I find out who committed this atrocity. I need your help, but right now you are not being at all helpful. I need a straightforward answer. You must have seen something, boy. Who did this to your village?"

Bono's brave facade cracked with each word that fell from Culann's mouth.

"Ummm, I don't know. My brother, he, uhhh ..." Bono fought to find the words.

Her maternal instincts coming to the fore, Fionna was at the boy's side in an instant, embracing him in her arms. With a cold look at Culann, she stroked the young lad's red hair.

"There, there," she cooed. "It will be fine. You don't need to answer his questions until you are ready. It must be hard for you after all you've been through."

Suddenly the words bubbled out. "I tried to stop them! They came from the sea. My mommy told me to hide in the cellar with Michael. We didn't want to, but Daddy ordered us to. My brother and I went downstairs and hid by the furnace. We could hear the shouting and screaming. Finally, my brother told me to stay put and that he would go get Mom and Dad. I waited down there for him and Mom and Dad to come back. I waited a long time. Finally, I had to go potty, so I snuck upstairs. That's when I saw them and I hid until he found me." Bono pointed to Tadg.

"*What*, boy? Who did you see?" the elder Tuatha asked with a strain in his voice. His soul-mate gave Culann another frigid stare, but the young boy didn't seem to notice the tone of the Tuatha leader's voice.

"You know, *them*, Erik the Red," Bono restated, this time his youthful anger coming to the fore. With his small hands balled into fists, he unwrapped himself from Fionna's embrace and faced the Tuatha leader.

"Who?" Culann said, not quite sure that he had heard the boy right.

"Erik the Red, you know, Monty Python," Bono proffered, obviously struggling to find the right words to tell the ancient leader what he wanted to know. Suddenly, his face brightened, "The Vikings," he stated resolutely, his face beaming with his success, "They did it."

Then, just as quickly as his defiance had risen, the horror of the previous day's events resurfaced and Bono broke from Fionna's arms screaming, "Michael. Mom. Dad. Where are you?"

With a burst of youthful speed, he broke from the circle of Tuatha and ran back into the village. Two of the Tuatha raised their bows and took aim, but Culann waved them off.

"No. We need him alive. If we are to figure out what has happened to our world, we will need one of its inhabitants to tell us what is going on. Tadg, take two men and bring the boy back here," Culann ordered.

"'Need him alive' indeed." Fionna glared at Culann. "I had better go with them. I think that I can calm him down. Perhaps a woman's touch is needed in this instance. Young children usually respond well to their mother. I don't think Bono has quite outgrown his mother's embrace."

With a wave of his hand, Culann signaled for them to be off. He heard Fionna's voice raised to the men: "If you harm one hair of that lad's head...." He smiled, then frowned.

The Vikings. Culann had fought Vikings before. They were fierce warriors and worthy opponents. Obviously, Vikings had raided this village, horribly torturing and slaughtering its inhabitants. Young Bono had seemed to know the Viking's leader, a warrior named Erik the Red. It was just like the humans to turn on each other like this — they were a perverse and militant race.

Culann glanced up to see his life-mate with Bono draped over her shoulder. He could tell from the boy's swollen face that he had been crying hard. It was obvious that children in this day and age weren't used to the violence that his people had taken for granted.

Fionna looked so at ease with Bono that it pleased Culann. It made him happy to see her so content. With a glance at Bono, now sleeping in his wife's lap, he smiled. Not all humans were so bad, it seemed.

* * *

Brea walked through the halls of Parliament with Sean at her side. He had really been a rock for her in these last few weeks. When the world got crazy and everything turned upside down, he had been there, listening to her troubles and soothing her in that way only he could. His hand gently massaged her neck as they walked, melting the stress away. Brea didn't know what she would do without him. She was renowned for her leadership skills, her ability to utilize everything she had and make the most of it, her ability to win. Sometimes, however, Brea felt so small, so weak, and so ineffective. It was at times like that when she turned to Sean. He was tall, strong, silent, a pillar of stone in the middle of her troubled life.

She glanced up at Sean and squeezed his hand silently, in that way that said I love you between the two of them. "You know, I never could have made it without you," she whispered, putting on a face for him that no one else would ever see, or for that matter believe existed in a woman as strong and commanding as Aubrey McDaniell.

An explosion knocked both of them to their feet and the main lights flickered and went out. Groping toward the walls, Sean and Brea were on their feet when the emergency generator kicked in, bathing the hall in a dull red glow.

"Quick, this way," she motioned to Sean, while the two of them pulled Berretas from their hidden holsters.

From a hall to their right, they heard cursing and an inhuman cackle of glee. Suddenly, something burst forth from the wall right in front of the two humans. All Brea had the time to register was a flutter of wings and bright orange eyes before the creature rushed past them, a torch fluttering merrily in its hands.

"And it's off to the library we go, he-ho!" it chortled as it flew off down the main hallway.

Quickly, Brea and Sean set after the little faerie with two security guards close on their heels. The glow of the creature's torch and its cackles of insane glee made it easy to chase through the halls.

They were running back the way she and Sean had just come, and Brea knew there was a dead end ahead where they could capture the mischievous gremlin. The pursuers turned the corner and saw the wall ahead.

The little faerie didn't seem to be letting up at all. Then Brea realized her miscalculation: the thing had flown right through the wall when they first encountered it. Kicking in a burst of energy, she closed the gap between herself and the faerie. Too late.

The fey creature hit the wall at break neck speed — and stopped with a small squeak. Brea, Sean and the two guards surrounded the creature. It seemed to be out cold.

"What happened?" whispered Sean.

"Sometimes their powers fail them behind our lines, just as our guns sometimes fail behind theirs," Brea replied.

"Good timing for us."

Brea chuckled. "So much for the old disappearing act."

* * *

"Culann, can I have my own horse to ride?" Bono asked fervently, eyes wide with excitement. "And a sword. Can I have a sword too?"

"You are too young to wield a sword and ride a horse," Culann returned with a smile, "but perhaps Tadg could teach you something about them later when we stop for lunch."

"Awesome, that would be really cool," Bono replied, his voice filled with anticipation.

"I rather think that you will be a bit warm rather than cool by the time I get through with you, young whelp, but I would be delighted to teach you a thing or two about the sword when we stop for lunch," Tadg grinned back at Bono.

"Speaking of eating, I'm starving. Could we stop at a Burger King or somethin'?" Bono swiveled his head around and smiled plaintively at Culann, who was riding behind him on the horse.

Culann laughed. "I know of no burghers who deem themselves kings in these parts, and I doubt whether they would feed us if we went there, my boy."

At the thought of one of the human rulers opening up his house to feed the Tuatha, the rest of the band roared in mirth.

"For that matter, why don't we go and sup with the King of Ireland while we're at it?" Tadg quipped, slapping his leg and causing the whole band to re-erupt at the young boy's expense.

"You guys are weird," Bono stated, shaking his

head. "I just wanted something to eat."

"Ignore them, Bono dear." Fionna consoled him with a smile. "They've just had too much fresh air and are a bit over-exuberant." Someone mentioned nectar of the gods, and the whole band continued to cackle with glee while Bono stared straight ahead and pouted.

Finally, the band stopped to rest next to a small brook. Tadg brought down some pigeons which he roasted over an open fire. At first, Bono wouldn't eat the pigeon meat, mumbling about how he used to feed the birds in the park and there was no way he was going to eat the birds from the park. Fionna reassured Bono that he wouldn't have to eat the park birds, and that she would provide him with something else. She then took one of the birds that Tadg had killed, went out of Bono's sight, deboned the bird, and returned with the deboned meat, which Bono dubbed "chicken." This he devoured in monstrous bites and swallows.

As the troop rested, Culann realized that he didn't have any idea where he was going. It felt *so* good to be out in the open air that he had not stopped to think about his destination. Things had changed considerably since the last time he walked the face of the earth, and he felt like a stranger. Ireland was no longer the home he had fought for; it had been warped by the humans, changed, deformed, and the Earth wept at her own condition. Anger welled up inside Culann. There *had* to be a way to set things right. Magic *had* called the Tuatha-de-Dannan from their underground tombs. Culann *had* to believe that the Earth was responsible for this. But what was he to do now?

Bono? The boy had lived here. Though he was young, he seemed admirably bright for a human. Perhaps he would have an idea of where to go.

Culann slowly rose to his feet and walked over to where Fionna was sitting with the boy. Bono was wolfing down the last scrap of meat, his face full of grease. Culann smiled.

"I've been thinking, young man, that I need to find out where things stand in the world so that I can help to set them right again. Do you know where I might go to do this, Bono?"

Bono stopped wiping the grease from his hands and twisted his face up thoughtfully. "I guess I'd go to town — that way," he pointed, indicating the smooth, black-rock road they had been travelling on since the village.

"Is the town, over that way, big?" Culann asked, hoping the lad would expand upon his answer.

"Oh, yeah! They have a Baskin-Robbins, a movie theater, a department store and all kinds of other neat stuff!" Bono exclaimed excitedly.

"What do basking robins have to do with anything? And stores that you leave?" Culann was mightily confused. "Do they have a system of government in this town?"

"Baskin-Robbins is where you get ice cream and why wouldn't you want to leave a store? Do you want to live in one?" Bono responded.

Culann shook his head. He would just have to ignore the things he didn't understand, and hope he could discover some clue in this town as to what was happening in the world. The Earth's pain had not let up since Culann had awakened and he wanted desperately to fight whatever was causing it.

With a sigh, he rose and signalled for his warriors to prepare to ride. With Bono now riding in front of Fionna, the warband headed off down the road to the west. As usual, Tadg rode off ahead to scout. Culann had always felt that anything that was too dangerous for his family to do was too dangerous for any of his people. Besides, it was a job that Tadg performed admirably.

They had ridden for about half an hour when Tadg rode back with news that a party of mounted men was approaching from the west. The enemy numbered about the same as the Tuatha, but Tadg thought he had not been seen — the warband would have the element of surprise.

Culann scanned the terrain, looking for some advantage. There were no places from which to ambush the approaching warriors, so he decided to use the elevation of the hill they were currently on to give his archers an advantage in case the enemy charged their position. The added height of the hill would allow his archers to shoot farther and also tire the attacking enemy. Meanwhile, Fionna prepared her spells and took up a position to the left of Culann. He motioned for his band to spread out along the ridge, then turned to wait for the enemy to appear.

He heard them before he saw them; the clatter of their horses' hooves on the hard black road created quite a din. Silently, he signalled his band to be ready. Up and down the line, arrows were nocked as both horses and Tuatha waited restlessly.

The enemy party appeared from around the bend. At Culann's signal, thirty bows were made ready and aimed at their targets. The leader of the opposing group stopped his riders and surveyed the arrayed Tuatha. After a moment, he shouted over the intervening field, "Greetings. I have no quarrel with you. Perhaps we could meet and discuss this like civilized beings."

The leader pointed towards the center of the field. "I'll remove my weapons and meet your leader over there."

Culann watched as the man unbuckled his sword belt, handing it to an aide, and proceeded to dismount and walk toward the center of the field. There was something strange about him, which Culann couldn't place. There was also something familiar about him, even though his appearance seemed alien. The hair on the back of Culann's neck prickled with anticipation. As the man got closer, Culann could see that his skin was dark — dark blue! Silver hair framed his face, accenting the blue and giving the man a noble veneer. Then Culann sensed it — magic! Its energy coursed through Culann like a cool summer breeze. This man, or whatever he was, had a potent magical aura around him.

"This man may be able to provide the answers we are looking for, Tadg. Fionna, keep the boy safely behind the lines and ride away with him at the first sign of trouble. There is something strange about these warriors." Culann unbuckled his own sword belt and dismounted. With a brief whisper of love to his soulmate, Culann turned and strode into the field to meet the strange blue-skinned man.

Culann approached cautiously, but without evidence of fear. Inside, though, he was ready to spring into action at the slightest provocation. He could feel the magic more strongly. As the Tuatha came near, the other man smiled, his white teeth made all the more evident by the dark hue of his skin.

"Greetings, my lord." The musical quality of the man's voice caught Culann off guard. "My name is

Delyndun, chief wizard to my Lord Thorfinn Bjanni, the master of this realm. I hate to be so bold, your lordship, but you do not seem to be of this world. I sense a magic in you that I do not feel in the other inhabitants of this realm." The elven wizard pronounced each word crisply, indicating a man who was not only used to talking, but also one who had been well educated. That, along with the fine cut of his clothing, seemed to indicate that he was a man of wealth and power, perhaps a landed noble.

Culann thought for a moment and replied, "You are right, Dellydin, my people are of a race far different from the humans who inhabit this isle. Long ago, the humans fought my race for possession of this island and drove us into hiding. Slowly and insidiously, they drained the magic from the world, leaving my people to die. Now, we have awakened with the return of the magic to the world and we are out to reclaim what is rightfully ours."

"Ahhh," Delyndun made this sound like a purring cat. "I see we have a common objective then. You see, my Lord Bjanni has come to conquer this world and establish a realm of magic here. It is *his* magic that you feel in your world now. The humans, as you call them, are a stubborn lot, refusing to give in to the inevitable. But, alas, their fight is a futile one and soon this island, along with the rest of their world, will fall to the unlimited power of my master. Perhaps our people can work together against these humans?"

"Perhaps," Culann said cautiously, "but I would like to speak to your lord first. Our objectives do indeed seem to be along the same lines, but I would have to see where my people fit into your lord's plans before I would commit to any long-term alliance. Until that time, however, I think we can avoid hostilities and work together."

With a smile, Culann stretched forth his hand in friendship, which the elf grasped energetically. A cheer erupted from both sides and the Tuatha lowered their weapons. The two forces rode to their leaders' sides and were soon mingling and sharing introductions. After an impromptu meal provided by Delyndun's magic, the now-united forces prepared to move out. Culann helped his wife get Bono situated in front of her on the horse. The poor lad had fallen asleep early in the evening, the excitement and fresh air having taken its toll. When he felt that the boy was secure, Culann mounted his own horse and led his band after the elven wizard.

As they rode, Culann noticed that Bono's sleep was restless, with occasional mutterings and starts. Fionna watched over him carefully, softly caressing the boy, trying to bring comfort to her human charge.

And Culann let the pain of the Earth melt away into a renewed purpose as he rode toward his destiny.

* * *

Brea walked across the room. Pieces of the carpet's padding showed in places where her repetitive pacing from side to side had worn away the fabric. She glanced over to where the small faerie was sitting, eying her movements with unconcealed glee. The little bastard knew that Brea couldn't physically harm him: most of the traditional methods of interrogation were of little use when your subject was a magical being. Brea just couldn't seem to make it feel pain or fear for its life.

Turning on her heel, Brea went back to face her

prisoner. The faerie was a little under three feet tall, with sky-blue skin, short, curly black hair, and eyes the color of tangerines. Its laughter was like wind chimes while its voice reminded one of the dulcet overtones of a woodwind. When the faerie smiled, its teeth glistened in the light. Brea had seen just about enough dulcet glistening for one day.

"Damn you," she screamed at the being, grabbing it by the arms and shaking it as hard as she could, "if you smirk at me one more time, I swear by all the saints I'll rip your little blue body limb from limb."

The tinkling sound of its laughter enraged Brea and she tugged at the arms with a vengeance, but they stretched like putty beneath her grasp. In frustration, she threw it at the wall. Tumbling through the air in a feat of graceful aeronautics, the faerie floated to the ground and stood smiling back at Brea.

"Now, now, stormer, we mustn't lose our temper, must we?" The faerie held its fingers to the top of its head, rolling its eyes around and snorting and grunting like a beast. Its antics seemed to drive it further into fits of delirium and it rolled into a little ball, giggling insanely.

Brea had to get out of there. She couldn't withstand its tauntings anymore without physically hurting something and the one thing she wanted most to hurt was immune to anything she could think of. She would just have to come back later.

"Don't forget to do your paperwork now, stormer. Perhaps you can learn something and beat some intelligence into that thick head of yours. Or aren't you able to write, stormer?" The creature prolonged the last syllable and slurred it into a shriek of laughter.

"You can eat this paperwork, you slimy little bastard" Brea screamed, hurling her pen and clipboard at the blue creature and turning to head for the door.

A sharp squeal of pain brought her up short. Turning around, she noticed the faerie clutching its arm, all thoughts of laughter gone. Then Brea noticed the pen on the ground next to the faerie — dark blood visible on its tip. Silver! Of course! She had forgotten the myths about some faerie's aversion to silver. Glancing around the room, Brea spied the letter opener which had been given to her when she had been promoted to captain. Rushing to her desk, Brea grabbed the letter opener, brandishing it like a knife, and wheeled around toward the faerie.

"So, silver is your Achilles heel, is it?" Brea waved the letter opener in the faerie's face. The creature's cringe and wide-eyed fear were a welcome change from the taunts she had been subjected to for the past day. In terror, the faerie scampered into the corner.

"Now we'll see if there is anything you wish to tell me about your plans in Ireland."

"Mercy, mistress, oh mercy, please, fair lady. I didn't mean to taunt you, oh no, not me. Anything you wish to know, beautiful lady, anything, but please don't hurt me with that wicked implement!" The creature cringed, desperately seeking to expose the least amount of its body by squeezing itself into the corner.

"That's better," Brea stated. "Now, I need to know why you were sent to sabotage our electrical system."

"Oh, please don't hurt me, I'll tell you everything, everything! It was in preparation for a raid, a raid I tell you. Oh no, don't hurt me, I know much, you'll see," the pathetic little creature whimpered.

"I need details. When, where, how many, for what purpose," Brea pressed, knowing she had the upper hand for the moment and wishing to take advantage of it.

"I need a map, a map, fair lady and I will show you all," the faerie pleaded.

With an eye still on the creature, Brea retrieved a tactical map of Ireland from her desk. Placing it in front of the faerie, she threatened it again with the letter opener, "Where, you pathetic worm? Tell me, or as God is my witness, I'll slice you open from one end of your slimy blue body to the other. And don't try to lie!" she added before the faerie could speak. "We have — uh — spells to tell if you lie!"

"Oh, that won't be necessary madam, please, I'll show you," it gulped and traced a trail with its finger on the map. "There, that is where the raid will take place."

Brea looked to where the creature pointed. The road from Castlebleyney to Ardee? A seldom-travelled road, especially of late. How could this piece of ground in the middle of nowhere be important?

Brea touched the letter opener to the fairie's skin, and fancied she saw smoke arise. "Why would your master want to 'raid' a piece of land in the middle of nowhere?" she barked.

"Oh, please, no, stop, stop. He wants to plant the next stelae, to bring back the magic."

Ah, that made sense! Brea had heard talk of these stelae: some of the enemy had come over to the human's side, bringing with them knowledge of the stelae and its importance. With a stelae strategically placed, the magic of the invading forces would take over the land, leaving the defender's weapons useless. If the attackers had managed to plant a stelae this deep behind human lines, over half of Ireland would have been cut off from the government in Dublin. Chaos would result and the defenders could be wiped up piecemeal. But now, the IRA would be waiting for the invaders.

"When and how many," Brea demanded, though she barely needed to threaten the faerie anymore, it was so cowed.

"In two days at midnight; oh, don't hurt me. Twenty riders on horseback. That is all I know, you've got to believe me. They hope to control the crossroads and gain the upper hand in the conquest of this territory. The attack on your machines was just a ruse in hopes that you would withdraw your defensive patrols to protect this building while the raid took place. Please don't hurt me. I've told you everything. Oh, please," it blubbered, until its moans for mercy became incoherent.

Brea wasn't paying much attention to the little faerie now. Two days. There were preparations to be made. Maybe *this* time those invading bastards would see what it felt like to be on the receiving end of an ambush. Whistling a little Irish ditty, Brea threw the letter opener onto her desk and walked out of the room.

After Brea was gone, the faerie stopped its blubbering and looked up. When it saw that no one was around, it reached out for the fallen pen. Smiling evilly, it broke the pen in half. It gasped with the pain, but its grimace became a low laugh. When one had important misinformation to impart, pain was irrelevant. Myths, indeed!

* * *

The world was a changed place. Up ahead, Culann could see one of the human relics, abandoned along the side of the road. The huge machine glared at him in its impotence, its eyes dark and sightless. Culann felt a twinge of fear at the sight of this creature, even though Delyndun had assured him that the machine was dormant and no longer a threat. It seemed that the magic Delyndun's people had brought into the world made the machines of the humans inert.

Somehow this seemed wrong. Even though the machines were alien, they belonged to this world. The sight of them sitting dead along the road made the whole world seem dead, as if she had cast off her current occupants but kept their belongings. Perhaps time would remove all traces of the humans, but their loss would be felt until then. Yes, a long time must have passed since Culann and his people had begun their slumber — so long that Culann felt like the derelict machine by the road. As the Tuatha rode by, he saluted the machine and wished it a speedy journey to the afterlife.

Ah, but Delyndun's people planned to restore Ireland to its former state, destroying all the foreignness that the humans had wrought on its soil and bringing the magic back to the Earth. Culann clenched his fist around the reins and smiled — it seemed that for the first time in Hibernia's history, the Tuatha-de-Dannan were going to side with the invaders.

Culann looked over to where Bono rode in front of his wife. The boy was unusually quiet. He stared at every silent town they passed and every derelict machine the troop came upon. Much of Bono's spirit seemed to have fled with the world that he was a part of. As comfortable as Culann was with the magic he now felt around him, Bono seemed edgy, frightened, and ill at ease. This would change with time, Culann knew. The boy was young, he could adapt. The new age of magic would be one in which Bono could grow up unfettered by the failings of human society. Culann vowed to himself that he would set things right in Hibernia and raise Bono as his own.

A rider from the front of the mounted party approached Culann.

"Your lordship," he saluted smartly, "we approach my lord's camp. Your horses will be taken care of by my people. We will allow you to set up your camp and eat a good hot meal before you meet my lord. Is this satisfactory to you, your lordship?"

Culann nodded his head wearily and the rider reined his horse around and headed back to the front of the group. Turning to Tadg, Culann told his eldest son to spread the word among the warband that everyone was to accept the hospitality of Delyndun's lord, but remain wary in case things weren't as they seemed. Culann was inclined to embrace this new magic which had permeated this part of the world, but his instincts told him never to accept things at face value. There was a twinge of wrongness in the magic Culann was feeling, something that he couldn't quite place. He would just have to be careful.

The party crested the hilltop and Culann caught his first glimpse of Delyndun's camp. As he had expected, it looked much like the Viking camps from days gone by. Culann had noticed some Vikings mixed in with Delyndun's band, but when queried, the wizard had never heard of Erik the Red, so Culann had decided that these Vikings were most likely not the ones who had committed the massacre at Bono's village. There must be hundreds of different Viking villages. He wouldn't let the mistakes of one village color his dealings with the rest. He would have to mention Erik the Red to Delyndun's lord when he met the man, demanding aid in bringing justice to the foul murderer Erik. If Culann ever found the Vikings and Erik — he glanced over to where Bono sat staring in wonder and fear at the encampment below him — so help him, he would cut down every one of the bastards and leave their corpses for the gulls to pick at.

The two warbands wended their way down into the encampment, the sound of the surf becoming apparent over the noise of the bustling camp. Culann ordered his men to set up near the outside edge of the Viking camp, in case things got messy and they had to leave quickly, though he didn't voice his musings aloud. After the Tuatha had eaten, water was brought for them to wash the trail's dirt from their bodies and Culann caught a short nap before Delyndun arrived.

"I hope the accommodations are satisfactory, sir?" the elven wizard said, proffering the query as some sort of obligatory greeting. "If there is anything else that my lord can provide you with, you need just ask. If it would please you at this moment, sir, my lord is awaiting your presence in his tent."

"These accommodations are more than satisfactory, Delyndun." By now, Culann had learned how to pronounce the elven wizard's name correctly. "I will join you in a moment after I find my son. Could you please give me a moment alone with my soul-mate?"

Nodding his assent, Delyndun slipped out of the tent to wait for the Tuatha leader.

Turning to Fionna, Culann delicately held her hand. "I will be gone to meet the leader of these humans, my dear," he softly said, allowing his hand to caress the smooth skin of her face. Fionna's eyes reflected the love and caring that Culann felt for her and they embraced for a moment before Culann reluctantly held her at arm's length. "I will return, my love, you must believe that, but above all, keep the boy safe. I am a grown man and am more than capable of taking care of myself, but the boy needs our help if he is to survive to see manhood. I doubt that anything will happen, but one cannot be sure in these strange times. May Danu watch over you, my love, and if I am to die, may we meet again on the shores of Tir-na-nog."

"My love, I will watch over the boy and wait for your safe return. I have an uneasy feeling about this though, Culann. Something isn't right here. Be careful, soul of my soul, and return to me." Fionna's words trailed off to a whisper and she turned her head away to hide her tears from her soul-mate.

Culann touched her hand for a moment, then left the tent to get Tadg. He found his son eating with the men and with a nod of his head, Culann headed back to where he had left Delyndun, Tadg following in his father's footsteps.

Delyndun led them through the camp toward the large wooden building at its center. As they progressed through the encampment, Culann caught snatches of old sea songs and glimpses of dice games, where Delyndun's men divided the spoils of war — living for today, for tomorrow they might be dead. Culann became caught up in the fervor of the camp: soon, his band would see battle and finally the wrongs of the past would be righted in blood. Yes, he could see himself, sword dripping blood as the bodies of his enemies floated in the surf at his feet. It was glorious.

"My lord." It was Delyndun. "We are here."

Culann came out of his reverie. They were standing before a large, wooden building. The structure had been built from wood salvaged from other buildings, perfectly signifying the way in which the invaders meshed with the Hibernia of today. Two guards stood to either side of the front door, which was covered with a blanket with the words "Hard Rock Cafe - London" woven into it. Light and smoke drifted under the edges of the blanket, as Delyndun motioned for the two Tuatha to go inside.

Culann tensed. This would be the moment of revelation. If Delyndun's lord was the Erik the Red whom Bono had mentioned, then the chances were good that Culann and Tadg wouldn't leave this building alive. Culann's hand drifted to the pommel of his sword and his eyes shot a look of warning to Tadg before he nodded to Delyndun and entered.

The interior of the structure was also a hodgepodge of stolen luxuries. Boxes were piled upon boxes, while their contents lay scattered about as if discarded randomly. A smoky grey haze hung over the room, giving it an almost surreal feel. It took a moment for Culann's eyes to adjust to the light. As they did, his eyes immediately locked onto the imposing figure sitting amid a pile of cushions on the far side of the room. Culann sensed that this was a man who had sent countless thousands to their deaths. The scars of many battles wove their unique patchwork across the man's face, giving him an aura of authority and danger. Culann was relieved to see that the Viking's hair was a shining black and not the red he had feared. Still, Erik the Red's name could have much darker implications.

The Viking's eyes met Culann's and for the first time in his life, the Tuatha felt like he had met his equal. It was Culann who looked away first.

Delyndun addressed the immense Viking. "My Lord

Thorfinn Bjanni, may I have the pleasure of presenting to you his Lordship Culann and his son Tadg, natives of this land and potential allies against the human inhabitants who war against you." Delyndun motioned for Culann to take a seat to the left of the Viking chief. Tadg took his place on his father's right. This done, Delyndun bowed low and backed off to take a seat at Thorfinn's right hand side.

"Greetings and welcome, my guests. I trust your ride here was enjoyable?" the Viking lord rumbled, his voice a deep-throated growl. "Delyndun here says that you fight the same humans with whom I am currently at war. Is this true?"

Culann measured the chieftain for a moment and replied, "It seems that way, my lord. Many years ago, the humans of this land drove my people from the face of Hibernia, forcing us to live underground. But not only did the humans steal our land from us, they also destroyed the magic which was our nourishment. When the magic reawakened in the land, we decided to again ride the surface world and regain that which the gods rightfully gave us."

"Ah, so it was *the magic* that brought you to us. It was *I* who brought the magic to this world, so it is because of me that you have been awakened. I come from another world, where magic is as common as trees and grass. Your world resists the magic that I bring and thus we must forcibly conquer it. With each parcel of land we take, our magical influence is extended." Lord Bjanni smiled.

"But it was not always so," Culann pointed out, "for once upon a time, the Earth herself breathed the magic of the land and her spell of life was visible in every living thing. When the humans turned away from the

Earth and her magic, they drained her and left her barren and sterile. You may be bringing the magic *back* into the world, Lord Bjanni, but it is hardly new or foreign."

"Your magic is gone, though. Mine is alive and well. It seems that without the magic I bring, your people will perish, Culann. The success of my invasion seems to be even more important to you than to me. For me, it is a matter of gaining more power. For you, it is your existence. Come, Culann, it is simple enough: join with me and the magic will be yours forever."

"Perhaps, Lord Bjanni, perhaps," Culann mused, gathering his thoughts together. "Do you know of a small fishing village to the west of here and of a Viking chieftain named Erik the Red?"

Thorfinn pursed his lips thoughtfully for a moment. "No, I'm afraid that I don't know of either one. However, I'll have Delyndun check through the ranks of the sub-chieftains to see if such a man can be found. I am rather new to this position, my Lord Culann, and not all the chieftains and sub-chieftains at my disposal are known to me."

Culann detected no hint of deception in Lord Bjanni's voice. "I'd appreciate that, my Lord. I have a matter of importance to speak with him about."

"Very well. Delyndun, see to it." The great Viking waved toward his aide and paused for a moment, sizing up Culann's mood. "So it seems we have a common goal, Lord Culann. If I succeed in conquering this island you call Hibernia, then the magic that was taken from you will be restored. With your help and knowledge of Hibernia, my task will be that much simpler."

Signalling for Delyndun to pour some mead for the

four of them, Thorfinn waited until the elven wizard had passed the filled cups around and then proposed a toast. "To Lord Culann and his men, my newest allies, together may we drive the rats who live in this land to its farthest shores and drown them in the crashing surf."

Silently, Culann nodded his assent and drank down the cool mead. For the moment, it seemed that allying with Thorfinn would be the best course of action.

Thorfinn finished first, crashing his flagon down upon the table.

"Now, as a sign of good faith, I'll show you my latest scheme," the barbarian chieftain smiled. "It has taken some time, but I was finally able to let some false information 'fall' into the hands of the enemy. Tomorrow, one of their leaders, a troublesome woman named McDaniell, will ride with some men to ambush *me*. Unfortunately for her, *she* will be the one who is ambushed.

"My source 'leaked' information which should lead her up the trail here." Lord Bjanni pointed to a map on the table. "If I've gauged this woman correctly, my Lord Culann, she will lead the force herself. I don't believe for a moment that she would leave such an important mission to an underling. But I will be waiting for her here with a force more than twice the size of hers and the little cockroach will be squashed."

Thorfinn slammed his hand onto the table and grinned over at Culann. "She is the humans' spiritual leader. It is only through her efforts that the humans are at this moment tentatively united. Without her to keep the shaky alliance in place, it will crumble and make it a simple matter for us to conquer the humans. She is all that stands in our path of victory! How would you like to ride with me on this little adventure, Culann, and get your first chance to taste of that revenge you've been craving?"

Culann smiled at the Viking leader. "I have been waiting for this moment for more years than you would believe, Thorfinn. We leave at dawn then?"

Culann held his hand out to the Viking, who engulfed it with his own hairy hands.

"We leave at dawn. It will be a long ride and I want to have plenty of time to set up the ambush."

With a last swig of mead, Culann left and made his way back to his warband's encampment. Father and son walked side by side, each lost in visions of the following day's battle. Culann put his arm around Tadg's shoulder and the two walked in a comradely fashion back to their tent to a sleep that would be alive with clashing swords and whistling arrows.

* * *

Dawn came to the Viking camp at an early hour, as men prepared their weapons and mounts for the coming battle.

"Fionna, I want you and the boy to stay behind." Culann used that tone of voice which said that his decision was final.

However, Fionna wasn't in that sort of mood. "So you think you can just march off to your death and leave me here to mourn your passing? I'd like to remind you that I am the most skilled sorcerer among our people. You *need* me for this battle."

"Then who is going to take care of Bono? The boy cannot be brought into battle, that much is certain." The question pierced to Fionna's maternal instincts and she faltered.

Culann didn't wait around for her reply. He knew he had won this round. Fionna would stay with Bono, even though it irked her. The boy's welfare was in her hands now and she took that very seriously.

The Tuatha leader walked amongst his warriors, exchanging barbs and jokes with the men as they eagerly prepared. The pent-up energy of many centuries was released into a flurry of activity, as each warriors' weapons glistened razor-sharp and their armor sparkled in the morning sun.

Culann felt good — he felt alive today. Today was the day when all the wrongs would be righted. His people would be avenged. Culann was born a warrior and he would die a warrior, hopefully with the blood of his human enemies wet on his blade.

Raising his hands into the air and breathing in the salt air, Culann let loose a bellow of sheer joy: "Remember Cath Maige Tuired!" The Tuatha's body quivered with excitement as the battle cry of his people boomed over the encampment, to be echoed back by his warriors thirty-fold. Today, many humans would travel to Tir-na-Nog or wherever their gods led them.

A commotion in the Viking camp caught Culann's attention and he turned to watch Thorfinn emerge from his wooden house. Standing on the front steps, the Viking chieftain urged his men into a battle frenzy with a stirring speech that caught up Culann with its enraptured praise of battle.

"Erik the Red," a small voice broke through Culann's thoughts.

Turning, the Tuatha leader noticed Bono at the edge of their tent, his eyes wide with fear and his mouth hanging open. The boy's body was shaking.

"Erik the Red," he intoned again in that flat, emotionless voice.

Culann followed Bono's eyes to where they stared at Lord Bjanni. "Are you sure, Bono?" he prodded the youngster.

"Erik the Red," Bono again replied, nodding his head fervently.

"No! You are wrong! He's *not* Erik the Red. He's our ally, our comrade. Look!" Culann grabbed the boy and held his head so that he would have to look at the Viking lord. "His hair isn't red! He can't be the Viking who massacred your village!"

The young boy tried to shake his head, still staring at the distant figure of the Viking chieftain.

Culann started to pick the boy up and shake some sense into him when Fionna's voice cut in.

"Stop that immediately! Put that poor boy down!"

Her words pierced through the haze. Culann slowly set Bono down.

Fionna put her arms around the boy and spoke soothingly to him. "Are you sure, Bono dear? Are you sure that's the man?"

With fear evident in his eyes, Bono nodded his head. "Yes. That's Erik the Red. He killed Michael and my parents." Burying his face in Fionna's shoulder, he started to cry.

"He's got to be wrong. How can this be?" Culann fumed.

"Children see things differently, Culann. You must remember that Bono puts things into words that make sense to him. Erik the Red is the name that Bono gave to the Viking who killed his parents. He has no reason to lie about this."

"He might be mistaken!" Culann barked. "He's just

a boy."

Fionna stared at him, then touched Bono gently on the brow. "Weep," she said to the boy, and he did.

She began to hum the words to a spell, her brow knit with concentration. Moments later, she looked up.

"In the real presence of the man of Bono's memories, this spell is easy. There is no lie, and no mistake. That is the man whom Bono saw kill his parents."

Culann felt a knot in his stomach. He had nearly made an alliance with a butcher, a foul creature who had tortured and mutilated the bodies of women and children. Bile filled his mouth as he again turned his head and stared at the barbaric Viking as he riled his men up for war with battle cries and songs of victory. Lord Bjanni may indeed have brought the magic back to Hibernia, but Culann could not condone what he had seen at Bono's village. There *had* to be another way.

Looking back toward Lord Bjanni, he saw the man in a totally different light. The inhuman gleam in the Viking's eyes revealed the murderer that he really was. The battle lust that filled Culann only moments before became a leaden feeling of disgust.

Culann remembered last night. An important human was being led to the slaughter. Glancing again at Thorfinn, Culann made up his mind.

* * *

Thorfinn could feel his body throb to the chorus of voices raised in a mighty tumult of battle lust. Yes, this is what he lived for. Battle. The smell of victory. Ahh. Quivering with excitement, Lord Bjanni let his emotions go and screamed a defiant cry of exultation.

"Excuse me, my lord."

With a swing of his hand, the great Viking lord knocked the messenger off his feet, sending the man sprawling to the ground.

"What do you want? Why do you disturb my preparations?"

"My lord," the messenger slurred through broken teeth, "the earth elves are gone, sir. They left no word. Just slipped out of camp."

In a stride, Thorfinn was at the messenger's side. Lifting him into the air, he stared at the man with mad eyes. "Are you sure, man? Speak or I'll tear you limb from limb."

"Yes, my lord," he gasped, "I saw the vacant campsite myself. Lord Delyndun sent me to fetch you."

With a cry of rage, Bjanni threw the messenger to the ground, where his broken body lay still.

"Curses and foul excrement on those slimy bastards. I knew I could never trust fickle elven women to go forward into a fight. If I catch those slinking scoundrels, I'll show them what magic is all about."

Panting hard, the great Viking chief brought his emotions into check. First, there was the matter of the stormer woman. There would be plenty of time later to deal with traitorous earth elves.

* * *

Her men would be in position well before midnight. Aubrey glanced at the sun as it hovered on the horizon, seeming to wait for the Irish warriors to reach their destination before sliding over the edge of the earth. Swiveling in her saddle, Brea made a mental count of her men. Good, all thirty of them were still with her. Since the invasion, bands of men were known to have been picked off, man by man, by horrible creatures out of nightmare. One of Brea's patrols had encountered such a beast. Few had lived to tell of that experience. It was nice to know that the Fates had at least given the Irish a fighting chance this time out.

Then an arrow whistled through the air, thunking into a horse two men up from Brea. The horse's scream of pain spooked the other horses. Immediately, the air was filled with curses and horses' whinnies as the column of men fought to regain control of their skittish mounts. More arrows whistled through the dusk air, some finding their targets in the milling Irish men. Brea brought her horse under control and moved it to the side of the trail.

Up to the left, Brea saw the charging Vikings and warned her troops, "Ten o'clock! Dismount and use your guns, but don't rely on them. When they get close, switch to swords and spears."

She didn't waste her breath with more orders — the time for that was gone. Kicking her foot over, Brea dismounted on the far side of her horse. When she had her feet firmly planted on the ground, a slap in the flank sent the beast back down the road. Brea took cover in the bushes as she glanced around, taking stock of their situation. Five men down and four injured, leaving her with 21 men. A quick look at the charging Vikings and Brea knew that the Irish were probably outnumbered 3 to 1.

She sent a silent prayer up to the Virgin Mary that their guns would work as she readied her own rifle. Its report was followed closely by the crumpling of a Viking. Around her, Brea heard the cracks of a number of guns, but not enough to turn the tide. Brea pulled the trigger and another Viking fell, but they were getting too close now.

Then she saw it. Running in the front of the advancing Vikings was the beast that had been terrorizing the IRA's scouting patrol for months — the beast of the shadows. Its orange eyes seemed to spout flame as it loped down the hill toward Brea. She leveled her gun and fired, but the bullet must have missed the creature for it kept coming. Another shot — this one Brea was sure went right through the creature. She began to breathe rapidly.

Her spear! Dropping the gun, Brea picked up the spear with the silver-plated tip. After her experience with the blue faerie, Brea had asked her weaponsmiths to plate the tips of some spears with silver in case the patrol met with any magical creatures.

Gripping the spear with two hands, Brea awaited the charge of the black beast. The monster was almost upon her. With grim determination and all the strength she could muster, Brea screamed, "For Ireland!" and buried the spear in the hurtling monster's chest. The momentum of the creature's leap took them both down, but Brea managed to keep her grip on the spear and the monster's slashing claws at spear's length. Her muscles strained with the effort.

For a moment, the black beast stopped struggling and Brea began to think that it was dying. Suddenly, it righted and began pulling itself up the spear's length towards Brea. Fear froze her to the spot as she watched, fascinated by the gruesome feat. What could only be a low laugh escaped its mouth as the beast readied its claws to finish her.

A blinding flash of flame erupted where the beast had been. Brea turned her eyes away. She could smell her own burning hair as an unearthly scream echoed through the vale, causing the other warriors to pause in mid-fight. Through the silence came the cry, "Remember Cath Maige Tuired!"

Spots swirled before Brea's eyes as the sounds of fighting resumed. Near her, a man gasped, "It's the bloody Tuatha-de-Dannan!" Brea's vision began to clear. Across the battlefield, a new group of riders on white horses had entered the fray, their intricately crafted helms gleaming orange in the day's last light, their silver swords moving like fire, mowing down the ranks of the Viking horde.

Dropping the burnt stub of her spear, Sean spotted her rifle. Bringing the stock to her shoulder, Brea scanned the battlefield for a target. On the ridge to her left, Brea saw two battles. One involved a blue-skinned man and a woman of surpassing beauty. The flashing of lightning and fire could only mean that a magical duel was being fought.

The other battle was between a Viking of immense size and a Tuatha-de-Dannan whose elaborate helm identified him as their leader. For a moment, Brea paused to wonder at the sight of the myths from her childhood fighting in all their glory right there in front of her. Then the Viking beat through the elder Tuatha's defenses, his axe cutting a slash through the leader's side, ending Brea's moment of wonder. In pain, the Tuatha screamed his challenge again, "Remember Cath Maige Tuired!"

Her decision made, Brea raised her rifle and brought its sights to bear on the Viking leader.

* * *

Culann's thoughts were ones of grave determina-

tion. With all his strength, Culann parried upward, blocking the attack of the Viking leader. Never in his life had Culann fought such a monster of a human. He tried to riposte past the Viking's defenses, but was met with the man's off-hand dagger. A stone moved from under Culann's feet and he stumbled, just for a second, but that was all that Thorfinn needed to break through. Culann gasped as the steel cut through his chain and broke the skin near his ribs. Pain welled up, but the Tuatha fought it down. He had to continue. To show even a moment of weakness would mean his death with such a skilled opponent.

A familiar scream sounded from behind him. The smell of burnt flesh assaulted his senses. Fionna! Every fiber in his body told him to turn and help his life-mate. But if he turned, he would be lost too. Suddenly, the Earth's pain flooded through him. Fionna!

He staggered. In front of him, he could see Thorfinn size him up, smile, and prepare for the final strike. Summoning all his strength, Culånn tried to bring the sword up to meet the attack, but his arms wouldn't respond to his brain's efforts. Raising his eyes, Culann stared at the sword which carried his death.

A report echoed through the valley. Thorfinn staggered, but did not appear wounded.

"Finish him, damn it!"

A woman's voice came to him across the battlefield. His sword. Mustering reserves of strength from some untapped part of his soul, Culann raised his sword to finish off the Viking chieftain.

A brilliant flash of light illuminated the night, blinding Culann. He fell to the ground with a groan. When his sight returned, all was dark. His mind reeling with the pain, Culann sank into oblivion.

* * *

Brea saw the flash, but had no time to wonder. A sound to Brea's left brought her attention to the battle at hand and she barely had time to level her gun before a Viking warrior was upon her, bowling her over as the gun went off at point-blank range. The shot either missed or didn't finish the man and he pummeled Brea's head with his fists, the weight of his body effectively pinning Brea to the ground. Blackness began to creep over her when Brea felt the handle of a dagger near her right hand. Grasping it with her last strength, she brought it down on the Viking's head with an audible crunch. Then darkness set in.

* * *

When Brea awoke, the smell of blood filled her head. She rolled the dead Viking away, breathing deeply from the release of the crushing weight. It was dark. Making her way out of the ditch, Brea saw a large fire on the hilltop with figures moving around it. The cries of the injured men drifted to her over the night air. She noticed the fatigues of the IRA among those at the fire. *We won!* The revelation did little to relieve the fatigue that numbed her brain. Wearily, Brea made her way toward the fire. As she approached, a voice challenged her from the darkness. Before she could reply, the man cried out, "It's the Captain. She's alive!"

In moments, Brea's men were gathered around her, helping her to the campfire. There, she recognized the Tuatha-de-Dannan leader. Sadness was etched on every feature of the Tuatha's face. A young human boy cried quietly in his lap.

Brea smiled and stretched out her hand to this myth come to life, "Thanks for your help, sir. My name's Aubrey McDaniell."

Slowly, the Tuatha leader raised his hand and grasped Brea's. "You're welcome, young lady. Thank *you* for saving my life. I am Culann. And this," he stopped and looked tenderly down at the youth in his lap, "is my son Bono." Another Tuatha appeared at the elder's side. A smile graced Culann's lips for a moment. "And this is my eldest son, Tadg." The younger Tuatha smiled briefly and bowed. Pain and loss were apparent on his face too.

"It would seem that you've lost somebody close to you," Brea observed.

"My soul-mate died at the hands of that damned blue-skinned bastard." Anger filled Culann's voice, overwhelming his grief for a moment. Tears filled his eyes.

"I almost trusted them. Because they had the magic. It never dawned on me that magic could be used for such evil. Not until it was too late. During the battle, I could feel the Earth's pain as their magic killed both Tuatha and human alike." He pounded his armor with his fist and gazed forlornly into the evening, his heavy breathing mingling with Bono's quiet sobs. "She was all I lived for and now she is dead. The world has changed, young lady, and there is no longer room for legends such as us. *You* are the new breed, Hibernia's new children. It is your job now to free the Earth from this abomination which has torn her asunder. She has chosen *you*."

Reaching into a pouch by his side, Culann withdrew an ornately carved horn and handed it to Brea. She held the horn up to the firelight. It was ancient, the runes that adorned its sides older than the human race itself.

"That is the Dord Fionn, young lady. When Hibernia is in its time of greatest need, blow upon it and the Fianna led by Finn MacCool himself will come riding to your aid. Blow carefully, though, for the magic will only work when Hibernia itself is in its direst need. Choose wisely."

With those words, Culann rose, cradling the now sleeping Bono in his arms. "We must leave now. Our duty here is done. We must find out what place, if any, we have left in this world." Turning his back to the fire, the elder Tuatha started to leave.

"What of the boy, Culann? He is human, is he not?" Brea queried.

Turning back to the IRA soldier, Culann shook his head. "The human boy died when the Vikings killed his parents and my soul-mate. Now there is only my son."

Turning away again, Culann slipped into the night, his soldiers silently following him until the darkness had swallowed up all evidence that the Tuatha had even existed.

* * *

The moonlight reflected off the waves as they crested and broke upon the rocks at the base of Malin's Head. Culann sat alone at the summit. He gazed up at the stars, seeking to fathom the worlds which lay beyond this one. When that failed, he returned to Earth and sighed.

Hibernia had changed. Many centuries had passed since the magic had first gone out of the world and the Tuatha had gone into their self-imposed exile of sleep.

Those centuries had shaped the world into a place where magic and legends didn't belong.

Yes, legends. For that was what the Tuatha-de-Dannan were. Legends. Fairy tales to be told to young children before they went to sleep. Myths. His people never even existed in the eyes of the world's current inhabitants. Perhaps they were right. Perhaps his people were as much an abomination to the Earth as these invaders now were.

Culann had begun to understand the Earth's cries of pain. It was the return of the magic the invaders had brought that had caused the Earth such torment. The humans of Hibernia were as much children of the Earth as the Tuatha, perhaps even more so in the present age. Whether the awakening of the Tuatha was caused by the Earth herself or the arrival of this alien magic, Culann didn't know, though he was beginning to favor the latter theory.

It seemed that the Tuatha could help, though, at least in a small way. As long as the invaders existed on the Earth, she would be in pain. This, Culann couldn't stand. He had lost his love to these invaders and he would be damned if he was also going to lose the Earth he loved so much.

But with the death of the invaders would come the end of the magic and probably his people too. Of course, that was how it should be. His people didn't belong any more.

A noise behind him startled him out of his thoughts. Quietly, Bono sat beside his father. Reaching over to ruffle the youngster's hair, Culann smiled. The boy would always remind him of his departed soul-mate. She had died to save this boy's people, as would all of his people in the months to come.

Bono looked up and smiled at his father. "You'll never guess what I found, Dad. A frisbee. I'll have to show you how to play sometime." Then the young lad put his head in Culann's lap and stared at the heavens. Culann followed the boy's gaze. Overhead, a falling star blazed gloriously for a moment before blinking out of existence.

Like my people, Culann mused.

Bono stirred in his lap. Bono, who was now one of his people. Hmm. Lying back, Culann surveyed the stars with his son. Perhaps myth *could* become reality.

* * *

Brea sat silently on the hill with Sean. She had been very quiet since the battle with the Vikings. Sean had been by her side, night and day, giving her the quiet assurance that she needed. She sighed. It had been a long day and tomorrow would be an even longer one.

They had found no sign of the Viking leader or his blue-skinned wizard when the battlefield had been searched the next day. It seemed that the war was still on.

Overhead, a falling star caught her attention. Somehow, it made her think of the Tuatha-de-Dannan. Reaching into her knapsack, she pulled out the magical horn. Dord Fionn, the Tuatha leader had called it. She ran her fingers over its carved surface.

"When Hibernia is in its time of greatest need, blow upon it," the Tuatha had told her. Well, Brea couldn't think of a more dire time than now.

With trembling hands, Brea raised the horn to her lips.

Tales of the Night Walker

Grant S. Boucher

CHAPTER 1
London

London. It's the kind of place where you not only risk losing your life, you risk losing your soul. I ought to know. I've traveled the cosmverse, tracking and recovering everything from a sword of power stolen by an overzealous collector to a man's personality, locked in the depths of a demon lord's diamond. Still, I ain't seen nothing like this place.

I still use my robes when I move through this part of town, even though the Night Walker officially retired years ago. I might have taken my chances when I was a few centuries, or even decades, younger, but now things are rough on the night streets of London … too rough.

That night marked the beginning of my last case. Sure I said I retired years ago, and I did. But sometimes a challenge comes along that even an old geezer like me can't resist picking up. It's not just the challenge, mind you. I never did take a case that wasn't a challenge.

No, this one had potential. Potential rewards, that is. And not your typical pile of rubies or a useless magical trinket either. We're talking potential immortality, a comfortable retirement, and ... well, I'm getting very far ahead of myself now. Let's start at the beginning.

My first name is Algerius, and my last name is none of anyone's concern. If you haven't guessed already, I've been something of a cosmic private investigator for the past four hundred years, give or take a decade. I'm famous as I've never failed to solve a case. This allowed me to command some rather outrageous fees in my later years. With those fees, and a little royal assistance, I recently acquired a small castle on the banks of the nearby Thames. It used to be called the Tower of London, before the universes collided. I think it was a museum of sorts.

Just as an aside, my first case upon arriving in the new world was recovering some valuable jewelry that had been stolen from this museum. In exchange for my services I was knighted and, more importantly, I got the deed to the Tower (sans the royal jewels, of course). That case was worth coming out of retirement and so's this one. Anyway. After some extensive modifications, it's habitable now. I'd tell you more about the whole affair, but that's another story.

So, I'm an old elf ex-detective. Did you guess it already? Keep up, you've got a lot more to learn. I was known as the Night Walker to those of many underworlds and no stranger has ever seen my face, or the rest of me for that matter, while I was on a case. Sure, the common folk bump into me every day on the street, but to them, I'm just another midnight-blue-skinned creature. And with some of the horrors walking London these days, what's so unusual about a run-of-the-mill elf?

At night, I used to travel about the rooftops, invisible to the naked eye. My robe is proof against all forms of organic vision. It's even covered my ass from the living dead once or twice. When anyone does see me in my costume (i.e. only when I let them), my outfit is pitch black. High-heeled leather boots, loose cotton trousers, and a billowing black shirt complete my ensemble. I wear a mask, too. No big deal, just a metal faceplate enameled in black. Not only does it conceal my true identity, it serves as a frontal helmet and adds a little ominous echo to my voice to boot. Sure it's a bit melodramatic. But four hundred years ago, it sent shivers up your spine faster than you could say "Uthorion."

Looking back on it now, it seems foolish. Quite frankly, it's a wonder I lived through it all. I'm an Ayslish elf in an area of Core Earth about the size of a city. If I go anywhere near Buckingham Palace, I get sick and have to trek out to the country. Believe me, it isn't a reflection on the local royalty. So, I thought I'd be glad to go into seclusion for a few years, take on and train an apprentice. I thought surely that would keep me busy in my waning years.

But watching my apprentice perfect his limited skills year after year, I couldn't help but get more and more interested in hitting the rooftops again. Nothing like a novice to make a professional feel bold. And the old memories, and their accompanying recurrent nightmares, grew dimmer and less horrifying in the depths of my aging mind.

So, when I got the letter, I was more than ready to take the case. And this one seemed like a piece of cake. What better way to get started again? This time, however, I promised myself I'd take good notes. It's time I published some of my more harrowing adventures for posterity. The knights and barbarians are getting too much press these days.

So there I was walking through London again, on my way to meet a Lady. I was looking forward to the crowd's reaction. She knew I was coming of course, but no one else did. That was always the best part of a case in the old days.

The London fog was a bear as usual, and the real creeps always come out when the fog's heaviest. The Black Pagoda's generator was working that night, so business was good. As I passed by the broken plate glass window, the red neon sign revealed an ogre's familiar face. Gr'vak the Butcher was looking right at me. He couldn't see me, of course. Good thing, too. He was looking strong these days. I broke that filthy nose of his years ago on our natural home world, and somebody had slashed his ear since then. Since the cut was fresh, I assumed the human skull Gr'vak was proudly using for an ale mug was all that remained of that minor altercation. You've got to admit, it makes a statement.

There's something about shades of red neon on an ugly ogre's face that makes my stomach twist. Always has.

I hadn't been down at the docks in a while. Sort of like riding a horse I guess. Once you get used to it, you never really quite forget the feeling.

The Lady's ship was the *Demon Queen*. All the Orrorsh boats had friendly names like that. Must have something to do with the climate. I found it at Dock Five.

This time, I was not alone on the docks as the local guard was out in force. The boat should have begun unloading a half an hour earlier, so something was up. My blood started rushing like the old days.

Everyone else was stuck waiting around, even the guards. The captain wasn't letting anyone on just yet. I wondered why and thought I'd take a look.

A rusty crane dangled like a gallows over the *Demon Queen*. Normally I would have flown, but my special boots were being polished that night. I made a mental note to get a hold of a spare set of boots after this adventure, just as I always carry a spare invisibility cloak. That bit of forethought has saved my life more than once.

I leapt to the top of the crane's control box; I think they call it a cab. Although I was still pretty nimble and my balance was as good as ever, I decided not to press my luck with aerial somersaults this time. I walked up the long arm of the crane with the ease of a cat. As I climbed, however, the unused crane's age began to show. As I was falling uncontrollably towards the ocean, I realized I should have taken the water route to begin with.

It was already too late. The crane smashed into the deck of the ship with a thunderous crash and three guardsmen dropped off the gangway and into the drink. Their metal armor would have drowned them, were it not for their comrades who were already coming to their rescue. I knew they'd be okay.

None of the passengers were on deck, of course, as everyone was still down below. I was soaking wet, but all right otherwise. This wasn't going to make a good first impression.

Fortunately, the guardsmen chalked the collapse of the crane to old age. Little did they realize the irony. At least my presence still remained a secret.

I grabbed hold of the side of the ship and my special gloves gripped as easily as ever. Like a water spider I effortlessly made my way up the bow of the ship.

As I climbed, I spied two portholes. As they were the only ones on the ship with light coming out of them, I decided to investigate. Even though I was dripping water like an old sponge, I was still invisible.

The first window was filled with rich passengers. No one stood out at first glance. I couldn't tell which one had come here to hire me.

The second window was a much more gruesome spectacle. A humanoid shape was lying under fine linens that used to be white. I couldn't tell whether that blood belonged to my meal ticket, but my gut feelings told me not.

At just that moment, the chief inspector finally showed up. He was slow, fat, and Egyptian — probably from the Nile Empire. You could tell by his make-up that he wasn't much of a lady's man. He didn't seem pleased about being awakened for this.

The chief threw the bloody linens to the side, and two of his men headed for the upper deck. I privately hoped they didn't pick my side of the ship to lose their dinner. I slid aside for a moment and looked up. I was lucky. The other side of the boat was closer to the stairs. Their comrades were laughing at the sickened men, but those laughs were fake. I knew none of them was feeling brave anymore.

I slid back over to the porthole; the chief was still pawing the body. This was surely the work of an animal, or someone who thought that way. It was a fresh kill, soft and flexible. The insides of this ex-person were missing, ripped from the abdominal cavity like an oyster from its shell. That human husk used to be a man, or a very hairy and ugly woman. At least I now knew the victim couldn't have been my client. Since I hadn't seen anyone crying in the outer room, he must have been alone, or perhaps not very well liked.

I could read the chief's lips, a skill I highly recommend to all aspiring detectives. He agreed with my conclusions. Smart man — but foolishly he ordered a search of the ship. I had seen enough anyway, so it was time to make my public entrance.

After a few minutes of hanging around, I dried off sufficiently and the crowd thinned out. Everybody on board had to leave their name and intended address with the fat chief. Naturally, I made a mental note of everyone and everything, just in case. At the same time, I was hoping my memory was as good as it used to be.

I knew her immediately when I saw her. She was young, athletic, and tanned. Her clothes were rich, but strange. I had heard they dress different in Orrorsh. Long black hair like raven's feathers cascaded down her shapely back and she moved with noble confidence and poise.

For some reason, she hadn't been in the cabin with the rest of the passengers during my tour of the portholes. I doubt I could have missed such a woman in that crowd.

As she reached the bottom of the gangplank, I appeared before her. She was hardly startled at all, so she must have done her homework before hiring me. The rest of the dock was empty, so for a while I feared my trademark entrance was wasted.

She startled me more than I'd like to admit. It wasn't just her confidence, but her face. Lipstick red as fresh blood clashed violently with eyes as blue as a sunny day. They were the kind of eyes that ripped into the mind and transfixed even the most jaded of men.

Fortunately, she couldn't see my face. Unfortunately, she could see my eyes. I felt absorbed in her and knew suddenly that this was not going to be as easy a case as I had first imagined.

"The Night Walker, I presume." She spoke like an aristocrat, with firmness and grace. Not unexpected, after all, as she was from one of the richest families in Orrorsh — before the cosmos was sundered, of course.

"Follow me, please, my Lady. The docks are not safe for long at this time of night." I covered up my mild arousal well, and it made my voice seem deeper than it had in years.

She held out her hand, like she knew the routine already. That made me uncomfortable. As I looked back toward her, I saw the fat Egyptian chief standing on the dock. He had lit a cigar in the interim, and it was dangling precariously from his fat, blackened lower lip.

As I took her hand, we disappeared into the night's thickening fog together. All I could think about was the look on the fat man's face, and how my grand return to the den of thieves had not gone completely unnoticed.

CHAPTER 2
Her Black Shadow

She was the kind of person that trouble followed like a black shadow. In the old days, her family had helped turn Sydney into one of the world's major industrial centers. All of a sudden, through no fault of their own, the entire universe ruptured about them and Sydney became one of those unfortunate places where human beings are little more than food.

The story goes that her whole family was murdered by unspeakable horrors in the weeks just after the attack. She was out camping in the wilderness when the sky over Sydney changed colors, and only salvaged what she could upon her return. Now, days are better, and her remaining wealth is used to keep appearances up. Her shoes are old and marked and have seen much better times.

As we relaxed in my parlor at the top of the Old Tower, I skipped getting down to business in lieu of discussing tonight's excitement on the ship.

"Miss Selene, I guess I won't start the evening by asking whether you had a nice trip."

She smiled. "Well, actually, it was quite enjoyable until the very end, Mr. Walker."

People from other countries and strange dimensions always made the same mistake regarding my public ID. I have never found a better way to be addressed by my clients, and my enemies always had more colorful phrases for me, within their limited vocabularies of course.

"What do you know about the murder? I have a professional curiosity, you understand."

"Well. I had never met Michael — I mean Mr. Van Cliven — before, but these trips are always so long, and usually the men are all married."

She had a sly smile that was leading somewhere personal.

"I think I understand," I continued, hoping to elicit some more intimate information.

"Gorgeous man. Strong, athletic, mature." She paused and gave me a coy glance. "Sort of built like you actually."

"Why, uh," I stammered, "thank you, Miss Selene." I was getting that feeling again. After all, there's more to retirement than writing one's memoirs.

"Well, I'm a single woman, and I like things a certain way. I don't leave anything to chance, not even my men."

"So tell me more about the late Mr. Van Cliven."

"Good lover." She paused while I felt embarrassed.

She frowned, and a delicate tear appeared in her left eye. I was noticing that her pupils had pearl white slashes throughout as she broke down in front of me.

"What is it with me?" she began. "Everyone I ever love ..." Suddenly she got angry and looked up. "Hell, any man I even *liked*! They all end up running away or dying on me."

I held out my arm and she leaned forward immediately. She felt soft, warm, inviting. As her tears started soaking through my shirt, I was thinking some very unprofessional thoughts.

Suddenly, a grim, bearded face appeared from around my chair. His eyes were burning red with the light of the fire and his teeth were yellow with age.

As my latest client went from tearful sobbing to terrified screaming, I began introducing her to someone she'd learn more about in the next few days my apprentice, Dongo.

"Hi, boss. I just fixed the furnace. Want me to light it?"

Despite his yellow teeth, he always had the smile of a child and it was what always endeared him to me.

"That's great, Dongo, but I think the fire will be warm enough tonight. Tomorrow night we shall see the evidence of your handiwork."

"Great, I'll get some coal tomorrow mornin'."

"That will be fine. Dongo, let me introduce you to Miss Sylvia Selene. She'll be staying here with us for a while."

As Dongo walked away from my side, the lady realized for the first time that my faithful assistant wasn't kneeling or crouching behind my chair.

"But you're a dwarf!?" she stammered.

"Yep!" Dongo affirmed proudly. "What's the matter? They don't have any dwarves in Orrorsh?"

"No, I guess they don't," she said, recovering her composure rapidly. "Down there, anything smaller than an ogre ends up dead."

Dongo wasn't fazed. "So how come you're alive?"

Neither was the lady. "I'm smart ... and I hang around with big men."

"Good policy," chimed Dongo as he headed off into the darkness.

"I didn't know you had an apprentice," mumbled Sylvia, half in wonder, half puzzled.

"Most people don't," I reassured her. "The less people know about you, the better. His anonymity has saved my life more than once."

"I'll bet it has."

"Oh, relax. He's as fine a dwarf as exists ... in this cosm at least.

"But let's get on to business. This boat murder has nothing to do with why you're here, right?"

"No, certainly not. The chief thinks some sea creature came on board and just happened to rip up my would-be lover. If the monster was after me, he sure was a stupid beast. I ask you, do I look like a man?"

She stood up and dropped her coat. I haven't seen a

body like that since the demon lord caper I mentioned earlier. Now that really was temptation.

The fire was burning bright behind her, making that dress little more than colorful window dressing. She had more curves than a corkscrew … a real femme-fatale.

"No," I began slowly, not wanting to say the wrong thing. "I certainly don't think so. You're a red-blooded woman to be sure."

"Red-blooded woman," she mused as she sat down. "I like that. Sounds gruesome. You know, the monster ripped out his insides, and his…," she looked down, "… you-know-where."

"Ahem, yes. Did you … see the body?"

"Yes I did. Pretty horrible, but I've seen worse. I'm from Orrorsh, you know. There are a million words for terror in the language of Orrorsh."

I was liking her more and more every minute. Maybe I should draw this job out a little. The job! Hell, I didn't even know what the job was yet. This doll was poison in my soul. I'd never been this off-the-ball before.

"Speaking of Orrorsh, it's time you told me what I've been hired for."

"Very true, since you're being paid by the day. This is a little hard to explain, but that's why I sought you out. You see, someone's stolen my immortality, and I want it back."

"Your immortality?! You only mentioned a neck-lace in your letter."

"Yes, well, that's what I mean by needing someone like you. A local yokel might not even believe me, let alone know where to begin if he did. You've handled magic, and dealt with the powers of darkness, and I'm afraid I might need that kind of experience."

"The powers of darkness. Hmmmm." I only hummed aloud when I was worried. This wasn't supposed to be so damned dangerous. Damned dangerous? I laughed politely to myself.

"Well, I'm not sure such forces are involved, mind you, but this is a powerful artifact, and only a fool would part with it cheap."

"And keep his life, of course."

"Of course."

"Well, what can you tell me? I'll want to know everything … tonight." After all, I needed to find out what the real story was.

In short, she related to me the following tale: During her wandering travels after the death of her family, Sylvia learned much about the new things that went bump in the night. After a short stay as a vampire's unwilling potential consort, Sylvia took upon herself the admirable task of disposing of the lusty scoundrel. The woman's got guts to be sure, and they're well packaged.

According to her tale, he burned up nicely. One of the items she recovered from the vampire's hoard was a necklace that, ironically, the vampire didn't have any use for. This heavy silver chain with a silver ankh like those found in ancient Egypt had the power to suspend natural bodily processes indefinitely. What does that mean? It means virtual immortality. No eating or sleeping is necessary. The body never ages. Diseases never get to multiply, and, thus, never take effect. A miracle device, apparently useless to its former master.

Naturally, Sylvia made better use of the necklace, but wasn't able to keep it for long. According to her, it was stolen by a very talented thief who probably didn't know what he was getting at the time, but who certainly wouldn't give it up easily now. Sylvia used much of the vampire's treasures hunting him down. As she was closing in on the wily criminal, he hopped aboard the next ship to London.

The thief's name is unknown, but he travels by the alias of the Ghost. Only the best criminals, and detectives for that matter, live long enough to earn a reputation like his. The guy was famous for getting into the most impossible places and relieving them of their rightful contents. Imagine that? It explains how he managed to steal a necklace right off of a living person. It also explains how he managed to live so long. My first guess was shapeshifting, but he might be able to shift dimensionally as well. In any case, it was going to be no picnic.

Sylvia offered me a ruby whose worth was beyond calculation — the very last of her fortune — as payment. I accepted, of course, but demanded a far more valuable payment as well: dinner tomorrow night. She accepted as I headed out the window. When a client insists you begin immediately, and offers you payment like that (the dinner, not the ruby), you learn to do without sleep for a week at a time. Dongo remained in the Tower to protect her. I had no need of him that night.

That night, the Night Walker flew alone.

CHAPTER 3
Full Moon

There was a new full moon out. It was my lucky night as I knew I'd have three or four days of perfect hunting time.

The easiest place to start was the docks. Just like the

Demon Queen, another ship from Orrorsh must have docked there a few days ago. One of the passengers was the Ghost, and it shouldn't be too hard to figure out which.

I used to break into the Harbor Master's offices almost nightly. We had a game we played. By this time, everyone in town should have known I was back in action and I wanted to see if he remembered.

The lock I picked in three seconds. I grabbed a long stick, and ran it through the handle of the door. As I stood to the side, I pulled the stick in just the right way to unlatch the door.

With a spring-loaded crash, a very sharp iron spike shot through the glass. Head height and rusty, it was very nasty indeed. I had won the game again. My advantage was brains, guts, and experience. His was that he only had to win once.

Inside the filthy office was the usual collection of old smut magazines and empty whiskey bottles. The files were organized in the same crazy manner, and the whole place smelled of rotten fruit. A trash can overflowing with apple cores finished the picture. Some things never change.

The only ship that fit the bill arrived three days ago. After eliminating all the women, I was left with twenty-two men. Normally, I wouldn't have skipped the ladies, except for the fact that the Ghost is notoriously chauvinistic and most decidedly male. Fourteen of the passengers were using their return tickets, leaving only eight one-way tickets from Orrorsh. Three of those tickets were "under 18" special fares, their hold-ers far too young to have made the kind of reputation the Ghost had. This left me with five good leads. It was time to head downtown to visit my friend the Chief

Inspector.

Old Smiley's office was the third one from the right, two stories down. His light was on, as always. Making my usual entrance, I leapt in through the open window and somersaulted into the center of the room. This time, however, I didn't get any laughing applause. This time, someone was pointing a gun at me. Someone big, fat, and Egyptian.

"So, Mr. Hot Shot," he wheezed sickeningly, "I see you've decided to drop in and welcome London's new Chief Inspector personally. Well, thank you very much. But next time you do that, I'll shoot first, introduce myself second."

"Cut the crap." I decided to play it tough. "I need some information, and I'll offer you the same deal as I had with Smiley. You help me out, and I'll help you out. You let me collect what I'm looking for, and you get to keep the criminal in your jail and take the credit."

"I like those terms, alright, but right now you've got nothing to offer. I'll need something before you get your information, Night Walker."

He put down the gun and sat back in his chair. It groaned in dismay.

I played my card. "What would you say if I offered you the Ghost?"

The cigar he had just placed in his mouth never got lit. It was drooping slightly from his fat lip.

"The Ghost, huh?" His cigar dropped into his lap. "You mean the thief from Orrorsh?"

"He's in town, and I've got five names for him." I showed him the list.

He looked over the names and reached for a pen. He started scratching out one of the names.

I reached over and grabbed the paper before he was

finished. "What the hell do you think you're doing!?"

"You only need four names, Mister Gentleman Detective. Number Five's downstairs. Want to see him?"

"I certainly would. What's he charged with?"

The chief laughed evilly. "Oh, nothing yet. We're just holding him … for questioning."

We headed downstairs, into the wretched dungeon they called a jail. The rats ruled this place, not the town guard. I drew all sorts of stares as I moved through the building. Hell, half of these men weren't even born when I was in my prime.

The chamber we arrived in was cold, wet, and smelled of death. The chief pointed to a dimly lit room ahead.

"He's in there. Let me know if you learn anything from him."

When I entered the room, I realized with horror what "downstairs" had meant. Lying on a slimy stone slab was the dismembered remains of my suspect number five. Even from yards away, it was obvious that the poor man had been ripped to shreds by some horrible beast or beasts.

Even worse, behind me I heard a half-dozen men draw their swords. As I turned, I saw the chief standing behind his newly-arrived guards. I had been double-crossed.

"Night Walker," the chief began, "you're under arrest on suspicion of murder. Surrender or die. You have five seconds to lay down your arms."

I had been set up in the worst way. He didn't really suspect me of murder, but just holding me for a while, without bail, was certain to be my death sentence. If the prisoners didn't get me, the guards would. Guess somebody lost the difference between the good guys and the bad guys during the past few years.

I wasn't sure why he wanted me dead, but I suspected that his replacement of Smiley hadn't been a friendly one. Maybe he thought I was partial to the old fool, or maybe he wanted to hold a kangaroo court for the sake of his political career. Maybe he thought I was going to start cutting in on his action in the area. Maybe he was up to something crooked he didn't want me to find out about. In any case, he had something to prove, and this was the way he wanted to do it.

So what did I do? Went on the offensive, of course. I threw down a couple of smoke bombs and ditched back into the morgue room. I reintroduced myself to my dead friend and got an idea.

When the guards arrived, they got an eyeful of terror. A mangled arm and a rather chewed up head were flying towards them, seemingly with a life of their own. As I tossed the parts, the men scattered, and I cut through the middle.

"You asses," yelled out the chief of the asses, "he's invisible again! Get out here and cut him off before he gets away."

I whispered "Too late, lard ass," in his ear as I grabbed his smoking cigar. He spun around and swung wildly as I dropped the cigar down his pants.

The guards were still readjusting their undergarments as I headed up the stairs. On my way out the door, I heard the scream of a man whose biscuits were burning.

Revenge is sweet.

CHAPTER 4
Suspicion

On my way back home, I had a lot of time to think.

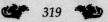

The death on the ship might have been sheer coincidence. After all, someone had done a much nastier number on that guy in the morgue. But the fact that the poor guy was also on my list was certainly nothing I could ignore. Someone — or more likely some*thing* — else was after that necklace. And whoever or whatever it was played for keeps. When I reached home, I had some new questions for Miss Sylvia Selene.

She was sleeping in my bed.

I had asked Dongo to put her there just in case the murder on the boat wasn't a coincidence. Not only was the highest part of the tower the safest part from the outside, it was also a sneaky way of keeping my clients where I, or my trusty sidekick, could watch them. She was radiant in the light of the full moon. Her perfect complexion glowed a soft pale blue.

As I stood in front of the open window, my shadow crossed her face, and she stirred. She must have recognized my silhouette, for she showed no sign of fear.

Smiling, she asked, "So, do you want your bed back, or can we share?"

Normally, I wouldn't have said a word, but there were some things I wasn't quite clear about, and the lady had some of the answers.

"We'll see, Miss Selene. I need to ask you some things about the murder tonight."

She seemed hurt. "Now it's 'Miss Selene' is it? Well, I'm not hiding anything. What do you want?"

She straightened up in the bed, pulling the thin sheets around her. I moved to the other side of the room and pulled up a chair. With the help of the full moon outside, her words were made true: she was hiding very little. I paused for too long a moment.

"Well?" She asked petulantly. I recovered my composure quickly as I remembered the evening's events.

"Tell me more about Mr. Van Cliven."

"Is that it? Jealousy? Please. The trip was long. I was bored. He felt good. That fat inspector who came on board when we docked wouldn't get off my case about Michael either."

"That's it?"

"He was murdered in my cabin, for crying out loud! I was the one who … who found him. I was on deck the whole time. I swear. I swear."

She broke down and started crying. Something in the pit of my stomach started to relax. With a flash of insight, I understood the connection. I moved over to the side of the bed and put my arm around her.

"I'm sorry, Sylvia," I began feebly. "Another man was murdered tonight, just like Mr. Van Cliven. He came in on the boat with the Ghost. I didn't see the connection."

She stopped crying for a second, "What … connection?"

"Van Cliven. His death wasn't a random stroke of chance. For some mysterious reason — something to do with your necklace I would guess — that monster was looking for *you* in that cabin."

She started to cry again. "But I didn't even *have* the necklace! Why did Michael have to die? You see? Every time I love somebody, they end up going away."

She wrapped her arms around me and I tried to undo the damage I had wrought. It would serve me right if she chose to hire someone else.

Instead, she looked up at me with those big blue eyes and said only "Help me."

As she gently lifted my mask, I did not resist. When she saw the shade of my skin, and how it glistened in the moonlight, she did not stop. And when she planted those ruby red lips upon my own, I succumbed.

As we made love like two demons possessed, all I could keep thinking about was Michael Van Cliven, and what always happened to anyone who chose to love Miss Sylvia Selene.

CHAPTER 5
Modus Operandi

I always wake up long before my women. After you've woken up even once with a dagger at your throat, you learn to sleep light. While Sylvia slept off one hell of a long night, I headed downstairs to begin a new day's work.

Dongo gave me that "not again" look, and I snarled convincingly back at him. He never liked anyone coming between the two of us, and he knew what kind of effect women have on me. He says I lose my edge. I say I just lose some sleep. This time he had no grounds to worry — I hadn't felt this good in years.

"Dongo, make a copy of this list. Just the four remaining names — the last guy was eaten last night."

"Eaten?" gulped Dongo.

"Yeah. Jugular slashed. Guts devoured. Flesh shredded like grated cheese. You know, eaten."

I love the look on Dongo's face when I gross him out. He had seen worse in his many years of faithful service, but to him, hearing it said was always worse than seeing it first hand. An overactive imagination, I suppose. As he walked out of the room, I could not help but love that silly little dwarf.

Sylvia surprised me by coming down the stairs seconds later. She was wearing only the black shirt from my costume. It was barely long enough to cover her. As she planted a soft kiss on my cheek, Dongo returned, threw my copy of the list on the table and started heading for the stairs down.

"Dongo. You take the first two. I'll get the second. Report to me at midnight, okay?"

He was out of sight by the time I finished giving him his orders, but I heard an affirmative grunt nonetheless.

As Sylvia straddled me in my chair and lowered herself on my lap, we decided to make a late morning of the day.

I left Sylvia cleaning up in the kitchen, as I headed out to check the street gossip about the murder. I locked the door behind me, just in a case the monster didn't only hunt at night.

The street always has the best information. The guys who are too scared to work over during the night in my Night Walker guise are always easy to talk to during the day, when I am disguised as a mild-mannered elf with a little too much curiosity. I always keep myself armed and wear my non-trademark magical items for safety, however. The thieves trust me completely, a relationship I have maintained for decades.

I needed to find out about the Ghost and whether or not he had a monster or two on his payroll. Naturally, the place to start was London.

It didn't take long to find what I was looking for. The monster apparently made quite a lot of noise, and a nasty mess as well, placing that body I ran into on the slab in the morgue. The attack had taken place right out in the open. Dozens of ogres, trolls, humans, — even town guardsmen — stood by while a huge wolf ripped a man to shreds in the heart of Hyde Park. The wolf was over six feet long and five feet at the shoulder, if the witnesses had exaggerated by the usual amounts.

Apparently, the beast appeared at the entrance to a pub across the street, and moved in quickly on its intended victim. Even when the man escaped into the street, and the town guard attempted to step in, the beast had only one thing in mind. The supernatural wolf effortlessly knocked down creatures five times larger than itself during the hunt. When it finally caught the poor devil, he was mercilessly torn limb from limb. Curiously, unlike most canines, the wolf tore out his groin first, then ripped off his arms. Only after the man's screams had mercifully ended did the beast tear out his throat and chew off his head. Surely, there was calculated method in this madness.

So now I had a better idea of what I was up against, but I still knew nothing about the Ghost.

One of the four remaining men on my list was this beast's master, and Dongo was already out watching two of them. I had a fifty-fifty chance of nailing the bastard myself tonight.

By asking around, I learned that one of the men, a mercenary by the name of Milo Grethan, was entirely too young to have established himself as a major criminal figure. In fact, his home base was here in London, and he had only just returned from a prolonged vacation, having purchased a one-way ticket for both his trips to and from London. On the other hand, my remaining suspect showed much more promise.

Nobody knew much about Mr. J. P. Stogh, as he was certainly not from around London. A graying merchant in his late 50s, J.P. was a man who was not only old enough, but rich enough to have been a successful thief for the past few decades. Better yet, he made quite a point of establishing the fact that he had "magic" for sale at his rooms. While that is certainly a profitable trade, it is also a shady and dangerous one. Changing into my costume, I decided to pay Mr. Stogh a visit.

The Great Griffin Hotel was both ritzy and expensive. Invisible, I needed but one glance at the register to know where to go. As I proceeded up the stairs, I noticed that every floor was appointed with linen closets, standing coat racks, and individual request boxes next to each and every door. A quality establishment to be sure.

As I reached the third floor, the cleaning lady was moving from room to room, but she was moving in the opposite direction. Lucky for me, she must have already finished, which meant J. P. wasn't home this fine afternoon.

The magically protected lock took all of four seconds to crack. As the maid entered the last room at the end of the hall, I slipped inside. The curtains were drawn and the room was dark and colors are not represented well in dim light, so the gory scene had an almost psychedelic air to it. In all my years, I hadn't seen anything worse than this.

The walls were splattered with blood and brains, as if some horrible game of stickball had been played with the poor man's head. Mr. Stogh's memories and dreams were staining wallpaper traced with crushed red velvet. The monster was ahead 3-0 now.

I kept down my breakfast by sheer will alone, and found the rest of J.P. in the bedroom. He had been caught sleeping, of course, but there was no sign of forced entry. This puzzled me for many minutes, as I searched through the apartment. Even stranger, the place had been searched, methodically and professionally. Pillows had been slashed, chairs were overturned, and desk drawers had been emptied of their contents. Even stranger still was the fact that a number of relatively valuable items, including rubies, gems, and magical potions, were lying about untouched.

The beast had an accomplice, or more likely a master, at its side during the crime. However, because the blood was on the pillows but had not entered through the gashes in the material, I determined that the search had taken place after the murder, not during, or before. And the gashes were made by a blade, not by claws. I was beginning to get a handle on the Ghost's modus operandi.

Suddenly, a scream echoed behind me. As I turned, I saw the maid collapsing in the hallway. Normally, this wouldn't be a problem. However, I wasn't invisible at the time, and I was pawing through the place like I belonged there. Also, I'm pretty easy to identify in a line-up—always a drawback of having a costume.

In the old days, I could have talked my way out of it. But I no longer had friends among the town guards, and now I even had enemies.

A criminal would have killed the woman while she was lying down. A criminal would have escaped and left no witnesses. A criminal would have been able to get out of this easier than a good guy. Shame I'm one of the good guys.

I ran out of the door as half a dozen rent-a-cops came charging up the stairs. Where were these overpaid pencil pushers when one of their guests was being ripped to shreds? I knew the roof exit would be locked, and to pick it would require precious seconds I did not have. I am not immune to bullets, despite all legends to the contrary.

The guards must have heard their now-invisible quarry come crashing down the stairs. They were not nearly as pencil-pushing as I had first believed. They all fired their guns and stabbed with their swords mercilessly.

Three of them were shot or wounded by each other, and my invisibility cloak was surely ruined; the coat rack lurking underneath fared no better.

Those precious seconds of confusion and friendly fire gave me the time I needed to pick the lock to the roof exit and don my spare invisibility cloak. Once on the roof, I leaped off, and glided down unseen amidst a gathering crowd of curiosity seekers.

As I passed among them, I realized I'd better check on Milo Grethan the mercenary — not to ask him questions about last night, or to find the missing necklace, but to warn him of his impending doom.

CHAPTER 6
My Luck Runs Out

Milo was pretty simple to find, or at least his home was. It seemed to be a very popular place for all-night parties, so most everyone under 30 knew where to go on a Saturday night.

This time of day, however, Milo was certain to be asleep. His only chance for salvation was his playboy, party-man personality. If Milo was someplace else last night, entertaining some young lady perhaps, then the Ghost and his fiendish henchbeast might have had a hard time getting to him. I wasn't even going to worry about the other two men I had put Dongo on. There was a better than even chance my faithful assistant was throwing up about now, somewhere in the darker recesses of London.

Invisibly, I flew up to the rear window of Milo's penthouse apartment by the Thames. I've lived in worse to be sure, when times weren't so profitable ... and dangerous. I was in luck: the rear window was ajar. Inside, I could hear a man humming in the shower. The air was thick with steam, and wrinkled clothing was on the floor. The sheets on the bed hadn't been touched. I had guessed correctly: Milo hadn't spent the night here.

As I opened the door, the steam blinded me temporarily.

"Milo," I called out to the voice, "I am called the Night Walker, and I've come here to warn you. Your life is in danger."

"No, my friend," came the chilling response, "it is your life that is in danger."

Stepping forward out of the fog was a large, fat, familiar Egyptian figure. This time, however, there was no cigar ... only a gun.

I was staring down the barrel of a standard issue police revolver, the kind that's easily concealed when under cover. Small caliber, no range. But hell, it's not the size of the hole that gets you ... it's the hole.

"Mr. Grethan is in protective custody, and you, my friend, are in a lot of trouble. You're going to drop to the ground right now, or die trying to escape. If you haven't anything to do with all of this, then what have you got to hide?"

I knew he wouldn't shoot me. He'd much rather take me downtown and feed me to some smelly troll scum rounded up especially for the occasion. No, he wanted me alive, that was for sure. Besides, no matter how much of a pig this guy was, he was supposed to be a chief inspector. Shooting a man in cold blood, even a suspect, was against everything he supposedly stood for. Besides, I reasoned, I was invisible.

As I ran out the door, I heard laughter, and then a shot. I didn't start to feel it until I was already leaping out of the window. As the water started rushing towards me faster than I had expected, I realized I wasn't in control of myself anymore. As I began to black out, I realized that steam was one of those things that rendered my invisibility quite useless.

CHAPTER 7
The Ticking Clock

The cool water of the murky Thames shocked me back to consciousness. I was wearing a bullet-proof vest (one of the few useful inventions of this planet), so it was not the bullet itself that hurt me, but the shock of the blow. The bullet had hit dead square in the center of my back, which knocked the wind out of me something fierce. When I emerged, dazed and confused, from the icy waters, I was several blocks downstream. No doubt the inspector was still patting himself on the back for my untimely demise. Fortunately for me, the police are notorious for closing a case faster than they can munch a doughnut. My brush with death had bought me the most precious commodity of all: time.

As I returned home late that evening, however, I learned that twice in the same day, my luck had run out. My front door had been jimmied, and inside I found something more sickening than anything I had ever seen in all my years.

Dongo was dead. His head was grotesquely displayed atop the very same kitchen table we ate breakfast at that morning, and indeed every morning for a year. Stuffed inside his mouth, and secured by a dagger through his tongue, was a note, bloodied but readable. I didn't even bother looking for Sylvia. I knew what the note said even before I read it.

Forget about the necklace and the girl lives. Remember Dongo.

The Ghost

There's something about the death of your partner that leads to certain emotions. Before tonight, I never would have said aloud that I loved the little runt. However, for the first time in four centuries, I cried. I hadn't cried since I hurt myself as a child.

Now, my decision to come out of retirement was staring back at me with a bloody vengeance. And Dongo's look this morning, telling me "Hey, Boss, the lady's poison," was echoing in my mind. He was my partner and right now, avenging his death meant more to me than Sylvia, money, or even that damned silver necklace.

Misery can drive you mad. But madness can give you an edge, the edge of fearlessness. I always had put on a brave face and shoved horrible, frightening things aside with a quick wit and a mask over my face. But now I was truly fearless. For the first time in my history as a crime fighter, I added a gun to my collection of on-hand weaponry. I was out for blood as well tonight.

May the best beast win.

CHAPTER 8
The Great Hunt

There were only two names on the list that I had given to Dongo. Since his list was conspicuously absent among his disheveled effects, I assumed quite logically that one of those remaining people was in fact the Ghost. Dongo had, of course, stumbled on to this fact during his surveillance. While Dongo always was the best at watching people, he was also certainly one of the worst at hiding from them. And who knows what supernatural powers that unholy hound possessed. It had tracked men across the city and had shamelessly ripped them to shreds. Poor Dongo never had a chance.

The first stop was a dead end. The town guard was only just arriving. The moon was full enough to see that another murder had just taken place inside. This time, the man's wife had been forced to witness the terrible spectacle. I knew she'd never be the same again.

That left only T. Byron Esprit, and I knew I was in luck. He was the easiest of all to find, as his family owned a historically famous mansion on the outside of town. Although he was known to travel extensively, and had the majority of his family roots in Orrorsh, I had left him to Dongo, feeling he was much too high profile to be our man. Naturally, in retrospect, I realized that he was just the kind of man who makes the best underworld kingpin. Never at home, always an alibi.

However, unless the hound could fly or teleport, he couldn't possibly beat me to the mansion. It was on the other side of town, and on the other side of the mighty Thames. The blood was still running down the windowpane at the last place, so I couldn't be that far behind. I knew if I could reach the Ghost before his trusty wolf returned, I had a much better chance of breathing tomorrow morning. Dealing with them separately would give me the edge I needed. If they were together, I was a goner.

Only one light was on in the entire mansion. A lone lantern flickered in a room at the very top of a tall tower rising from the heart of the estate. The window was closed and the shades were drawn, but inside a man's figure was pacing to and fro. I timed his movements, and at just the right moment, I crashed through the window.

I was soon sitting atop a rather frail old man in his late sixties. He was dressed in nobleman's robes, and he wore a rune-covered sword at his side. Around his neck was an ornate silver necklace with an silver Egyptian ankh.

The ankh had a narrow, pointed base and a smooth round circle at the top. It seemed as unremarkable as any necklace I had ever seen. It was even a bit gaudy by modern standards, like the jewelry the ogres and orcs wear.

I pinned the old man's hands easily as he struggled to get free. There was only one problem with the entire scenario — he was screaming for help. He wasn't yelling for his personal guards, or even his great wolf. He was yelling for the town guard!

"Shut up!" I commanded him, for a number of selfish reasons.

"Please, don't kill me," he whimpered. "You can have the necklace. Just don't kill me."

It was pathetic. Was this a ploy? Was he stalling for time? Was this aging criminal genius playing with my mind? Something inside me said he was sincere. But then again, I had been wrong more than once today.

"Where's Sylvia?!" I demanded, having already noticed a barred door to the east.

"Who?" he asked. His eyes showed true amazement and bewilderment at my question. This was the kind of look that got you released from custody during questioning for murder. It was nothing but honest.

Against all my instincts, I let him stand up.

He got up slowly and backed up against a wall. I drew my gun, but he never made a reach for his sword. He rubbed his wrists until the blood was flowing freely again.

"What have you done with Sylvia? The woman who owns the necklace?"

"Oh, her. How should I know, you damned fool? I left that bitch on the docks of Orrorsh."

"For crying out loud! Are you, or are you not, the Ghost?"

"That I am," he said with a gentlemen's bow. "And I will make the educated assumption that you are none other than the legendary Night Walker."

I was almost liking the guy, until I heard a bump in the closet next to me.

"Okay, then who's this?!" I called out confidently as I headed for the door.

He moved towards me with sheer panic on his face. "No, don't!"

With my right hand, I drew my gun and held him at bay. With my left hand, I slid the bolt back and threw open the door. A knife blade slashed from the darkness. It missed by a mile. I turned and pointed my gun, ready to fire.

I almost killed a ten-year old girl. She was small, fragile, and terrified. I was hopelessly confused.

"She's my granddaughter," he explained weakly. "Please, do not harm her. She has nothing to do with any of this. Take the necklace and go. Leave us in peace and I will never bother you again.

"You see, for all my fantastic capers, this was the one thing no thief ever could steal, before now. This was my last chance at immortality. Don't you see?"

As he took the necklace from about his neck, a huge pair of canine jaws appeared around his arm. The Ghost screamed. The child screamed. I slammed the door on her and threw my back against the wall.

The old man's arm was severed in one bite, and a shower of arterial blood coated the room. His arm dropped to the ground, his fingers still twitching with recent life about the necklace of immortality.

The wolf was huge — larger than the witnesses described. It had a glorious black coat that glistened silkily in the moonlight. The greying hair underneath the chin was stained in new blood from the previous evening's kill. For a moment, I marvelled at its exquisite technique … its raw animal grace.

Then it went for his groin. The old man dropped to the ground in shock as the monster ripped his manhood apart. As he lay there twitching, already dead from the shock, the ruthless and horrible beast went for his throat, with the mindless intention of completing the kill.

At that moment I knew the beast was indeed too much for me to handle alone and I panicked. I holstered the gun and grabbed the necklace, and for a moment an old man's arm came with it. As I leapt out the window, I knew immediately that the wolf was coming. I could feel its hot breath behind me as I glided towards the ground. I didn't look back. I didn't want to see how close it was to me. Like looking down when you're at the top of something very tall, I felt it was better not to know.

As I hit the ground, I heard a heavy thud and a dog-like yelp very close behind me. I might have gained a few seconds, providing I didn't lose my footing also. I ran like I had when I was young, but my lungs were already screaming. I wasn't young, and my lungs had been through enough today.

I swung my cloak about me and scaled the spiked iron fence surrounding the estate. I thought maybe my invisibility would help me. Maybe it couldn't jump the fence in one great leap. Maybe it didn't want me at all. Maybe I should just drop the necklace. Maybe … maybe the dog wanted a bullet in its brain.

I dropped and rolled, drawing my gun like a professional shooter. Unfortunately, my finger never even got to squeeze. The beast hit me like a ton of granite, and my gun flew out into the street.

The monstrous canine jaws started tearing at my groin … and then stopped. As I clutched myself in pain, the great wolf raised its head slowly, as if undecided in its next action.

Suddenly, the look of madness returned. I raised my hands in front of me as the beast leapt for my throat. It wasn't attacking methodically, like it had the old man and the others. Maybe this was because I was wearing the necklace now, I didn't know.

It took all I had to defend myself and my fingers weren't going to last for long. The wolf was thrashing wildly, like a creature possessed.

I was quickly losing my strength, and my own blood was staining my eyes. My right thumb was lying lifeless on my throat, and my left wasn't far behind it. The horror above me knew this. It tasted blood again and knew it had won this battle also. As it stepped back away from my face, it looked down evilly into my eyes. Those eyes … they were supernatural. Eyes as blue as the day, but with gashes of white running throughout. They stood in sharp contrast to the red blood dripping from the jaws above me.

The monster reared its head again, and I knew where it was going. As I braced for the shock of involuntary castration, a sudden clarity swept through my head. Blood red? Sunny day? Pearly slashes? I would go to my grave with a terrible secret. The last one of my career.

I craved a weapon in hand — any weapon would do. Something to give myself the illusion of defending myself. And then I remembered the necklace. Instead of vainly blocking my face and throat with my blood-ied stumps for hands when the beast came to complete the kill, I dropped them to my chest. The monster was mad with the blood rage of the kill, of course, and only took this as an opening. As it lunged wildly for my throat, I twisted the necklace with both hands, bracing the rounded top against my sternum. The force of the beast driving the sharp end of the necklace into itself knocked the wind out of me as well. If the monster survived my clever attack, I was going to be unable to muster another.

The necklace had driven deep into the cheek and jaws of the beast, and the wolf's searing blood covered my face and neck. Our blood mixed and, oddly, a dull red smoke began rising up from the ground.

The wolf was thrashing about blindly, as if I had struck its heart or had burned it somehow. My neck-lace might have penetrated deep into the skull, into the monster's eye or brain, but I doubted it.

Suddenly, a dozen gun shots rang out around me. At first I thought this was some strange reaction to the intensity of my own pain, but the wolf recoiled, stunned and in shock. I looked up, and saw a handful of fresh holes in the monster's silky black coat. My saviors raised their guns again, but the beast seemed unimpressed. When I raised the necklace, however, the unholy beast fled, wounded but not killed.

As the pain and loss of blood overwhelmed me, my adrenaline rush began to subside. I fell back in the grass in a daze of hazy red smoke. The necklace clanked heavily around my neck.

I remember seeing a young man take a sample of the wolf's blood and place it in a test tube. He took a vial of some foul-smelling sulphurous compounds and mixed the reagent with the blood. The blood sparked with a magical light, and the man's proud face lit up with a smile.

"Told you," he called out to footsteps approaching me, "werewolf."

As the footsteps inched closer, I knew I had no way to defend myself now. I was going into shock for the first time in two centuries.

Above me appeared a fat, Egyptian face. He leaned over me, dropping hot cigar ashes in my face. He picked up my missing thumb and started twisting it in front of my face. As he squeezed the last remaining drops of blood out of it and on to my face, he beamed with a broad smile.

"Missing something, Night Walker?" I couldn't answer him. "That's one nasty werewolf you fought there. Nastiest one I've ever seen in all my years. Wouldn't happen to know who it was, would you?"

He paused. "No. I guess you wouldn't."

I didn't even have the strength remaining to nod my head.

CHAPTER 9
Femme Fatale

I found her very late that night, in my bed. She

claimed to have escaped from the Ghost, and I bought it, or so I pretended. I figured out every angle of the past few days' events while we made incredible love until morning.

Sylvia was a werewolf, of course. Every full moon she gained the power to become one of the most hideous and vicious monsters in the known universe. She could choose when and where she metamorphosized, but she had to do it at least once every evening with a full moon. That is, unless she was wearing that necklace. You see, besides keeping you from needing to sleep or eat, or age for that matter, it also had the beneficial side effect of halting all other bodily processes, including involuntary "shapeshifting."

She'd seduced most of the men with her natural human talents, then torn them apart after the loving was over. No breaking and entering required.

She must have killed Mr. Van Cliven for her own reasons. Maybe he got a little too rough one night on the boat, or maybe she had to kill every once in a while or go insane. Maybe she was just a little kinky. In any case, I remembered that no one was mourning his loss in that cabin that night. Perhaps he wasn't a very nice guy.

But then she killed Dongo to throw me off the track and to keep me from finding the Ghost before she did. The poor old man hadn't harmed a soul in decades. As I read more about him in the years to come, I found we had more in common than not.

I knew werewolves only had to change once every moonlit evening, so she really didn't need to kill anybody. Especially not Dongo, and certainly not me. I guess she felt she needed that necklace worse than she needed me.

Speaking of the necklace, the town guard thought it was just another one of my magical devices. They still respected the concept of personal property — at least they did once I had had a talk with the inspector, and promised him I could put a stop to the killings that very night. He must have been desperate, because he agreed to give up his vendetta against me if I could accomplish this thing. He gave me twenty-four hours.

In any case, I had been eyeing that necklace for myself. Surprise, surprise. I had been seriously thinking of retiring for good this time. I still had a lot of money, my health (*sans* a thumb or two, but a good healer might be able to help), and my good reputation.

So, was I going to let her play me for a sucker now? No, not by a near shot.

I gave her one last chance to prove herself. I told her she could have the necklace in the morning, claiming I had some obligations down at the headquarters of the town guard the next day and the necklace remained a piece of material evidence.

If she really cared anything about me, she'd wait. If her blood lust was uncontrollable, and I had been just another dupe of this lycanthropic vamp, she'd never let me live until morning.

As I pretended to drift off to sleep with her in my arms, she was also going to answer the one lagging question on my mind: did she have to kill all of these men to survive, or did she just choose to do so? I made sure I was wearing the necklace all night.

She was very, very good. I waited for hours for her to make her move. I knew she was awake by the shallowness of her breathing and the fact that she was not moving around in her sleep. The more unmoving she remained, the more obviously awake she was. I'm glad I was wearing the necklace, or I would have drifted off. I caught myself thinking she might really be asleep, but as dawn was approaching I felt her soft and delicate finger gently working their way along my chest. Was she admiring the necklace, or was this just a feeble attempt at thievery? As she slid her fingers back and forth about the chain of the necklace, I felt her hand hesitate and then withdraw. Had she changed her mind? Was there some spark of redemption going through her mind?

The low growl that issued from an area dangerously close to my loins answered that question once and for all. She was shapeshifting quietly, in a matter of seconds! I had always thought that the process was a violent, excruciatingly painful process that gave victims lots of time to react and run away. I realized that all of my suppositions had been based on fictional film and literary accounts, and that Sylvia could not possibly have been as effective as she had been unless indeed the opposite had been true.

There was no use in pretending now, as the bed was beginning to shift down with the new mass she was gaining in her animal form. I opened my eyes and was stunned as I watched the woman I loved become a beast of death before my very eyes.

I panicked. I instinctively reached for the gun I had secreted beneath my pillow with my right hand! This was the same hand currently swathed in bandages and missing a thumb. Ever try and grab and fire a weapon without a thumb? My instincts nearly cost me my life, and my selfish gamble was becoming infinitely more dangerous than I had expected.

This time, she went for blood. As I began switching my body from right to left in order to facilitate the recovery of the gun with my still functioning left hand, I felt the jaws of death clamp about my forehead.

The hot breath and rabid foam began to choke and blind me as the monstrous canines began tearing into my temples. The sharp necklace, which I had wielded so effectively in the fight before, was being stepped upon by one great clawed paw. There would be no repeat of my clever stroke here. My gun, its barrel brimming with bullets cast of pure silver, was my only chance.

It was a test of will now. Could I grab, aim, and fire the gun using only my left hand, before she opened up my skull and began savaging my mind like she had Mr. Stogh's?

I had the gun. But as I brought it about, I heard the horrifying sound of bone chipping and cracking. The beast was breaking through, and my own blood was clouding my vision. Not knowing the outcome of my action, I hoped for the best and pulled the trigger.

Fortunately, at close range, any shot is a good shot. I only grazed her in the shoulder, and as I had seen before, a normal bullet carried neither force or mass to cause this beast even a moment's hesitation. But the silver bullet was a searing poison in her blood, and the creature reacted to it like a man would. It hurt, and it hurt bad.

The beast slipped off the bed and pulled me and the upper mattress with it. We all fell upon each other and my own linens were tangling me up at the precise moment when I needed to finish the kill! I fired again blindly, and, as I heard no yelp of pain, I assumed I missed.

Just then, another sheet rose up and hit me square in the chest. My gun flew out of my hand. This time, however, the deadly linens saved my bacon, as they remained caught on the corner of the bed, and stopped the beast in mid leap. I fell back into the corner of the room, but the beast was not atop me.

As the monster tore through the sheets with tooth and claw, I lunged for the great shape with the necklace as my weapon. Driving it deep into the body, the monster's reaction was indeed gratifying. While the beast howled like a demon from Hell, I grabbed the gun and levelled it at my quarry.

The beast emerged from the sheets a second later and levelled its gaze at me, and my gun. I smiled at the monster like Dongo always had for me and said, "she's poison, boss." The great wolf leaped in vain as a hole opened up in the top of her skull — a hole lined with silver.

EPILOGUE

That would have been the end of my long illustrious career, had the local paper this morning not read "Murdered Men Become Werewolves!"

The Ghost was alive and loose and this time I could be sure he was no gentleman thief. I never did find out how he had plied his trade in the early days. Could he change shape? He could now. Could he fly, turn invisible, or walk through walls?

The possibilities became infinite as the ultimate criminal became the lifelong nemesis of the universe's only "Immortal Detective."

But that's another story.

DON'T MISS THESE OTHER GREAT

PRODUCTS!

Adventures and Supplements

☐ Cylent Scream $12.00
☐ Storm Knights Guide $15.00
☐ The Temple of Rec Stalek $12.00
☐ City of Demons $12.00
☐ Central Valley Gate $12.00
☐ Infiniverse Update Vol. 1 ....$18.00
☐ Kanawa Land Vehicles $15.00
☐ Creatures of Orrorsh $18.00
☐ Los Angeles Citybook $18.00

Novels

☐ Storm Knights $4.95
☐ The Dark Realm $4.95
☐ The Nightmare Dream $4.95
☐ Tales of the Nile Empire $4.95

**If you can't find the game product you want
at your local hobby shop or book store,
use the coupon below.**

— — — — — — — — — — — — — — — — — —

West End Games
RR3 Box 2345, Honesdale, PA 18431

Please send me the items I have checked.

I am enclosing $_____

(please add $3.00* to cover postage and handling for the
first item and $1.25 for each additional item).

Send check or money order — no cash or C.O.D.'s please.

Name:_____

Address:_____

City:_____

State:_____Zip:_____Tel:(____)_____

*For deliveries to Canada, add US $5.00 for the first item ordered and US $2.50
for each additional item.
Allow 4-6 weeks for delivery.

The Infiniverse is Waiting...

The story of the Possibility Wars continues as heroes and High Lords clash to determine the reality of Earth. Infiniverse *lets you take a part in that story.*

What is *Infiniverse*?

Infiniverse is a 16-page monthly newsletter that introduces you to new characters, creatures, miracles, spells and adventures within the realms of *Torg. Infiniverse* is a forum for players and readers to ask questions about the Possibility Wars and get answers straight from the game designers and authors who hold all the secrets.

You Can Win the Possibility Wars

By compiling results from *Torg* roleplayers all around the world West End Games can compute how well Earth is defending itself against the High Lords. YOU get to influence the direction of the Possibility Wars by telling us what happens in YOUR campaign. In return, you'll receive a response form with new dangers and benefits based on your campaign's successes and failures.

How Can I Get It?

The cost of *Infiniverse* is only $25 for 12 issues (outside of the U.S., $30). Simply send a check or money order along with your name and address to West End Games, Dept. 20605, RR 3 Box 2345, Honesdale, PA 18431. We'll start your subscription right away and every time you play the *Torg* roleplaying game, you have the option of sending your results to us via a West End response form (included in *Infiniverse*). Even if you don't participate in the interactive game, *Infiniverse* is still the best source of new information about the ever-changing universe of *Torg: The Possibility Wars*.